Catch the Moment

Euanie MacDonald

PIATKUS

Copyright © 1998 by Euanie MacDonald

First published in Great Britain in 1998 by
Judy Piatkus (Publishers) Ltd of
5 Windmill Street, London W1P 1HF

This edition published in 1999

The moral right of the authors has been asserted

A catalogue record for this book is available from the British Library

ISBN 0 7499 3110 8

Set in Times by
Action Publishing Technology Ltd, Gloucester

Printed and bound in Great Britain by
Mackays of Chatham PLC, Chatham, Kent

To Celia and to Sinclair, with thanks

Part 1

Courting Fortune's Favour

Prologue

Ayrshire, 1892

A chill wind cut through her thin coat and she shivered. 'What's that?' She lifted her face and sniffed like a wee terrier dog. The wind carried with it a distinctive smell, a clean, fresh, tangy odour. Annie licked her lips and found they were salty. She had never known the sea, so she couldn't guess what it was, but for the rest of her life she would remember its first sharp presence and briny taste.

Chapter One

'Oh, Mither, we're goin'!' Annie Ramsay grabbed the curved edge of the leather carriage seat.

With a yowl that battered the eardrums, the train made ready to move out of St Enoch's station, belching a cloud of smoke and hot cinders above the crowd waving goodbye. Metal ground on metal, buffers jerked and clashed as the engine shivered in impatience for the brakes to be released. Annie had never heard such a hellish concentration of noise, even from the horse-drawn trams that criss-crossed her native city.

'I believe someone is trying to catch your eye, lass.' Doctor Murchieson peered out of the window over horn-rimmed glasses. 'Isn't that one of your brothers?'

A half-grown lad wearing a patched jacket and ragged trousers bespattered with flour lopped up to the carriage waving wildly.

'Aye, it's Sandy, I thought he couldn't come! The baker must have let him off right enough.' Fear forgotten, she jumped to her feet and ran to the window, leaning out dangerously far till he could hold her hand.

'Annie? Ye're goin', ye're really goin'!' Sandy said desolately, rubbing away the tears that had begun to trickle down his face with an angry gesture. 'Och, Annie! Annie!'

'It'll be alright, Sandy. Dinnae greet. Maybe they'll let me come hame for Hogmanay.'

'Do ye think so?'

'Aye,' she lied, gulping hard and trying to smile.

The train lurched forward and he let her go. As it pulled slowly out of St Enoch's station, Sandy ran alongside panting

4

and as he lost ground, she saw him mouth her name over and over.

'Annie!'

Sandy stopped where the platform ended, but his misery followed her. In seconds his skinny frame had dwindled to a dot.

'Cherrio, Sandy!' she whispered and fumbled in her pocket for a rag. As she scratched away her own grief, the train braked, then picked up speed again. 'Oh jings!' She grabbed the window sash as the movement threw her slight form off balance.

'Close that window, lass, before you end up on the rails,' said Doctor Murchieson, frowning over his glasses.

'Right ye are, Doctor, I will in a minute.' She craned desperately for a last view, but the station was gone and with it her last contact with home.

'Sit down, Annie!' The doctor got up and pulled the window closed. Subdued, she took her place beside him as the train roared arrogantly into the shabby suburbs of the great city where the girl had spent her entire life.

'I should think so too!' a well-dressed woman on the far side of the carriage commented acidly, eyes narrowed with undisguised contempt for the girl's darned coat and patched button-boots. 'Some folk have no idea of how to behave in public places, neither they have! Rif-raff, hanging out the window shouting and snivelling like the scruff they are ... disgusting.'

'Quite right, Helena.' Her companion nodded and turned primly to Annie. 'Shouldn't you be in third class, child? This is for first class passengers only, you know.'

'I ken that,' Annie replied with a toss of her curly head.

'Well then, I suggest you take that ... er ... thing ... and leave, before the guard comes up the corridor and throws you out?' The other woman gazed pointedly upwards.

On the rack above their heads, Annie's little bundle wrapped in an old shawl looked out of place beside the three other passenger's sturdy leather trunks and embroidered carpet bags.

'Mind yer own business, missus, and I'll mind mine,' Annie replied with a cheeky toss of her head.

'Would you believe the nerve of it?' The women gave each other an affronted look. 'I'm calling the guard right now, Helena!'

'The lass is with me, ladies.' Lowering his paper, Doctor

Murchieson intervened politely but firmly. 'Her ticket is paid for in full, just like your own.'

'There should be a law against it, so there should!' The women hissed. But Annie was too busy thinking to care.

A month, just a month since I even heard of Clachan's Farm. Now I'm going to live there! Annie's head spun with the amazement of it. She felt bewildered, excited and more than a touch afraid. It was a lot to take in and she had resolutely tried not to think much till it was upon her. At fifteen years and nine months, Annie Ramsay from the Gallowgate, who had only ever seen a cow on the condensed milk advert by the tram-stop, was being carried off in the Stranraer ferry-train to become a milkmaid in Ayrshire. She shivered involuntarily and sank a little deeper into the cold leather seat.

Even when her mother had tied her few belongings into a neat bundle last night and shed a tear or two over them, Annie hadn't really thought in her heart that she would be leaving, probably for ever. Now she was on her way, and to what she wasn't sure. Her grey eyes darkened and she gazed intently out of the window at the blackened tenement walls and backyards of the great city.

Tribes of children played hide and seek among the flapping lines of washing bravely defying the flying cinders of the Ayrshire train. Annie watched them flash past. This was the world she knew, and she clung greedily to its familiarity.

Opposite, Doctor Archibald Murchieson hid behind the *Glasgow Herald*. His impulse to get Annie Ramsay to a life where she had a chance of survival had been the spontaneous reaction of a generous heart. But now they were on their way, he hoped he hadn't burdened his old friendships, one of them in particular, with a wee cuckoo in the nest.

'Och no, Archie Murchieson,' he told himself firmly as doubts crowded in, 'you did the right thing. And if it doesn't work out, well it was an act of Christian charity and that's that. Anyway Geordie Clachan and Bess Crawford are couthy folk with no airs and graces about them, despite the good living Geordie makes. It's not as if I was sending Annie to Craigdrummond House! Still ...' The worry nagged on and he closed his eyes, paper forgotten. 'Maybe I haven't been entirely wise.'

'My patients always seem to live on the top floor!' Archie

6

Murchieson had grunted as he climbed the steep tenement stairs that dismal February morning. 'Och well, at least it's daylight and I can see where I'm going ... more or less!'

'Och, it's you, Doctor.' A man passed him on the way down, cracked workman's boots echoing on the bevelled stone steps. 'Yer no goin' to see oor Annie again?' He paused with a frown that hovered between belligerence and defence.

'I am that, Jamie, and how is the lass?'

'No bad enough for spending guid money on doctors.' Jamie Ramsay pulled out a blackened clay pipe and stuck it between ragged teeth.

'This visit is on my charity list,' Murchieson replied firmly. 'Are you still in work, Jamie?'

'Aye, at the docks, Doctor. It's great to have a pay comin' in, so it is.' He pushed a strand of grubby curly hair from his eyes.

'And going out again,' the doctor commented dryly.

'Och, ye ken I need a wee dram ...' Jamie shifted uneasily.

'Yes I do know, Jamie Ramsay, and only too well.' Doctor Murchieson sighed. 'We are in the last decade of this century, before long it will be the year of our Lord nineteen hundred, the dawn of a New Era of Progress and Hope, but some folk will no doubt still spend what wee bit money they have in the public house instead of on their wife and bairns.'

'Aye well ...' Jamie shuffled and looked down at his boots. 'It's all right for you to talk,' he growled. 'Doctors don't have the same worries as folk like us.'

'Is that a fact?' Doctor Murchieson raised his eyebrows ironically, then shrugged. 'Och, I suppose there's no point in preaching, Jamie.' He shook his head, resigned. 'You're not a bad lad, at least when you're sober. And I know fine you agree with me in your heart, if not in your thirst. Just watch the drink, man, you've bairns to think about.'

'Aye right enough, well I'll be on my way, Doctor, the shift'll be startin'.' Jamie Ramsay tipped his cap and clattered off as fast as he could.

Murchieson carried on up past the noxious communal toilet on the next landing and rattled on Ramsay's door. A worn, worried woman opened it, wrapped in the comfort of an old plaid shawl with identical twin girls of five or so, snotter candles dripping, clinging to her skirts.

7

'Morning, Mistress Ramsay, is my favourite patient better?'

'Och aye, she's fine. Ye needn't have come back, Doctor. And the place is a mess, so it is.' Apologising with every step, she led him into the kitchen.

'Don't bother yourself, Mistress Ramsay. It's not easy keeping a room and kitchen like a palace when you have five bairns and your man to share it ... and you do better than most,' he reassured her. 'Well then, how's Annie Ramsay today?' Murchieson asked the girl lying on a truckle bed in the corner.

'I'm fine, Doctor.' Her cheery smile lit up the fever-bright grey eyes, pale face and cheeks with an unhealthy flush. Near the foot of the bed, a kettle putt-putted steam into the damp, stuffy air of the crowded kitchen. A line of patched workman's clothes hung limply on the pulley above her head.

'Well, you've certainly improved on the last time.' With a smile, he squatted down and took her pulse. 'Now let's listen to your chest.'

'Can I get up the day?' Annie asked anxiously. 'The other lassies are coverin' the best they can, but the foreman'll replace me at the 'baccy factory, if I don't get back soon. I canny miss any more shifts, Doctor.' The effort of speaking ended in a cough that left her gasping for breath.

'Och, my poor lassie, that place with be the death of her!' Mrs Ramsay gave a keening wail. 'Annie, that's always loved to sing and now she can hardly draw a breath! I've tried to find her some other place to work, Doctor, but there's nothin' going the now. Wi' Annie bein' that clever, she wanted to stay on at the school and maybe get a trade,' the woman fretted, 'but ye ken we needed the money.'

'I understand your position,' Murchieson sighed, 'I've known the lass nearly all her short life and she's bright right enough, and with a lovely voice ... it's a pity she can't use the talents God gave her. But then, these streets are full of folk who could do better given half a chance.' The doctor straightened up, standing thoughtfully for a moment. He put his stethoscope carefully into the black bag, then went on decisively, 'In fact, Mistress Ramsay, one of the reasons I came back was to talk to you about Annie's future.'

'Whit do ye mean?' Mrs Ramsay's face clouded in anxiety. Life had not been kind and she instinctively feared the worst.

8

'This time she's got away with it,' the doctor replied gravely. 'Her chest is nearly clear despite the cough. But next winter she might not be so lucky. I'm treating her for chronic bronchitis now, like I've done every winter for the last five years and it gets worse each time. Last January when she developed pneumonia, we all thought we'd lost her.'

'I ken that.' Mrs Ramsay took her daughter's hand in a helpless, protective gesture.

'Well, I've already half a dozen cases of tuberculosis in this street,' Murchieson went on with a resigned grimace. 'If the lass doesn't get out of the tobacco factory and this place soon, she'll be next. I'm just amazed she hasn't caught it yet.'

'Och, I've heard there's some folk cannae get it,' Mrs Ramsay said hopefully, 'maybe Annie's one of them, Doctor.'

'Yes, some folk have a natural immunity, but there's no guarantee Annie's one of them.' He walked over to the window and looked down to the muddy yard far below. The crowded tenements formed a gloomy, black square in the sooty February drizzle. Weak light filtered down from low, dark clouds and hardly penetrated the muddy alleys. 'In any case, with her lungs as they are, Annie needs fresh air and good food, Mistress Ramsay, or she'll die quickly of pneumonia if not slowly of TB.' His tone was grim.

'But I haven't two bawbees to rub together, ye ken that, Doctor!' The poor woman's eyes filled with tears. 'The oldest laddies are workin', but they just have laddies' pay and hardly cover their keep. Wi' the twins so wee, and our Jamie no able to pass the pub, there's nothin' left over.'

'I know that fine.' Doctor Murchieson sat down at the rickety table where a loaf and a dish of lard were placed neatly side by side on a clean, cracked plate. 'And I know you do your best.' His gesture took in the bit of well-washed net curtain across the window and the worn oilcloth on the floor. 'That's why I've racked my brains and finally come up with a suggestion which I hope will work. That's the real reason I'm back today.'

'Aye?' Mrs Ramsay instinctively pulled the twins towards her as if she felt her world was about to be threatened. They stood staring at him wide-eyed and silent, all three. In the corner, Annie pulled herself up on one elbow to listen.

Doctor Murchieson continued, 'I met an old friend of mine at

9

the Kilmarnock District Burns supper last week, just hours after I'd seen Annie at her worst, so the lass was in my mind.'

'Well, imagine that!' Mrs Ramsay said in surprise. 'Ye've aye had a soft-spot for oor Annie right enough, Doctor.'

'I have that,' he agreed, smiling over at the bright-eyed girl who shone like a jewel in this poverty-stricken setting. 'But normally I don't interfere in the lives of my patients ... beyond giving sound advice where needed, of course,' he added ponderously.

The woman nodded. 'I ken that, but ye do what you can. Ye're well thought of in this street, so ye are, Doctor.'

'It's nice of you to say so,' Murchieson's kind, plump face coloured with pleasure. 'Anyway this time I've decided to make an exception for Annie's sake.'

'Whit do ye mean an exception, Doctor?'

'My friend,' he explained gravely, 'is the tenant of a big farm in Ayrshire. He has a fine dairy herd, as well as rearing sheep and horses.'

'Sorry, Doctor Murchieson, I don't follow ye ... whit is a dairy herd?' Mrs Ramsay looked puzzled.

'That's coos for milk, Mammy, they send it up to Glesca in great big urns then we buy it in wee jugs from Robertson's milk cart,' Annie volunteered.

'That's right, lass. Now maybe you have a better picture, Mistress Ramsay,' the Doctor said as he turned back to the bewildered woman. 'And I can get Annie fee'd and trained as a dairymaid in Ayrshire, if you and her father are willing to let her go.'

'But Ayrshire is miles away,' her mother protested. 'My cousin went to Ayr once. She says it's no a bit like Glesca, there's nothin' but sea and fields and that. And they all talk funny.' She shook her head. 'Och, no, Doctor, thanks for thinkin' about Annie, but no, my bairn isn't goin' among strangers, to work wi' beasts and things.'

'Leave her in the tobacco factory and she'll be going to another place, Mistress ... permanently!' Doctor Murchieson was blunt.

'Och, don't say that!' Annie's mother blanched, hand flying to her throat. 'Look, I'll talk to Jamie. Er, would she get any pay?' she asked tentatively.

'Of course, Mistress Ramsay! Slavery went out a while back.'

10

He smiled. 'Annie would get a fee as they call it. It's not a lot. Farm workers are not the richest in Scotland. I believe for an untrained lass it's about three pounds the half-year.'

'Three pound? That's no much!' Mrs Ramsay protested. 'She gets ten shillings a week in the 'baccy factory and it's goin' up now she's learned to roll the leaf.'

'And what did she earn this week, or last? Or the two months she was ill last winter?' he pointed out.

'That's a fact, Doctor ... nothin',' Annie broke in. 'Ye don't get pay when ye're on the sick ...'

'Exactly,' Dr Murchieson agreed and turned back to her mother. 'And her fee would increase each year. She would probably also be paid a wee bit more in kind.'

'Kind? Whit's that, Doctor?' Mrs Ramsay asked with a puzzled look.

'A sack or two of oatmeal for porridge, for instance, a cheese ...'

'Och.' Annie's mother shrugged in disappointment. 'Is that all?'

'Of course you wouldn't have her keep to think about,' Archie Murchieson plodded on. 'All in all you would be no worse off than with her in the factory and she would certainly benefit.'

'I think the doctor's right, Mammy, anything would be better than being sick all the time,' Annie piped up from the corner.

'Och, no, Annie hen, Ayr and them places are too far. We'd never see ye. It's kind of ye, Doctor,' Mrs Ramsay shook her head decisively, 'but she's no goin' and that's that.'

'What farm is it, Doctor?' Annie broke in stubbornly.

'Clachan's Farm,' the doctor replied. 'Geordie Clachan is a fine farmer and a fine man. He's a widower these many years, with a lad of eighteen or maybe a wee bit more ... och time passes that fast I can't keep up!' he shook his head.

'Aye but if our Annie did go ... and I'm not sayin' she can,' Mrs Ramsay added as Annie sat up, face hopeful, '... who wid look after her if that fairmer is a widow-man?'

Doctor Murchieson beamed. 'His housekeeper, Mrs Crawford, is an excellent body. She runs the place with a rod of iron.'

'Aye but would she be good to my bairn?' Mrs Ramsay's face clouded again. 'Annie can be a right wee madame at times, but she's a good lassie. I'd no have her ill-treated, neither I would, by some stranger. It's bad enough when Jamie gets a bit too much in him and thumps the lot of us ... but he's her faither and that's different.'

'Different, is it?' Doctor Murchieson muttered, but swallowed his irritation. 'Mistress Ramsay,' he went on patiently, 'I know the lady myself these many years, from when she was a lassie in fact. Aye, she's strict, there's no denying, but she's a kindly soul at heart. You need have no fear for your lassie's welfare at the hands of Mistress Elizabeth Crawford, Mistress Ramsay.'

'Och well, maybe I could talk to Jamie,' she still sounded doubtful.

Annie sat up, choking back the cough that threatened everytime she moved. Her voice came out in a hoarse, but determined wheeze. 'There's no need, Mammy, Daddy doesn't ken the first thing about farms, he'd jist say "aye" or "naw" depending on how much whisky he has in him when ye ask.' She turned to the doctor. 'I'll be comin' with ye, Doctor,' she said firmly and settled down again on the hard, rag pillow. 'Clachan's Farm? Aye, that sounds just fine for me.'

Now they were on their way. Doctor Murchieson looked at the girl opposite, gazing intently out of the train window, fascinated by the passing world she had never seen before. 'Och, man,' he shrugged and went back to his paper, 'what's done is done!'

Chapter Two

They clanked and juddered to a halt for the thirteenth time. Annie had counted every stop, watching the turmoil round-eyed as passengers scrambled in and out, yelling and fussing. Och, it's like magic the way they get all sorted out and nobody gets killed by they big wheels, so it is, she mused.

'Craigdrummond Junction! Next stop, The Maidens!' bawled the guard.

'Wait a minute! Craigdrummond! Isn't this me, Doctor?' Annie jumped up anxiously.

'Indeed it is, lass. That's it, mind your feet on the bar.' Doctor Murchieson puffed as he helped her jump down the steep drop to the low platform.

Only a few people were getting off, but there was chaos enough as they lifted out crates of chickens, bags, bundles and a squealing pig.

The guard walked along the length of the train shouting instructions at the top of his voice above the intermittent howls of the impatient engine. 'Watch ye don't burst they sacks!' He chaffed a carter who tossed the last bales and bundles into the goods-van. 'Is that us then?'

'Aye, that's the lot for the Stranraer ferry from Craigdrummond House,' the carter replied, dusting his hands.

Doctor Murchieson leaned down with Annie's bundle. 'Here you are, lass. Mistress Crawford knows you're on this train, so don't worry if you have to wait a while, somebody will be along for you before dark. Tell her and Mr Clachan that I send my most cordial respects and I'll be calling in September as usual.'

'Aye, I'll tell them, Doctor,' Annie answered bravely, hoping that she didn't look nearly as scared as she felt. She stood there clutching her bundle as the platform cleared terrifyingly fast, carriages disappeared and the train belched and puffed away.

'Haw, mister!' she cried after the retreating back of the last soul, an old farmer hunched on a cart. Unhearing, he and his scraggy horse plodded off, taking the final sign of life with him.

Annie had never felt so alone. Tentatively she looked around. The sight gave little comfort. Craigdrummond Junction was only a halt for lifting and leaving passengers and freight, without even a ticket office or waiting room for shelter. There was a bare bit of platform and big signal box further down the line by a level crossing. Now the train had gone, the junction seemed placed in the middle of nowhere.

Annie peered up at the treacherous March sky where dark clouds were beginning to scud in from the west as first signs of evening appeared.

'Maybe nobody will come, I'll be stuck here till the next train comes. Och, Mammy, Daddy! The doctor said that's not till tomorrow and I haven't any money for the fare anyway!' she said aloud and tried not to let the terrifying thought plummet into panic.

Taking a deep breath, the girl put down her bundle and straightened up, lifting her chin in a characteristically determined gesture. She looked beyond the junction to the countryside. Great rolling ridges of distant hills ran the length of the horizon as far as she could see. Between these and the railway track, a desolate moor stretched menacingly. Here and there, scattered boulders rose grim and dark, casting weird shapes onto the dark green moss. Shifting streaks of reflected colour ran crazily to and fro like demented spirits as the wind tossed cloudy shadows from above.

'I wish I hadn't bothered looking!' Annie whispered under her breath, overawed. She had never seen such fearsome emptiness before. This wasn't like Glasgow Green or even the Kelvin Park where nature was well under control and there were always plenty of folk around. She longed for the dingy lanes and dirty alleys of the city, for the crumbling, familiar tenements of the Gallowgate and the noisy, rattling trams in the busy main streets.

A chill wind cut through her thin coat and she shivered. 'What's that?' Suddenly she lifted her face and sniffed like a wee

14

terrier dog. The wind carried with it a distinctive smell, a clean, fresh, tangy odour. Annie licked her lips and found they were salty. She had never known the sea, so she couldn't guess what it was, but for the rest of her life she would remember its first sharp presence and briny taste.

'Yip! Yipp ...' The cries of seabirds floated eerily on the clear air. Minutes crept by and the sky slowly darkened with the gathering storm. Now and then she felt the prick of hail on her cheeks. 'Oh, what if it starts to thunder!' Annie remembered gruesome stories she had heard in school of people being struck by lightning. Things like that always seemed to happen in dangerous places. And this vastness was dangerous.

'Och, I want to go home!' she muttered aloud, biting her lip to stop it trembling. She looked for somewhere to shelter, becoming more and more scared as her imagination ran riot. Only the signal box broke the desolation. There was no sign of life. Annie's heart sank further. Still, the box gave most hope, she walked towards it, clutching her bundle, curly chestnut head bent into the rising wind. But when she got there it was as empty and unfriendly as the alien countryside around it. Annie could have wept.

She stood shivering getting colder and colder, then with a sigh she crouched by the signalbox, singing a street ditty under her breath to keep up her courage. 'Oh, I'll gie you a dress o' red, a stiched roon wi' silver thread, if you will marry, arry, arry, arry, if you will marry me ...' It gave little comfort and her voice died away as the bitter wind with its erratic bursts of biting hail seemed to seek her out and cut through the threadbare coat. Time dragged on.

'Are you Clachan's lassie off the Stranraer train?' A voice suddenly came from nowhere making her jump.

'Owya!' she looked around but saw no one. 'Oh, Mither! The place is haunted wi' ghaistes and ghoulies!'

'Did ye hear me, lassie?'

Annie looked up towards the sound and saw a cheery face leaning out of the signalbox window. She blushed at her own daftness. 'Aye, I heard, but I didn't think there was anybody in there, Mister. The door was locked when I tried it a minute ago.'

'There wasn't anybody. I went straight home to get my piece once the train left. I just came back,' he replied in a sing-song, unfamiliar accent. 'You were that busy round the other side, looking over the bonnie Carrick hills, you didn't hear me unlock the door.'

'Is somebody coming for me from Clachan's Farm, Mister?' Annie raised anxious grey eyes to the signalman.

'That's what I'm trying to tell ye, lass. Thampson the carter will be back in a wee while and he'll take ye over the moor. He's just delivering some stuff to Rannoch's Farm. Ye can see the tallest chimneys from where ye're standing.'

Annie's eyes followed the direction he pointed. Suddenly she realised there were signs of habitation after all amid the barren moor and hills. Smoke from what must be Rannoch's farmhouse blew in long streamers as the rising wind caught it. Funny she'd never noticed that before. Her natural optimism came rushing back. Maybe Ayrshire wasn't so desolate after all.

Her spirits rose even more when the cheery voice continued. 'Come round the back and join me for a wee minute. I said to the missus there was a wee lass off the Stranraer train for Clachan's. "Och, no," she says, "Thampson aye sits and gossips for hours at Rannochs wi' the cook, the lassie will be frozen stiff and fainting wi' hunger before he comes back." So she put an extra bit bannock in my piece for ye.'

'Och, that's great! I'm coming!' Annie ran round and in through the welcoming open door. A tin mug of strong black tea brewed on the iron-wrought top of the charcoal stove and a jammy slice of fresh bannock later and she forgot about the hail rattling more frequently now on the window, heralding the growing storm.

'Right, lass, here's Thampson for ye.' The kindly signalman led her down to the platform where the carter pulled up an hour or so later.

'Good luck to ye, Annie Ramsay. Ye're right cheery company, so ye are,' he called as he turned to leave.

'Thanks, Mister.' Annie waved and grabbed her bundle as a blast of hail-laden wind nearly lifted her off her feet. She struggled the last few yards over to the cart.

'Up ye come then.' The carter threw her bundle in the back under a tarpaulin and helped her onto the seat beside him. 'We'll use this one for ourselves, it'll help a bit.' He pulled up a big sheet of greasy canvas over a makeshift frame and she shrank gratefully into the partial shelter it provided.

'Gerrup!' The carter's big Clydesdale horse snorted and clomped heavily off the platform and onto the rough track which, to Annie, seemed to run forever to nowhere.

The wind gusted and whistled, causing the canvas to flap and billow like a sail. They trudged the long miles across the moor as the evening closed steadily in. At first the carter whistled cheerily, then driving rain replaced the intermittent hail and he concentrated on keeping them on track through the growing darkness and the endless wailing of the icy wind.

Annie wished she was home, she wished she had arrived, she wished she was anywhere but on this miserable journey. She thought it might be possible to be wetter and colder, but she didn't think she could be and still live.

'It's no far now, lass,' the carter said glancing down at the shivering girl. 'We're nearly off the moor and then it's only minutes to Clachan's Farm.'

'What's that over there?' Annie saw the lights of a great house glow ahead in the darkness.

'That's Craigdrummond House,' Thampson replied. 'The Laird lives there.'

'The Laird?'

'Aye, Sir Urquhart Cameron of Craigdrummond to give his full and due title. He owns the farms for miles round here.'

'Does he own Clachan's Farm?'

'Och aye, Geordie Clachan's family have been tenants for generations, and can hold their heads up wi' pride in Ayrshire, but that's what they are, tenants just like the Rannochs where I was delivering.'

'Can the Laird throw them oot?' Annie remembered the bailiffs arriving many times at the close to evict recalcitrant tenants.

'Throw them oot?' The carter laughed. 'That would be the day! He would have to find a good excuse to break that agreement. And he'll get none from Geordie Clachan. The Laird never has to wait for his rent from Clachan's Farm.'

'But could he?' Annie persisted.

'Och, lass, I'm no lawyer,' the carter replied. 'All I ken is that generations of Clachans have farmed there. And Geordie is a landowner himself in a small way, ye might say, being that he's bought extra fields here and there over the years from freeholders

17

and farms them too. And what's it to do with you whether Geordie Clachan is tenant or owner?' he demanded.

'That's where I'm goin' to work!' Annie said importantly with a pert lift of her wet face.

'Aye, I guessed that's why I'm taking you there. I didn't think ye were a candidate to be Lady of Craigdrummond, or of Clachan's farmhouse for that matter,' the carter replied dryly.

'Why not? My Mammy says we're all Jock Thampson's bairns when it comes to the bit!' Annie replied dryly.

'I hope not!' The carter laughed uproariously and slapped his wet thigh. 'That's my name, Jock Thampson! Still it's a good question ... why not?' He smiled at the spirit of this small, shivering bundle of wet ragged clothes with the sharp questions and quick replies. 'But ye better watch yer manners with Mistress Crawford, she'll no put up wi' cheeky wee lassies,' he warned direly, 'even if they are from Glasgow.'

'Och, I'm no that cheeky, at least no much,' Annie said sheepishly and lapsed into frozen silence. 'Owya!' she yelped as a highly-sprung carriage pulled by two fine horses flew past in a clatter of hooves and flying stones. 'Och, that made me jump!'

'That's from Craigdrummond and heading back there. Maybe it's the Laird. It cannae be Miss Alexandra at this time of evening.'

'Who's Miss Alexandra?' Annie asked. 'She has a right bonnie name.'

'Aye, called after Alexandra, the Princess of Wales ... she's bonnie as the day herself is Miss Alexandra, and full of charm when she feels like it, but wi' a temper ye wouldn't believe if ye cross her ... or so I'm told by folk that works there ... not that I ken her myself,' the carter added hastily.

'Is this Miss Alexandra, Mistress at Craigdrummond?'

'In a manner of speaking,' he replied. 'Lady Cameron died having a late bairn a few years back and the Laird hasn't been the same man since. Miss Alexandra is sixteen, so aye, I suppose ye could say she's the Mistress of Craigdrummond for want of another. Unless the master marries again. Though he doesn't seem inclined so far,' he added with a shrug.

Annie fell silent again, incurious about those who had no bearing on her new life which was coming inexorably closer with each clop of the big horse's hooves. She grasped the bar of the

18

wind-break with a frozen hand and wondered for the hundredth time that day about what lay ahead.

'Well here we are,' Thampson announced at last, pulling up with a 'woa' and a grunt. The Clydesdale whinneyed to a stop in the dark farmyard. Except for a lit window, it seemed as deserted as the railway junction, but then the dogs began barking and to the left a door opened, spilling bright light into the miserable night.

'What's yer name again, lass?' the carter asked as he lifted her down.

'Annie Ramsay,' she answered looking apprehensively beyond him to where a tall, imposing figure draped in a long black cloak came bustling towards them.

'Well here she is, Mistress Crawford.' The carter grinned. 'A wee bit drookit and cold, but none the worse I'm sure after a plate of broth. I'll leave her to ye, Mistress. Well, cheerio and good luck to ye, Clachan's Annie.'

'Cheerio,' she called back, wishing she could go with him.

'I'll be away then, Mistress.' The carter touched his cap respectfully with a hopeful look at the package in the house-keeper's hand.

'Goodnight to you, Thampson,' Mrs Crawford replied. 'And here's a wee lump of butter for Mistress Thampson, with your fee.' She beckoned to Annie. 'Right, lass, follow me.'

'Aye, Missus.' Annie tried to keep up.

As the light from the window touched the girl, Mrs Crawford suddenly stopped, bent down and peered into Annie's frozen face. 'In heaven's name!' she gasped in astonishment. 'What has Archie Murchieson sent us? We were expecting a lass to train as a dairymaid, but you look more like a wee drowned Glasgow rat to me! Does he think I'm running a charity for his waifs and strays?' She gave a disgusted sniff.

Annie shifted her bundle uneasily and wiped her dripping face with the back of her hand. Chilled to the bone, she shook uncon-trollably from head to foot, teeth chattering.

'Och well, there's no point in you standing out here,' Mrs Crawford shrugged in exasperation, 'I won't have your death on my hands. And from what I gather, you're halfways to being consumptive already! You might as well come in, though I'll be sending you right back to Glasgow in the morning. Dairymaid indeed!'

Och, maybe it's just as well if I go back to the Gallowgate, if they don't want me at Clachan's Farm. And I'm no a wee drowned rat! Annie thought indignantly, but remembering the carter's warning, she bit her tongue. There was no point in making things worse. 'Och but I can't go back!' she moaned softly in despair. 'I went and gave up my job in the 'baccy factory!'

It looked as if her great adventure at Clachan's Farm was over before it had even properly begun. Glumly she followed the housekeeper's irate figure through the farmhouse door wondering what on earth she was going to do.

Chapter Three

'Michty!' Astonished, she stopped on the doorstep, gawping and forgetting her icy feet and hands, or her hurt feelings, as the brightness and warmth enveloped her.

In the centre of the glowing room was a long scrubbed table, the biggest Annie had ever seen. A giant oil lamp glowed in the middle, casting bright light around like a halo. It was laid for supper with sturdy plates and tankards jostling for space along the two long sides. At each end a single place was set in splendid isolation. One had a finely carved chair marking it out as the head. Three huge loaves of bread still steaming from the oven sat, each on its own board, flanked by slabs of creamy butter and frothing jugs of buttermilk as big as the ones Annie had seen in the Gallowgate dairy.

On the big black-leaded iron range in the corner, a pot of mutton broth bubbled loudly, throwing a delicious aroma into every corner of the room. Potatoes sat waiting in great containers to join the soup on the stove. Annie goggled, she hadn't seen that much food together in her whole life.

'Well, don't just stand there dripping water all over the floor!' Mrs Crawford said acidly, taking off her own long cape and hanging it up on a hook behind the door.

'Sorry, Missus.' Annie pulled together her scattered wits and asked as politely as she could, 'Where shall I pit ... er ... put my coat?'

'On the wee hook at the bottom, you'll never reach the others.' Mrs Crawford sighed and patted her neat brown hair which was just showing touches of grey here and there. She smoothed the white apron over her ample, well corseted figure. 'Now let's have a proper look at you.' She took the girl's shoulders firmly, turning her towards the light with astonishingly strong hands. Trickles of water ran down Annie's forehead from a cluster of damp curls and dripped off the end of her short nose. She felt very small and very inadequate.

'Aye, well, you're not much to look at, even in the light, are you?' Mrs Crawford said briskly, 'And there's not a pick on your bones!' Annie winced as the strong fingers pinched her arms. 'Are you sure you've finished school? What age did you say you were, child?'

'Nearly sixteen, Missus. I've been working in the tobacco factory for two years.' Annie tried not to be intimidated by this powerful woman, but, still shivering with cold and apprehension, she was certain she would be on the first train next morning.

'Hmmm, you don't look a day over eleven or twelve ... Och, mind you I suppose you'll be a mite better once we get you cleaned and dried and put some supper in that wee skinny body! Well, we're stuck with you whatever you are ... at least till the carter comes back tomorrow... I wonder if the nine o'clock train from Stranraer is running yet? Och, Archie Murchieson, what have you done this time!' Mrs Crawford raised her eyes to heaven. 'Lezzie!' she shouted so suddenly, Annie nearly jumped out of her skin.

'Coming, Missus!' A strapping young woman with a round, cheerful face appeared through the door at the back, 'I was just in the pantry. Oh tae hang!' Leezie didn't try to hide her surprise. 'Is this the lass off the train?' Her voice was laced with disbelief. 'I thought the Doctor said she was to work wi' the milkin'! That wee thing will no be able to drive the kye back to the byre, let alone milk one!'

'Aye, she's not quite what we were expecting,' Mrs Crawford agreed dryly.

Annie stood miserably while they talked about her. She wanted to cry, but bit her lip hard so she wouldn't. They could say what they liked. Sticks and stones will break my bones, she repeated the old rhyme to herself, but words will never hurt me! But they did.

'I never thought she was goin' to be a bairn like that,' Leezie added.

'I'm not a bairn,' Annie's head shot up and her eyes flashed.

'I'm sixteen in June. That makes me a wumman! I could learn, so I could, if ye wid just gave me a chance!'

'Aye, well, that's a matter for me to decide and I'll do so when I have done far more important things. like finish supper.' Mistress Crawford turned to the maid, 'We'd better get her sorted out before the men come in from the byre. Get the bath, Leezie.'

'Och, what are ye doin?' Annie's eyes widened with shock and she squeaked a horrified protest as a tin bath was dumped in front of the range and she was unceremoniously stripped to the skin by the two women.

'You don't think you're sitting down to eat with civilised folk in that condition?' The housekeeper rubbed a bar of carbolic over her from head to toe and held her firmly as Leezie doused her liberally with tepid water.

'I had a bath!' Annie lied gamely. 'I don't need one!'

'Not lately, by the look of your neck!' the housekeeper said. 'Maybe you're planning one to celebrate the New Century... but that's not for another eight years!' Mrs Crawford gave her another going over with the pungent soap, stinging her eyes and making her hop. 'We've done for the lice this time, but if I'm daft enough to let you stay... and there's no saying I will... you'll have to wash your hair every day for two weeks and comb it with the fine-comb to get rid of the nits.'

'But boogies is nothin! Everybody has wee visitors, so they have!' Annie spluttered through another flood of soapy water.

'Not in Clachan's Farm they don't!' The housekeeper lifted her out as if she was a collie pup and Leezie wrapped her in a rough white sheet.

'Take her up and loan her one of your shifts, Leezie, and a pinny till tomorrow.'

'But my shift will be far too big, Mrs Crawford!'

'Och, don't argue, girl!' Mrs Crawford said irritably. 'Tie it in place with the pinny, just fold it up round the waist so she doesn't trip and she'll do. Get on with it, or the men will be here and not a scrap of food on the table!'

'Come on, wee lassie.' Leezie propelled a clean but humiliated Annie out of the kitchen into a spotless interior hall where every bit of brass shone dully in the light of wall-candles and a smell of beeswax oozed from polished wood. Overawed and wide-eyed, obediently she followed the big, country-girl up the stairs to the chilly top of the house where the servants lived. A set of stairs went off to the right.

'What's up there?' Annie asked curiously.

'That's up the men's quarters, the lassies are only allowed up to clean,' Leezie replied. 'This is us lassies up here.' She led the way to the left and stopped in front of an attic door. 'You'll be in here the night. I'm next door and then along at the end there's Maisie.'

'Who's that?'

'The other dairymaid.'

'Will she be showin' me what to do?' Annie asked hopefully, unable to believe she would be sent right back.

'Not the now. One of the laddies will have to help ye to begin with... if you get staying! Mistress Crawford's not too happy wi' the Doctor sending ye, but she's aye fair,' the older girl commented shrewdly.

'Whit does she no gie me a chance for?' Annie said in a small, hurt voice. 'Jist a chance. It's not much to ask.'

'Annie, lassies queue up to get workin' at Clachan's Farm,' Leezie replied gravely. 'We work hard... right hard wi' no slackin' and farm hours are long. But we're paid a fair rate and we're never starved or beaten, or worse. Some fairmers take advantage of farm lassies, but there's no jiggery-pokery here, if ye ken whit I mean...' Leezie gave her a meaningful nudge.

Annie nodded. 'Aye, ye had to watch for that in the 'baccy factory as well. Some of the foremen were at ye all the time.'

'And lassies are set for life once they've worked at Clachan's Farm. When ye've been learned something here,' Leezie went on, 'ye can do it right.' She looked at the girl sympathetically, not wanting to dampen her hopes, but feeling she should know the true situation. 'I just want ye to ken why she's no as welcoming as ye'd hoped, Annie,' she said. 'The Missus only took you because the Doctor asked her special and we happened to be needing somebody. She knew ye would be a city lass wi' no idea of beasts or byre, but at least she was expectin' somebody a bit bigger and stronger...'

'But...' Annie was about to argue when she caught a glimpse of herself in a big framed mirror at the top of the stairs. A small, shocked face peered back, topped with bedraggled, wet curls.

The darned sheet wound round her underfed body emphasised her slightness. She could see she was nobody's idea of a sturdy farm girl. 'So I'll no be staying then. Is that what ye're saying, Leezie?' she concluded.

Leezie's round face became thoughtful. 'Maybe aye, maybe no. Like I was saying, Maisie's away home to Alloway, her mither is sick. That's lucky for you both ways.'

'What do ye mean both ways?' Streetwise Annie was instantly alert.

'Well maybe Mistress Crawford will try ye out right enough, because they're desperate short-handed in the byre and she kens the fairmer wants another hand right away.'

'Why else am I lucky what-do-yer-call-her ... Maisie's no here?' Annie insisted.

'Och, ye'll find out soon enough if you're still workin' when she gets back.' Leezie shifted uneasily as if she'd said too much. 'Just watch it wi' her, that's all. You'd better get dressed before ye freeze.' Leezie noticed her shivering. She lit a candle from the one in the hall and then opened a narrow door, showing Annie into a tiny room the size of a broom cupboard. 'This is for you ... tonight anyway.'

'On my own?'

'Aye.'

Annie crept in. A narrow iron bed covered with a pristine, but well darned patchwork quilt, took up almost the entire width. At the far end, a chest of drawers was jammed under the little window. It never occurred to Annie that the room was tiny, in fact it seemed huge for one person to have all to herself. She had never slept anywhere alone in her life. The prospect was more than a little frightening.

Dressed in the strange over-large clothes, with a mob-cap covering most of her damp curls, Annie followed Leezie back to the kitchen a few minutes later. This time the inside door was open and the hall was full to overflowing with men of every shape and size, talking in the unfamiliar dialect of Ayrshire. They were busy taking off their muddy farm boots and untying the leather thongs that kept their trousers from the mud.

Annie stood behind the door, keeping well out of sight, waiting, her stomach in a knot. One by one the men disappeared into a back room and she could hear the splashes as they washed the day's

25

work from their hands and faces. Gradually they drifted into the kitchen chaffing, laughing and sniffing the air appreciatively.

At last they were all inside and without warning the door was closed with a bang, robbing Annie of her hiding place.

'Mistress Crawford,' a male voice said loudly, 'what's this then, has Maisie been out in the rain while she was away and shrunk?'

The rest fell silent. To a man they stared at the newcomer.

'Och no! Mistress Crawford, tell me my eyes are deceivin' me,' a cheery-looking, ruddy-complexioned man finally spluttered in disbelief. 'Surely this can't be the new dairymaid?'

'Indeed that's what she's supposed to be, Dougie,' answered Mrs Crawford gravely. 'Though I doubt the kye will be over impressed!'

Suddenly all the men started laughing. Annie stood there, red to the hairline, wishing the farmhouse floor would open and swallow her.

Swamped by big strapping Leezie's old clothes, Annie should have just looked ridiculous. But, blushing beetroot with miserable embarrassment, she stood her ground against the mocking laughter of strangers. Her hair had almost dried and defiant dark chestnut curls crept out from the mob-cap, softening the broad forehead. Annie's determined little chin went up and she refused to allow the angry tears that glittered in her grey eyes to flow.

Bess Crawford saw the unexpected strength of character in the gesture and wondered. For all he's soft-hearted, Archie doesn't usually have bad judgement ... och, maybe I'll give the lass a chance like she asked after all, she mused. A week won't do any harm while Maisie's away, and then at least I can tell Archie she had a fair trial when I send her back.

'Right,' she said to the crowded room, 'If you're all washed and ready, then supper's on the table.' Men and maids sat down, hungry and appreciative of the simple, wholesome fare spread before them.

'Och, what am I supposed to do?' Annie Ramsay stood in the middle of the big farm kitchen and felt panic grip her.

'Come on, Annie.' Leezie's strong hand grabbed her arm and guided her unceremoniously to a place near the bottom of the supper table.

Bess Crawford nodded approval, and checked everyone else

26

was in place. She kept good order at Clachan's Farm where her reign was supreme. 'Where's Ian?' for a moment she didn't see her nephew, then she noticed him crouched down having a word with old Charlie before taking his place. Och he's a good lad, she thought and her face softened, revealing without being concious of it, the soft-spot reserved in her heart for the boy she had virtually brought up. Ian was her dead sister's son, and as dear to her as if he were her own ... almost more so since she had sacrificed so much for his sake. The day the child was four they buried his mother. When everyone had left after the fine funeral tea Bess had prepared in the back-room, her brother-in-law turned to her with desperation in his face and voice. 'Bess, could you leave Ayr and take over the farmhouse?' Geordie Clachan, helpless and grief-stricken didn't stop to think she might have had other plans for her own life, now her elderly husband had left her a comfortably-off widow and a respectable time had passed in mourning.

'Well ...' Bess had half expected the request, but her well-rehearsed refusal stuck in her throat when he asked. Clachan's Farm was big, with a whole army of lassies and men working there. A firm female hand was essential at the helm, that she knew, if she didn't take over, Geordie and Ian would have to manage with the help of some incompetent maid! She had strong ideas on that sort of thing.

'The farm itself is no problem,' Geordie echoed her thoughts. 'But Ian needs a proper home and a mother, not some lass looking after him between flirting with the farmlads. Och, Bess, I have no heart for re-marriage. There was many that said I was too old for Jean when we wed.' He sighed deeply. 'Who'd have guessed I would have been the one left to carry on alone? Nobody could ever take her place for me, nobody.' The big farmer's eyes filled with unshed tears.

Bess gazed down at the bright-eyed boy clinging to the long folds of her mourning skirt and looking up at her with her dead sister's great brown eyes that could melt a heart of stone.

'Aunty Bess, are you going away like Mamma?' he asked sadly. 'Can you not get her back from heaven, Aunty Bess?'

'Please, will you stay, Bess?' Geordie stood there, sad and broken, hair seeming to have turned grey already in a few sorrowful weeks, now his rose of summer was gone.

Bess Crawford thought of Archie Murchieson, with his kindly

heart and canty smile. Marrying William Crawford had brought
her security and comfort, but little happiness ... at best. She had
made a mistake once and had been given a rare second chance.
But even before she told Geordie that she would think about it,
Bess knew the decision was already made.

Fourteen years later she was still at Clachan's Farm and poor
Archie had long ago moved to Glasgow, burying himself in the
problems of his poverty-stricken patients. He had never married,
still hoping that she would find a replacement at the farm now Ian
was nearly a man, and the edge had long gone off Geordie's
grief.

'Are you ready, Bess?' Geordie Clachan's voice cut across her
reverie.

'Aye, indeed,' she smiled and swept to the end of the table.
The others stood up and bowed their heads as the farmer led the
solemn grace.

Ian Clachan listened as his father's words rolled across the
generous board but his eyes slid unbidden to the diminutive
stranger beside him. Unexpectedly touched as the others laughed,
his heart had gone out to the brave little figure in the ridiculous
garb.

Years later Annie thought about that first meal in Clachan's
farm. Everything seemed strange and unreal, but at the same
time, sharp and unforgettable.

Mr Clachan presided over the men's end of the table and gave
the signal to eat when grace was over. The farmer was a big man
and older by far than the housekeeper. Geordie Clachan had a
weather-beaten face, thinning grey hair, eyes that were both firm
and shrewd and a booming laugh. Though the housekeeper would
decide her fate as Leezie said she did with all the lassies, Annie
understood instinctively that Geordie Clachan was a man to be
reckoned with. The men, all ten of them, were at the same time
both familiar with and deferential to him. There was no doubt
who the boss was on Clachan's Farm.

At the other end of the table, nearest the range and with the
two girls next to her from the right, the housekeeper sat in state,
handing round the soup tureen and following it with plates of
steaming potatoes laced with buttermilk and garnished with
lumps of rich fat mutton. Each man demolished plates of food
that would have kept the whole Ramsay family for a week.

28

Annie watched in awe, sitting in silence while they chattered and ate around her. She was grateful she had been placed next to Leezie, who hissed instructions about passing the plates and made sure she ate and used her cutlery.

Unused to such abundance, her stomach growled in protest. Still she did justice to the sturdy portions dished out to her by the older girl. I might as well get stuck in if they're going to send me home tomorrow, she thought cheekily as the food restored her spirits. Now and then she peeped timorously down the table, dropping her eyes as soon as someone caught her looking.

There seemed to be no special order among the men, old and young mixed democratically. A few of them were scarcely more than lads. There were two about Sandy's age she guessed. They swaggered and tried to follow the expressions and conversation of the older men and more than once got a look from the house-keeper that froze idle boasting in its tracks. Opposite Annie was an elderly man who slurped his soup loudly and wheezed like a puffing billy. Annie shot a look at the housekeeper when he made a particularly loud noise, but she seemed completely unaware. Annie thought that was strange, since her sharp eyes noticed everything else that went on.

'It's auld Charlie,' a voice whispered in her ear as she stared at the old offender. 'Mistress Crawford says he can't help making noises since he lost his teeth, and we should respect him for the man he still is as well as the one he was ... but God help one of us if we slurp!'

Annie turned to look at her companion on the right for the first time. He was a lad older than herself by a few years, she guessed, big and strong, with a bright face and the steadiest eyes she had ever seen.

'Sorry, I didn't ken I was staring,' she murmured shame-facedly.

'Charlie was the best shepherd in Kyle when he was younger,' the lad continued. 'Even now, he's the only one that can go out on the Craigdrummond Moss in a midnight storm or fog and find a stray ewe in lamb without even a lamp to guide him.'

'What's the Moss?' Annie asked.

'It's a dangerous bog. It looks all right to those who know no better, but if you put a foot wrong you can sink without trace. Many's an animal has been lost in the Moss and folk too. They

say it's haunted with the spirits of those who have died there ...
howling in the night!' he teased, grinning as her eyes widened.

'Ye're kiddin'!' Annie blanched.

'No, I'm not. So, what do you think of Clachan's Farm?' he
added conversationally, tearing off a chunk of bread and wiping
the last drops of buttermilk from his plate.

'I don't know,' she whispered truthfully. 'Right now I only
wish I was back with Mammy in the Gallowgate ... Mistress
Crawford says she's sending me home tomorrow ... but I don't
want to go,' she added illogically. To her shame she heard her
voice tremble.

'Och, maybe she'll not send you away.' He seemed to understand how she felt, despite her confusion. 'And if you do stay,
then you'll soon get used to it. I've been here all my life and I
can't imagine anywhere else I'd rather be in the world than
Clachan's Farm.'

She turned and looked fully at him, puzzled by his self-assur-
ance, polite voice and manner. 'What do you work at?'

'Och, a wee bit of everything.' He shrugged. 'I have to learn
all about the farm, but just now I go to agricultural school in
Glasgow during the week to learn about new ways to use the land
... and how to do the books ... farming is changing fast these
days. I stay in digs in Kelvinside, but I'm back on weekends and
the holidays. My faither says I can leave the books when I'm
eighteen, that's only a couple of months away. Och, I can't wait!'

'Which one's yer faither?' Annie looked round at the group of
men.

'That's him at the top,' the lad nudged his head to where the
farmer sat in state. 'I'm Ian Clachan.'

'Oh, is that a fact,' Annie replied and lapsed into awkward
silence.

That night she lay in the narrow bed, clutching a carved bird
Sandy had made for her from a piece of firewood. Mrs Crawford
had confiscated everything else, including the shawl that made up
her bundle, till her few clothes were washed and rid of fleas.
Annie wished they weren't so fussy, but she had more to worry
about than that. Even the silence bothered her.

As the house settled for the night, she could hear Leezie snore
gently in the next room, then the bed creaked as the older girl

rolled over and the comforting grunts stopped. Rain drove against the window pane and the wind howled like a hundred ghouls and ghasities.

Annie crept down to the foot of the bed and peered through the tiny window. Outside was only blackness and the shifting weird forms of trees tossing wildly against the pale wet moonlight. Despite her resolve not to think about sad or scary things, Annie remembered Ian Clachan's tales of spirits on the Moss. As she crawled under the blanket again, she longed for the noisy tenement, where arguments, snores, cries and laughter could be heard all day and night, joining with the wails of bairns and the bursts of drunken song from some returning reveller.

'Och, this is a terrible place!' Suddenly she missed her family so much it hurt in her chest, just as if a knife was sticking there. Mammy, Daddy and the twins would be tossing and muttering in the big back-room bed, with the boys snoring behind the curtain in the kitchen wall bed. Her own truckle bed that was put up by the range at night, 'Where is that?' she wondered suddenly. 'Maybe the twins have it now.'

Annie pulled the coverlet up over her thin shoulders and lay knees almost to her chin. Och, I'll never sleep here, were her last thoughts till Leezie roughly shook her shoulder in the darkness of early morning.

'Mrs Crawford is waiting in the kitchen, Annie,' Leezie announced. 'She's decided what's going to happen to ye.'

Chapter Four

Miss Cumming could feel a migraine coming on, a bad one. She pressed a sweating hand to her forehead. It had been a difficult day. Alexandra Cameron seemed to be impossible to please.

'What old-fashioned rubbish! Next time, we'll go to Glasgow for my summer shoes!' she said loudly to the suppressed fury of the shopkeeper.

'Mistress Alexandra, these shoes are the latest mode. They were made by Lees of Maybole from this year's patterns. They're exactly the same as ones being sold in Sauchiehall Street in Glasgow!' Mr Kennedy said stiffly.

'Lees must have got their patterns mixed up, or you've mistaken your stock! These are no different from the ones you showed us last year,' Alexandra snapped.

Alexandra's governess hissed under her breath, 'If you make remarks like that, dearest girl, people will think you haven't been properly brought up!'

'Oh, I think they won't make that mistake, Cumming.' She tossed her golden head, crowned with a neat blue-ribboned hat. 'Everybody in Ayr knows exactly who I am.' She looked with detachment at the shop owner and his assistants who had neglected every other customer and pulled out just about every shoe in the shop for the girl's scrutiny.

'And what you're like,' the governess muttered. Looking after the only daughter of Sir Urquhart Cameron of Craigdrummond, was a prestigious post and a well paid one, but her charge was anything but easy. Alexandra had always been a little hysterical, Miss Cumming thought, but since her mother had died two years before when she was fourteen she had become much worse.

Almost overnight she had changed from a lively, if easily over-wrought, young girl, into a demanding and difficult one of very uncertain temper. On the threshold of full womanhood, but not quite there. Miss Cumming felt the fault was not entirely Alexandra's. Her father seemed in no hurry to let her finish and make a proper debut.

Cumming watched anxiously as Alexandra's face flushed with the tell-tale signs of growing irritation. If only her father understood how the girl suffers from waiting around for him to remember and decide her fate, the governess worried. If only he would spend a wee minute with her talking about her future. I'm sure that would do her more good than all the fine shoes in Ayrshire. But he's not been the same man at all since poor Lady Cameron died. What Alexandra needs is a new mother not a governess ... a firm hand ... stability! Miss Cumming had no doubts about it. 'Are you sure there is nothing, Miss Alexandra?' she asked aloud.

'Nothing! Oh, let's have tea and go home, Cumming.' Alexandra, got up amid a pile of discarded shoes. 'There's not a pair I would be seen dead in.' Holding out her foot for the assistant to replace her high boots of fine calf leather. The girl fumbled nervously. Alexandra tutted, then with a toss of her head flounced out.

'Just a minute, Miss Alexandra,' the flustered governess called after her, but Alexandra had gone. She turned. 'Oh, I'm sorry, Mr Kennedy, it looks as if she doesn't want to try on anything else.'

'It's all right, Miss Cumming.' Kennedy gritted his teeth and managed a strained smile. 'Do you want us to send over a selection of the ones she ... er ... didn't altogether reject, to Craigdrummond?' He added anxiously, 'Like we did the last time? It's no bother.'

'Yes, do that, Mr Kennedy, and include some fine kid shoes suitable for indoor use ... afternoon tea, soirees and the like.'

'Certainly, Miss Cumming.'

'Er ... thank you.' The woman nodded and flushed at the man's grim expression. 'I think Miss Alexandra is a wee bit tired today.'

'Of course, Miss Cumming.' Kennedy didn't let his feelings show till they had left the shop. 'Tired? Tired my foot!'

33

Thumping the desk, he let his pent up frustration out in a rush. 'That young lady is nothing but a spoiled brat for all the Cameron titles and her faither's money! And don't you breathe a word of what I've just said!' He turned furiously to his weary assistants. 'Or you'll be looking for another job. Now get this lot sorted out!' He stormed into the back shop.

'Yes, Mr Kennedy,' the girls chorused after him, stifling giggles till he was well out of hearing. It was nearly worth being run off their feet to see their miserable boss so hopping mad.

In the private salon of the Grand Hotel, Alexandra Cameron bit into a crumbly scone, smothered in rich Ayrshire butter. Her sour moods rarely lasted, especially if she got her own way, and now she was all charm. 'Sorry, Cumming, I'm just not in the humour for shopping today, why don't we go home when we've finished tea?'

'Certainly, Miss Alexandra,' the older woman replied patiently, 'I'll send a boy over to the mews to fetch Wilson with the carriage now if you like. But we haven't got the material for your ball-dress yet.'

'The Hunt Ball's not till September.' Her nose wrinkled with scorn.

'The seamstresses will need a wee while to make up that fancy pattern your aunty sent from London, especially if it's done in that creamy white crepe she recommended. Mind you, I think it's far too grown-up for a lass of sixteen,' Miss Cumming added with a disapproving sniff. 'Styles like that might be fine for young girls in flighty cities like London, but not in respectable places like Ayrshire.'

'And you're too old-fashioned for words, Cumming!' The blue eyes danced wickedly. 'Anyway I want to look grown up, after all, I'm sixteen now and in a way this will be my "debut" ... not officially of course, that's still to come.' Her pretty face became dreamy. 'Papa must let me "come out" this year ... I'm getting so old! Just think, Cumming, I can have dances and "at homes" down in London with Aunt Lispeth and then I shall get married,' she added the last words with more than a touch of defiance.

'Alexandra Cameron!' Miss Cumming was shocked to the core of her respectable being. 'You're far too young to be talking about marriage. It'll be finishing school first and you know it.'

'That's what you think!' Alexandra said pertly. 'I've waited

34

long enough. No, I'm coming out! Then I'll marry the first man who asks ... the first very rich, handsome man, of course ... someone who will adore me and let me do exactly as I please!' She laughed so the staff turned round and looked, then quickly looked away again, one didn't stare at gentry.

'Alexandra!' Miss Cumming blanched. 'Don't talk like that, it's not seemly!'

'Fiddle!' Alexandra was unrepentant. 'I'd do anything to escape Craigdrummond and dreary old Ayrshire. Most people I know are stuck here for ever, till they get carried out in a box drawn by six black horses! Even then it's a short trundle down the road to Craigdrummond Cemetery and be left to moulder for ever!'

'Och, dearie me! Maybe your father should marry you off as soon as he can!' The sharp words were dragged out of the woman. 'What you said about Craigdrummond is just wicked ... and your poor mother lying in the family tomb at the kirk ... och, I don't know what's got into you, you used to be such a lovely girl ...' She trailed off, blinking rapidly and sniffing into a big white handkerchief.

'Cumming, you take everything too seriously,' Alexandra put her slim, white hand over that of the older woman. 'But it's true. Since Mamma died, I never see Papa. He's always away in Glasgow these days. I get so depressed ... then I get angry ...' she trailed off and drummed her fingers in a nervous gesture for a long moment, then went on with a frown, 'Oh, I might as well marry as soon as I can.'

Miss Cumming looked down at the pristine tablecloth with its fine embroidered thistles and crowns and said nothing. She understood what the girl meant only too well. After a minute, she raised her head and said briskly. 'Well then, if that's your idea, you'll have a chance to meet some eligible young Ayrshire men at the Ball. The "creme de la creme" of Ayrshire will be there.'

'"Creme de la creme" or the "best of the buttermilk"?' Alexandra's blue eyes danced.

'Oh come now, dear, there are some charming lads in Ayrshire and there may be some coming from further afield ... even Glasgow or Edinburgh! Anyway this is the first ball that your father has allowed since the dear Mistress died, so you'd better make the best of it ... though don't be bold with the young men, Miss Alexandra ... modesty is a virtue to be treasured. And in any case, I think nineteen or twenty is time enough for a young gentlewoman to be wed,' she added with a sniff, still upset by her charge's precocity.

'What nonsense!' Alexandra laughed. 'Twenty is ancient ... one foot in the grave! But for once you're right, it is a fine opportunity to show myself at the ball ... goodness knows when there will be another at Craigdrummond. Papa wouldn't have agreed to hold this one only it's his turn to be President of the Ayrshire Hunting League and it was expected of him. Hmmm ...' A reflective look came into the blue eyes.

'Oh, please don't make a gossip of yourself, Miss Alexandra ... that's not what I meant at all,' the governess flustered.

'Yes, why not?' Alexandra ignored her. 'I can exercise my charm on the Ayrshire swains as a practice for better things in London! So, what are you waiting for, Cumming?' She put the china cup down with a sharp click. 'If I'm to look the part of Craigdrummond's lady, we'd better find some suitable material for my dress.'

Oh no, groaned poor Miss Cumming inwardly. Why didn't I just keep quiet?

Hours later they sat side by side in a well-sprung Craigdrummond carriage, clattering comfortably down the coast road. A huge parcel of cloth was perched with other packages on the opposite seat. Gusts of wind shook the carriage with increasing force as the spring storm gathered from the West and slowly hid the majestic outline of the Isle of Arran from sight. By the time they had reached the edge of Craigdrummond Estate, the rain had begun in earnest.

'There's a telegram for Miss Alexandra,' the butler said as they hurried in from the foul weather that looked settled well in. 'It's from the Laird.'

Alexandra ripped open the cover. 'Papa says he's coming back later this week,' she said with a puzzled look on her face.

'That's nice, dear.' Miss Cumming took off her heavy coat and hung it up.

'Yes, but I don't understand,' Alexandra went on slowly. 'He has never let me know before.'

'Annie,' Leezie called down the byre where the younger girl was scrubbing out a pen. 'Mistress Crawford says leave what you're

36

doing and come inside. Dougie can finish it. You've to get changed. I've looked out some house-clothes for ye. They're from Bella that left last year. She was wee as well.'

'Whit for, Leezie?' Annie leaned on the brush. 'Mistress Crawford said I wouldn't be needed in the house.'

'Aye, well ye are. Mistress Rannoch and Miss Betty are coming over the day, so you've to help cleaning the house and maybe serve them as well wi' me. Nellie the house-maid is sick. It'll take the lot of us to get the place ready in time!' She gave a dire shake of her head. 'Mistress Rannoch would notice a speck of dust a mile off, so Mistress Crawford is always in a fine frazzle before she comes.'

'Who's Mistress Rannoch?' Annie asked, wondering what sort of creature could put indomitable Mistress Crawford in a frazzle.

'She's Mistress Crawford's best cronie. The two of them are thick as thieves ... now don't say I told ye this,' Leezie's round face broke into a wide grin '... but they are aye trying to put one over on each other. It's a right laugh sometimes, so it is.'

'Whit do ye mean?'

'Well, Rannoch's and Clachan's are the biggest tenant fairms on the Craigdrummond Estate ... and in fact the biggest in Kyle. So, the two ladies see themselves as leading local fairming society, if ye like.'

'Aye, so whit do they do? Have milkin' competitions?' Annie giggled.

'Och, you Glesca folk are daft, right enough, so ye are!' Leezie cuffed her lightly. '... But ye're right in a way, the fairmers keep an eye on how the fairms do every year and nearly have a fit if one does better than the other at lambin' time, or gets a peck more corn frae the fields. For the ladies it's mostly things like if Mistress Crawford arranges a wee sale of work for the kirk, Mistress Rannoch has to have a soiree for the Scottish Missions to Heathens in Africa ... ye ken whit I mean?'

'Aye ... but there's something else I don't understand,' Annie said as the girls crossed the farmyard together.

'Just one thing?' Leezie laughed.

'Och, you!' Annie grinned, liking the cheery housemaid more and more. 'It's about Mistress Crawford, ye say she's a crony of this Mistress Rannoch ... so she's not just the housekeeper, is she?'

'Och no, she's a lot more than that. Mistress Crawford is in charge of everything that the Master doesn't do himself,' Leezie explained. 'Ye see, Mistress Crawford is the late Mistress Clachan's sister, she's family not servants.'

'Is that a fact? Does she have a man?' Annie couldn't imagine the terrifying figure as a blushing bride.

'Not now. She was widowed years ago herself and never remarried. Listen, here's a wee word in yer ear, Annie, before ye go another step in Clachan's Farm.' Leezie looked down solemnly at the girl trotting by her side to keep up. 'The Missus has given ye a chance, but she doesn't have time for wasters, like I telt ye, she has the pick of Ayrshire. You had better be a good lassie and do yer bit every minute this week. She's very strict about work and comings and goings. If she catches any of us skippin' on the work, she docks our pay. And if ye do anything worse ... like messin' wi' the lads ... or stealin' ... givin' up cheek ... ye ken ... you're out and no sorries either!' Leezie's eyes grew round as chestnuts.

'Oh jings, I'd better watch it!' Annie thought of her reputation for giving smart quick answers. The foreman in the tobacco factory was foaming at the mouth sometimes, but she was a good worker and popular with the others. Her shift always seemed happier and did better than the others, especially when she led them in cheery songs as they flagged towards the end of a long day, so he let it go. Mistress Crawford was another case altogether. Annie knew she had to do well this week, she just had to!

After the visiting ladies had taken high tea, Mistress Crawford leaned out of the kitchen window and cornered her nephew as he crossed the yard. 'Oh there you are, Ian. Would you take Betty for a wee stroll, she's dying for a breath of air?'

'Aye.' Ian looked none too pleased. 'But it can't be for long, Aunty Bess, I've still the long-rigg to check.'

'Och, Ian, try to be nice to Betty, there's a good lad. You don't want to hurt the lassie's feelings now do you?' Bess cajoled, dropping her voice so the visitors wouldn't hear.

'All right.' He shrugged. 'Tell her to come.'

As she withdrew her head into the kitchen, his aunt sighed. 'Poor Betty, she wears her heart on her sleeve for Ian so she does, but he never seems to notice!' Ruefully she watched as the young woman, her homely face alight with pleasure, followed her nephew's tall figure up the hill and almost having to run to keep up.

'Don't they make a fine pair, Mistress Crawford?' Betty's mother joined her at the window.

'Indeed they do, Mistress Rannoch,' Bess Crawford replied firmly. 'Indeed they do. It seems no time at all since they were bairns crawling through the heather.'

'Aye, Betty is soon eighteen,' her mother said with pride. 'That's just the age to be thinking about serious matters.'

'So it is.' Bess knew well what was coming, she and Elsie Rannoch regularly ploughed this particular acre and neither tired of it.

Elsie Rannoch gave a contented sigh. 'I might be her mither, but I'll say it anyway, our lass will make a fine farmer's wife so she will ... you've tasted her bannocks, haven't you, Bess?'

'Many's the time, Elsie. She has a fairy's touch with the bannocks, that lass.'

'Och, it's a shame Rabbie and me were not blessed with a son to take over in the fullness of time, Bess. But, like I'm forever saying, it's an ill wind that blows naebody any good ... the lad who marries Betty ...' she trailed off with a meaningful purse of the mouth.

'Aye, and Ian will inherit after Geordie,' Bess put in her bawbee's worth. 'Clachan's is a sound farm. Aye, the books are a sight to see at the end of the year. A fine sight.' She paused. 'Mind you, big farms are the fashion these days. Geordie says the farm papers are full of it.'

'So they are.' Elsie nodded gravely.

'And the Big House seem to like the idea. Did you hear that the Laird's factor offered a good contract to the tenant that took over auld Wullie Johnson's place and joined it with his own when the auld man died?'

'I heard that too,' Elsie nodded.

'... And what if Betty doesn't find a lad to take her fancy?' Bess asked though she knew the answer already.

'Och, you know fine that Rannoch's tenancy would revert to Craigdrummond,' Elsie replied sharply. 'But that will not happen, Mistress Crawford! There's many a lad showing more than interest in our lass now she's coming of an age to wed.'

'Och, I can believe it, she has such a nice nature and she's that good with bairns is your Betty,' Bess agreed in a soothing tone.

'But Rabbie and me are choosy ...'

'And so you should be with a fine lass and a fine farm,' Bess nodded.

Mollified, Elsie went on, 'Did I say we were thinking of sending her to Glasgow for a month or two, Bess?'

'Not a word.'

'Aye, there's a school for daughters of folk with decent standing in society like ourselves.' Elsie Rannoch preened just a little. 'You know what I mean ... merchants, farmers and the like. It's not like the gentry do, not a finishing school exactly, but it adds a wee bit of polish to a lassie's manners. And our Betty is maybe a wee bittie lacking in the social graces ...' her mother trailed off.

It will take a bit more than polish to make Betty in anything but a plain, healthy dumpling of a country girl, Bess thought, but kept the opinion to herself. Not that Ian should be looking for anything more, she added silently, Betty Rannoch will make a perfect wife for him one of these days ... and the lassie worships him, so she does. Despite their regular sparring, she and Elsie Rannoch were of one mind about Betty and Ian's future. Aloud she replied with just a touch of condescension, 'Och, Betty is fine as she is, but maybe in any case it's not a bad idea, Elsie, a school could be the making of her ... like you say, a wee bit extra on the social side ... Now, Elsie, when are you and the lass coming over again?'

'First Monday of next month as usual if that suits you,' Mistress Rannoch replied, looking after the distant figures sharp against the heathery hillside. After a moment she added with careful casualness, 'But can't you bring Ian and Geordie over for a wee soiree before then ... as well as you coming on your own for the second Thursday as usual? It's for the Ayrshire Bible Fund for India. We're thinking of inviting a pianist down from Ayr and maybe having a recital ...'

'I'll do my best, and I'll certainly come myself.' Bess nodded, 'Though you know the men are not so keen on soirees as we ladies are. But I'm glad you reminded me, Elsie, I meant to tell you that I'll be organising a bakery stall at the end of the month for the Sunday School trip ... they're going to Alloway for the day on the train. The estate workers bairns look forward to it that much ... it's the only pleasure some of them get. Will you do a batch of your currant scones ... and maybe a couple of seed cakes?'

'Delighted, Bess.'

The two women wandered back to the back-room where Annie and Leezie were tidying away the remains of the cake, buns and shortbread.

'Is that a new lassie?' Elsie Rannoch's sharp eyes spotted the newcomer at once as Annie slipped out, burdened by a huge tray. 'She looks a bittie on the wee side, Bess. I thought you said you were after a dairymaid the last time we were over.'

'Archie Murchieson sent her from Glasgow a couple of days ago,' Bess answered with a wry smile. 'One of his waifs and strays ... you know what a soft heart the man has! Aye, she's meant to be a milkmaid. To tell you the truth I nearly sent her right back again ... but I decided to try her this week and I have to admit she's not doing badly in the house today. Still we'll see if she's any good with the kye before I commit myself to keeping her ... willing lassies are two-a-penny.'

'So they are.' Mrs Rannoch nodded. 'Now tell me, have you heard anything more about what's going on at the Big House?'

'Craigdrummond ... not a word, is something afoot?'

'By here and there is, Bess,' Mistress Rannoch's eyes lit up, delighted to be the bearer of news. 'One of my pantry lassie's sister works up there in the kitchen. You'll never believe what she told me!'

'Oh?' Despite her annoyance that she was not the first to know, Bess bent a willing ear as they finished another pot of tea. 'Do tell, Elsie ...'

Miss Cumming, anxious and perspiring, rushed over as Alexandra cantered into the stable yard with the groom who had accompanied her on her afternoon ride. 'Dress for the drawing-room! Your father wants to see you at once, Miss Alexandra!'

'So he's come?'

'And with guests! Och, we should have bought those new shoes in Ayr, I knew it!' The governess flapped and fussed as Alexandra dismounted and handed over the reins of her pony.

'The drawing-room?' Alexandra's eyebrows shot up in surprise. She was not unused to finding her father had arrived with unexpected visitors, he had done so many times before without telling her. But she wondered with a little tickle of apprehension why he had suddenly sent her a warning and was asking for her now. Usually when he had friends for dinner or to hunt, she was excluded. There was no place for her in his male, adult company.

With Miss Cumming fluttering about like a demented bee, offering advice and dropping sashes and flounces in her concern, Alexandra tried to look her sixteen years. But despite her best efforts, she failed miserably. Her wardrobe was still that of a young girl, not a woman and her hair hung loose and undressed caught back with a simple ribbon. The short skirt which barely reached below her calves, made her feel childish and gauche. She wished yet again that her father would react to her pleading and not leave her hanging eternally between childhood and the adult world.

'Alexandra, may I introduce Lord Edward Baird of Ballantyne,' Sir Urquhart Cameron drew his daughter forward as she hesitated at the door of the drawing-room.

'Miss Cameron, a pleasure to meet you.' An imposing, well-dressed man of around her father's age or a little younger, bowed, raising the young girl's hand briefly towards his lips. He gave her a cursory glance, then retreated to the fireplace where he had been leaning.

'And Mr Ronald Leslie of Bearsden.'

'A pleasure, Miss Cameron.' Stout and cheerful, Leslie also lifted Alexandra's hand in a courteous gesture. 'What a pretty lass you have, Urquhart! Didn't tell us that, did he, Ballantyne?'

'Indeed not,' the other man replied politely.

Alexandra winced in embarrassment.

'Alexandra, my dear,' Cameron's voice changed subtly and she was instantly alert. 'This is Mr Leslie's sister, Lady Maria Lennox.' The Laird drew forward the third person in the room with an air of proprietorial yet diffident pride. Alexandra stiffened, she had never heard him speak like that before.

A good-looking, slim woman, dressed modestly, though in the height of fashion, rose from in front of the fire and held out a soft, delicate hand. 'How nice to meet you at last, Alexandra.' She smiled warmly. 'Your father has spoken so much of you, I could hardly wait for this opportunity to become acquainted.'

'Lady Lennox.' As Alexandra bobbed a curtsey, she felt the woman's green-blue eyes bore into her with unnerving intensity.

'Lord Ballantyne, Mr Leslie and, naturally, Lady Lennox, will be coming to the Hunt Ball in September, Alexandra. I thought you might all like to meet well in advance.' Cameron smiled, his sad features softening and reminding her heartbreakingly of how it had once been in Craigdrummond.

'Thank you, Papa, how kind.' Alexandra would have given a great deal to keep that note of warmth in her father's voice.

'There is one thing more,' Urquhart Cameron began, then hesitated.

'Come, Leslie,' Lord Ballantyne broke in, realising it would be tactful to withdraw. 'If Urquhart has no objections, I'd like to take a look at his new guns before dinner. Keeper's down there, I suppose, Cameron?'

'Oh, please do,' he shot a grateful look at his friend. 'Brown is at your disposal if you want them primed. Lady Lennox and I will join you in a moment.'

As the two men left, he turned to his daughter.

'Lady Lennox and her aunt, Mrs Braidie, will be staying here for a few weeks before the Ball,' he said. 'Maria has kindly offered to help with the arrangements. She will also help me receive the guests, since you have not officially "come out" yet, my dear.' The words hit Alexandra like a bolt of lightning.

'Oh, I see.' Alexandra quickly dropped her eyes to hide her shock and disappointment. Deep in her over-imaginative heart, she had pictured herself at long last in proper attire, standing alongside her father as Mistress of Craigdrummond to welcome the guests. Oh, papa, how can you let a total stranger stand at Craigdrummond's doors? That's my place! Her thoughts tumbled round in her head furiously, her earlier vehement desire to escape from the House quite forgotten.

'It's a pleasure, Urquhart, not kindness on my part.' Maria Lennox turned smilingly to her host, unaware of the reaction the news had aroused in his daughter. 'And I'm sure Alexandra and I will get on famously. You didn't tell me what a very pretty girl she is either. I can see that she will make someone a lovely wife one day.' She took in the childish frock and loose hair. 'Though I can understand that you want to keep her young as long as possible ... fathers never like to see their daughters grow up.'

The words were kindly enough, but even in her anger, Alexandra flinched at the searching, appraising look in the older woman's eyes. Maria turned to the girl, placing a hand on her arm. 'Your father would like me to stay here for about two weeks before the Ball, Alexandra,' Lady Lennox went on. 'We can get to know each other very well then, can't we, my dear?'

'Yes, Lady Lennox,' Alexandra replied expressionlessly.

Maria Lennox turned back to the Laird with a soft smile playing round her mouth. 'We can talk about such details when you come up to Glasgow nearer the time, Urquhart. Oh, I can hardly wait!' Her fine eyes glowed. 'It will be so interesting to plan the evening and instruct your housekeeper and cook ... after all, I may as well get used to Craigdrummond!' she lowered her lashes demurely.

'Is that a ray of hope for a lonely widower at last?' The teasing note in Cameron's voice riveted Alexandra to the spot and the feeling of dread in her stomach began to grow. 'It's so very generous of you, Maria, to spend the time on our little event,' he went on. 'And I hope you understand how much I appreciate it, my dear.'

'My dear friend, as a widow, one is always glad of ways to pass the empty days,' Maria said with a twinkle in her eyes which belied the sad words.

'I'm sure your days are never empty, Maria,' Cameron said huskily.

Alexandra stood there forgotten as the two gazed conspiratorially at one another across the room. After a few moments her father pulled his eyes away from the attractive widow and dismissed his daughter with a cheerful wave of his hand. 'Well, good night to you, Alexandra, I expect supper and Miss Cumming are both waiting for you in the schoolroom. Do thank Lady Lennox for her kindness. Perhaps she might even allow you to accompany her when she talks to the staff about the Ball.' Sir Urquhart seemed unconscious of the fact he had wounded Alexandra deeply. 'It will be an excellent opportunity for you to see how things should be done.'

'Thank you, Lady Lennox,' she muttered between clenched teeth, making an effort to control herself. Resolutely she stared at the finely woven carpet without seeing it, emotions in a turmoil.

'Not at all, Alexandra, it will be my pleasure,' the older

woman answered with a smile which hid her own discomfort at the young girl's obvious anger.

'I hope you really don't mind Alexandra trailing along, Maria.' The fond look was back in the Laird's eyes.

'Of course not, Urquhart. A motherless girl can have no idea how to manage the servants. She will need to know that and more, if she's going to run her own household one day. And you seem to have neglected that side, my dear!' she said in mock reprimand. 'This will only be the first of many little things we can do together, won't it, Alexandra?' She turned to the girl who stood ramrod stiff by the door, poised for flight from this growing nightmare.

Not if I have anything to do with it! Alexandra thought defiantly. Under her father's eyes, she replied politely enough again, 'Yes, thank you, Lady Lennox. Good-evening, Father, Lady Lennox,' and withdrew.

'No! No! Never!' Alexandra stood outside the door in the empty hallway, in a state of complete chagrin. She clenched her fists. 'How dare that scheming woman try to take Mamma's place?' she asked herself angrily. 'Well, she might have dug her claws in Papa, but I won't see her taking over my life ... God help her if she tries!

Clachan's Farm,
June 4th 1892

Dear Sandy,

I promised to write to Mammy once I got settled, but since she doesn't read that well I thought you were the best one to get the letter. It is nearly three months since I came to Clachan's Farm and I am beginning to feel as if I was here for ever so I do.

At first it was awful hard, the kye (that's what we call coos in the Gallowgate) are awful big and there is a lot to milk. The farmer and Dougie the dairyman laughed themselves sick when they saw me trying to copy Dougie milking the first time, but I got the last laugh. My fingers are stronger than they look from all that work packing in the 'baccy factory and once I got the hang of how to do it, I can work nearly as fast as him already. The kye like me to do the milking because I don't nip. If ye nip they try to kick ye and that's not funny. Dougie showed me a great big dunt on his leg that he got when he was a laddie from a coo he nipped. I sing to the kye when I'm milking and they seem to like that. The farmer has put another man helping with the kye now till Maisie the head milkmaid gets back next week. Everybody says she's a right sharp one and you have to watch her. I'm no looking forward to that. Sometimes I help in the farmhouse and that's not bad either, but I like the beasts the best. Ian, the farmer's son is a kind laddie, though he's nearly a man, being the same age as yourself, Sandy.

I was sixteen yesterday but I didn't tell a soul. It was a wee bit lonely, so it was, with work and nobody knowing. Tell Mammy that I'm fine. I hope Daddy is still in work and that and keeping enough back from the pub for Mammy. Give Isa and Bella a sweetie each from me and tell our Eddie he'd no last five minutes here because they don't half make you work. The food is great, you'd love it, so ye would. Mistress Crawford says I'm bigger than when I came. I'm still a bit scared of her, but she's fair so she is.
Your loving sister,
Annie Ramsay

'Well Annie, imagine, it's nearly Midsummer and you're still with us,' Mistress Crawford commented as the girl struggled over the back hall with the pail of fresh milk she had sent for.

'Aye, Mistress Crawford.' The housekeeper rarely exchanged small talk with the staff and streetwise Annie, smelling trouble, stiffened.

'In here, lass. Aye, in the kitchen ... I'm not going to eat you!'

'Right ye are, Missus.' Annie's heart sank as her worse fears were confirmed.

'Annie, the fairmer and I have been talking, so I want a wee word with you about your future. Maisie will be back soon and this needs settled before she does. Come along, now, what are you gawping at?' She took the pail and swung it easily up onto the wooden ledge by the big Belfast sink in the back hall.

Annie paled as she followed the tall woman into the kitchen. The first few weeks she had been waiting every day for Mistress Crawford to carry out her original threat and send her back to Glasgow. It was ironic that just when she had begun to relax, the question had actually arisen. Now Maisie was returning, maybe they had decided they could manage without her after all. She stood, eyes wide waiting for the housekeeper to deliver her fate.

'I thought you would be worse than useless when I saw you standing there by Thampson's cart, dripping all over the yard,' Bess Crawford began in her usual forthright way, looking steadily at the uneasy young girl. Though still small and delicate-boned, in the few months she had been there, Annie had begun to blossom into a fine young woman with the tough but healthy exercise and good food of Clachan's Farm. 'Archie Murchieson wasn't so daft after all.' Mrs Crawford gave a secret smile.

'I ken ye thought ye'd got a bad bargain, Missus,' Annie nodded ruefully, watching the housekeeper's face for signs of impending doom. Instead she was in for a surprise.

'That's true, but I was wrong, Annie, you've done your bit right enough, though with your city ways it hasn't been easy.' The older woman almost laughed aloud at the memory of Annie's look of blind panic when the first herd of cows was driven in for milking. 'We all thought you would turn and run when Dougie lined the kye up and handed you a pail. But you stood your ground and the dairymen all say you've got the makings of a fine milkmaid. The fairmer agrees with them too. He thinks you're a cantie lass.'

'Oh, is that a fact?' Annie gasped.

'And I'm pleased that you're learning fast to help in the kitchen and round the house,' Mistress Crawford went on. 'You've a quick mind and a willing heart, and that's better than all the inches in the world.' The housekeeper spoke in an even tone, not making too much of the praise she was giving.

'Och, thank you, Mistress Crawford,' Annie stammered, red to the ears. Bess was strict as a rule and sparing in her praise, this was unexpected indeed.

'Aye, well, don't expect me to repeat the honours every five minutes, Annie Ramsay! You've a lot to learn and I've a few complaints as well,' she added dryly. 'That sharp wee tongue of yours for one thing ... I've heard you cheeking some of the men ... though the daft galoots seem to find it funny and egg you on.' She pursed her lips. 'You'd better be more careful or somebody might just bite your tongue off for you! It's lucky that you've never made the mistake of answering me back!' she added with a frown.

'Oh, I'd never do that, Missus.' Annie flushed.

'I hope not, or your feet wouldn't touch the ground between here and Glasgow! And when Maisie arrives, you had better keep your smart replies to yourself as well, Annie, for she won't like them.'

'Aye, Missis. Will I be working wi' her?'

'Indeed you will, lass. Maisie will be in charge of you from now on, not Dougie. I'll be watching carefully to make sure the two of you work well together. Some lassies have found Maisie a wee bit difficult, or so I am told. But just don't come running to me with tales, lass. I won't put up with it. We want to keep Maisie at Clachan's and that's that.' The house-keeper was uncompromising. 'Do you understand, Annie? No cheek and no tittle-tattle. As you've heard me say many's the time, my motto is "Hard work always pays". So do your bit and you should be safe enough, but remember it's last in first out if we have to choose.'

'I promise, Missus.' The white cap bobbed. 'Am I getting to stay, then?' Annie asked in a small uncertain voice, quite unlike her usual cheerful, cheeky tones.

'For the time being,' Mistress Crawford nodded. 'Your mother will be getting your "quarter's fee" next week. We've a messenger going up to Glasgow on some other business, he can hand it to her then. Is she at home?'

'Aye, the twins haven't started the free school yet ... but after that, Mistress Crawford, will I still be staying at Clachan's then?' Annie's slight body was tense.

'Well, I'll fee you first till September,' Mistress Crawford replied. 'From September, if you're still a good lassie and worth keeping, you'll be fee'd for a half-year at a time.'

'Thanks, Missus! Oh thanks very much! And I'll no forget, "Hard work always pays"!' Annie left the kitchen and skipped across the hall and into the byre where Ian Clachan was helping Dougie muck out. Work was work for master and man alike in Clachan's Farm and Ian knuckled down with the rest when he wasn't at college.

'Ye banks and braes o' bonnie Doon, how can ye bloom sae fresh and fair ...' she warbled as she danced round the two men holding the edges of her working apron.

'What's the singing and dancing for then? Are you thinking of joining the Ayr Music Hall troupe, Annie?' Ian pushed a strand of hair from his eyes and smiled as she suddenly did a little jig, heavy working boots clunking on the byre floor.

'I'm stayin'! I'm stayin'! "Hard work always pays"!' she sang and did a little twirl. The white apron billowed out round her and sprigs of dancing chestnut curls escaped from her cap.

'Is that a fact?' Ian replied with a dry little smile that hid his stab of pleasure at Annie's joyful spontaneity. He always felt the sun had come out when Annie Ramsay was around, with her bright face, lovely voice and cheery nature. 'So Mistress Crawford thinks you're not just a useless wee Glasgow sparrow after all.' Ian couldn't resist teasing, knowing she would rise to it at once.

'Och, you!' She stopped dancing and stood hands on hips, slender body arched in outrage. 'I'm getting to know this farm as well as you, Ian Clachan.' Annie tossed her head, forgetting the promise she'd made to curb her tongue.

'Did ye hear that, Ian?' Dougie laughed at her cheek.

'Och, aye, Dougie, and who am I to argue with a woman of such gifts. Here she is, ladies and gentlemen,' Ian made a mock bow to an imaginary audience, 'brought to you from Glasgow at great expense by Doctor Archibald Murchieson on the Puffing Billy, the star milkmaid, tricked out and ready to take the Twentieth Century by storm. Yes, good folks,' he went on with a flourish, 'she can do a song and dance and milk the kye at the same time ... I present, Clachan's Annie!' He finished with a rattle on a milk pail. Both men laughed till they cried, as Annie, red in the face, danced up and down with fury.

'Och, ye're nothin' but a pair of Ayrshire eejits, wi' muck all over yer boots!' she yelled. With her chin in the air, she marched out.

'Annie, there ye are.' Leezie cornered her before she reached the dairy. 'Mistress Crawford sent me after you. She forgot to say that Maisie's coming back tomorrow.'

'Right ye are, Leezie. I'll do my best to get on wi' her.' Annie came back to reality with a thud and tried not to show her apprehension.

Leezie had no such qualms. 'Och, it's been great without that

49

one causin' trouble,' she said with a heartfelt sigh. 'I just wish she wasn't coming back so I do. I'd no be in your shoes having to work wi' her, Annie, neither I would. She's a bad lot that Maisie, so she is!'

Chapter Five

'So you're the scruffy, stunted wee skelf everybody's been snig-gerin' about!' a spiteful voice broke into Annie's sweet song as she milked the next evening.

'Is that a fact?' Annie straightened up and turned to face the newcomer, patting the warm rump of the cow to reassure her she would finish the job in a minute. 'And you must be Maisie. They telt me you had a tongue that would clip clouts!'

'Oh did they, whoever "they" might be?' Maisie's small eyes narrowed and she stood with arms akimbo. 'Well, now ye're sure, ye'll know to watch yer step and no answer back to yer elders and betters.'

Annie's heart sank. Despite all the warnings, she hadn't handled this encounter well. Leezie and just about everybody else had told her that Maisie was a spiteful bully who tried to get everyone into trouble while she fawned on Mistress Crawford. Annie had decided to go easy, get the measure of the young woman when she got back and see how they could rub along. Now she had ruined the whole fine plan within the first minute of meeting her. 'Och, well,' she told herself silently, 'I'll just have to keep my head down and hope she forgets.' Maisie's next words dispelled that wishful thought.

'And just remember, wee scruff, I'm in charge of the milking in here. Ye've had an easy time keepin' in wi' the men, showin' off, singin', dancin' and playin' the helpless wee lassie! But that's over. I ken your kind, and I'll be watchin', so I will!'

'I haven't been playin' the wee lassie or showin' off!' Annie protested, thinking of the hard work she had done over the previous months. 'I do my bit.'

'Oh aye?' Maisie sneered and picked up a pail. 'Well, let's see how ye compare wi' a real milkmaid.' She sat down and her fingers flew as the milk shot in loud bursts into the pail. However good Annie had become, she was undoubtedly no match for this expert. No wonder Clachan's kept her on despite her unpopularity. Annie decided that tact was the best part of valour.

'Ye're right.' She smiled disarmingly. 'I've a lot to learn, but you're more than welcome to teach me.' With a nod, she sat back down and began her own slower, steady movements.

'Aye.' The older girl looked put-out for a moment, then said in a nasal whine that set Annie's teeth on edge, 'And jist keep the music hall acts I've heard about for those that want it. I like tae milk in peace and quiet!' With a sniff, she turned her back and continued till they had done the job in almost half the usual time.

Maisie left Annie to finish last cow. 'See that the pails are emptied and cleaned!' She nodded over towards the dairy where the milk was poured into giant churns to settle before the cream was removed for butter.

'Aye,' Annie replied, glad to be left alone at last.

'I thought the place was empty, it's that quiet.' Ian stood leaning on the barn door. 'You're usually in full voice by now, Annie?'

'Aye, well no the day.'

'Maisie's back then?' Ian guessed at once from Annie's subdued demeanour.

'Aye, she is that.' Annie replied non-committally, as she cleaned the last of the milk pails and tidied the shed for the night.

'Don't let her bother you, Annie,' he advised. 'We all ken that Maisie is a right spiteful lassie at times. Och, but it's just her nature, she can't help it. None of the men take any heed when she starts. And you should do the same.'

'I'll try,' she said to please him, but her heart was in her big working boots. Clachan's Farm had seemed to her to be paradise over the last few weeks. Now she had to learn that even paradise has its serpents.

'Good lass.' He grinned, picked up his pitchfork and crossed the yard whistling.

Annie watched him go. He was the nicest lad she had ever met in her life, she thought. Even some of the sonsie lads in the 'baccy factory who had chaffed and teased and got as good as they gave, were not a patch on Ian Clachan ... aye, her eyes shone, the very nicest.

Maria Lennox had been fond of her first husband, but it had been a gentle marriage of adoration on his side and grateful devotion on hers. Many years older, Sir Albert Lennox, had given her undemanding security, position and respect. Maria had not resented that her brother had inherited all of their parents' modest fortune, but it had been a relief to be married so well since she had little to bring with her as a dowry. When Sir Albert died, leaving her a comfortably provided for widow at twenty-seven, she had mourned him sincerely, but without deep grief. Now she was as deeply in love as a woman could be and knew that her affection was returned. Still she hesitated to commit herself to Urquhart Cameron.

Alexandra's refusal to be anything but coldly polite, made her wonder if she might regret taking the girl on. More worrying was the underlying instability she saw in Alexandra's sudden mood swings and seeming inability to grasp reality.

'Dear Urquhart seems unaware of that side of his daughter,' she told her aunt, Mistress Braidie.

'Oh, I'm sure he knows she is a little er ... nervous, though men tend not to acknowledge these things,' her aunt replied slowly. 'Miss Cumming believes that's maybe why he has been in no hurry for Alexandra to make her debut ... hoping she'll grow out of the tantrums and moods. But he can't keep the poor girl in short skirts for ever!'

'No indeed,' Maria said thoughtfully. 'Oh well,' she sighed. 'I'll keep trying.'

After a long summer of being rebuffed at every attempt to conciliate, tentatively Maria voiced her doubts to an increasingly impatient Urquhart.

'So that's it!' he sounded relieved. 'And I wondered if you had ceased to care for me.'

'Never,' she whispered, eyes falling before the desire in his.

'Then you must marry me! And soon!' Urquhart said joyfully. 'I am sure your concern over Alexandra is much exaggerated, my dear. She is just easily overwrought ... always has been ... nothing more ... my sister Lispeth is exactly the same. Look,' he said firmly, 'leave Alexandra to me, I'm sure she will be delighted once she gets used to the idea. And I know she will benefit from your influence once you are established as the Lady of Craigdrummond.'

'Oh, as you wish, Urquhart,' Maria allowed her love for the man to smother her remaining misgivings.

'We will go to Craigdrummond this very weekend.' He smiled. 'And I will tell Alexandra then.'

Alexandra had known all summer in her heart that there was an 'understanding' between her father and Maria Lennox. Though Sir Urquhart Cameron said nothing, the signs were clear. Each time the Laird and Lady Lennox came to Craigdrummond, Maria seemed to have wormed her way in deeper in the Laird's affections. Alexandra expected to be summoned in formally for an announcement any time. Jumpy and irritable, she was difficult and petulant with everyone around her.

'I hate her, Cumming, and that stupid old auntie she drags along as a chaperone!' she moaned as they went for the final fittings of the dress being made for the Hunt Ball. 'They're both so mean to me!'

'Oh now, now, Miss Alexandra,' Miss Cumming shushed. 'You're not being at all fair. Lady Lennox is only trying to be helpful, and I don't know how you can say Mistress Braidie is mean, she rarely comes out of her room when she's here. I shouldn't think she's passed more than the odd word with you.'

'Lady Lennox is always telling me what to do!' Alexandra refused to be mollified.

'Well, you have to admit that despite my efforts, some aspects of your training have been sadly neglected. I never could get you to practise your embroidery or learn the finer points of etiquette. You're not the easiest pupil in the world when you set your mind against learning something, dear.' Miss Cumming sighed heavily.

'One minute she's saying that I'm grown up,' the girl snapped, 'And it's about time I mended my manners or no one will marry me ... the next she's pointing out that I'm only a child and should do exactly as she wants. Is that fair?' She pouted, wallowing in self-pity.

'I think the poor woman has the patience of a saint with you, Miss Alexandra. You argue against everything she suggests all the time ... at least when your dear Papa is not there!'

'See,' Alexandra burst out, 'she's even turned you against me!'

'Oh, dearie me!' Miss Cumming felt out of her depth as usual. 'Listen, Miss Alexandra, once you've "come out", you'll no doubt find her easier to get along with, you'll be more equal, if you know what I mean. And if someone is to blame for you not making your debut this year ... and I'm not saying there is ... then it is your dear father, not Lady Lennox. Give her a chance, dear, you'll need an ally when I leave in September to take charge of the Lamont children. Be fair to her too,' she pleaded. 'Lady Lennox isn't that old, she's barely thirty according to Mistress Braidie. Being landed with a girl of your age must be a daunting prospect.' Miss Cumming looked down at her own ringless hands and asked quietly, 'Has your dear father mentioned anything yet ...?'

'No, but I think he will soon. He said something yesterday about having a little talk before the Ball. I don't care.' But Alexandra's eyes were bleak as she couldn't help thinking, it would have been different if Mamma were alive, I'm sure she would have let me do exactly as I want. In the years between, she had built up a romantic and mostly unrealistic picture of her dead mother.

'Anyway, I'm sure your Papa will sort things out now I'm leaving, whatever happens with Lady Lennox. Though I'm not one to criticise,' she added carefully, 'I think it is overdue. In a way I agree with you, a young woman of your age doesn't need a governess, just finishing school, then a proper debut and finally a good marriage.'

'I thought you were against marriage,' Alexandra said.

'Not at all, it's just that you seem to want everything at once,' Miss Cumming replied.

'I do.' Her eyes narrowed. 'Everything!' Suddenly her mood soured again. 'Oh must we go for a fitting today? I feel so closed in, so caged and trapped!'

'Of course we must,' Miss Cumming said gently.

'Oh alright!' she finally agreed with bad grace.

'Good,' Miss Cumming drew a sharp sigh of relief. The dress was lovely, in a delicate creamy white, with a gathered neck and deep flounces down to Alexandra's ankles. It had a closely fitted bodice which showed off her trim figure and made her look far older than her years. Alexandra loved to whirl in front of the dressmaker's mirror. In her imagination she was already dazzling the well-bred youth of the County and being acclaimed the 'Belle of the Ball'. The governess smiled contentedly to herself, she knew her charge's good humour would be restored as always when she slipped into the graceful folds.

Urquhart Cameron stood with his back to the window of his study. Brilliant light steamed in from the northern sun which was just beginning to sink in the warm August evening. Idly he noticed clouds were gathering from the sea, boding ill for the next day.

Below, gardeners were weeding, clipping and raking the great drive in anticipation of the forthcoming ball. All was as it should be. Almost.

'You sent for me, Papa?' Alexandra said, answering his summons with a heavy heart and a shiver of apprehension. His face was in shadow against the bright light behind him and she couldn't see his expression. Lady Lennox was nowhere to be seen.

'Er ... Alexandra,' Cameron began with uncharacteristic hesitancy, 'I have something to tell you, though I imagine it will not come entirely as a surprise.'

'Yes, Papa?' Alexandra raised quizzical eyebrows and tried to keep her hands from trembling.

'Lady Lennox, Maria, has done me the honour of accepting my proposal of marriage. We will be married next month. She will acoompany me to kirk tomorrow and sit beside me in the family pew, which will be a traditional statement of my intentions by all at Craigdrummond. I will make an official announcement at the Ball, when I present her to the company.'

Though she had been expecting an announcement, now it had come the finality was overwhelming. Her throat was tight with emotion. That woman would be moving in as Lady of Craigdrummond. 'Oh no, Father!' she cried, her face flushing with emotion. 'You can't marry her!'

'What on earth do you mean? Of course I can marry Maria ... and I expect your full cooperation, Alexandra!' Embarrassed at her reaction, Cameron spoke abruptly and with a coldness that brought her momentarily to her senses.

56

'Congratulations then, Papa,' the reply came out at last, brittle and terse. She turned at once to go.

'One moment, Alexandra, I haven't dismissed you yet,' the Laird said sharply. 'Maria believes that the news of our marriage may not be as welcome to you as we both hope. Until this moment, I could not believe this to be true.'

'If you want to marry Lady Lennox,' she said in a tight voice, 'then it doesn't really matter what I think, does it, Papa?'

Cameron drew a quick breath, although Alexandra was known to be sharp with others, she had never answered him before in such a manner. 'I don't like your tone, Alexandra. Maria is right!' Cameron inadvertently made matters worse by his unintended misquote, 'You are rather immature for your age and in need of a firm hand.'

'Immature!' Alexandra drew a sharp breath.

Before she could say more, her father went on, 'I admit that the fault is largely mine, I have not made any arrangements for you till now. Neglected you, perhaps, in my own misery after your poor mother died ...' He moved away and looked out of the window across the great moor. After a long moment he sighed and turned back to the tense girl, still standing rigid and defiant. 'Come, Alexandra, let Maria be a mother to you, my dear. I am sure your Mamma would want us all to be happy together.' For a man accustomed to give orders, Cameron made a tremendous effort to be conciliatory.

Alexandra looked at her father. He so obviously wanted her to agree and, though she longed to please him, the familiar devil in her refused to be persuaded.

'I'm sixteen, Papa, I don't need a new mother.' She tossed her golden head and pouted.

'And you're subject to your father till he decides otherwise!' he snapped, stung by her inflexibility.

'It's Lady Lennox's fault!' She threw consequences to the wind. 'Since she came, I've begun to hate Craigdrummond, hate it! I will never accept her, Papa!' Her voice rose hysterically.

'Now stop that, Alexandra!' Her father's face tightened. 'If you hate Craigdrummond because of Maria, then we had better do something about it, because she is certainly staying. Perhaps you would be happier going to finishing school at once?'

'I don't want to "finish", I want to get married. Then I'll be free of the lot of you!' The childish fantasies spilled out and her eyes filled with angry tears.

'Married?' Her father looked astounded. 'You're far too young to consider that. And I intend seeing that you behave properly towards Maria, or you'll find yourself in serious trouble, Alexandra.'

'I don't care!' She was beyond sense and restraint.

'I am not arguing with a spoiled child.' His face darkened and he said with a stern expression she seldom saw, 'You are confined to the house for the next few days. Instead of kirk, you will do bible reading at home. I would like to forbid you to attend the Ball, but that would set tongues wagging. You are immature. You need a lesson and a sharp one.'

Alexandra was shocked out of her mounting tantrum. Her father never spoke like that to her.

He looked thoughtfully at her standing there, red-faced, quieter, but still defiant. 'She tells me that your dress has been made up to a pattern which is a little old for you, a London style or something, isn't it?'

'Yes, Aunt Lispeth sent it,' she replied more warily, sensing something even more unpleasant than being confined to the house was to come.

'Oh, Lispeth is such a butterfly, that must be where you get it from!' he raised his eyes to heaven. 'Well,' he went on grimly, 'I am ordering you not to wear the new dress, Alexandra. Instead you will wear something which is more suitable for a girl who has not yet made her debut. You may chose one of your best gowns together with Miss Cumming. She can show the final selection to Maria for approval. Goodness knows you have plenty of garments in the wardrobes. But the new one remains in wraps till you show yourself grown up enough to deserve it.'

'Papa! No!' she cried and stamped her foot in a new flood of anger, frustration and disappointment. But there was nothing she could do, he was adamant. As she rushed out of the room in tears, she passed Maria Lennox in the hall.

'Alexandra, dear.' The older woman held her by the arm. 'What on earth is the matter?'

'What do you care? This is all your fault! You would do anything to humiliate me, anything!' she stormed. 'I'll never accept you here in Craigdrummond, never! I'd rather die first!

And don't expect me to dance at your wedding for I won't go!'

Maria Lennox raised an eyebrow and let her go. 'Oh I don't think such a melodrama is called for, Alexandra,' she said softly. 'I think all that is needed is a little change in your attitude, then we could get on famously. Come now, we don't have to make a battle of things. We both love your father, we can both make him happy, can't we?'

Alexandra stood glowering, eyes filled with angry tears and Maria tried again, 'Look, I understand that you don't want a mother, dear. Oh maybe I've been trying too hard to fill that place and if so, I'm sorry, but I could at least be a sister, if you would just let me.'

'I don't want a sister either!' she retorted feeling gauche and stupid in the face of the other woman's reasonable calm.

'Oh well, Alexandra.' Maria shrugged, realising it was best not to press her further. 'Don't say I didn't offer.' She moved away, silk skirts rustling, and opened the study door.

Cameron turned to her at once, his voice full of love. 'Ah, Maria my dearest, I'll be so proud to show you off to my friends and peers at the Ball, and to the Craigdrummond tenants at kirk tomorrow as my future wife!'

Heart filled with jealousy, Alexandra heard the warmth in her father's voice. It faded to a murmur as the door clicked shut. She felt excluded, lonely and humiliated.

Bitterly, she made her way to the fine bedroom with its rose satin drapes and thick Paisley carpets. She threw herself down on the soft quilted cover of her bed. For an hour she sobbed as if her heart would break, then she got up. There was no sign of charm in the blue eyes now, instead they were hard with deep resentment.

'I'll make them both rue this day,' Alexandra Cameron vowed to the empty room. 'If it's the last thing I ever do!'

Chapter Six

'It's no good, Leezie,' Annie moaned as they dressed for church. 'I've tried everything I can, but Maisie is as rotten as ever.'

'She's the same wi' everybody, Annie,' Leezie consoled.

'Aye, but you can keep out of her way in the house, I'm stuck with her. She girns at me all the time,' Annie went on, her grey eyes troubled, 'And when she can't pick fault with my milking, she complains to Mistress Crawford behind my back, saying that I'm lazy and that. And she tells back barefaced lies about me as well.' Annie's face flushed with anger at the injustice. 'She told the Missus yesterday I wouldn't do my turn swilling clean the floor after we'd done wi' the kye. And it wasn't true, neither it was.'

'Did Mistress Crawford call ye in for a row?'

'Not yet.' Annie sighed, tucking rebellious curls under the simple bonnet she had been given to wear on the Sabbath.

'There ye are then,' Leezie replied triumphantly. 'If she had listened to Maisie, she would have had ye in right away. She never waits wi' a row, Mistress Crawford.'

'Do ye think so?' Annie sounded relieved. 'Och aye, maybe right enough.'

'Forget Maisie, Annie. Mistress Crawford kens what she's like. And she kens ye do yer bit.' Leezie peered at her best hat in the dusky mirror, admiring the green ribbon she bought from a tinker who came to the farm the week before. 'This looks nice, Annie, doesn't it?'

'Aye,' Annie agreed absently, still worrying that Maisie would not let her forget her presence so easily.

'Oh jings! There's the trap for the fairmer's family already.

We better cut across the hill!' Leezie grabbed her hand and the two girls ran downstairs and out into the yard where Mistress Crawford, Mr Clachan and Ian were already climbing onto the polished open carriage.

'Hurry up, you pair! I won't stand for Clachan's Farm folk being late for kirk! Maisie and the house lassies went ten minutes ago,' the housekeeper's voice carried after them as they fled, taking the short-cut across the moor that would get them to Craigdrummond kirk quicker than those who were travelling in more style.

The Sunday morning was bright and clear, full of bird-song and the fragrance of wild flowers. Heather sprang up again as their flying feet lightly pressed and passed. Wild thyme filled the air with bitter-sweet scent. Pausing to catch her breath, Annie looked round at the hills which had once seemed so menacing and over at the green Moss where glints of water here and there warned of hidden danger. The sea was out of sight, but the smell of it was carried on the breeze. After almost six months, it had all become familiar to Annie and more beloved with each day. The dark streets of Glasgow seemed very far away.

They made it to the kirk before the carriage even turned up the long drive. Bobbing a curtsey to Mr Menzies the minister, the girls filed in demurely to their place in the Clachan Farm pews. Beside them, looking scrubbed and starched, sat the rest of the unmarried workers, including Maisie who sniffed in annoyance as they squeezed past. Behind them were two whole rows filled with the married men from all the Craigdrummond Estate and farm cottages, with their wives and many children.

Annie marked the day's psalms in her hymn-book and watched out of the corner of her eye as Geordie Clachan, Ian, and Mistress Crawford arrived, taking their special places at the end of the row. Ian winked cheerily and made a face when he thought nobody was looking. It was so comical Annie nearly disgraced herself by laughing aloud. Och, it feels good being part of Clachan's Farm, she thought happily.

What's this then, Ian Clachan? Bess Crawford stiffened and said to herself, as she saw her nephew watching the little stray from Glasgow with a daft fond expression on his open face. I don't think Betty Rannoch would be too pleased to see that look

61

in Ian's eyes for some other lassie, she thought. And neither am I! She felt a stab of razor-keen apprehension.

In the short time Annie had lived at Clachan's Farm, her childish, starvelling figure had blossomed into womanhood like a flower in the desert after rain. Annie Ramsay was rapidly turning into a comely young woman. No wonder Ian was watching her.

Och, Bess, don't be daft, she told herself. Geordie would never give his blessing to a mis-match like that and Ian is too good a lad to go against his father's wishes. Betty will bring a fine farm with her the day she weds. And what farmer's son would not consider that? But the look in Ian's eyes ... aye it was a worry ... Bess turned imperceptively so Annie came into the corner of her vision without seemingly being observed. Hastily she buried her head in the psalm book as Annie felt her scrutiny instinctively and glanced round. It had been enough, the pure worship she had seen in the little milkmaid's face as she caught Ian's eye was enough to tell her all she needed to know. And it wouldn't do.

Opposite, the Rannochs sat surrounded by their own folk. Betty's round face flushed with pleasure when Ian came in with his father. She had no illusions that he gave her a thought unless prompted. The situation didn't worry her a jot. I've got the farm coming to me, she gave a secret, happy smile, and Ian knows where his best interests lie. He'll make a fine farm out of joining up the two when Faither and Geordie Clachan decide to stay by the hearth instead of ploughing the fields.

'Psalm twenty-three,' the minister intoned.

'The Lord is my Shepherd ...' he led in his fine baritone.

Betty picked up her psalter and her head came up defiantly as the congregation joined the minister in the opening psalm. Anyway, I'll make him as good a wife as he can hope to have, even if I'm not the bonniest lass in Ayrshire. One day I'll be standing there. Her eyes swept possessively over the rows of Clachan pews. Aye, once he comes back from Glasgow for good. That's when I can make him notice me ... and so I will.

The notes died away, then suddenly a little ripple passed through the waiting congregation. The Laird's family from Craigdrummond House had arrived and there was a new face among them. As they swept down the aisle, Annie peeped curiously from under her lashes. The Laird led as usual, but this time

62

his daughter was not by his side. Instead on his arm he proudly bore an attractive woman, dressed elegantly as befitted the House of Cameron. Pretty Alexandra was nowhere to be seen.

Bess Crawford bided her time till Annie was alone with her in the kitchen. The girl had proved to have a light hand with baking and the housekeeper often called her in to help if she finished early with the cows.

'Ian's a right good lad,' she began as her nephew's tall figure passed the window and he waved cheerily.

'Aye,' Annie stiffened, her quick mind detecting something else behind the seemingly off-chance remark.

'You ken that Ian is walking out with Betty Rannoch, Annie?' Mistress Crawford patted a lump of dough into shape.

'Is that right?' Annie kept her attention firmly on the bowl of flour and eggs.

'Nothing has been announced yet,' Bess went on. 'We want to wait till she's twenty before they show themselves in kirk together, though that's not so long now, just a year or two. Then the engagement will be short.'

Annie stopped and looked at her in puzzlement. 'Ian hasn't mentioned anything about marrying soon.'

'And why should Ian Clachan discuss his private affairs with a milkmaid, Annie?' Bess said with deliberate emphasis on the last word. 'I'm only warning you for your own sake, lass.' She left the baking and turned to face the girl who had reddened at the words.

'I'm sorry, Missus,' Annie replied, 'but I dinnae follow ye?'

'You're getting a bit too sweet on Ian, Annie,' she said bluntly. 'Just don't get any ideas, lass. Plans are already well underway between the families for the wedding.'

'I haven't been trying to catch Ian, Missus!' Annie mumbled in blushing embarrassment, tinged with guilt that Bess had somehow realised she adored the farmer's son.

Bess hurried on, 'I'm not saying you have, Annie, but I want you to be careful that you don't encourage him without thinking. It would be a poor way to repay our kindness for taking you in off the streets of Glasgow and giving you a decent life.'

'Och, I wouldn't let you down!' Poor Annie wished the floor would swallow her and end this unexpected nightmare.

'Aye,' Mistress Crawford went on, 'Ian is right fond of Betty in his own way. They have kenned each other since they were bairns. A Rannoch marrying a Clachan is the match we all want, not some mis-alliance with a penniless waif.'

'Och, Missus ...' Annie cried.

Bess hurried on ignoring her protest, 'And they won't be waiting too long, Annie, once their engagement is official. Ian will have to get into the way of dealing with both farms as soon as he can. In any case we think it's as well to let them wed young, so they can have their bairns while they are able to enjoy them.' She rushed on again before Annie, blinking back humiliated tears could comment, 'Aye, Geordie is pleased and so am I, not to mention the Rannochs, of course. None of us want to see Rannoch's Farm going to a stranger. Do you understand about the estate inheritance rules, Annie?'

Annie shook her head. 'Leezie said something about them once, but I'm not sure what she meant,' she whispered.

'Either Betty marries and the lease goes to her husband when Rabbie retires,' Bess explained, driving the point home with a minimum of words, 'or they have to give it up since Betty cannot take over, her being a lassie.'

'Aye, well, I'll make sure ye have no cause to worry about the farms on my behalf.' Annie hoped her voice was steady.

'Good, I just thought you'd like to know how it is,' Mistress Crawford said. 'I ken you and Ian like each other's company, Annie,' her tone was brisk. 'I've seen you walk up the cliffs with him on a Sunday afternoon. And I'm not the only one who's noticed, I expect.'

'We just talk, Missus,' Annie said, grey eyes pleading.

'I'm not suggesting there is anything more than innocent friendship between you,' Bess went on, 'but others might not be so charitable. Even if Betty was not involved, it's not right for a farm lass to be so close to the farmer's son. Just keep your distance, Annie, it saves any gossip and any misunderstandings.'

'Aye, so it does.' Annie turned back to her baking, heart heavy and throat so tight she almost choked.

Bess wasn't finished. 'Do I have your word then, Annie, that you'll keep away from Ian?' She turned the girl round and searched her face with a stern expression that brooked no shirking an answer.

'Aye.' Annie blinked back tears.

64

'Then we'll say no more about it!' Bess nodded, letting Annie go and feeling she had done her duty well.

The fine weather broke next day. Sunny summer days suddenly seemed far more than just a lark-song away, even the nights appeared to draw in faster. Determined mizzling rain settled in from a grey heavy sea.

Annie and Dougie, dripping wet, carried in slabs of fine butter to the Craigdrummond kitchens, then went back to the cart for great churns of cream which they could barely carry between them.

Staggering under the weight, Annie's eyes were everywhere. Maids and men rushed carrying china and silver by the armful preparing for the Hunt Ball. The noise was deafening. Folk passed each other at speed with sure-footed accuracy, missing catastrophe by the merest margin.

The milkmaid gawped as staff rushed up and down stairs to the newly reopened ballroom, carrying tables, chairs, candelabra and acres of fine linen.

Dougie laughed at her awed expression. 'Aye, Craigdrummond House is a fine sight is it no, Annie?'

'Oh aye,' she stepped aside to let a bustling maid rush past.

'Och, it's good to see they dustsheets comin' off,' Dougie added. 'There's been nothin' but gloom about the place since Miss Alexandra's mother died, but times are changin' at last.' He placed a rough hand on Annie's shoulder and propelled her out of the mainstream of human traffic. 'You stay here, lass, till I find out how much buttermilk the head cook wants for the baking.'

'Aye ...' Annie backed into an alcove and unashamedly feasted her eyes on the organised chaos around her. Beyond in the hall she could see skivvies carrying silver cutlery, dull from the great stores, and sweating to make it shine under the sharp gaze of Davie Murray, the imposing butler. Floors everywhere were being polished and the glittering glass covers round the gaslight mantles were buffed to the point where it hurt Annie's eyes to look at them. Maids chattered, footmen whistled, the cooks perspired as their tempers became tinder short. Ranks of scullery-maids kept well beyond ladle-reach as they peeled, chopped, strained and stirred.

'Come on, lass, the work is just beginning, you'll be back a dozen times today!' Dougie called her out of her dream.

Time after time that day in the relentless drizzle, they took their place in the long line of covered carts which trundled endlessly up from the Craigdrummond Estate farms. Piled high with sacks of flour, sides of meat, mountains of vegetables, eggs, butter and cream, they came as if from a cornucopia.

Struggling to protect a great tray of straw-cushioned eggs, Annie pushed her way through. Blinking in disbelief, she caught a glimpse of crystal chandeliers, burnished to a million diamonds, being carried between footmen. Grim-faced with concentration they placed each foot carefully, lest they should trip on the way up polished marble stairs up to the ballroom. 'What in the name of the wee man will they think of next?' she murmured wide-eyed. Clachan's Farm was familiar comfort and hard work, but this was opulent richness beyond all belief.

Red-eyed and bitter since she had stayed at home on Sunday, Alexandra Cameron sulked in her room. It was so rare of her father to actually punish her, that she had resentfully done her bible readings, knowing he would certainly follow it up. Now, two days later and far more upsetting was the question of the ball dress. Despite all pleadings, Urquhart was still adamant she should not wear it.

Maria Lennox had left Alexandra well alone, realising that now was not the time to force a relationship. 'She'll come round in time, dearest,' she'd said as she tried to reassure Cameron, who was still angered by his daughter's intransigence and worried by her nervy, hysterical outbursts.

'I sincerely hope so,' the Laird muttered in irritation, 'maybe a year or two away is just what she needs ... a change ... a firm hand ... you know.'

'We'll talk about it after the Ball, my dear.' Maria smiled. 'Let's not let family differences spoil our big evening, Urquhart.'

'Of course not, dear love.' Cameron lifted her hand and gently kissed her fingers, looking deeply into her eyes. 'And we'll set a date next month, Maria. I want it to be very, very soon,' he whispered softly.

'As you wish, Urquhart,' she blushed and nodded. They gazed at each other, Alexandra and her objections forgotten.

* * *

Alexandra drew her dress out of its protective linen covers and looked tearfully at the pretty material and the lovely flowing skirt with the rosebud gathers round the hem. 'How could they forbid me to wear it? How could they be so cruel? Lady Lennox just wants to be the centre of attraction at the Hunt Ball! I'm sure it was her idea to make me dress like a child. I hate her! Hate her!' she said resentfully to herself and refused to admit she might have brought the punishment on her own head.

She went back to the windowseat where she had sat all day, grim-faced and refusing to be drawn into the excitement as the house prepared around her. Idly she gazed down at the scuttling figures as they came and went. Annie glanced up at the lit windows of the family rooms, but neither girl marked the other.

Sometimes Alexandra wished she was a servant too, their lives seemed more purposeful than hers.

Below, Annie's small chapped hands, slid slimily on the buttermilk churns as she and Dougie wearily heaved in the empties. Finally they were done and heading gratefully back to the warmth of Clachan's kitchen. Annie glanced over her shoulder at the fading lights of Craigdrummond glowing like jewels through the descending mist. 'Aye it's bonnie,' she murmured, 'and what a carry-on inside. I wonder if they'll be ready in time? I'm dying to see whit it will be like tomorrow.' She couldn't believe order could come from such chaos. 'Och well, pies for supper,' her stomach growled in happy anticipation.

'Come now, Miss Alexandra,' Miss Cumming coaxed her charge towards dinner. 'Don't sit here wallowing in the miseries. The Laird won't change his mind about the dress, or about the new Lady of Craigdrummond. You'd better make the best of things. How about that pretty blue we had made up just last month? No one has seen it yet. You could look really sweet with a few more trimmings added to the bodice and hem.'

'Sweet!' she hissed. 'I don't want to look sweet, I want to look grown up. Nobody will notice me in that thing, it doesn't even reach my ankles.'

'Well, we could add a little flounce round the bottom, that might do the trick,' the governess said doubtfully. 'I'm sure your Papa wouldn't mind that.'

'Oh forget it! There's two days yet before the Ball. If I can't wear my new dress, I don't care what I wear. Maybe I'll go in my shift!' Alexandra replied rudely.

'Alexandra!' Miss Cumming was aghast.

'I'm going out for a ride on Blanche.' Alexandra felt she had to escape or she would burst. The dappled mare had been a gift from her father on her last birthday and was her favourite mount.

'Come now, not this evening.' Miss Cumming objected. 'The weather is miserable and the grooms are all busy getting ready for stabling the guests' horses. There would be nobody to accompany you and you're not allowed out alone. Anyway it's getting late.'

'Oh I suppose so.' The girl shrugged and let the matter go as suddenly as it had arisen. Turning back to the window, she cupped her chin in her hands and gazed out at the mizzling blanket of fog and rain.

Miss Cumming was relieved her charge seemed calmer. 'Well, I'll just go and see if Mistress Braidie would like a wee cup of tea.' She got on well with Maria's elderly chaperone and they shared many a gossip over scones and a pot of best Ceylon or Earl Grey.

'Et tu, Brute! She who is not for me is against me!' Alexandra whispered in her melodramatic way. For a few moments she sat still as death, then got up, her face resolute and secretive. Carefully she hid her riding coat under a shawl and made her way through the house, avoiding the areas of main activity. In minutes she was out in the wet yard. She slipped on her coat and tucked the tell-tale golden curls under a plain snood.

Unnoticed she walked round the corner to the quiet stall where her horse whinned happily to see her. She patted the smooth flanks. 'Saddle Blanche,' she called to the young stable-boy from the corner where he was lifting hay onto a rack.

'It's a wee bittie late, Mistress ...' he faltered.

'Saddle Blanche!' she snapped.

'Right, Miss Alexandra,' he touched his forelock and did as he was told. One of the older men might have objected, but Alexandra knew this lad was too much in awe of her to do anything but what she said.

'At last!' Alexandra felt the wind on her face and the sharp sting of rain on her cheeks, but even so, her heart lifted as she trotted then galloped into the thickening mist. Suddenly all the cares and fears over Maria Lennox and the future diminished. She hoped nobody would notice she was missing, but deep down she didn't care. The desire to get away from Craigdrummond for a few hours alone was paramount. Alexandra laughed aloud. 'I'm free! Come on, Blanche!' She gave the horse its head, disappearing into the protective whiteness of the misty evening.

Chapter Seven

The letter from Glasgow lay on the desk by the big bible in the back room all afternoon. It had come when Annie and Dougie were over at Craigdrummond and Mistress Crawford waited till they came back from their last trip and supper was set, before telling Annie where to find it. 'Jock Thampson brought it over from the junction with our post. Imagine someone writing to you, Annie,' Mistress Crawford sounded surprised. It was seldom anyone but she or the farmer himself received a letter and then not every week.

'Och, it'll be from our Sandy, Mistress Crawford. I wrote away back in June, so I did.' Annie gave a little happy hop and rushed in to read it the minute she was given leave.

Glasgow,
23 August 1892

Dear Annie,
I am sorry to tell you that Daddy was kilt in an accident at work last week. Mammy said we were not to tell ye till he was buried because we haven't the money to bring ye up for it and that it would not do any good anyway since nothing can bring him back, neither it can. Mammy had just paid the wee insurance for the funeral so he didn't have to go to a paupers grave and he would have been glad of that. A bit of metal fell from the boat they was buildin and it kilt him. Our Eddie is joinin the navy so he can send his money to Mammy. That should be good because ye ken what a lazy eejit he is and never does a hands turn. I have asked the baker if I can have extra shifts with the cakes and that and

70

he says aye since I do a man's work as it is and have a good hand with the scones and the pastry. We can manage but money will be tight so it will. Mammy is awfy cut up so she is. The twins don't understand what has happened and keep asking if Daddy is at the pub which cuts Mammy to the quick so it does. I'm sorry I am no as good as you at writing Annie, be a good lassie and send us a wee letter now and then to cheer Mammy up. She was glad to get yer money and it must be nearly time for the next lot she says. If things is this bad, it will be pledged on tick before it comes and she is right.

Your loving brother,
Sandy.

Annie read Sandy's untutored scrawl twice before the message sunk in. Tears welled up in her eyes. Jamie Ramsay might not have been the world's most responsible father, but he had been no worse than many in the poverty-stricken tenements. The Ramsay bairns often went to school with frozen bare feet and empty stomachs, but so did everyone else. And if he took their meagre pay once they began to work, it was his right, she thought. And though his temper was ragged when he'd been boozing, none of them had every been black and blue from routine beatings like some of their friends.

'Daddy was never that rotten when he had a wee dram too many,' she said aloud as she wiped her face with the back of her hand. Och, Mammy will miss him, so she will! *Oh my luve is like a red, red rose* ... she remembered how he had danced her mother round the crowded kitchen last Hogmanay. His whisky-laced tenor ringing round the shabby room as he serenaded her for all he was worth while the family looked on, laughing their heads off.

What hurt most, was not really the loss of Jamie, but the realisation that she no longer belonged. The family had grieved without her and had not even tried to bring her home for the funeral. A great sense of loneliness began to rise from deep inside, till it choked on a sob. She put the letter down beside the bible and bit her lip so hard she could taste blood.

Behind her the door opened and Maisie's thin whine cut across her sorrow. 'Mistress Crawford says what's keeping ye? We

71

can't wait all night for a wee scruff like you before the fairmer can say grace!'

'Leave me alone, Maisie! I'm no coming.' Annie turned away so the older girl couldn't see the tears.

'Aye ye better come, or ye'll pay for it!' Maisie pushed her hard on the shoulder from behind.

'Clear off, ye rotten bitch!' Annie whirled round, tears lost in sudden spitting fury that made the older girl recoil.

'Och, please yerself!' Maisie drew back, scared by the expression in Annie's face. 'We'll see what Mistress Crawford says about that, so we will! You're in trouble, so ye are!' Maisie slammed the door, heading straight for the kitchen, her face beetroot.

Annie couldn't face explanations and the sympathy that would surely follow, the bustle and cheer of the big kitchen. She left the letter by the bible and slipped into the hall. Nobody was about. Her working coat, with its protective cape of heavy leather across the shoulders and back, hung limp and still damp from the rain. Underneath, her big farm boots were cleaned and waiting for the next morning's work. She put on the boots, swung on the coat and tied a long scarf of strong homespun wool round her hair and neck with automatic precision.

Tears blinded her as she stumbled into the yard. Outside it was still barely light, but the mist from the sea and the rain had created a thick pall of eerie whiteness which swallowed up the land. Glad of its anonymity, Annie bent her head and walked away from Clachan's Farm towards the ridge of the moor. By now she knew the area round the farm like the back of her hand, even in the mist. Aimlessly she clumped along the rough track, sad thoughts tumbling in her mind. She was sixteen on the verge of full womanhood, but this was the first time she had to cope with the finality of death. It was hard to bear.

'Where's Annie?' Mistress Crawford asked when Maisie came back.

'Och, that one!' Maisie had recovered her nerve and made the most of the opportunity. 'She's in a right bad mood, so she is. She turned on me like a wildcat and was right cheeky as well. She even said she wasn't coming into supper, Missus.'

Mistress Crawford shook her head, 'That's not like Annie.'

'Aye well so she did, Missus!' Maisie insisted.

'In that case she can go hungry! I'll speak to the young lady later on.' Mistress Crawford's face darkened, but she didn't want to make a scene there and then with all the men looking on and waiting hungrily to eat. 'We may as well start, Geordie.'

'Aye.' Geordie Clachan bowed his head and said grace and they began their meal.

Ian was puzzled, Aunt Bess was right, it wasn't like Annie Ramsay to behave like that at all. She had a quick tongue, but never sulked, though he'd noticed she had been a wee bit distant with him lately. Och well, you never know with lassies! he thought as he shrugged and ate.

Alexandra Cameron had never come this far from Craigdrummond alone. After the initial mad gallop, the exhilaration had worn off and she was becoming steadily more and more worried. In the growing mist nothing looked familiar any more, after a while she decided wisely to give Blanche her head and let her turn home, as the mare seemed inclined to do.

'Good girl!' At first the horse headed resolutely back, apparently following the way they came. She chose forks in the paths that criss-crossed the moor without hesitation. Alexandra sighed with relief. Then she stiffened, realising with a shiver of shock and fear that they had already trotted past an unmistakable boulder formation, rising from the side of the path. 'Come on, Blanche,' she muttered, patting the horse's neck as much for her own comfort as that of the beast. 'Don't take us round in circles. Home, back to Craigdrummond, girl.'

Blanche whinnyed uneasily and shied at a stunted tree which loomed suddenly out of the shifting mist. 'Easy, easy,' Alexandra crooned, trying to keep her voice calm as she clung on.

The horse trembled and bucked, but Alexandra held her well and she steadied. After a while she relaxed her grip a little as the horse began trotting happily again. Suddenly from the whiteness a grouse rose with a raucous cry, flapping frightened wings in front of the nervous mare. Blanche reared in fear and bolted off the track and onto the open moorland, with Alexandra clinging on like grim death.

The end came fast and soon, Blanche tripped on the heathery

terrain and threw her burden heavily onto the moor, while she galloped off into the impenetrable mist.

Alexandra lay there winded and shocked. Slowly she raised herself, wincing at the aches that seemed to come from all over her body. Unsteadily she got to her feet, wet, muddy and thoroughly frightened. One ankle hurt, but the high boot supported it like a bandage and she hobbled forward. After a few steps she stopped in hopeless bewilderment. She could see nothing, nothing at all, to guide her home. A sob rose in her throat. The moor itself held no great fear, but Alexandra was Craigdrummond bred, she knew the Moss was somewhere around and at all costs she had to avoid it.

'Oh I wish I'd said where I was going,' she cried to the unyielding silence, but she knew nobody would think of checking for her horse yet at the Craigdrummond. They would all think she was somewhere indoors sulking as she had been doing for days. It might be hours yet before anyone really missed her, unless Blanche made it back without her and the grooms raised the alarm.

'It's all that woman's fault,' she raged aloud against Maria Lennox. 'Well, maybe I shouldn't have come out alone.' After a while she admitted to herself that Maria could not be completely blamed for her present predicament. She sat on a stone, forcing down mounting hysteria as she tried to work out which direction she should take. The blanket of soft, grey stillness gave nothing away. It was impossible to guess where Craigdrummond lay.

'Come on, Alexandra Cameron, you can't sit here all night!' she told herself and got up. 'Ouch!' The ankle hurt, but still bore her weight. Slowly she hobbled forward, trying to check every step in case she was getting near the Moss.

Alexandra had never walked far in her life, except on shopping expeditions. Even then the carriage always waited patiently outside the shop they were patronising. Weariness, combined with the ache from her twisted ankle and bruised body, began to take its toll. 'I must keep going,' she told herself silently. Stumbling along she became more exhausted and more careless. The temperature was low on the misty moor even in late summer. Instinctively she knew if she stopped she might never start again.

The ground felt spongy and reminded her of the lurking danger. She shivered in terror knowing a mistake could be fatal.

The Craigdrummond Moss was between her and Craigdrummond if she strayed too far to the west. Directions were impossible to gauge in this white blanket. The Moss might be waiting for her ahead, deathly still and evilly green in the shifting, treacherous mist. She might be almost upon it now.

Annie heard the horse before she saw it. It had the hesitant steps of a beast unused to being alone. Her months at Clachan's Farm had taught her much about animals and, to her surprise, had awakened a talent for handling them, big and small not just the cows she worked with daily.

'Come on then, my bonnie.' Blanche trotted down and came whinnying happily to her call. She held the reins of the trembling beast and saw the empty saddle, all ready for a female rider. 'And where's your mistress, lass?' She forgot her own sorrow in sudden concern. 'Did you run away? Och, ye're a bad girl, so ye are!' Annie assumed the animal belonged to one of the farms that nestled in sheltered corners across the hills and moorland. It never occurred to her that the beast might be from Craigdrummond House itself.

Slowly she began walking back to the farm, leading Blanche and talking to her reassuringly. Annie had walked a long way in her sorrow, but had stuck carefully to the paths and was confident of the road home. 'Maybe somebody will ken where you come from at Clachan's Farm, lass,' she said softly to the horse who snorted and nuzzled her neck.

'Whit in the name of the wee man was that?' Annie froze as an eldritch shriek carried across the moor from the direction of the Moss. She stood trembling for a moment in superstitious dread, then chided herself firmly, 'Och, Annie Ramsay, ye'r beginning to let Ian's daft stories go to yer brain. It was probably a stoat wi' a rabbit.'

'Oh, Mither!' The screech came once more and died on a hideous note of horrible fear. Annie started to run back towards the farm, dragging the horse with her. Whatever was out there, she wouldn't wait for it to come and get her. Suddenly she stopped as a terrible thought hit her. She looked at the empty saddle and then, pulling the horse with her, left the safety of the track and headed straight into the falling darkness and the mist, in the direction of the fearful cry.

75

'Is anybody there?' Annie shouted nervously over and over again. But only silence surrounded her. Trying to remember everything old Charlie had taught her about keeping a sense of direction when searching for a beast in the dark or in a mist, she carefully counted her steps and covered a wider and wider circle. She kept a fast point in some odd shaped boulders and picking out as many other landmarks as she could from a bush here or a stunted tree there. Every so often she stopped and listened, hand on Blanche's muzzle to keep her quiet.

At last she heard it, a desperate moan of terror and exhaustion. 'Is anybody there?' she yelled as loudly as she could. 'Answer if ye can, I'm coming to get ye!'

'I'm here!' the reply quavered faintly through the mist. 'For God's sake come quickly, I can't hold on much longer, it's got me by the legs. It's pulling me under!'

Deliberately slow, despite the urgency, Annie Ramsay crept forward. She knew if the Moss had a victim in its deadly grip, it would be even happier with two. 'Keep calling,' she yelled, 'any noise at all will do. Repeat something over and over ... anything just to guide me in!'

'I'll try!' From the impenetrable gloom came the strangest load of gobbledegook Annie had ever heard from mankind. They hadn't taught her French verbs in the Gallowgate elementary school. But it was good enough for the job. Steadily she followed the weird words. 'I have to be careful now, I'm nearly there,' she called encouragingly. 'I'll have ye out, don't you worry, just you keep talking.' Annie spoke with more optimism than she felt.

The ground became unstable under her feet and the horse shied nervously. 'Aye you're no daft, bonnie lass.' Gently she stroked the horse's muzzle. 'Wait here now, nibble a wee bit scrub, that's right. I won't be far away.' Annie let Blanche go, knowing she wouldn't stray far, now she had been found and calmed.

Getting onto her hands and knees, she called again. 'Go on talking, hen, talk and talk, I'm nearly with ye.'

'Je suis, tu es, il est ...' Alexandra repeated and repeated the words as the horrible sucking felt stronger and stronger round her legs. Her grip was slackening as she tired.

Annie could see her at last, almost up to the waist in the bog and clinging to two boulders that jutted out incongruously from the glistening moss. Alexandra had dragged herself as high as she could onto the rocks, but the bog held her too firmly to clamber further without help.

Annie knew she had to get her secured first and then out of the sucking green slime. The rocks stood like an island, but were too far away for her to reach. How can I get near enough without sinking in myself? She thought for a moment with the clarity and speed of desperation. Aye, it might work ... old Charlie says he's done it wi' ewes!

Quickly she took off her sturdy farm coat and laid it flat, leather side under, like a raft on the slimy, treacherous ground. She wound the long, sturdy scarf from her hair and neck. 'Hold on, I have to use the horse as well,' she called to the victim.

'I can't, hold, on,' Alexandra ground out between clenched teeth.

'Aye, ye can,' Annie said calmly and encouragingly. 'This'll no take a minute. Now be a brave lassie, I'm coming.'

Blanche came to her call. Annie undid the reins, looping their combined length round her own waist and tied one end to the saddle prow. 'Don't you bolt, or ye'll be the death of me and this poor lassie,' Annie crooned to the frightened mare. 'Ye don't have to come nearer, neither ye do, just stand nice and steady.'

Annie lay flat on the coat, and crept forward. The Moss sucked at the edges, but failed to pull it or its burden under. Carefully she stretched out her hand, at last grasping the right wrist of the other girl. 'Don't let go of the rock with yer other hand yet,' she said sharply. 'But when I tell ye, then you grab my arm with it.' She looped the scarf found her own arms linking them with the right wrist of the girl and then pulled sharply on the rein. Blanche fearing she was being drawn towards the Moss began, as Annie hoped, to back nervously away.

There was a hideous sucking noise and both girls cried aloud with pain clinging to each other, as the strong woollen scarf bit into their arms and the Moss at first refused to give up its prize.

'Keep a grip of me!' Annie shouted.

'I am. Oh God, make the wretched bog let me go!' Alexandra screamed in pain and hope.

They clung together like leeches as the frightened horse pulled them slowly clear. Annie used her own feet to help with the last few feet and sprang up to calm Blanche once they were both on firm ground.

Alexandra lay panting and sobbing in shock on the heather, filthy and slimy from head to foot, unrecognisable as Craigdrummond's heiress. 'Can you get us out of here? I don't know where I am and it's dark as well now!'

'I can try,' Annie replied bravely, rubbing a trickle of blood from her own bruised arms.

'Have you cut yourself?' Alexandra peered at the younger girl's arm and saw her properly for the first time. 'My God,' she said in surprise, 'you're quite small, but ...'

'I ken,' Annie said with a weary grin, 'I'm stronger than I look. My arm's alright,' she shrugged. 'I'll no die of it the day.'

'What's your name?' Alexandra asked this stranger who had dragged her from certain death.

'Annie Ramsay.' Then she added with a wry smile, 'But nearly everybody calls me Clachan's Annie.'

'Why?' She was intrigued despite their odd predicament.

'Jock Thampson the carter called me that when he left me off in Clachan's farmyard the day I came to work there. It just stuck. Have ye hurt your foot?' She saw Alexandra wince as she tried to walk.

'Yes, I did it when I fell from Blanche, but it's much worse now. I think struggling in the Moss has damaged it even more,' Alexandra admitted through clenched teeth.

'Aye ye could be right.' Annie ran an expert hand round the swollen foot as if she was feeling the vulnerable leg of a calf. 'If I unlace the boot, ye'll have to do without it, for it won't go on again. This will double its size right away.'

'Please open the boot, I don't think I can stand the pain much longer,' Alexandra asked humbly. Despite her injuries, she was impressed by the bright confidence of the younger girl. It commanded a respect in her she rarely gave to subordinates. None of the maids at Craigdrummond ever treated her with such lack of deference, or genuine concern. Probably her attitude will change the minute she knows who I am, Alexandra thought with a stab of sadness. Everybody's does.

Annie dispelled that idea straight away with her next words which showed she knew exactly who she was dealing with. 'Aye, ye're right, it's best to take it off.' Annie began to unlace the ruined fine leather boot. 'But I think we'll no make it to Craigdrummond, Mistress Alexandra, Clachan's Farm is nearer.'

'As you like,' she murmured. Released from the boot, the foot began visibly increasing in size. 'Sorry, but I feel quite strange, can you give me a hand?' She leaned on Annie and tried to get up, but began to sway helplessly back and forwards.

'Aye well ye can faint once we get back to Clachan's ... you're no faintin' here, or we're both in dire trouble, Mistress.' Annie said curtly. 'Let's have ye!' She draped Alexandra's arm across her shoulders. 'Now, right up onto the horse!' With a tremendous effort that left her own head spinning, Annie pushed her unceremoniously into the saddle. Balancing the swaying figure as well as she could with one steadying hand, she gritted her teeth and led the two of them back through the gloom and onto the track, blessing old Charlie for his tutorship at every step.

Annie had managed to drag her ruined muddy coat from the bog and it hung filthy and wet across her shoulders, giving little protection. But she hardly felt the cold, so intent was she on getting the two of them to safety. She had no idea of time, how long the rescue had taken, or even how long she had wandered about earlier in her sorrow. Darkness had taken over the mist entirely. Wearily she guessed it must be around ten or eleven o'clock.

Not a word more was spoken between the girls on the slow plod back. Annie thought once or twice that her companion would fall out of the saddle, but somehow she managed to keep upright. She thought she would die of tiredness herself if they didn't get to Clachan's soon.

Finally they clopped into the dark farmyard and the door was thrown open at once. The men streamed out, torches blazing and dressed for a search. Ian was first over. 'Faither, Aunty Bess, come here quick,' he shouted to Geordie who had run out followed by Mistress Crawford in a state of unusual agitation and disarray. Leezie trailed behind, red-faced and eyes swollen from crying.

'Thank heaven!' Leezie cried when she saw the bedraggled arrivals. 'It's Annie right enough ... all covered in muck and glaur! Oh tae hang! Would you look at that? Mistress Alexandra's with her on her horse. They're black as the ace of spades the pair of them.'

Ian Clachan reached the girls first. 'Ian, I'm awfy tired.' As Annie pitched forward into his arms, she had a last odd thought before blessed darkness overwhelmed her. 'What on earth is Doctor Murchieson doing here?'

Chapter Eight

'What are ye doing here, Doctor Murchieson?' Annie muttered when she opened her eyes hours later. 'And what in the name am I doin' in the kitchen?' Somehow they had got her undressed, washed and into a day-bed by the big range, without her being any the wiser.

'Mistress Crawford thought it was warmer for you here. And as for me,' he said with a smile, 'I just came to visit my old friends as I always do during my annual holidays ... and to consider yet another Ayrshire property ... not to mention seeing how wee Annie Ramsay from the Gallowgate was coping with the beasts and folk on Clachan's Farm.' His eyes twinkled and the smile broadened. 'And what did I find ...?' he waited, head tilted like a squirrel, for her reply.

'What did ye find, Doctor?' she asked on cue.

'The whole place in an uproar, Geordie and his men about to scour the fields and moors, Mistress Crawford white to the gills, Leezie having hysterics, Maisie howling that it wasn't her fault ... and no Annie to be found!'

'Och, the mist was terrible,' Annie's eyes widened. 'I thought it was one of Ian's ghaisties when I heard the first cries. Here, listen, is the lassie from the Big House all right?' Annie raised herself anxiously as memory flooded back.

'Miss Alexandra's fine, lass, and owes you a debt she can never repay if we've understood the situation right ... though you've to keep it all under your hat, I believe. Miss Alexandra gave us a garbled version before I tied up her foot properly and we took her home. Up at Craigdrummond they hadn't even missed her when Geordie and Bess took her back. What a to do!'

'Och, it was old Charlie she should thank,' Annie said blushing, 'he showed me how to see the Moss doesn't swallow ye up.'

'Your letter from Sandy started the search, Annie. Ian found it in the back room.' The doctor took her hand sympathetically. 'I'd known about the sad event all along, of course, since I attended your poor father and wrote out the death certificate, but I never imagined you hadn't been told.'

'No,' Annie shook her head sadly. 'There was no money for me to come up to the Gallowgate anyway for the funeral. Sandy and them thought it was best to wait before they told me, or I'd be sure to insist on coming. How's Mammy? Sandy says she's fine, but is she, Doctor?' Annie's lip quivered.

'Your mother is coping well, Annie, never fear, and the boys have rallied round.'

'Aye, Mammy has the twins to think about. Och, maybe I should go back and help her. I could get my old job back in the 'baccy factory, I was a good worker, Doctor, the foreman said I was. And I'm stronger and bigger now after being on the farm. My lungs are just fine.' The grey eyes filled with tears but she blinked them back.

'Listen, Annie, you're better off here. Your Mammy gets your pay every three months. There's never short time or half-shifts on a farm, so she wouldn't get much more if you were still rolling tobacco. And what would they do on Clachan's Farm without you, eh?' Doctor Murchieson patted her arm avuncularly. 'Mistress Crawford is pleased with you and the Farmer too. Indeed they all seem to have taken to you, Annie, you should have seen the state of everybody when you were missing.' The doctor's tone was kind and positive, cheering Annie to the very core of her heart.

'Did she? Were they?' Annie thought of the warning the housekeeper had given her. Annie had tried to keep away from Ian since, to the poor lad's clear bewilderment. Maybe Mistress Crawford was reassured after all.

'And why not?' The doctor, unaware of any tension between Annie and the housekeeper demanded, adding stoutly, 'You do your work well as I understand things.'

'Och, maybe ye're right, Doctor. Mammy would have me to keep as well as the rest.' She hesitated for a moment then rushed on, garrulous in her relief. 'And I'm glad ye think I should stay, because I have to thank you for sending me here, Doctor Murchieson. I've never been happier in my life, neither I have.' Emotional weak tears, spilled down her face onto the pillow. 'I want to stay at Clachan's Farm for ever, till the day I die, so I do!' Even wi' Maisie picking at me all the time ... even if I'm not allowed to be pally with Ian any more ... those less happy thoughts slipped in unbidden.

'Well, why not?' Doctor Murchieson smiled. 'And one day you may well be courted by some of those strapping lads sitting round the supper table ... you could do worse, Annie.'

'Aye.' She dried her eyes and blushed.

'Oh and by the way, you'll be seeing more of me in future,' the doctor commented casually as he checked her pulse and then listened carefully to her breathing. 'I've taken the plunge this time and bought a practice in Girvan.'

'Girvan is nice. I was there wi' Leezie and Dougie at the fairing. Is yer house right by the sea?' Annie had become passionately fond of the wild coastline that stretched from Ayr southwards. Every chance she got, she walked on the heather-covered cliffs above Craigdrummond strand with the sharp wind in her face and her heart as light as thistledown.

'It's right on the front in fact! I'm leaving Glasgow very soon, Annie, coming back to my native hills and moors, within the sight and smell of the sea.'

'Och, that's great, Doctor, but who'll look after Mammy and the bairns?' she asked anxious again and plucking at the coverlet.

'I've sold my practice to a young doctor who has lots of fine new-fangled ideas. Aye, John Chisholm is progressive right enough. He believes a lot of humanity's ailments begin in the mind and the soul, not the body!' An indulgent smile played round his mouth as he went on, 'But even so he's a decent soul who knows the value of a dose of salts and a goose-grease poultice. Never fear, they'll be well cared for.'

'Now don't you go tiring Annie, the poor lass is done. Do you realise it's two in the morning?' Mistress Crawford came in, smiling and chiding her old friend, dark skirts rustling and pinny as pristine white as ever, despite the events and the hour. 'We'll be lucky if she doesn't come down with pneumonia.'

'Och, Bess, you know me better than that,' Archie Murchieson protested. 'I wanted to check the lass as soon as she came round.

Anyway Annie is just tired, nothing more, her lungs sound better to me now than they've ever done, Ayrshire is doing her the world of good ... you can take the doctor's word for that!'

'It's because I know the doctor so well that I'm saying it! Once you get started blethering, you don't know when to stop, Archibald Murchieson!' She playfully tapped his comfortably full waistcoat with a reprimanding finger.

Annie lay there agape, not able to believe her ears as the formidable housekeeper and the great doctor teased each other like a pair of youngsters at the Midsummer Fair. Suddenly they remembered her presence and lapsed self-consciously back into their usual formality.

Aye, aye, thought streetwise Annie. A practice in Girvan and more visits here. I think Mr Clachan better watch out or he'll be losing his housekeeper. Och no! she drew herself up sharply with a weary little giggle. The Moss has addled my brains. They're far too old the pair of them for that sort of nonsense. And with that charitable judgement, her eyelids drooped again and she fell fast asleep again in front of the glowing range.

Maria Lennox stood beside her fiancé, glowing with unfeigned happiness. On this so special occasion, she wore a splendid ball gown of dazzling azure silk that swept the floor and showed off her slender shoulders and neck. A fine pearl choker, Urquhart's betrothal gift, shone against her white skin and a great sapphire ring weighed down her slim hand. She received the compliments and congratulations of the company graciously.

'And how is poor Miss Alexandra, Sir Urquhart?' yet another guest asked the Laird. Alex had almost managed to overshadow the couple's big announcement after all. Ayrshire's gentry was all agog and wanted to know how the young Mistress fared.

'Oh she's fine, Mistress Baillie. Shaken of course, and the foot will take some time to heal, but really the lass is none the worse for the adventure ... it was lucky she was found quite quickly, it can be cold on the moor at night,' Cameron explained for the hundreth time.

With Clachan's agreement, they had decided to keep the details of Alex's adventure within the family. The story had gone out that she had been carried off by the bolting horse and thrown, then found by a farm worker. How she was found or by whom, was not mentioned, or how near she had come to death in the Moss. Even the workers on Clachan's Farm had been given an edited version of the events and Annie herself was sworn to silence.

Alexandra missed the Hunt Ball entirely, so she didn't have to worry about being seen in a childish dress. With the bruises all over her young body and the state of her swollen ankle, she lay in her room feeling sorry for herself as music sounded below, mingling with the laughter and bustle of arriving guests.

'Get out my dress, Cumming. The real one, not that silly blue. At least I can pretend I'm going!' she quavered in a little voice full of self-pity. A burst of laughter echoed up the stairs to torment her and rub salt in the wounds. 'Do fetch it! Cumming, did you hear?' The hysterical note began to rise.

'Yes, dear,' Miss Cumming shushed her. But in a moment the governess was back, looking worried. 'I'm afraid it's not there any more, Miss Alexandra.'

'Mistress Lennox probably had it destroyed,' she said bitterly. 'Not that it matters now anyway!' Turning her head into the soft pillow, she tasted the salt of her tears as they trickled down her bruised face.

'In here a minute, Annie.' Some weeks after the rescue, Mistress Crawford called a restored and hard-at-work milkmaid. 'There's a message for you.'

'For me?' Annie's stomach tightened in fear, the last message had been the one about her father's death.

'Och, it's nothing bad,' Mistress Crawford reassured her.

'Oh!' Her slender body slumped in relief. She climbed out of her boots and padded into the kitchen in her knitted woollen hose. The early September day was warm and the room was heavy with the smell of fruit. Mistress Crawford and the kitchen-maids had been working all week bottling the rich harvest. 'Apple and blaeberry pie tonight!' Annie's mouth watered.

'Right you two, away you go.' Mistress Crawford dismissed Leezie and Nellie, before turning to the milkmaid once they were alone. 'It's a message from Craigdrummond, Annie.'

'From the Big House for me?' Her eyebrows shot up.

'Annie, you've been a canny lass and kept the full tale of your night's work on the Moss to yourself, like we instructed,' she said quietly.

'Aye, I ken the lassie at the Big House must be feeling right daft,' Annie replied, chestnut curls bobbed madly round the edge of the mob-cap and loosened, falling down almost into her eyes. 'Sorry, Missus,' Annie saw the housekeeper's disapproving frown and she poked them in again before going on, 'And the Laird will no be wanting the world and his wife gossipin' about Miss Alexandra.'

Bess Crawford hid a smile, Annie sounded like a wise old woman not a lass of sixteen. 'That's right,' she said. 'And the Laird's factor sent for Mr Clachan today to say you should be given a reward, Annie.'

'A reward? Imagine that?' Annie's eyes widened.

'Aye, well, Mr Clachan told him that it shouldn't be anything which would draw attention to what happened out there. And they agreed with that, of course.'

'What do you mean, Missus?' she frowned.

'Well, the factor thought of giving you a pony, or a complete new set of clothes, but Mr Clachan said it would seem strange for a wee milkmaid to come cantering up to kirk on a fine horse, or start walking about in silks and satins. Somebody might start asking questions. And they want Miss Alexandra to put the whole business behind her without all sorts of stories circulating.'

'Aye, I can see that, so what was decided, Missus?'

'A dowery.'

'A dowery?' Annie's eyebrows shot up.

'Aye.' The housekeeper flushed remembering the last time she and Annie had spoken privately like this, but she went on steadily enough, 'Mr Clachan suggested that the best thing was to put the price of a pony in the bank for you. You can have it as a dowery when the time comes for you to wed. You'll have a tidy nest egg.'

But not enough to make me worthy of Ian Clachan, Annie found herself thinking, then she immediately pushed the ungrateful idea away. Though she had been upset and low after the housekeeper's talk with her, she bore no resentment. The warning had not been entirely unjustified ... maybe it was even more timely than Bess Crawford realised. Instead she replied, 'That was kind of the Fairmer, but I'm not sure marriage is for me, I saw enough of what it does to folk when I lived in the Gallowgate, Missus.'

'Ah well, you might change your mind on that in the years to come,' Bess Crawford gave a tight smile.

'Och, but I couldn't keep it for a dowery anyway.'

'Why on earth not?' The housekeeper asked in astonishment.

'Sandy said in his letter that things is hard in the Gallowgate. Ye better send it to my Mammy instead.' Annie knew she couldn't live with the knowledge of hardship at home if she had money of her own. 'I've everything I want here and if I change my mind about being wed, then somebody will maybe take me without a dowery.'

'I'm sure they would, Annie, though it won't be possible to give your family the money.' Despite her concern over Ian, Bess Crawford liked Annie and was touched by her thoughtfulness. 'The Laird said it should be only for your direct benefit. You can't touch a penny for five years, neither can anybody else, though it will gain interest nicely for you.'

'Dandy!' Annie hadn't a clue how bank accounts worked, but if the Laird's factor had fixed it, it should be safe enough. 'Well, if that's all, Missus, I better get back to the kye.' She climbed back into the heavy boots and cheerfully clomped off into the farmyard, singing happily and without another thought to the dowery or anything else but the job in hand.

'And there's one who would take her without stick or clout to her name if his father would let him.' Bess Crawford frowned to herself as Ian came across the yard with a pitchfork over his shoulders and joined the girl, tweaking one of her curls. She saw Annie glance guiltily back at the kitchen before the two young people were joined by Dougie and all three disappeared, laughing and chaffing, into the byre. It was impossible to expect them not to meet in the closed, busy world of Clachan's Farm.

It's a pity that the lass has nothing, she thought, for otherwise they get on right well ... Och, in the name of heavens what am I saying? She was shocked at her own thoughts. Now listen, Bess Crawford, stop that daft idea before it starts! Rabbie Burns might have said, 'The mark is but the guinea stamp, the man's the gowd for all that', but a farmer likes to think of a bit of land coming when there's a wedding afoot. Ian is spoken for with Betty Rannoch. She added aloud, 'Joining the two farms makes a lot of sense ... a lot of sense!'

'What makes sense, Bess?' Geordie asked as he came in carrying a side of lamb.

'I was just thinking that Ian could go a long way before he'd get a better farmer's wife than Betty Rannoch,' she said firmly.

'Aye, we all ken that.' Geordie smiled and shook his head. 'But you and Elsie Rannoch seem to be taking this all a bit too fast lately. There's no rush, Bess, let the lad grow up and live a wee bit before he takes on too many responsibilities.'

Bess flushed. 'Well, Elsie and I think it's better to wed young and have bairns while you can enjoy them,' she blurted out before remembering Geordie himself had married late.

Good-naturedly he shrugged and laughed. 'Och, you women, always matchmaking. We menfolk haven't a chance. Well, here you are!' He threw the lamb on the slab by the sink. 'There's a nice bit of meat on this.'

'There is that!' She prodded it with an experienced finger. 'I'll roast some shoulder tonight and maybe do some pies with the shank.'

'Aye, well I'll be off to the rigs.' Geordie left her to her thoughts.

She stood pensively gazing out of the window as he went whistling up the hill, letting her thoughts run on. Whatever Geordie says I'd like to see Ian settle and my own work done here. I'd be happy with Betty in charge, she's a capable lass and she adores Ian. Och and I'm sure he's fond of her, at least up till now he has not made any objections to the idea of wedding her. Still in a way it's a pity he's met temptation at an age when lads are inclined to be rash ... Annie Ramsay is bonny and getting bonnier by the day, there's no denying ... And I know what marriage can be without love, though I think I've earned a second chance ... she trailed off, staring into space, lost in her own thoughts.

'Och, you're becoming daft in your middle-age, Bess Crawford,' she pulled herself up aloud. 'Geordie is right, maybe we shouldn't push Ian and Betty too fast. Archie will wait, he always has!' With a decisive nod, she snapped out of the mood which was threatening to become sad and turned back to the business in hand.

'Are ye ready wi' the apples, Missus?' Leezie's voice broke in from the still room.

'I am that! And then there's this lamb to butcher, Leezie.'
Mistress Crawford stuck her neatly dressed head round the door.
'Get Nellie to boil the bottles before the apples start turning
brown!'

Once the ball was over and the festivities finished, Cameron and
Maria prepared to leave for Glasgow. There was much to do
before the wedding and he had to see his lawyers about bridal
settlements and the like. By the bride's choice the simple ceremony would take place in Craigdrummond Kirk, but for this
Cameron wedding there would be no great list of distinguished
guests, just a few close friends, Maria insisted and Urquhart
lovingly agreed.

Urquhart's farewell to his daughter was fond, but firm. Her
almost fatal antics had finally forced him to come to some decisions about her future.

'You realise I hope, Alexandra, that this latest escapade has
quite made up my mind.' The Laird looked down sternly at her
pale form on the day bed.

'Yes, Papa,' she murmured tremulously, quite unlike her usual
lively self.

'. . . So, I am arranging for you to go to finishing school in
Paris for two years or so, from October.'

'Paris? But can't I just go to Aunt Lispeth and "come out"
instead, Papa?' she pleaded, looking as pathetic as she could.

'No, Alexandra,' Cameron made an effort to keep the irritation
out of his voice. 'You won't be making your debut. Sixteen is too
young, even for a sensible girl and that's hardly an epithet one
would apply to you, especially now.'

'Papa!'

He raised a hand to stop her protest. 'You have a lot to learn,
my dear, before I would dare let you loose on polite society. A
finishing school will polish your manners and improve your atti-
tudes, then perhaps we can think of Lispeth presenting you at
Court.'

And I'll be well out of the way of you and precious Lady
Maria Lennox at Craigdrummond! Alexandra thought bitterly.
Two years away from all that was familiar was a rather frightening prospect. 'Will I be coming home for holidays?' she asked
with a tremble in her voice that wasn't altogether feigned.

'Not during the first year or so, but at the discretion of the parents after that. The Misses Berry have strict rules about going home too soon ... they insist that it simply upsets the young ladies. Maria and I will visit you as often as we can, and of course approved friends of the family may drop in too. You won't be lonely,' he said heartily.

'It seems a long time,' Alexandra's voice was still tremulous.

'Oh, there are others to keep you company and there is a considerable amount of cultural travel too. You'll get a fine rounded education.'

'Did Lady Lennox choose the school?' she demanded bitterly.

'No, I did. It was recommended by the very best authorities,' her father replied sharply. 'The decision to send you to Paris and for how long, is entirely mine. Please stop blaming Maria for things you bring on yourself, Alexandra.'

She knew from his set expression that there was no point in arguing. 'Can Cumming come with me?' she asked in a tiny lost voice.

'Miss Cumming has already made arrangements for her future, as you well know,' Cameron answered shortly. His eyes were like his daughter's in colour and now they were equally stubborn. 'In any case Miss Cumming is not trained to serve as your maid,' he added with an air of finality.

'So I'm on my own?' Alexandra moaned.

Cameron ignored the wail. '... But you will need a maid when Cumming goes. Most girls of your age and position would have normally already had a lady's maid,' he went on thoughtfully, pacing up and down the pretty room. 'I've been remiss there too.' He sighed deeply. 'It's the sort of thing your dear mother would have seen to. Oh well,' he shrugged, 'we have to do something about that soon, I suppose. The school takes only a few girls at a time and prefers each one to bring her own attendant. I know,' his face cleared as if he had managed to shake off a burden, 'I'll ask Maria to choose someone to go with you, it should be easy enough to arrange in time.'

I don't want that woman to choose me a maid! Alex thought defiantly. 'Can't I choose for myself, Papa?' she asked demurely. 'I'm sure Lady Lennox has others things to bother with.'

'Perhaps.' The Laird was relieved she seemed to have taken her banishment quite well. He'd expected tantrums and tears, so he was ready to make concessions. One maid was much like another to him. All the girls at Craigdrummond House were from the village and decent enough.

'Please, Papa.'

'Yes, but only if you choose one from among the Craigdrummond House girls, there is no need to look further afield. And choose someone with experience ... ask the house-keeper, perhaps. Just make sure it's not impossible to train her in time before you go,' he warned. 'Now I must be off.'

'When is the wedding, Papa?' Alex called after him as he walked to the door.

'Two weeks time.'

'So soon?'

Urquhart ignored her comment. 'Maria wants a quiet cere-mony here in the kirk.' His strong features softened. 'There will be just immediate family attending and you, if you are in a respectful humour ... though I've heard you are rather shy about coming,' he added dryly. 'Maria's brother, his wife and a few other friends, Edward, Lord Ballantyne for one, whom you've already met, will be best man.'

'Yes, I remember him.' Alex also remembered the bored look on his face as he bowed over her hand in the drawing room where she first met Maria. Everything that evening was tinged with her shock at meeting the hated woman who had ruined her life, she thought with a deep stab of resentment.

'Maria is right to insist on modest arrangements since we are both widowed,' he went on. 'But naturally we will hold some simple celebrations for the tenants when we get back from our honeymoon. That will be expected.'

'I suppose so,' Alex muttered, imagining Maria taking homage due.

Urquhart warmed to his theme. 'We will travel for a few weeks round Europe immediately after the wedding. The Riviera should be fine in September and not too full of the Prince of Wales' entourage! Yes, Nice would be a pleasant place to start our life together.' His eyes glowed and Alex felt another stab of jealousy.

I wish he'd never met Maria Lennox! she thought angrily.

Despite her father's white-faced shock and Maria's genuine concern when she was carried home by Geordie Clachan and

Mistress Crawford, the girl still refused to accept the inevitable gracefully. But Alexandra was not completely without tactical skill, she knew if she showed unwilling to go to the wedding, her relationship with her father would be damaged for ever. She guessed Maria must have told him what she said about not coming, but not the full story since he seemed more amused than angry. Anyway she did not want to miss out on everything, even if only a simple ceremony in Craigdrummond Kirk!

'... And of course I will come to your wedding, Papa. How could you think otherwise?' She didn't quite meet his eyes.

'That pleases me, Alexandra. Now I must go, the carriage is waiting.' Cameron smiled and turned at the door. 'I told Miss Cumming that Maria and I will come down from Glasgow again next week. She intends to be bring her wedding outfit and since time is short, I believe she has made some arrangements about yours. We can talk more on your finishing school then.'

Alex leaned back on the chaise-longue and shifted her injured foot uneasily as she contemplated her new future. At least in Paris, not Glasgow or Edinburgh, she thought, as a tickle of excitement bubbled up to dominate the apprehension. I wonder what it will be like? she mused. I've never been away from Craigdrummond for more than a few weeks at a time and never stayed with anyone except Aunt Lispeth once in London after Mamma died.

At Craigdrummond Alexandra Cameron was a very big fish in a little pond. When she passed people noticed and jumped to attention. Alexandra had a suspicion that Paris might not be quite the same. The prospect both thrilled and frightened her.

Chapter Nine

'No chance of an invitation to the kirk for this wedding, Bess,'
Elsie Rannoch said with a touch of huffiness. 'You would think
just as a matter of decency, they would have asked the main
tenants' families. It's customary for us to witness a Cameron
marriage. Rabbie and me feel quite snubbed! And Betty's right
disappointed, aren't you, Betty?'

'Och, not really, er ... I suppose so, Mamma,' Betty
Rannoch's homely face clouded as her mother shot her a sharp
look.

'Well, I don't really blame them having a quiet do,' Bess
Crawford replied. 'There must be still sad memories for the
Laird, marrying again in the same kirk as before. Och, I remember visiting Jean and Geordie when the Laird married Miss
Alexandra's mother ... Jean and Geordie had a place in the kirk,
but I just watched from outside, not living on the Estate at the
time. She was a bonny bride ...'

'Aye, we saw her ourselves, Rabbie and me ... from the back
of the kirk wi' the other tenants!' Elsie said with heavy emphasis
on her status.

'Miss Alexandra is very pretty,' Betty ventured a comment.

'They say she has got the best of her mother's looks and the
Laird's,' Bess agreed.

'... But not her mother's sweet nature. I've heard Miss
Alexandra is still as jealous as a ferret over the new Lady.' Elsie
Rannoch sat back with the air of someone having the last word.

'Aye, well she'll have to get used to it, Elsie,' Bess gave a
disapproving sniff. 'For there's no changing the Laird's mind ...
and why should he be swayed by the tantrums of a silly lass?'

Annie carried in another tray of fresh tea, scones and short-bread and placed it on the table. 'Here ye are, Mistress,' she said. 'I've added an extra spoon of Assam like ye said.'

'Serve Betty first,' Mistress Crawford instructed her. 'She likes it weak.'

'Aye, Missus,' Annie carefully poured the delicate liquid into Betty's china cup and handed it to her.

Bess watched out of the corner of her eye, but Annie gave her no cause for concern. She treated Betty in exactly the same cheery way she treated any other guest she served. Aye, well maybe the message has got home, she thought, but still ...

'She's learned fast, that wee lassie,' Elsie remarked as Annie took the empty plates and left.

'Aye, she has that,' Bess nodded. 'But it's like I said when you noticed her the last time, willing girls are two a penny ...'

Maria Lennox was stiff with apprehension when she arrived at Craigdrummond the following week. Much as she loved Urquhart, she felt the strain of coping with his difficult, spoiled daughter. Underneath she was sure Alex must have many good qualities, how could she not with such a father? But they were not displayed for her benefit. Some of the local gentry she met at Craigdrummond, spoke well of the girl and praised her charm and gay personality. Pity I've never seen that side of her, Maria thought ruefully.

Once the maid had unpacked and Maria had freshened up after the journey she went to look for the girl, catching up with her in the drawing room where she was sitting in her favourite windowseat, chin in hand. Making sure none of her anxiety showed, she greeted her warmly, 'Ah, there you are, Alexandra. I hoped to find you here since I remembered you like this room.'

'Yes, I'm here,' Alexandra sounded grudging. 'I saw you arrive in the carriage off the Glasgow train.'

'Well, it's lovely to see you, dear ... oh, and your father and I were so glad you decided to attend the wedding after all.'

'I could hardly miss it!' Alex said shortly, feeling shameful pleasure when she saw Maria's face fall at the abrupt retort.

Ah well, Maria thought in resignation. Maybe Urquhart is right, a couple of years in Paris will make a difference, though I think it was a little hard to send her away so quickly. Oh well, she shrugged, Alexandra is his daughter and he knows her best, I just hope she doesn't blame me for it all.

Alexandra stood for a moment looking forlorn. Maria felt a surge of pity. She could see the battle that seemed to be always storming within Alexandra between her conflicting needs and desires. Suppressing her own uncertainties, she smiled warmly and said in a conspiratorial voice, 'I have a surprise for you, Alexandra.'

'A surprise?' Alexandra was taken aback.

'Yes, a surprise, come to my rooms.' Maria took her arm and led the way into the guest-wing where she and her aunt would be staying for the sake of propriety, until after the ceremony.

'What is it?' Intrigued despite herself, Alexandra followed willingly up the stairs.

'Would you like to see my wedding costume?' Maria asked gently.

'Er ... yes ... thank you.' Short of outright rudeness, she hadn't much choice but to agree. Anyway, she adored clothes and was rather curious.

'There it is.' Maria threw open the door of the shadowy room and pulled back the curtains letting a flood of autumn light into the darkness.

'Oh it's lovely!' The admiring words were wrung spontaneously from the girl who loved fashion by instinct despite her limited experience.

Maria being a widow had chosen a sober mid-blue for her wedding, but the costume, displayed to full advantage on the tailor's dummy, was made of a beautiful flowing velvet and was stylish to the last detail. The perfect 'A'-line of the dress was adorned with row after row of tiny tucks, to follow the shape of Maria's neat figure. The design was completed by a waist-length fitted jacket with 'leg of mutton' sleeves, trimmed with satin cord and decorated with glowing pearl buttons. Sitting beside it were a pair of perfect shoes in dark-blue kid and lying on a cushion were high-buttoned gloves in the same colour. A tiny hat of matching velvet, trimmed with a froth of tulle and exquisite miniature flowers with pearls set into the centre, was balanced gracefully on a stand nearby.

'I'm glad you like it.' Maria blushed with real happiness.

'Of course, who wouldn't? Miss Cumming said you'd chosen

94

my dress too.' The resentment was back in Alexandra's voice.

'Yes.' Maria nodded, face inscrutable. 'I thought you should have something suitable and, since you've been so poorly, we thought it best to go ahead without the bother of coming up to Glasgow for tiresome fittings.'

'I see.' Tight-lipped, Alexandra barely hid her anger. Dress fittings were anything but tiresome to any young woman and fine Maria must know it. I expect you want me to look like a little girl, so you can look the proper motherly part! she thought hatefully. With an effort she bit back the angry words, knowing if she said anything now Maria might pass it on to her father.

'Here it is.' Maria pulled back the curtain round an alcove wardrobe where a solitary dress hung on a padded hanger.

'Oh!' She stood dumbfounded. There, in all its glory, was exactly the same dress style she had so wanted to wear for the ball, but this was made up in a material more suitable for day-wear and with a higher neckline. It was done in a lovely shade of forget-me-not blue which contrasted wonderfully with her future step mother's own choice. An exquisite frilly blue pelerine hung over the shoulders to the waist. The dress was a dream come true.

'Do you like it, Alexandra? We borrowed the dress from Craigdrummond while you were bed-ridden after the fall and used it as a pattern for this one. I hope you don't mind ... it should fit you.' Maria flushed anxiously. 'I was afraid to say before now, in case our "make-over" was unsuccessful and you would have been disappointed, but I think it is wonderful, don't you?' Hopefully she offered the olive branch again.

'Yes, it is beautiful, thank you, I like it very much,' Alexandra replied shamefacedly and for the first time since she had met Maria, there was no underlying meaning to the words.

'Well, it's not much but I suppose it's a start,' Maria told herself with a little thrill of pleasure. The memory was to sustain her through many of the traumas that lay ahead.

Obeying the Laird's request for a low-key event, the estate workers had gathered in a respectful group outside the kirk just to give three cheers for the couple, watch the gentry come out and then disperse.

'Michty me, Miss Alexandra looks right bonnie.' Leezie nudged Annie.

'Aye, so she does,' Annie nodded. Suppressing a giggle, she thought, And she's a dammed sight bonnier than the last time I saw her covered in muck from the Moss. But, sworn to secrecy, she kept those thoughts to herself.

'Och, we might as well go now they've left for Craigdrummond House in the carriages.' Leezie peered after them. 'Ye cannae see a thing.'

Alexandra was too taken up with excitement to notice Annie among the others when they came out of the kirk, but she gave a vague disinterested wave towards the estate workers as was expected of her. Despite herself, she really enjoyed the wedding, dressed in her lovely new gown. It was the first really grown-up garment she possessed and she adored it. Above all, the attitude of the male guests pleased her, saying more than any words that she was now a woman and an attractive one at that. Even Lord Ballantyne, who was nearly as old as her father, danced attendance, Alexandra thought happily.

From the moment he looked at her properly inside the kirk during the ceremony and his eyes widened with shock, the older man had stayed by her side, catering with obvious pleasure to her every whim and fancy. He even promised to call in when he was next in Paris and take her out for chocolate in the Bois de Boulogne.

Alexandra thanked him prettily. She understood at once he saw her with different eyes, and was not acting from avuncular interest. It was her first taste of the womanly power to come and it was heady.

Ballantyne's presence and attention made Alex far more gracious to Maria than she might have otherwise been, much to her relief. But now the big event was over. Lord Ballantyne had gone to his London home and the happy couple were on their way to Europe. Alexandra felt flat, sad and anything but grown-up.

'Come on, Alexandra, let's go to Ayr for a little outing.' Miss Cumming saw the old nervy depression settle on her charge and wondered how on earth they would pass the time till her parents got back. Och, I'll be glad when I go to Lamont's and take care of younger bairns again, the governess thought. This was getting too much for her.

Even after a day's shopping, Alexandra's spirits were low. The two of them sat silently in the carriage back to Craigdrummond and when they got there, the big house was empty and forlorn.

'It's strange, Cumming,' she said. 'Before now, I've been here often alone, but this time is different. I guess it's because I'll soon be leaving. I won't be Alexandra Cameron of Craigdrummond again for a long time.' Two years seemed like a life-sentence.

'Did you hear the latest from Craigdrummond?' Mistress Rannoch asked Bess Crawford over tea in Rannoch's front parlour.

'Well ...' It irritated Bess that Elsie always seemed to have the best stories first these days.

Mistress Rannoch rushed on, rubbing her plump hands together in feigned outrage, 'It's said that Miss Alexandra struck one of the grooms with her riding whip! It's been hushed up, of course, but she wouldn't have done it if the Laird was here.'

'Och, Elsie, I can hardly believe it!' Bess looked shocked.

'Aye, well, I had my own doubts,' Mistress Rannoch helped herself to a slice of Dundee cake, 'but it's supposed to be right enough. The lass I told you about that works there, she heard from one of the grooms who works with the lad!'

'Och, maybe it's just as well that lass is going to that foreign finishing school,' Bess said grimly. 'Somebody has to teach her manners. She wouldn't do that in my farmhouse, gentry or not.'

'Indeed,' Elsie Rannoch nodded agreement. 'My feelings entirely, Bess. God help poor Lady Cameron when she gets back next week.'

'And God help Miss Alexandra if her father hears.' Bess Crawford pursed her lips.

In fact the incident had gained much in the telling and had been little more than an accident. But since Alexandra Cameron was more difficult by the day it was hardly surprising that folk were talking. The time passed slowly and she moped round Craigdrummond alternating between snapping at the servants and going unnervingly quiet. One minute excited that she would soon be leaving the sheltered life she had so despised and the next apprehensive and afraid. Now and then she rode out with one of the grooms in close attendance. She was forbidden to go alone for fear of repeating the escapade which had nearly been the death of her.

On a fine Sunday afternoon, when the moors were ablaze with purple and the berried rowan trees shone burnished bronze, she became restless and had Blanche saddled. At a sharp canter, she and the groom headed towards the sea. With the wind in her golden hair and the sun on her back, she felt a rare sense of contentment.

'Stop and wait over the other side of the hill!' Alexandra suddenly drew up and called to the groom. 'I want to dismount and spend a few minutes here alone.'

'I've no to leave ye, Mistress,' the groom insisted uneasily, looking around, but seeing no danger lurking in the fine autumn day. 'I'm sorry, but I'd better stay.' He shifted worriedly in the saddle.

'I'll decide for myself who stays with me, man.' Her face darkened. 'Wait over the brow of the hill. You can hear me call if there are any problems.' She rapped out, 'I'm not likely to come to harm in broad daylight, now am I?'

The groom, the one she had accidentally struck, looked uncertainly at her determined face and imperious manner. Miss Alexandra was formidable when she was in this kind of mood. And, aye it had been an accident, he thought. Well more or less. Years at Craigdrummond had also taught him that Miss Alexandra was unforgiving if crossed. 'Och well, just shout if ye need me, Miss, and I'll be there,' he sighed and trotted on.

Alexandra dismounted and led Blanche back to where she had seen Annie Ramsay sitting reading in a sheltered sunny hollow underneath a russet berried rowan tree. 'I thought it was you,' she called as she approached.

'I come up here after kirk when the weather is good. Sunday is my half-day off, though I do the evening milking as a rule,' Annie replied casually from where she sat without getting to her feet. She had seen the pair pass and heard the groom dismissed. It didn't surprise her that Alexandra had stopped.

'What are you reading?' Alexandra asked, peering curiously down at the little brown book Annie so carefully marked with a slip of polished leather and laid on the edge of her homespun Sunday dress so it wouldn't get dirty.

'The poems of Rabbie Burns ... our Ayrshire poet.' She smiled. 'I love to read them and think about how he felt. He came to Carrick many times, though he was born in Kyle. Maybe he roamed these very moors and cliffs, dreaming of Highland Mary or making up some lines of a poem... "Here is the glen and here the bower, All underneath the birchen shade..."' she quoted with a faraway look in her grey eyes.

'Oh!' Alexandra was completely taken aback. This diminutive lass seemed full of surprises.

'Isn't a milkmaid entitled to quote Burns?' She laughed at her astonished face. 'Why not, Miss Alexandra?' she added pertly. 'Rabbie Burns was a simple ploughman after all. And he was just as much at home in the fine drawing-rooms as in the byre!'

'I suppose so!' What surprised Alexandra most was the lack of servility in Annie, which her position as daughter of Craigdrummond so often commanded and which seemed to bring out the worst in her.

'I'm leaving Craigdrummond, Annie,' she said quietly. 'I thought when I saw you, I might as well take the chance of saying thank you for saving me from the Moss and also to say goodbye. I'm going to finishing school in Paris.'

'Aye, I heard that. Och, what a shame,' Annie replied sincerely. 'If I had to leave this place, I'd weep. I wish ye luck, Miss Alexandra, so I do.'

'Well,' she looked at her with an expression which was unreadable. 'I'll be off.' With a swish of her riding skirt and without a backwards glance, she mounted Blanche and trotted over the hill to where the anxious groom waited.

'Poor lassie.' Annie got up and shook off the heads of heather that clung to the homespun of her Sunday dress. 'I wouldn't have your life for all the bawbees in the bank!' Everyone at Clachan's knew Miss Alexandra was difficult and demanding. Leezie had said that rumour in Craigdrummond village had it that she was mad jealous of the new Lady Cameron and would probably make her life a misery. 'I'll bet that's really why they'll be sending the lassie away,' Annie concluded as many others did. 'Aye, I'm glad I'm only Clachan's Annie and no Craigdrummond's Alexandra!' The daft thought made her giggle as she began walking back through the heather.

'Annie, wait! Annie.' Ian Ramsay called, panting up the steep path.

'I'm waitin!' She paused.

99

'I guessed you'd be up here with your nose buried in a book.' He looked pointedly at the worn copy of Burns poems in her hand.

'So ye thought it was time to come and winkle me out!' she grinned. 'Are lassies no supposed to think, Ian?'

'Och, Annie, with Aunty Bess around I couldn't take that attitude ... and you of all people should know it! You've a great head on your shoulders. Even if you don't know the details of crops and things, you always seem to understand. I'm always telling you about my plans for the farm, listening to your opinion, and heeding it too ... at least when you're around to give it ...' he broke off with a reproachful look.

'Ye're a galoot, Ian Clachan, I was only kiddin' ye!' Annie grinned at his discomfort. 'So what are ye here for, more advice about crossin' new oats with the old? Or shall we try to invent a coo that can milk itself?'

'Och, you get worse, so you do, Annie Ramsay!' he said with a sheepish grin. 'And right enough I have a great idea for the long-riggs ...' His face tightened. 'It's just that ye never seem to have time for me these days.'

'Blethers!' Annie replied, but couldn't meet his questioning gaze.

'I thought I might walk with you if you were thinking of going up the cliff, we used to always do that.' Ian stood anxiously looking at her.

Annie's resolve to heed Bess's warning melted before the pleading look in his expressive brown eyes. Och, just once can't do any harm, she told herself silently. It's not as if we're up to anything.

'Well?' Ian's face fell at her hesitation.

'I wasn't ... och, but why not? The sun is shinin', Ian, and you're the best company in Ayrshire so you are.' Her smile was balm to his wounded feelings.

'Come on then, what are you waiting for, Annie Ramsay?' He turned towards the sea.

'I hope Mistress Crawford doesn't hear about this,' she muttered under her breath as she followed him up the brow of the hill.

Companionably, they climbed the rest of the way, standing finally side by side on the top ridge as they had done so many times before. Below in its magnificence lay the broadest reach of the Firth of Clyde, sparkling and gleaming in the dying autumn sun. Under their feet, orange, purple and gold, the heather and broom-strewn cliffs spilled down in great sweeps to the golden sands of the cove lying far below. Sea birds circled wildly, crying out their displeasure at the disturbance.

Annie felt as she always did up here. 'Ye ken, I think sometimes that I've died and gone to heaven when I stand on this cliff top. There can be no finer place on earth, Ian,' she whispered.

'No finer place at all,' he solemnly agreed. Side by side in comfortable silence, all else forgotten, they watched the sun gradually sink in the West. Its rays touched the sleeping soldier that was the Isle of Arran and lit up his great helmet, tilted in the waves. To the south lay the pudding basin shape of Ailsa Craig, which, legend has it, was thrown from Ireland by an angry giant. The islands seemed but a hand's reach away in the clear air.

'I could stay here for ever.' Annie smiled and reluctantly turned away as the last orange glow gave way to encroaching dusk and the islands faded.

'That's what I want you to do, Annie. I'm going to marry you,' Ian said so quietly she thought she hadn't heard correctly.

'What did you say?' Her eyes opened wide with surprise.

'I'm going to marry you, Annie,' he repeated, his weather-beaten young face grave.

'Ye're not serious,' Annie gawped.

'I am that!' Ian insisted. 'Faither says he'll start me with a wee wage from this very month. That'll go up every year till I'm earning like a man. By the time I'm twenty-five I'll be a full partner with him in the farm and then we'll divide the profits till he retires and I take over altogether. But I'll be earning enough to keep a wife long before that, Annie.' He caught her arm and pulled her against him. She felt as delicate as a foal. Lightly he brushed her curls with his lips.

'Och, what's all this blethers, Ian Clachan?' Annie drew away, her own heart beating like a drum and her face flaming. She had never felt such emotion before in all her young life, but she forced herself to say, 'How about Mistress Betty Rannoch? The whole of Craigdrummond knows you're meant to wed her. You're promised, Ian!'

'I ken they want me to marry Betty. It's always been the way. And I wasn't against the idea till I met you,' Ian added with care-

101

less honesty that poor Betty would have wept over, 'for I would love to farm Rannoch's with our own. There is so much we could do to improve production if we took the acreage together. Och, and Betty's no a bad lass ... but now I'd rather have you, Annie.'

'Ian, you faither would have a fit if you threw yourself away on a wee Glasgow scruff,' Annie said forthrightly. 'Annie Ramsay from the Gallowgate is no match for a fairmer's son!' She struggled to keep the bitterness from her voice, knowing it would only encourage him. 'That's what Maisie and many like her would say if ye started courtin' me.'

'I don't care what folk say. I want you. And I know you want me too, Annie, I know it!' Ian's mouth was tight and he drew her to him again. Her face buried in his chest, she smelled warm and manly. 'Och, Annie,' he murmured, 'Annie, I know you feel the same as I do!'

With her heart pounding, Annie knew that if she stayed close one moment longer, they would both be lost. 'Ye ken nothin', Ian Clachan!' She slipped out of his embrace. '...Come on,' she turned back to the farm, 'let's get back before Mistress Crawford is out looking for the pair of us with a brush! Whatever ye say, you're promised to Betty Rannoch and that's that!'

'I mean it, Annie.' His long legs kept up easily with her. 'I'm not taking Betty Rannoch ... we don't need their farm, me and you! It's enough with Clachan's.'

'Blethers!'

'Blethers nothing!' His voice had the determination of youth in its first great love. 'You're sixteen, Annie, I'm eighteen past. That's a good age for a lass and lad to start courting properly. We can maybe wed in the summer after next when I'll be twenty.' Ian had worked it all out.

'Ian Clachan!' Annie stopped and looked into his anxious, earnest and so very beloved face, her heart thumped till she felt dizzy, but she kept her word to Bess. 'We're both far too young to be talking about things like that. Even if your faither would agree ... which he won't ... ye haven't asked me what I feel, now have ye?'

'I thought from your face back there, that you felt the same as me ... was I not right?' he asked anxiously.

'I admit that ye're a fine lad and I'm honoured, Ian,' she said carefully, looking down at her worn shoes, 'but I decided a while ago that I won't be getting wed till I'm twenty passed ... if ever. In fact I'm not a bit sure marriage is for me. I saw too many lassies wed young in the Gallowgate and have a bairn a year without the wherewithal to feed or care for them. That's not what I want.'

'Annie, you know that wouldn't happen to you. We make a good living on Clachan's Farm, a very good living. You'd want for nothing and neither would our bairns. A farmer's wife is a fine thing to be. You'd have a place in society here, so you would.'

'Aye and that's another thing,' she said crisply. 'I'm not having anybody say that I trapped Ian Clachan into marriage for his money ... which is what they would say and ye ken that fine! You'd be better keeping to Mistress Betty Rannoch, she's your own sort.'

'I told you I don't care what people say, Annie, I'm set on you and that's that!' His face was as stubborn as her own.

Annie looked at him, wondering how on earth she could get out of this situation with Ian's friendship intact but still keeping the promise she had made to Bess Crawford. Suddenly her irrepressible sense of humour broke through and saved them both. 'Och, away ye go, Ian Clachan, your face is as red as a big boiled beetroot, so it is!' Despite the tension that had built up, she giggled and watched his own steady humour restore itself.

'Just give me a chance, Annie,' he said more quietly this time.

'I'll tell ye what, my lad!' She smiled. 'If at twenty-five I'm still unwed and if Mistress Betty has decided to pass ye by, I'll give the question fair consideration and let ye know.' Though by then you and she will already have a quiverful, her common sense whispered slyly in her ear and almost unnerved her.

'Then I'll wait, Annie,' he replied seriously. 'And that's a promise!'

'Aye and pigs will fly!' She forced herself to stay cheery and her laugh rang through the clear air. 'Come on, old man ... I'll be back before ye!' Off she ran in a flurry of skirt and apron, chestnut curls escaping from her Sunday snood.

'No you won't!' Ian joined the mad flight through the heather. Pointing down at a trap parked outside the kitchen door, Ian solved the problem. 'I see Doctor Murchieson is visiting again, I suppose I better go straight in and pay my respects.'

'And I'll just check the kye and see if Dougie needs any help,' Annie saw the chance to escape.

'Do you know the Doctor is courting Aunty Bess right seriously these days?' Ian added with a twinkle in his eye. 'My Faither says there'll be a wedding before long if the good doctor gets his way.'

'What! Do you think she will?' Annie gasped. 'Is she no a wee bit old for that sort of thing, Ian?'

'Och aye, she's forty-five if she's a day,' he agreed. 'But the doctor is no spring chicken himself and he's had his heart set on her since before she married the first time. He went off to practise somewhere, India I think, and missed his chance there. He's asked for her hand every year since she was widowed.'

'Well, there you are,' Annie said with a dismissive wave of her hand. 'If she's said no this long, she's no likely to change her mind now.'

'Don't be too sure,' Ian said thoughtfully. 'Now he's moved to Ayrshire, he's pressing his case harder.'

'Och, in the name! What would we do without her?' Despite the reserve that lay between her and the housekeeper since their discussion over Ian, Annie's heart sank. Nobody could run Clachan's Farm like Bess Crawford. She could imagine a chaotic household with Maisie bossing everybody around. Annie arguing wi' her ... and Leezie in a dozy state burning porridge ... and wee Nellie trailing behind making a mess of everything ... mixing new eggs wi' old ... and nobody in charge organising the household as it should be. 'Well, Ian,' she said aloud, 'much as I owe a lot to Doctor Murchieson, I hope she doesn't give in!'

'Och, I was only kidding, Annie, I don't think there's much danger,' Ian spoke with the certainty of youth that older folk could not be as carried away by love as he had been himself on the hill just minutes before. 'Aunty Bess is strong minded and likes her independence. I think Doctor Murchieson is wasting his time. He'd be better to look elsewhere.'

'Aye, well just you remember what I said to you about doing the same,' Annie couldn't resist teasing. 'I can't see you being happy turning into an old bachelor waiting for me to win a fortune and change my mind, which I won't,' she added with a toss of her head.

'Hmmm,' Ian grunted ruefully and watched her step lightly across the heather and turn down towards the byre.

Chapter Ten

Annie stood in a cheering, gawping crowd with all the other farmhands and tenants in an official welcome, as Urquhart Cameron arrived back from honeymoon to present his wife to the Estate.

'Craigdrummond welcomes its new Lady! Everyone is there, my dear.' He squeezed his bride's hand as their carriage turned up the great drive.

Well almost everyone, thought Maria, Lady Cameron, noticing there was no sign of Alexandra among the household which, dressed in fresh crisp uniforms, lined the magnificent stairs. 'Oh, there she is!' Relief flooded through her as her step-daughter appeared and took her place at the front.

Above all Maria hoped that the girl had got over her pique and they could begin on a good footing. The wedding had been so promising, she prayed it heralded the start of a better relationship between them.

'Welcome home, Papa!' It seemed as if Maria's wishes were fulfilled. Alexandra greeted her father with an embrace and the new Lady of Craigdrummond with a light kiss on the cheek. 'And welcome, Stepmother.'

'Thank you, Alexandra.' If it irritated Maria to be called 'Stepmother', she didn't show it. The poor woman feared there would be many such tests before she and Alex were friends.

'Well that's that,' Leezie sighed romantically as the family disappeared inside and the great doors closed. 'The Laird and his Lady, back again.'

'Not that it makes any difference to us!' Maisie sniffed. 'Folk like that wouldn't notice if they walked on your head.'

'Aye, well maybe ye're right,' Dougie chaffed, 'but I'll no be arguing wi' the free beer and whisky the night in Craigdrummond Square. What do you say, Fairmer?'

'Just don't come back singing, the lot of you, then getting up in the morning with heads like bags of Craigdrummond stanes,' Geordie replied with a smile. 'And that goes for you as well, Ian.'

'Aye, we'll be canny.' Ian had begun to take his place fully on the farm, and he was grateful to his father for subtly underlining his manhood.

'That's only for the men!' Maisie wasn't to be placated. 'There's nothing for us.'

'Och, you're always whinin', Maisie,' Leezie objected.

'Ye ken weel there's a do in the kirk hall tonight for the rest of us, Maisie, wi' cakes and scones and sweeties for the bairns,' Annie chipped in.

'Come on, the lot of you!' Mistress Crawford rounded up her flock. 'Back to Clachan's Farm. There's a byre full of kye waiting to be milked and I doubt if supper will be ready this side of next week!'

'Right ye are, Missus,' they chorused. Annie linked her arm with Leezie's as they headed off chatting and giggling towards the farm.

'And have you chosen a maid to accompany you to Paris, Alexandra?' Maria asked over a quiet family supper that evening.

'Yes,' Alexandra answered, looking from one to the other.

'What a nice surprise,' Cameron said kindly. 'We both felt sure you hadn't bothered.'

'Isn't it?' Alexandra smiled.

'Which one of the girls have you chosen?' Maria tried to recall some of the sturdy Ayrshire lassies that helped in the house. 'Rosie, perhaps?'

'Oh, I didn't think any of the girls here at Craigdrummond House were really suitable,' Alexandra waved a slim hand dismissively, still smiling, 'so I thought of one from the estate instead.'

'Well, as long as she is a Craigdrummond lass, that's fine, Alexandra.' Her father was pleased she had made a mature decision alone at last. 'And who is the girl?'

107

'Annie Ramsay, you know, "Clachan's Annie" as she's called!' Alex leaned back in her chair and watched their shocked reaction.

'The milkmaid who dragged you from the Moss?' Maria's fine brows rose. 'But, Alexandra, you're not serious. She's not the right type at all.'

'Of course not, a milkmaid is entirely out of the question!' Cameron agreed. 'What is this nonsense, Alexandra? I told you to choose someone at least half-trained!'

'Oh, why should I not have Annie? You've never met her, either of you.' Alexandra insisted looking from one to the other. She got up from table and stood by the chaise-longue face flushed and eyes over-bright.

Maria watched her with mounting concern.

'There are plenty of girls in the House you can chose from,' Cameron tried to sound reasonable, but he felt his temper go on edge.

'All the girls here are either stupid or annoying.' Alexandra held her ground and her voice rose. 'And as for being the right type, what is that? Annie is intelligent ... she even reads Robert Burns on her half-day off. I expect she could soon learn to be a lady's maid ... after all she learned how to milk cows when she came from Glasgow.'

'That's not quite the same, my dear,' Maria tried to sound soothing, but thought with horror of a milkmaid's rough worka-day hands trying to smooth Alexandra's fine linen ... if she knew how to sew or iron at all. 'Are you sure you have thought this through ...?'

'Yes, of course,' Alexandra nodded, lying. She hadn't thought of Annie at all till the name popped into her head when Cameron asked.

'Quite out of the question!' the Laird snapped.

'But we owe her something special, don't we?' Why Alexandra had suddenly decided on this course of action she wasn't sure, but now she had started she was determined to get her way.

'Alexandra, you're being ridiculous. It would set tongues wagging, even if it were feasible which it isn't,' Cameron replied in exasperation.

'Not at all, Papa,' Alexandra argued. 'She could be trained. By the time we came back from Paris, who would even think of the circumstances in which she was hired?'

'Cameron,' Maria broke in gently. 'Didn't you say things like this are matters for the lady of the house?'

He turned to his new wife with a look of relief. 'Of course! Can you deal with it, my dear.'

'Yes, I think so,' she replied gently. Then turning to Alex she asked, 'Are you really serious, Alexandra?' Maria felt instinctively that there might be more behind this than met the eye.

'I am.' She realised to her own shock that she was very serious indeed. Annie's capable cheeky cheerfulness and lack of servility had attracted and challenged her deep down. That was why her name came into my head all at once, she thought. With Annie, life wouldn't be boring.

Alexandra changed her tactics, and looked sadly from one to the other. 'Papa, Stepmother.' Her eyes fell and she almost wished she hadn't begun with such a provocative title for Maria. 'If I have to go away among strangers, send Annie with me, please.'

'No!' Her father paced the room. 'How could we do such a stupid thing. It would make a laughing stock of us all. Alexandra, you're impossible!'

'Urquhart, can we talk alone for a moment?' Maria asked urgently.

'Of course. Leave us, Alexandra,' Urquhart said brusquely.

'Yes, Father.' Alexandra didn't argue. She left, cheeks flushed, but with the feeling that her case was not yet lost.

As the door closed, Maria reached out and took his hand drawing him towards her. 'A moment ago you agreed this is a question for the lady of the house.'

'True,' he smiled down at her indulgently.

'Well, my dear, my intuition tells me that Alexandra means this. If "Clachan's Annie" or whatever the girl is called, is what she wants, then I think we could at least interview her. After all, two years is a long time away with no one of your own. In the unlikely event of the girl turning out to be suitable, then surely she could be trained discreetly in Glasgow ... then if she is altogether hopeless for the job, I can ask the training school to find someone else, though not from Craigdrummond. At least Alexandra cannot say we didn't try to understand.'

The Laird sighed in defeat and looked lovingly at his new wife. 'How can I refuse you anything, Maria, even something as preposterous as this? All right, we'll send to Clachan's Farm and see the girl. But if you decide she can go with Alexandra, then the transition must be handled with complete discretion. We don't want more gossip at all costs!'

'Oh you are generous, my dearest,' Maria kissed his hand and placed it against her cheek. In her heart, like the Laird, she believed Alexandra had made one demand too many and would have to live with uncomfortable consequences. 'And God help the poor girl, if she succeeds!' Maria Cameron thought with a surge of pity.

Across the moor at Clachan's Farm, the cows lowed and snorted as they were driven in for milking with Dougie whistling along as Annie sang, her sweet voice ringing across the clear evening air. In the midst of all the discussion among the gentry at Craigdrummond on Alexandra Cameron's future, it had not occurred to any of them what effect their decision might have on the lives and feelings of the folk on the farm, and particularly on the hopes and dreams of Annie Ramsay.

'Oh, Archie, thank goodness you've come today of all days!' Mistress Crawford gasped as her old friend dismounted from his trap.

'Well, that's nice of you, Bess,' Archie Murchieson smiled and handed over the reins to the groom.

'We need your help, Archie.' Bess Crawford was as discomfited as Doctor Murchieson had ever seen her. 'Annie was called to the Big House and sent home to make a decision!' she blurted out.

'Craigdrummond ...? Decision on what?'

'To become a lady's maid of all things!'

'A lady's maid? Annie Ramsay? What nonsense!'

'You heard me! It's all the fault of that Miss Alexandra!' she explained the situation as she led him into the big kitchen that was the heart of the house, especially when trouble arose.

'Archie, has Bess told you about Annie?' Geordie Clachan asked as he rose to greet the doctor, his face clouded and grave.

'She has that,' Archie replied with a sigh.

'You know the lass, what should she do?' Geordie frowned. 'She's all worried. She came back and asked for our help and

110

we've promised to talk it over and give her the best advice we can. They expect word this evening. I'm supposed to send a lad before six with a letter. Have you ever heard of such a thing, Archie, are they out of their minds up there?'

'It certainly sounds like it! But be careful about how you advise the lass. It's her future.'

'Well, I ken that and so does Bess, but it seems so daft ... ' the farmer hesitated.

'Geordie, strange as it seems to us all that they should make this offer at all,' the doctor said firmly, 'when it comes to it, it's up to Annie. Whatever she says, she has to make up her own mind.'

'You would think that the Laird of Craigdrummond would have more sense!' Geordie Clachan shook his head. 'Are they trying to make a fool of the poor wee lass?'

'I was telling Archie,' Bess Crawford broke in angrily. 'It's Miss Alexandra, she thinks that she only has to point at something and it's hers! But why on earth pick on Annie? She's not a toy to be used and discarded ... for that's what will happen when the novelty wears off! Lady's maid for heaven's sake!' Bess shook her head.

'Well, Archie's right, there's nought we can do about it except listen to what Annie feels herself now she's had an hour or two to think. But there is one thing we can do,' he said stoutly, 'if Annie refuses, we'll back her decision they can't make her go.'

'Can they put pressure on in other ways?' Doctor Murchieson asked.

Bess nodded thoughtfully. 'Well, all our girls come from Craigdrummond village, except for Maisie and Annie. The big House has first call on them.'

'Blethers! The lease on this farm is quite clear,' the farmer said firmly. 'The Laird can do nothing about the folk we take on here. Anyway we can fee other lassies and other labourers too at the Ayrshire Fair if needs be. I'll have nobody, neither Laird of Craigdrummond, nor anybody else, press a lass from Clachan's Farm into doing what she doesn't want to do!'

'Well said, Geordie!' Archie, lowered his rotund form into a comfortable chair by the fire. 'But first we have to ask Annie what she thinks ... and in fairness point out the advantages if she doesn't fully appreciate them. Her wage as a lady's maid would be at least double what she gets here and the prospects are even better in the future.'

'Och, she won't leave here whatever they offer ... whether or not she thinks she could do the job,' Mistress Crawford spoke spontaneously. 'Annie loves the farm and she has made good friends ...' she trailed off suddenly and turned away, busying herself making a warm toddy for the doctor.

Suddenly she began to put the problem in a different perspective from the others. Aye there will be one sad face in particular if she does decide to leave the farm, she thought ... but that might be for the best ...

'Call her in, Bess,' Geordie sighed. 'We better get this over with.

'I'm not going to Paris or anywhere else! And ye can tell them that's final!' Annie stood with folded arms in the middle of the kitchen. 'I like it here and I'm staying ... if ye will still have me.' She looked from one to the other uncertainly.

'Of course we will, lass!' Geordie spoke stoutly, 'You're a good worker and a decent girl. We think highly of you, Annie. Don't we, Bess?'

'Er ... of course we do,' Bess replied, then turned away again abruptly.

Doctor Murchieson saw the girl's confusion and felt in fairness he should explain the potential of the offer she was rejecting so vehemently. 'Think well on it, lass, before you say no. This is by any measure the chance of a life-time. Don't turn it down without full consideration ... though it would be a challenge and there is the possibility you might fail,' he cautioned.

'I ken that, but failing is not what worries me. Och, I don't need to think about it, Doctor. My heart is in Clachan's Farm,' Annie insisted, grey eyes serious.

'Are you sure now, Annie?' Geordie Clachan broke in. 'If you say no, they won't ask again. Wee milkmaids are not what they usually have to look after the daughters of gentry.'

'I'm sure, Fairmer.' The stubborn chin went up.

'Well, lass, I'll write a note and send your word back to Craigdrummond as they asked.' Geordie Clachan got up. 'And I can't say I'm sorry, I think you've made a wise choice.'

Mistress Crawford bent over the stove again, a frown on her face. She hoped Annie wasn't meaning Ian when she said her

112

heart's in the farm, though she feared so! Och, in the shock of it all, Bess thought, I forgot about her and Ian. She seems to be keeping away, but you never know! This would be a fine chance to solve the matter for once and for all. Och, I wish I had encouraged her to look more kindly on the offer before Geordie came in. Of the people in the farm kitchen, Bess was the only one now convinced that Annie should go.

'Annie!' Lurking in the hall, Ian grasped her arm as soon as she left the kitchen. He made no secret of his eavesdropping. 'I couldn't hear everything. Are you staying or not? Tell me right now, Annie, are you?' Anxiety robbed him of diplomacy. 'I ken what it's all about. Faither told me before you all went in.'

'I'm staying at Clachan's Farm. But don't let that give ye any more daft ideas, Ian!' She smiled and walked off towards the milking shed where Maisie was already installed and working.

Ian let out a great sigh. His heart lifted, he went whistling on his way.

'Oh aye,' Maisie snapped as Annie came in. 'Decided to turn up have ye? I wonder what Mistress Crawford will say when I tell her ye left me to do the most of the work myself, ye lazy wee slut!'

'I was talking to the Missus and the Fairmer,' Annie replied quietly. 'I don't think either of them will be over impressed with yer tale this time, Maisie.'

'Oh!' The older girl was non-plussed at Annie's strange attitude and let be.

Leezie rushed into the kitchen as supper was being prepared next night.

'Mistress Crawford! Mistress Crawford! Miss Alexandra is at the door with a groom asking for ye!'

'In the name of heavens!' Mistress Crawford dried her hands and rushed out after the flustered maid.

Alexandra Cameron, in fine riding gear with a slender whip in her hand, stood composedly looking round the farm yard with an air of detached casual interest.

'Come in, Miss Alexandra!' With a show of calm she didn't feel, she escorted the self-possessed young lady into the back room and bade her sit in the best chair by the fireplace. Fortunately the evening was mild and the place wasn't chilly, but

Mistress Crawford hissed at Leezie to light the fire set ready in the grate.

'Oh don't bother doing that for me, Mistress Crawford,' Alexandra said with a wave of a gloved hand, 'I've just come for a few minutes to speak to Annie Ramsay, is she here?'

'Yes, Miss Alexandra, I'll get her,' the housekeeper replied with a strange excited feeling settling into the pit of her stomach. Maybe the fate of Annie wasn't settled after all. 'The lassies are just about finished with the kye ... er ... cattle.' Mistress Crawford sounded as flustered as she felt.

'I'm in no hurry.' Young Alexandra Cameron's composure was unnerving as she sat there on the best chair near the big family bible.

Mistress Crawford closed the door and scurried in an undignified flap of skirts and apron across the yard and into the byre. 'Annie! Get out of your working boots and go into the back room!' she hissed to the surprised milkmaid. 'You have a visitor, lass.'

'A visitor, who is it, Missus ... oh jings! Nothin's happened to Mammy or the twins, has it?' Annie stood up, almost knocking over the pail in her anxiety.

'No, lass, it's Miss Alexandra. Shhhhh ...,' Mistress Crawford whispered, putting one finger over her lips, and shooting a warning glance to the far end of the byre where Maisie was milking, head bent, unaware of what was going on.

'Oh, I see!' Annie got up and followed. In the back hall she carefully removed her big boots and coat. Quickly peeking in the hall mirror, she tucked stray curls back under the mob-cap. Taking a deep breath, she smoothed her darned woollen skirt and went in.

Alexandra came straight to the point. 'Annie, why won't you come to Paris with me?'

'Because I'm not a lady's maid. I'm a milkmaid. That's what I ken and what I like doin'.' Annie was equally uncompromising. 'I love Clachan's Farm, Miss Alexandra. It's hard work here, but for the first time in my life I'm happy. Why should I want to change?'

'You'd have a better wage,' she coaxed, 'a lot higher in fact, none of the other maids at Craigdrummond earn anything like it. I could even persuade Papa to give you some more money if you think it's not enough. Maybe a little lump sum each year.'

'I'm sorry, Miss Alexandra.' Annie shook her head. 'It's tempting what ye offer, I'll admit that, but no thank you, money's no everything ... Why on earth do ye want me anyway?' She allowed her curiosity full rein in the odd circumstances. 'I've been trying to work it out and it makes no sense at all. There are plenty of girls at Craigdrummond, in Ayr too, who would jump at the chance of going with you and who would make better maids than me.' Annie's cheeky grin lit up her face. 'I've a right sharp tongue, so I have ... ask anybody ... and I've heard yours would clip clouts as well,' she added forthrightly. 'We'd be bound to clash ... Och, and jist listen to me! I don't speak like a lady's maid.'

'Accent is nothing.' Alexandra waived that objection with a flick of her hand. 'I could fix that for you in a week myself! And people who bow and scrape just make me mad ... Annie, I don't want anybody else, I want you.' The blue eyes fixed her compellingly.

'Ye still haven't answered me,' Annie insisted. 'Why?'

The Cameron heiress looked at the diminutive young woman standing proudly before her. 'You are the first person who has looked me in the eye and not treated me differently because of who I am. You took my life in those hands of yours and pulled me out of the Moss. Whatever Papa likes to believe, I know I would be dead now if you hadn't come past that evening. Our lives are linked!' she added dramatically.

Annie smothered a grin and replied firmly, 'I would have pulled out a calf in the same circumstances and taken the same risks. Don't let that night cloud your judgement, Miss Alexandra, get somebody more suited to the job.'

'Well they say when you save a life, you owe that person, not the other way round,' she said with a stubborn look on her face.

'What do ye mean by that?' Annie asked sharply.

'I would not be here if you had not dragged me from the Moss. So you are responsible for my life and you must stand by me now if I need you,' Alexandra spoke with conviction.

Annie flushed. 'Och, that's just blethers.'

'As you wish, but I believe it.' She stood and looked at her for a long, silent minute then seeing Annie returned her gaze without flinching, she changed her tactics. 'I'm going to be alone, Annie, and, though I won't admit it to Papa, I'm a little afraid.' She

115

went on in a low, persuasive voice, 'I want someone I can trust to share my new life with me. Nothing is the same any more since Papa married. Nobody cares about me any more. They just want rid of me, Annie.'

'Do ye not think you're making more of this than there is to make?' Annie asked shrewdly.

Alexandra's blue eyes suddenly filled with unshed tears. 'I don't know anything any more.' She took a step forward and grasped the other girl's hands. 'Come with me, Annie. I know I can trust you. I need a confidante more than I need a maid. Please, Annie, come with me.'

Alexandra Cameron was clever. If she had ordered Annie to go, threatened her, or those she loved, Annie would never have agreed, whatever she offered in reward. But this part pathetic plea, part subtle flattery, was probably the only way she could have got Annie to consider the prospect at all and she knew it.

'Och, ye don't know what you're askin'!' Annie thought of Clachan's Farm, of the sea, the beasts she tended, the wild, lovely moor and above all Ian and the folk she had come to care for ... Ian ... Ian. Firmly she shook her head. 'I'm sorry, I understand better now why ye asked, but I can't, Miss Alexandra.'

'Will you at least promise to think about it for a few days?' Alexandra asked, in the same, soft voice.

'Yes,' Annie reluctantly agreed. 'I'll think about it again, but I have to say I'm sure the answer will still be no.'

'Well that you'll reconsider, is something at least.' Tears disappeared like magic. Alexandra smiled and held out her gloved hand. Annie took it in her own rough one. 'So, thank you for that.' With a whirl of skirts, she was gone and Annie stood gazing into space till Mistress Crawford came quietly in behind her.

'I heard,' the housekeeper admitted without embarrassment. 'She really wants you, Annie,' she added softly.

'Aye she does that,' the girl nodded. 'Poor lassie, she seems awful lonely for all her wealth, so she does ... Mistress Crawford,' Annie turned towards her with an uncertain, anxious expression on her face. 'I don't want to leave Clachan's Farm, Missus ... you think I'm right to refuse her, don't you?' Annie desperately wanted reassurance.

Bess Crawford took a deep breath before she answered, thoughts spinning. Ian had been cock o' hoop all day since Annie had decided to stay and his obvious joy fuelled her worries. She knew that young men could be foolish in their fancy... Her mind spun with every possible horror. It wouldn't be the first time a farmer's son had got a farm lass with bairn and the girl and the bairn quietly looked after well away from the scene. But Bess had a feeling there would be no stopping him marrying Annie if that should be the case. From fourteen any girl was old enough in Scots law. And Geordie Clachan was an honourable man, he might insist that Ian accepted his full responsibilities.

Bess imagined trying to explain her own failure to run a proper household to neighbours and friends alike, as well as facing Mistress Rannoch's rightful wrath ... they had planned so much together for Ian and Betty ... and what about the doctor?

'What do you think, Missus?' Annie repeated, puzzled at her uncharacteristic hesitation.

'Well, like the farmer said, you'll never get another chance like it in your whole life,' she said slowly. 'For a lass from the Gallowgate that started with nothing, the chance to train as a lady's maid and travel in Europe is nothing short of a miracle. They're offering very generous terms, Annie, very generous indeed, especially considering you're completely untrained.'

'I ken that,' Annie hung her head. 'But I don't want to leave Clachan's Farm ... not for anything, Missus. I've promised to keep away from Ian!' the last was whispered painfully.

'But will he keep away from you?'

'I dinnae ken!' Annie kept her eyes on her feet.

Mistress Crawford saw her waver and played her strongest card, 'Forget Ian for the moment, Annie,' she said abruptly. 'The right choice on your part could bring benefits to others too, Annie.'

'What do you mean?' Annie looked bewildered.

'Your family, for instance. As Miss Alexandra's maid, the pay would be better by far than anything you'll ever get here, from what I understand at any rate and from what you've said.'

'My family?'

Bess knew Annie's loving heart well and pressed home. 'Aye, your family. Now your mother's a widow, she's having it hard isn't she, Annie, that's what you said, wasn't it? Just think of the

117

difference the money might make ...'

'I hadn't thought of that,' Annie paled.

'You told me your mother needs every penny she can get, doesn't she?'

'Aye.' Her heart sank.

'I tell you what, go and speak to your mother, Annie, it might make things clearer.' She put her hand on the girl's shoulder. 'I understand what a difficult situation you're in. None of us could ever have imagined that Miss Alexandra would have set her heart so strong on you. You heard Doctor Murchieson, it is a fine chance, lass, and one you'll never have again.'

Annie hung her head for a moment, then said with a catch in her voice, 'Well, I'll need a day off to go to Glasgow. Do ye think ye can manage? This Saturday would be easiest I suppose since ye can get extra help with the kye.'

'Don't worry about that ... go tomorrow since time is pressing. And I'll even give you your fare.' Mrs Crawford found it hard to hide her satisfaction that Annie was seriously considering the Craigdrummond offer at last.

'Och, ye're that good to me, so ye are, Mistress Crawford,' Annie said with a grateful flush. 'Strict but fair, they telt me when I came. That's why I trust yer advice.'

'I do my best.' Bess couldn't look at her.

'Aye, ye do that,' Annie agreed with a fervence that added to the older woman's discomfort.

'I'm glad you think so, Annie.' Bess Crawford suppressed a tingle of guilt. She knew she was doing the right thing encouraging the girl to leave Clachan's Farm ... of course she was.

Chapter Eleven

Annie noticed the dirt and poverty of Glasgow's back streets properly for the first time in her life. 'I've been spoiled in Craigdrummond. We have to work right hard, but the air is fresh and the streets of the village are clean.' She tried to avoid the gutters overflowing with mud and rubbish, but her sturdy Sunday boots which she had polished till they shone, were bespattered with muck more objectionable than that of Clachan's farmyard.

'Och, it's no fair that folk have to live like this, neither it is,' she muttered as she hurried along the Gallowgate, her feet following well-remembered streets. The tenements crowded in on her with their broken windows, stinking narrow closes and foul backyards. She longed to be back on Craigdrummond cliffs.

When she reached the close mouth, her heart beat faster with apprehension. She had sent a short note to say she was coming and she hoped they had received it ... but what if no one was in?

The stairs up to the top floor seemed shorter and she realised with pleasure it was because she didn't puff and pant any more. 'As the guid Doctor would say ... "Your lungs are in very good condition, Annie!"' She grinned, took a deep breath and rattled on the door. Her mother opened at once.

'Annie, hen! Och, come in! By here you've grown into a fine lass in Ayrshire, so ye have! I'd hardly have kent ye if I'd passed ye in the street.'

'How are ye, Mammy?' Annie fought to keep the shock from her face. Her mother seemed to have aged ten years since her husband's death.

'Och, I'm fine. Come in, come in.' She held open the door. 'Eddie's away the day, but Sandy's waiting to see ye, he changed his half day wi' a pal at the bakery.'

'I thought Eddie was in the merchant navy,' Annie's brow wrinkled in surprise. 'And there ye are, Sandy,' she smiled in pleasure to see her favourite elder brother.

'Annie, ye're in the pink, so ye are!' He gave her a hug, then abruptly turned and walked over to the window, looking out intently as if the drab scene below was suddenly fascinating.

Annie's puzzlement deepened at his obvious tension. 'Is something the matter? Sandy, Mammy, whit is it?' she asked slowly, looking from one to the other. 'Where are the twins? Has something happened to the lassies?' she demanded anxiously.

'Naw, the lassies are fine,' Sandy replied. 'They've jist gone over to auld Maggie's, ye'll see them in a minute.'

'Then what in the name is the matter? The pair of ye look as if ye're about to be hung.'

'Ye're no far wrong there,' Sandy sighed. 'Ye better sit down and I'll tell ye.' He came back to the table and drew out a rickety chair for her. 'Things are no goin' well, hen.'

'I thought ye were managing fine ... though maybe I was kidding myself.' Annie noticed with sadness how the once familiar apartment seemed even poorer now her father's wage had stopped coming in. The clock that had been her mother's pride and joy was missing. Annie guessed at once it had been pawned.

After the comfort and warmth of Clachan's the whole place stank of rank, pitiful poverty. The room and kitchen that had been home to her for so long, was tiny and cramped with the damp, sour tenement smell she had gladly forgotten.

'We were doin' no bad ... and your money is a great help,' Sandy explained, 'but then Eddie was injured in the navy. He's back home like Mammy telt ye.'

'Well, doesn't he get a wee pension or something if he got hurt?' Annie demanded.

'Och, Eddie's that daft!' Her mother pushed a stray lock of greying hair from her eyes. 'The eejit wasn't workin' when he got hurt, hen. He went out and got drunk and fell down some stairs fighting the navy police. He was kicked out, wi' no money comin' to him.'

'And the trouble is,' Sandy went on sadly, 'I haven't come out of my time so the baker won't pay me more, even though I do a man's shift.'

'And if that isnay enough,' Mrs Ramsay said in despair, 'We owe that young Doctor Chisholm, ye ken, he took over frae Doctor Murchieson?'

'Aye, the doctor telt me,' Annie replied. 'Were ye sick, Mammy?'

'Naw, he came in tae see Eddie when he was bad ... och, but he's a kind lad and says he can eat without takin' oor bawbees ...'

'I suppose he'll have to!' Annie thought of the amounts they and their neighbours must have owed generous-hearted Doctor Murchieson over the years. 'It's no wonder they have a devil of a job finding doctors to work the tenements,' she remarked, realising for the first time what an unintentional burden they and their like must be.

Deep in her misery, her mother ignored the comment and went on, plucking nervously at her worn skirt. '...But then it got worse, hen. Once he was up again, Eddie went and pledged ten shillings in tick in my name and didn't say a damned word till the frighteners came lookin' for it. I gave them every penny I had in the place tae get rid o' them, but it's no enough to pay back what he lent. We're still up to oor eyes in debt, Annie, and no a thing to show for it!' She began to cry in ragged sobs.

'It's as bad as Mammy says,' Sandy said gloomily. 'At least if we had the money to pay off all the tick, we wouldn't be worryin' all the time about the bailiffs ... or the frighteners comin' back and kickin' me and Eddie stupid just for the hell of it.'

'But ye would still be livin' from hand to mouth.'

'Aye, hen, so we would. Och, I feel that helpless so I do!' Sandy struck his hand with a closed fist. 'If only ...' he trailed off, shaking his head.

'If only what?' Annie asked with a horrible cold feeling clutching at her stomach and a growing ache in her heart.

'If only I had enough to pay off the money and get out of this hopeless mess for ever.'

'How can anybody do that here?' Annie asked, thinking of the mean streets and foul tenements.

'I'd open a wee shop.' Sandy's eyes lost their desperate look for a moment. 'Mammy could make sweeties and tablet, and I could make cakes and stuff. We'd work all the hours God sends, so we would and gladly. Then we could keep ourselves, the twins and Eddie. He's right useless so he is, but he's family and we have to look after him ... But it wid take a miracle, so it wid!'

'Och, Annie,' Mistress Ramsay came over and clung to her. 'I'm sorry this is no a welcome home for ye, but we're worried sick. Without your wee bittie money and Sandy's, we'd be in the poor-hoose already, so we would. As it is I dinna think we'll manage. I've said I'll pay off Eddie's tick at tuppence a week and they've agreed ... but it'll take years to clear wi' the terrible interest they're takin'. Me that's never been in debt in my life ... not even when yer daddy drank his pay ... we went without instead, so we did!' She burst out crying again, gripping Annie's arm convulsively.

With a great effort, Sandy shook himself out of his own despair. 'Mammy, leave off Annie now.' Gently he detached his mother's hands. 'The poor lassie didn't expect this sort of a welcome. Come on, make a wee cup of tea and she can tell us why she's come ... by here, oor Annie, like I said, ye're in the pink! And ye seem to have got bigger an' all.' He took in his sister's healthy complexion and comely, well-fed body. 'And me greetin' like a big bairn when ye left St Enoch's on the train.' He laughed for the first time since she had come home. 'Ye've landed on yer feet, Annie Ramsay.'

'Aye, I landed on my feet.' Annie looked at her brother. She and Sandy had always been the strong ones in the family, the hard workers, the two that bore the burden of supporting their mother in every way they could. Even as barefoot children it was Annie and Sandy who queued for stale bread at the bakers, or walked miles at dawn to pick fruit on Clydeside for a few coppers and a bag of half-rotten rejects. Now he was struggling alone with the unequal task of being the main breadwinner in the impossible chaos of poverty and hampered by his youth. She couldn't desert him and her mother now. 'And that's why I'm here,' she said. 'I've got some news for the pair of ye.'

Her mother got up and filled the big iron kettle, placing it on the dying heat of the old coal stove. 'Whit's that, hen?'

Annie took a deep breath and looked from one to the other. 'I just came up to tell ye that I've been offered a better position, wi' more money. It's no certain I'll get it yet, but if I do I think I ken how ye can get out of debt and open that wee shop as well.' She sat on her hands so they wouldn't see them tremble. 'See, Sandy, see, Mammy,' she forced a bright smile, 'miracles still happen.'

Annie walked up to Craigdrummond House as soon as she got back to Ayrshire and asked politely to speak to Lady Cameron personally with an important message.

'I'll take it.' The maid held out her hand.

'No, it's not a letter, it's the same as the last time I came with an important message only this time it's jist for Lady Cameron, nobody else. I ken Lady Cameron will want to see me if ye say I'm from Clachan's Farm,' she insisted.

In the face of Annie's determination, the maid gave in. 'Wait a minute and I'll find out.'

This was the second time Annie had been inside the family quarters of Craigdrummond House, she was too intent on the business in hand to even spare a glance for the luxury around her. Her sturdy boots clunked loudly on polished wood and marble as the maid led the way up stairs and along corridors hung with generations of Craigdrummond's Lairds.

They stopped at the sitting room where Maria and Miss Cumming were listening to Alexandra half-heartedly playing a Mozart concerto.

'Here's the girl from Clachan's Farm, Milady.' The maid bobbed a curtsey. Annie waited, white and tense in the corridor.

'A girl? I thought you said there was an important message from the farm,' Maria demanded.

'Aye, I'm sorry, Milady, there is a message, but she said it's not in a letter and it's just for you.' The maid flushed with embarrassment realising she had misunderstood the situation.

'Indeed? Then show her in,' Maria replied intrigued.

'Annie!' Alexandra stopped playing and got up when the girl appeared at the door. 'You've come back!'

'Annie? Annie Ramsay?' Maria's delicate eyebrows rose. After the girl's earlier refusal she had never thought to see her again. 'It's all right, you may go.' With a wave she dismissed the maid. 'Come in.' She beckoned Annie into the drawing room.

Maria gave her a searching look. Surprised at the strength of Alexandra's disappointment, Maria had tried to console her with promises of a maid from Glasgow, but had been rudely rebuffed. Since then her step-daughter had been almost unbearable to all of them including poor Miss Cumming who was at her wits end. Maria held back from complaining to the Laird for she knew he would be furious with his daughter. However, the state of affairs couldn't be allowed to drift indefinitely. The departure date was already close.

'I'll tell kitchen to hold supper a few minutes.' Miss Cumming discreetly withdrew, closing the door behind her.

'Well, have you a message from Mistress Crawford or Farmer Clachan?' Maria asked.

'I have a message from me, your Ladyship,' Annie replied with a grave expression on her face.

'Is that so?' Maria looked curiously at the diminutive girl, noting the intelligent grey eyes, straight back and proud bearing. As before, when she and the Laird had interviewed Annie, she was polite and deferential, but quite unintimidated, the realisation that Alexandra might have good reason for her unusual choice, had come as a pleasant surprise.

'If you still want me, I have decided to accept the offer you made to go wi' Miss Alexandra to Paris, Lady Cameron.' Annie said her piece without preamble. 'But there is something I want in return and without it, I won't go ... I won't go at all, whatever anybody says,' she repeated gravely.

'If it is terms of employment, then why haven't you asked to speak to the Laird's factor instead of me?' Maria smiled.

'Och no, men only understand money for what it is, women see past that to what it means. And anyway Miss Alexandra said you stood behind her wantin' me. No, Lady Cameron, it's you I need to talk to before anyone else comes in on this.'

'Well, you had better explain in that case.' Maria was amused at the farm-girl's uncompromising manner and words.

'My first year's money is to go to my Mammy in advance,' Annie began without further preamble. 'And she has to get keeping it whether or not Miss Alexandra has me as her maid for the whole year or just a week ... even a day!'

Annie was nobody's fool, Maria thought wryly. She has the measure of my step-daughter after all. This was no plaything for her to get bored with and discard.

Annie drew a deep breath. 'It has to be enough to pay off ten shillings tick wi' whatever interest is left, and to set up Mammy and my big brother Sandy in a wee confectioners and fancy cake

124

shop ... Otherwise I'll stay on Clachan's Farm where I really want to be.'

'Oh!' Maria Cameron stifled a laugh. It was one of the strangest transactions she had ever heard in her life. 'What do you say, Alexandra?' she took refuge in the question while she recovered her composure.

'Ten shillings plus whatever it is, wouldn't even buy a pair of my Sunday shoes and setting up a little cake-shop cannot involve so much money, Stepmother.' Alexandra hadn't a clue about such things, but she answered with confidence. 'Papa will surely think it's a sound bargain ... after all it will put me in good humour till I go, and then you'll all be rid of me for a couple of years! I suppose he'll think Annie's cheap at the price.'

She ignored her stepmother's embarrassed wince and with a complete change of manner, she turned to the girl and said softly, blue eyes alight with pleasure, 'Oh, Annie, I'm so glad you're coming!'

'Aye, I suppose ye are. But maybe the Laird won't agree to my terms,' said Annie non-committally.

'He will if you ask him, Stepmother!' Alexandra said in a tone both pleading and defiant.

'Oh, surely it is not impossible.' Maria gave in. She knew it was weak of her, but she wanted to please Alex. 'I'll have to speak to Sir Urquhart, of course.' Privately she thought, I can work all the details out with Urquhart later and make sure the little milkmaid gets her wish. After all, the amount is trifling to the Laird of Craigdrummond. Maria Cameron had an idea her husband would refuse her nothing she asked of him. Her smooth white cheeks flushed and transformed her from a handsome woman to a glowing beauty.

'Did you hear that, Annie? Isn't it wonderful?' Alexandra smiled broadly.

'I heard.' Annie didn't know whether it was wonderful or not.

'I'll speak to the Laird and, since time is short, you'll be hearing from us very soon, maybe even later today.' Maria addressed Annie who was standing watching her with grave, grey eyes. 'I feel sure what you've asked will be granted, Annie. After all, according to Alexandra, without you she might not be here.'

'Thank you, your Ladyship. If that's all, then I'll get back to the milking.' With a little bob, Annie withdrew.

She waited till the big house was well behind before she let her pent up feelings out. Choking back the sobs when Clachan's Farm drew close, she dried her eyes and walked with head erect into the big kitchen where Mistress Crawford was baking a batch of scones.

'I'm goin' if the Laird agrees!' Briefly, Annie told her of her decision. 'Eddie's got the family into debt and Mammy and Sandy need money to open a wee shop. It'll take more than a milkmaid's wages to do it all, so that's that.'

'Clachan's Farm will be the worse without you, Annie,' the older woman said sincerely enough, but deep inside she felt satisfied that her gamble in sending Annie home had paid off far better than she had hoped.

'Do you think so, Mistress?' Annie said glumly.

'...But I can see you have little choice, Annie,' the house-keeper went on quickly. 'Like the Doctor said, it's just as well to make the best of the opportunity while you have it. This is a fine decision. Congratulations, lass.'

'Thank you, Mistress Crawford.' Annie bit her lip hard. 'But it's a bit early for congratulations, they might say no to what I've asked.'

'Aye they might,' she replied. But not if young Miss Alexandra has anything to do with it, she thought, and it sounds as if the new Lady Cameron agrees as well, for whatever strange reason.

'Well I'm not goin' for less,' Annie said stubbornly.

'Now listen to me, Annie.' Bess took her by the shoulders and looked into her troubled face. 'Whether they take you or not, you've not to say a word about this business to Dougie or the lassies, not even to Ian. The Laird likes to keep things very quiet where Miss Alexandra is concerned. Only the Fairmer, myself and Doctor Murchieson need know why you're really leaving if you go.'

'But Ian kenned all about it the last time they offered.'

'I know that, but this time I'll warn Geordie to keep quiet. The fewer folk who know the better. Ian's a good lad, but he might say something without thinking and let the cat out of the bag. I'll just tell him and the farm-hands that you have to go back to Glasgow because of your mother. There's no need to spin any complicated tale. By the time Miss Alexandra is finished in Paris,

126

it will all be history. Folk get used to anything and fast once the deed is done! Now promise, Annie!'

'I won't say a word to anybody,' Annie replied slowly, '... not even Ian.'

'Good lass. It's for the best ... everybody's best.'

'Aye ...' Annie looked doubtful. 'But does that mean I'll no hear from anybody on the farm? Can Leezie no send me word now and then ... I could maybe just tell her ... she'll no say a word, Leezie's no a gossip, Missus? I'd just like to ken how folk are doin'.' Despite her best efforts, Annie's lip trembled.

Bess steeled herself against rising sympathy for the desolate girl in front of her. 'No, Annie, Leezie won't be writing, because she won't know where you are. But,' she added with a dry smile, 'I'll write myself if there is anything worth telling. Life is quiet here as you know.'

'Well, not always that quiet, Missus.' Annie shrugged in defeat. 'But if that's what you want, I'll no tell Leezie either.' Annie knew she couldn't argue with the housekeeper.

'That's what I want.'

'Aye, well in that case, I'll away and do my turn.' Annie took her coat, slipped into the farmyard and picked up her pail.

Slowly she made her way across to the familiar milking shed. Dougie had driven in the cows and they were patiently waiting in the stalls. Thank God Maisie is going to be late this evening, Annie thought gratefully. The other milkmaid had been sent on an errand to Craigdrummond village earlier in the day and wasn't due till nearly supper. If I'm lucky I might even be finished before she gets back, she hoped as Annie felt she couldn't face Maisie's barrage of digs and spite tonight.

As soon as she sat down, she put her forehead against the cow's warm flank and began to cry all over again. 'Och, Annie Ramsay,' she told herself after a bit, 'ye better stop greeting or you'll turn the milk sour wi' all the salt water you're adding.'

Still wrapped in her own grief, she didn't hear Ian come in behind her and stop to listen as she sobbed out her misery at leaving Clachan's Farm.

He went over and put a tentative hand on her shoulder. She stiffened, thinking it was Maisie, then turned, trying to compose herself.

'Och, Ian Clachan, ye shouldn't creep up on folk like that!' Annie wiped her eyes on the edge of her pinny.

'Annie, what is it?' he asked. 'Has something happened?'

'I'm leaving ... going back to the Gallowgate,' just in time she remembered her promise to Mistress Crawford.

'Has Aunty Bess given ye the sack?' he asked astounded.

'Och no, it's just family business. Please, Ian, don't ask!' she sobbed.

He knew of Annie's journey home, but not of Alex's second visit. Bess had sworn Leezie to silence about that. Ian didn't know why Annie was leaving Clachan's but, he could see it had cost her dearly. 'Don't go,' he whispered, face full of sadness. 'I can't bear the thought of Clachan's Farm without our Annie ... my Annie.'

In his sorrow, Annie could see the man he would become, and the knowledge of her own loss cut even deeper into her heart. She knew if she left he would be sure to forget the careless promises of youth, promises she had tossed aside so lightly and which suddenly seemed infinitely precious.

'I have to go, Ian, and maybe it's just as well ... ye should stick to yer own kind. Forget all that talk about trying to wed me. It would only cause trouble.'

'I've told you I don't care about what folk would say or do, I just want you, Annie,' he insisted.

'Aye, well I'm going, and that's the way it is,' she turned away and began milking.

'I won't forget you or my promise,' he said.

'Aye ye will,' her reply was muffled.

'Will you write?'

'No, it wouldn't be seemly, Ian,' she replied. 'It would only cause gossip if ye got letters from me.'

'I'll write to you,' he said stubbornly. 'I can get your address in the Gallowgate somehow. It's in the farm books.'

'No!' She said and turned from him. 'I don't want you to write. There's no future for us. Get that into yer daft head! Now away ye go, Ian, ye're only making it worse.' He saw her shoulders begin to shake again as she struggled for control.

After a few minutes he could take it no longer and silently withdrew, fleeing up the hill. Ian was a man now and nobody could ever see him cry, nobody and nothing but the wild cliffs and the wheeling seabirds.

'You're getting the shove, aren't ye?' Maisie's voice broke into her sorrow when the milking was nearly done.

Thank God I've stopped greetin' like a glaikit bairn, Annie thought as she went on drawing out the milk in steady spurts, trying to ignore her tormentor.

'Did ye hear me, scruff? Ye're out aren't ye ... shoved out?' Maisie wasn't going to let be.

'By here, if anybody gets the shove it should be you!' Annie stopped milking and got up. She didn't care any more what the other girl would say. She was losing the only place she had ever been happy and Maisie's viciousness seemed insignificant beside that.

'I'll give you a wee bit of advice before I go, Maisie.' Annie faced her squarely. 'You'd better stop creeping up Mistress Crawford's and the Fairmer's arse, whispering and spreading lies about folk, so ye had, or one of these days somebody will thump ye one.'

'Oh aye?' Maisie stood threateningly, arms akimbo. 'And who will that be? No a wee skelf like you anyway,' she sneered. 'Ye're jist a bit of stinking muck from the Gallowgate ... Mistress Crawford says ye're going back there. Aye, that's where ye belong. It'll be a different story for ye, so it will,' Maisie went on, oblivious to Annie's rising colour. 'Ye'll be back in the gutter, no running after the fairmer's son and trying to trap him, neither ye will!'

At the mention of Ian, Annie saw red altogether. 'Back in the gutter? Is that a fact? Well maybe ye're right about where I come from and where I'm going, and maybe ye're no, Maisie! But here's how folk from the gutter behave wi' spiteful targes who tell lies about them.' She lifted her pail, half full of steaming milk, and slung it over Maisie, soaking her from head to toe.

'I'm going to report ye for this! Ye'll get your last pay docked so ye will, I'll see to it, by God I will!' Maisie screeched in rage, as milk ran in rivulets down her face, skirt and legs onto the milking shed floor. 'You're a wee midden, Annie Ramsay!' She stormed off into the farmhouse.

Mistress Crawford looked at Maisie as she gasped out her tale of woe. A smile played round her normally stern mouth. 'Aye well, it's too late to dock Annie's last pay, Maisie,' she replied acidly, 'it's already paid. And to tell you the truth, my lass, what

129

Annie did to you was long overdue. Now get out and stop dripping milk all over the kitchen floor!' With that she turned her back on the furious milkmaid and went on rolling pastry for the evening's mutton pie.

For Annie the act had been cathartic. Her heart lightened and with the optimism of youth, she told herself that the time away would be over 'in the wag of a wee dog's tail'. 'Maybe they'll have me back at Clachan's when Miss Alexandra is finished with the school,' she told herself. 'Mammy should be set up by then wi' Sandy so they won't need my money the same and maybe Mistress Crawford will forget about me and Ian.' Annie tried to be positive. 'Och, I'm sure Paris won't be that bad. That tower they built when I was at school is supposed to be a sight for sore eyes. And if they agree to what I've asked at least it will be worth it! But what if they don't?' Immersed in her sorrow, she had not really considered that possibility.

Bending down, she mopped up the mess and cleaned and stacked the empty pails. Hope crept into the misery. 'If the Laird doesn't agree, then at least I can ask the fairmer for some extra work on my half day and try to pay off the tick. Mammy and Sandy could maybe manage then ... and I could stay here after all.'

Before the tiny thread of hope could strengthen, it was snapped. Mistress Crawford came to the door of the byre and called her over. 'They've sent a message from Craigdrummond, Annie. Tomorrow morning first thing you'll be on the Glasgow train. Miss Alexandra's governess will be waiting for you at Craigdrummond station and she'll take you.'

'Tomorrow?' Annie blanched.

'Tomorrow.' Her tone was firm. 'You're to be trained right away. They said just to wear your Sunday best. Miss Cumming will escort you to where you're going and stop to buy suitable clothes, a trunk and a uniform.' She put her hand on the girl's shoulder. 'You've to take nothing else, lass, except your own few knicknacks in a wee bag. Not another stick of clothing. Nothing.'

'Not even my second best?' Annie gasped.

'Not even that. You possess nothing that will fit in where you are going. It's all for the best,' Bess added firmly. 'Your life at Clachan's Farm is over, Annie.'

Part 2

Far, far from thee I wander here

Chapter Twelve

The noise, the seething crowds and the pungent shifting smells reminded Annie of Glasgow. She stood behind Alexandra on the platform of the newly enlarged and modernised Gare du Nord looking around with awe. Giant Corinthian cast-iron columns supported a vast high glass roof and the whole edifice was enclosed on each side by symmetrical wings that hid more platforms and offices. A strange brilliant metallic light cast harsh shadows and picked out rubbish drifting into a corner in the autumn evening wind.

'Don't just stand there gawping, girl!' hissed Miss Eugenie Berry who had accompanied them from London. 'You counted in the bags, now count them out.'

Obediently, Annie stood by checking as the porter Miss Eugenie had beckoned with an imperious gloved finger loaded their luggage from the guards van onto a cart. Pressing ahead through the jostling crowds, he led the way along the platform and out of the mêlée, with Annie's single modest trunk perched precariously on top of Alexandra's handsomely bound ones.

Outside, a line of cabs waited in the growing darkness, patient horses shuffling in the smoky air of late October. Annie glanced back and caught her breath. Even the front of the station was magnificent, with soaring columns and decorated with nine huge statues that would not have looked out of place on a castle.

'The statues personify the most important cities of France and Europe which are served from the Gare du Nord. Rather typical French whimsy!' Miss Eugenie explained loudly to Alexandra, who gave a disinterested shrug.

Annie saw any initial resemblance to Glasgow disappear like

autumn mist as they clattered out of the station and into the Boulevard de Magenta and then the rue Lafayette. 'Oh, just look at those shops, the cafes, the theatres ... oh, the lights!' Alexandra squealed with delight as the sights and sounds trotted past. Her blonde head bobbed to and fro and she peered out like a child.

'It's just electricity. A passing fad most likely. Surely you noticed in the station. Oh, you'll soon get used to it, we've all had to,' Miss Eugenie said with more than a touch of disapproval.

'Electricity! How wonderful.' Alexandra was thrilled. Everyone had heard of this amazing innovation, but this was the first time she had seen it operate so widely and to such effect.

'Paris has been pioneering the public use of electricity since the "Universal Exposition" three years ago,' Miss Eugenie sniffed. '"Ville Lumière" it calls itself, though I prefer gas-light myself. It's more genteel.'

Neither girl had ever seen such sharp, harsh wonderful light. Even the gaslights of Buchanan Street in Glasgow, or in London's Pall Mall, were dim in comparison. Paris's first electric lights had gone on in the Place du Carrousel, Parc Monceau and on the Buttes Chaumont in 1889. Now, five years later, they sparkled from the windows of fine department stores, and from stations, monuments, theatres and the Palais Royal.

'Do we pass the new Tower? Does it have electricity too?' Alexandra peered out of the carriage. 'Papa told me about it when he came back from the Exposition.'

'No, we do not pass the Tower, though we will have an outing there at some point,' Miss Eugenie conceded. 'But,' she went on with her habitual sniff, 'not everyone approves of Monsieur Gustave Eiffel's tower.'

'Ooh, can we go up?' Alexandra squealed. 'Is it dangerous?'

'Monsieur Eiffel has personally guaranteed indemnity if it should collapse or any one be injured, so I don't think it can be very dangerous,' Miss Eugenie replied cautiously. 'Nevertheless, I think it will be enough to see the edifice.'

'Why?' Alexandra demanded with a pout. 'I think it's silly just to look.'

'Ladies should moderate their voices and their opinions, Alexandra, dear, if Miss Stephanie and myself feel there is a danger to our young ladies, we will not countenance exposing you to it,' Miss Eugenie reproved.

Eugenie Berry hoped Alexandra wasn't going to prove difficult. Cameron of Craigdrummond was a name to drop casually in years to come and she and her sister were proud to receive such an important student. Proud enough for her to have gone all the way to London to escort Alexandra and her maid to Paris, but she was a trifle alarmed at her tendency to be over-excited and horrified by her horrible provincial accent. That will be the first thing to go! Miss Eugenie grimaced.

Annie sat opposite Alexandra and Miss Berry, squeezed against the window by those boxes and trunks which contained Alexandra's clothes and jewellery too fine to be risked in the luggage compartment. Michty! she thought as the glittering city unfolded in flashes of unimaginable colour and sights. The minister at Craigdrummond would surely say this place must be the work of the Devil himself! Och, but it's bonnie! Every bit as much as her young mistress, she was enchanted as they trotted through traffic so daring and fast it was a wonder they were not mowed down.

Out front, the driver roared imprecations at his fellows that made Miss Eugenie wince and be glad Alexandra's French was inadequate.

She need not have worried, both mistress and maid were too enthralled by the magic of this city of new-age light to care. Cutting sharply through the dusk, its clear brilliance sparkled from the most fashionable cafes and bars, thronged with artists and hangers-on, as well as ordinary folk. Paris flaunted all she had and showed herself to be a teasing courtesan by night, if a gracious lady by day. By the time they had reached the Seine and turned towards the wealthy Faubourg Saint Honoré they were too awed even to gasp any more.

The journey was over too fast for them both, but once their bags were unloaded and Alexandra had been shown to her suite, it was already late.

'We'll send up a supper tray tonight,' Miss Stephanie Berry explained after welcoming her new charge. 'Tomorrow you can meet the other young ladies, we only have a few at a time so we can give individual attention. Then we can begin to acquaint you with the routine of our establishment. Francine will see to your maid.'

135

Alexandra was unusually subdued as Annie served her in front of a glowing fire. 'Don't you like the place, Miss Alexandra?' Annie asked, glancing round at the unfamiliar French furniture and fittings.

'Oh yes, it's nicer than I feared,' she replied with a shrug. Certainly the rooms were well appointed and comfortable, and the supper was delicate and good. It was clear that the two Misses Berry spent at least a decent part of the large sums of money they charged on their students. 'It was all so exciting in the carriage, but now it just seems a long way from Craigdrummond,' she added in a small, lost voice.

'Och, you'll feel different tomorrow. You're just a wee bit tired,' Annie said briskly, pouring a glass of some lemony concoction and placing it gingerly on the little table beside her chair. She had been feeling a bit subdued herself. Also tired and hungry after the long journey, there was no chance of a rest for a while yet. Now supper was over she still needed to unpack the things Alexandra would need for the night from her evening case in the adjacent bedroom and help her to bed.

It didn't occur to Annie to moan, even to herself. Maids had to wait. Disciplined the whole of her short life, from the want of Ramsay's single end to the 'baccy factory and then the farm, Annie knew to be patient, hope that her turn would eventually come and put up with it if it didn't. She accepted that it would be hours before she managed to get something to eat ... if anyone remembered she hadn't had a bite since Calais.

She watched Alexandra slowly pick at the food, trying not to think how long it would be before she would be free to flop down on the narrow bed in the tiny room that Francine had briefly shown her in the maids' quarters at the top of the house. Her own modest trunk stood neglected there till her work was done.

'Annie!' Alexandra shifted restlessly in the easy chair. 'Do adjust the footstool, I'm so uncomfortable.' Wearily but willingly, Annie did as she was told. 'And those cushions!' Alexandra was proving to be a demanding mistress.

'I'll just go and unpack your things, Miss Alexandra.'

'No, stay here!' Alexandra seemed in no mood to be alone. 'Annie, you saw those posters on the boat about the anarchists who throw bombs in Paris, didn't you?' Suddenly she harped

back on a theme that had cropped up first on the train-ferry crossing between Dover and Calais.

'Aye,' Annie replied.

'Do you think they are still at large?' Alexandra sat, fork
poised in mid air, with a worried frown.

'Och, I'm sure they're all behind bars,' Annie tried to reassure
her. She learned it was safest to deal with Alexandra's nervous
fears quickly before she developed a full-scale drama from the
simplest things.

'The posters looked fresh to me.'

'Och, they were inside the main saloon, that's why they looked
so new. All the others will have blown away weeks ago,' Annie
tried to sound convincing. Till the boat, she had no idea either of
the existence of the Paris anarchists who had troubled the city
over the previous few years, but she had no intention of saying
so. 'Do you really think the Laird would sent you to Paris if there
was likely to be trouble, Miss Alexandra?' she asked with a
smile.

'Of course not!' Alexandra brightened up, tackling the terrine
du canard with gusto. 'I'm sure you're right, Annie, Papa wouldn't
risk me.' Then with a flash of resentment she added, 'Though
maybe the same could not be said about Stepmother!'

Annie made no comment, but busied herself with Alexandra's
hand luggage. In the few weeks she had been trained for
Alexandra's service and since, Annie had learned not only how to
speak properly and to serve, but also when to bite her tongue. At
first Alexandra's moods and tantrums had made her think about
leaving, but she held back, partly because of the respect she felt
for Lady Cameron who had treated her kindly, partly from
simple pragmatism. If I leave, she concluded, the Laird might not
honour his promise to pay Sandy and Mammy and I doubt
Mistress Crawford would give me an open-arms welcome back at
Clachan's Farm.

Clachan's Farm and Ian were memories to be treasured, no
more. Mistress Crawford had made it plain that chapter in her
life was closed. Och, in a way I can see why the Missus wants to
keep me and Ian apart, she thought many times. But it was hard.

Even before they left for France, Annie had made up her mind
to stick out the job with Alexandra patiently. I've nowhere else to
go, she told herself, so I might as well keep the peace and learn

this trade properly, it'll stand me in good stead for the day Miss Alexandra gets fed up with me. So far she had succeeded, but tonight her tiredness made her less careful than usual.

'Did you hear what I said, Annie?' Alexandra was not going to let her escape without comment.

'Och, Miss Alexandra, I didn't answer because I can't agree!' she responded, 'Lady Cameron is a good woman!'

Alexandra stopped eating, a piece of toast dramatically midway between plate and mouth. She shot Annie an angry affronted glance. 'I realise that you would not be here if my stepmother had not taken an unaccountable liking to you,' she snapped unfairly, quite ignoring her own part in the affair, 'But I don't want your opinion on her, Annie, unless I ask for it!'

'Aye, Miss Alexandra,' Annie sighed. 'Or unless I say what ye want me to!' she muttered under her breath. Aloud she added in an even tone, 'I'll just see to your night clothes.'

'Very well, I do feel tired,' she agreed. 'It's been a long day.'

'Och, anyway Miss Alexandra is nowhere near as nasty as Maisie,' Annie mused, opening one of the main trunks. 'In fact she can be right charming and a good laugh when she's in the mood. Maisie wouldn't have known a laugh if she met one on the Moss!'

She shook out the fine night-linen and spread them over the coverlet she had turned down on the well aired and generously pillowed bed. Gently Annie smoothed out a ribbon, 'And in any case I can't see me dowsing Miss Alexandra in a pail of milk whatever she says!' That daft idea brought a smile to her lips.

Good-nature restored, she went back into the sitting room, helped her mistress to undress, brushed her golden hair till it shone, catching it in a snood and settled her for the night. Finally, feet dragging from tiredness, she climbed the stairs to her little room.

Francine heard her come and came out in her nightdress, long hair plaited neatly. 'Here, this is for you,' she said in careful English, as she handed over a plate of bread and cheese and a pitcher of the same lemon drink Annie had served to her mistress. 'Poor girl, it must have been a very hard day. Mon Dieu! I think you need some food and some sleep.' Concerned, she took in Annie's exhausted face and weary body.

Annie felt grateful tears come to her eyes as she took the plate and sank down on the edge of her bed. 'Och, that's kind, thanks, Leezie,' she said.

'Leezie?' Francine asked with a puzzled frown. 'I am Francine Lamarche.'

'Sorry, but you remind me of someone I knew. A lassie called Leezie. You don't look like her.' Francine was small, dark-haired and neat. Annie heard her voice shake with emotion and she swallowed hard, 'I hardly know you yet, but I can see you're the same salt of the earth!'

Francine looked at her uncomprehendingly. 'I'm sorry, I do not understand. And I do not know your name, just that you are Miss Alexandra Cameron's maid.'

I was just trying to say thank you for the food, Francine.' Annie stood up and held out her hand in the formal gesture she'd been taught during the training in Glasgow. 'I'm Annie Ramsay,' she said. 'How do you do?'

'Welcome to Paris, Annie,' Francine replied with a warm friendly smile. 'I will be looking after you. I will call you at five-thirty, that will give you time to iron your uniform before work. Good night ... bonsoir.'

'Bonsoir,' Annie's first word of French came easily. Then she sat alone and ate the strange tasting cheese and crusty bread with a good appetite despite the late hour. Asleep as soon as her head touched the pillow, she dreamed of the fields, the hills and the Moss round Craigdrummond and the kye lowing softly as she drove them in for milking.

In the dark small hours, she woke in a sweat of fear from a nightmare where the Moss was pulling her under and Alexandra stood by watching, then with a laugh she turned and walked away, calling over her shoulder, 'Goodbye Clachan's Annie'. For a moment unsure of where she was, Annie repeated the words as if they were a mantra to calm her pounding heart, 'Clachan's Annie, Clachan's Annie'. But as full consciousness returned, she turned her face into the hard pillow and wept for the knowledge that Alexandra was right, Clachan's Annie was no more.

The next day, Alexandra arose fresh and bright, full of optimism and began her new life with gusto. Annie, under the direction of capable and helpful Francine, did the same. Neither of the young women looked back. There was too much to do, to see and to learn to spend time mourning the past.

Over the next year and a half, Annie watched Alexandra blossom and took more than a touch of pride in her mistress's beauty. Dressed in the latest fashion, hair arranged under a froth of tulle and flowers or framed by a neat boater, Alexandra Cameron was lovelier than ever. The Berry sisters had honed her Ayrshire burr to London drawing-room standards. She sounded what she was, a rich and lovely heiress. And if she was lazy when it came to learning French or reading chosen texts from the great writers, the part of her Paris education which she never neglected was how to dress well for her high station in life.

Paris in the 1890s was the undisputed centre of the fashion world, even if one of its leading couturiers was the English House of Worth. After the first insecure weeks, when, fresh from the country, this aggressively thriving city seemed overwhelming, Alexandra adored it. Her father had given the Berrys a generous dress allowance on her behalf and she made sure they used every franc. Very soon she also realised the power of her own beauty and delighted in it. Annie was her captive audience and as she regaled her with tales of conquests that gained much in the telling, she laughed gaily at her predictably shocked reaction.

'Well, maybe you and the other young ladies better watch it dropping hankies and notes. It sounds to me as if those young French gentlemen flock like bees to the honeypot every time you go to the Paris opera or ballet and not just there either. You can't trust some of them,' Annie warned direly.

'Oh fiddle-dee-dee!' Alexandra adored the covert flirtations the Berry sisters never seemed to notice. And one in particular. She thought of Jean-Marc who for almost a year now, had pursued her most of all. Comte de Ledignan, he signed passionate pleas and declarations of devotion. The dear Comte, who always seemed to know wherever she would be. How he managed to slip love letters into her muff in the ballet cloakroom, or under a cup of chocolate in the opera cafe, she could hardly guess. He must spend a fortune bribing attendants and waiters. Alex smiled secretly and sighed. So handsome and just a little dangerous with that glorious moustache and air of careless elegance! The country lads of Ayrshire seemed clumsy and gauche in comparison.

'I mean it, Miss Alexandra.' Annie saw her expression and knew her young mistress was off on one of her daft romantic dreams. 'Watch those Frenchmen!'

'And why shouldn't I tantalize them, Annie?' she asked, head tilted and eyes dancing, 'There's no harm in it! The sisters make sure we are well guarded.'

'The Laird wouldn't like it! And ...' Annie blushed.

'And?'

'I've heard they take things like that a bit too far given half a chance.'

'And how did you come by that piece of worldly wisdom? Oh, Annie, just look at you, you've gone puce as a plum. And what do you mean by "take things too far"? Come now, do tell!' Alexandra laughed at her embarrassment.

'Och, it was one of the Misses Berry's maids that told me about that sort of person.' Annie recovered her aplomb. At times like these, Alexandra not only enjoyed Annie's familiarity, she encouraged it. But though she responded, Annie was wary, for she knew that Alexandra's mood could suddenly sour and she would become imperious or angry. But this time there was something on her mind and she decided to risk a warning. 'Just be careful, Miss Alexandra,' Annie's expression was serious. 'The lassies downstairs say there are some right bad lots in Paris, even if they pretend to be fine gentlemen and no doubt some of them are right enough ...' she floundered. 'Och, it's just that you want to watch that Comte, or whatever he calls himself.'

'Whom?' She feigned surprise.

'Och, Miss Alexandra! You know the one that's always prancing about when you appear, according to what you tell me. Well, I wouldn't trust him up Craigdrummond Main Street on the Sabbath, as we used to say on Clachan's Farm. He tried to bribe me to give you a note yesterday, so he did.'

'Tried to bribe you?' Her eyes widened innocently. 'What an odd idea. I'm sure you're mistaken, Annie.'

'Aye, well I'm not mistaken, I ken when somebody is up to no good! He stopped me in the street. Och, the cheek of it!' Annie occasionally reverted to her old accent when she was worried.

'Well, if he gives you something for me, you should just pass it on, Annie,' Alexandra said with a pout and flushing. 'In any case he is a Count, of that I'm sure. And it's not your place to judge your betters!'

Annie saw the mounting colour and added, 'He didn't give me anything, because I wouldn't take it. We've been told by the Misses Berry that if we do that kind of thing we'll be sent home in disgrace.'

'Hmmm ...' Alexandra looked thoughtful, the sisters were maybe not as blind as she believed. 'Still, Annie, your first loyalty is to me!' she went on imperiously.

'Aye, so it is, but Count or not, I don't trust the man!' Despite the forthright words, Annie knew she was on delicate ground and made a spinsterish, disapproving face to distract Alex out of the sour mood that was threatening.

'Oh, you do look silly, Annie, just as if you had eaten a lemon! So, would you take messages for me if this Count was less ... dangerous?' Amused, her good humour was back and she smiled.

'Och, maybe I would,' Annie replied. Then she grinned and shook her head. 'But I haven't seen one yet in Paris I would give a bent bawbee for! They're a shower of French fancies!'

Annie had judged her mistress's temper right. 'What a description!' Alexandra was too entertained to be offended.

'Excuse me, Miss Alexandra.' Annie cocked her head, listening. 'There's somebody at the door. I expect it's Marie-Claire with the rest of your linen.'

'Or maybe with the post! Do answer!' She loved to get letters.

'Right away.' Annie straightened her pinny and composed herself, looking the picture of the well-trained lady's maid.

As well as arts, language, music, dance, dress and etiquette for the daughters of the noble and wealthy, the Berry establishment taught their personal maids the finer aspects of caring for the comfort of their young mistresses. Francine had never a better pupil than Annie Ramsay who drank in new knowledge with enthusiasm and used it with skill.

Alexandra accepted Annie's abilities without surprise or comment. 'Try out that new hairstyle on me, Annie,' she called after her as she went to the door. Holding up her golden mane, she peered in the mirror. 'I must look ravishing in my new outfit for the Opera.'

'Och, you know you'll look the prettiest in the place, whatever you do, Miss Alexandra!' Annie replied honestly.

142

'Peut-etre!' Alexandra's French grammar was still erratic, but she loved to use little phrases she thought sounded good.

'Merci, Marie-Claire.' Annie closed the door. 'You were right, Miss Alexandra, it is a letter.'

'It's from Cumming.' She tore open the envelope and quickly scanned the contents. 'She says she is delighted with her new charges ... poor Cumming, anything would be easy after me.'

Annie could well believe that, but said nothing. Alexandra's moods were undoubtedly fewer than in Ayrshire, now she had so many distractions around her, but she was never easy.

'Oh listen, Annie, she has visited Craigdrummond.'

'Och, that's fine. I hope your parents are well, Miss Alexandra,' Annie said politely.

'She says so,' Alexandra replied. 'Though it's a pity Papa cannot come over again.' Lady Cameron was already in late pregnancy and the Laird was worried about leaving her alone in Craigdrummond.

'Anyway, you'll be seeing Lord Ballantyne today. He seems to come regularly for the races.' Privately she thought, and not just for the races either.

'Yes, so I will, how nice.' She nodded absently. 'You know, it's not long before the baby is due to arrive.' She paused with a half-smile on her face. 'It seems strange at soon eighteen to have a little brother or sister.'

'Well, Lady Cameron is a young woman yet, I expect there will be a few more to follow,' Annie replied.

'You think so?' Alexandra looked at her. 'Poor Maria, I made her life quite miserable, didn't I?' she made a rueful face, but her eyes were watchful.

Annie replied without taking time to think, 'Well, you could be a lot nicer even now, though I think the poor lady was just happy you didn't bite off her nose when she came at Christmas.'

'Annie, you know I don't like it when you say things like that,' Alexandra's face darkened.

'You know my views,' Annie muttered stubbornly, then changed the subject quickly, 'Will you wear the blue or the gold when you join the others for a walk in the Tuilleries?'

'Oh, the gold this time.' Quicksilver Alexandra was happy again. 'I'm meeting Lord Ballantyne immediately afterwards. He says gold matches my hair.'

'Aye, so he does,' Annie said with a thoughtful nod.

'Do you ever hear from your rustic friends on the farm?' Alexandra asked, then added more carelessly than unkindly, 'They can write?'

'Aye, they can write!' Annie was stung, 'And better than those who have more advantages at times! Even poor farm-folk get a decent education in Scotland, Mistress!'

'Oh, Annie, the minute I tease you about that precious farm you're up in arms,' she laughed at her maid's flushed face. 'No wonder they called you Clachan's Annie. I remember what you said that Sunday long ago when I stopped with the groom ... do you miss the farm still?' she asked idly, as she tried on a dark woollen skirt, lined with silk and trimmed with satin ribbon.

'Just as much as the day I left.' Annie buttoned her young mistress tightly. 'But it would be a lie to say I haven't enjoyed this time here, Miss Alexandra. Seeing Paris and Vienna and soon Rome, it's something I'd never have dreamed of doing when I was a wee lassie living in the Gallowgate, or sitting in the gloamin' milking Clachan's kye. There's so much to learn, so much to do.'

'Such as?' Alexandra Cameron was intrigued that a maid should feel so interested in her surroundings.

'Och, there's not much more to say, the whole place just makes my mind boggle at times.' Annie thought of the sights, smells, strangeness, ugliness and beauty that was Paris. 'But I'm glad I'm me and not you.'

'What do you mean by that?' Alexandra turned in surprise, silk underskirt swishing.

'Well, I can go out on my half-day off or when you're doing something where we maids are not included and my work is finished, like this evening, for instance. There's not much free time, a wee bittie more than on the farm maybe, but I make the most of what there is to see Paris.'

'So, that's why you have learned French so fast, I did wonder when I heard you telling off the shoeboy for ruining my new calf-skins,' Alexandra mused. 'I hardly understood a word, though it was clear he did! Do you speak to French people much?' Her face clouded. 'We mustn't, unless the Misses Berry have selected them! "Ne peeeerlez pas avec lees Pareeesiens!"' she mimicked

Miss Berry's finicky English accent which came so strongly through her carefully constructed French.

'I have to in this place or I couldn't do my work,' Annie replied. 'I've learned decent enough French from Francine and the other lady's maids and I've bought a wee book or two on grammar from the stalls down on the Seine. But being in and out the basement, dealing with the laundry-maids, kitchen-folk and that, you can't talk as if you've just swallowed a French dictionary.'

'Oh, why?' Alexandra was puzzled.

'The lassies that work below stairs come from all over France,' Annie explained, 'and from parts of Paris you never visit, Miss Alexandra. None of them comes from well-off families, you might say. They're a bit like myself!' Her grin broadened. 'Some of the words I've learned you won't find in any dictionary, that's for sure! I suppose I speak "Gallowgate French" as well as "Big House French", if you know what I mean.'

'How lucky to be able to do things alone,' she sounded envious. 'Do you have friends, Annie?'

'I like Francine, the Misses Berry's maid, Miss Alexandra.' In fact Annie and the senior maid had become firm friends from the start. But Annie knew she had to be careful. Alexandra Cameron could be generous and amusing, but she had a possessive temperament, Annie had discovered, even with someone as insignificant as her maid. A word too many now and she might put a stop to the little freedom Annie had. 'Och, like I said, there's no need for a lot of friends, I'm too busy.'

'But do you talk to many people outside the Berry Establishment?' she persisted.

'Not so many!' Annie felt herself blush at the lie. Unbidden came the face of the mixed medley of folk she had come to know in the Montmartre cafe which Francine's brother owned.

When they had a whole afternoon or an evening free, the two girls visited Louis Lamarche. The walk was long, but neither was daunted as they made their way across the Boulevard Haussmann, past the station Saint Lazare then along the rue de Clichy to the still rather rustic, rundown charms of Montmartre. Once there, they helped out in the kitchen, served at table, occasionally stood behind the bar, or just sat, feet up by the big range, sipping hot chocolate, a drink to which Annie had become quite addicted.

The Cafe Chat Roux was her secret world and she did not want Alexandra interfering. Even a maid is entitled to a wee bit of her own life, Annie thought. She picked up a pile of linen and began counting her mistress's shifts, thinking about the realities of working for Alexandra and living in Paris. Though she still missed Ayrshire, Annie couldn't deny that she had come to love much that was this great enigmatic city of extreme beauty and horrifying ugliness.

If Francine was working and she was free for a precious hour or so, Annie would walk along the Seine past the bateaux-lavoirs, where washerwomen toiled endlessly and the gaily decorated bateaux-mouches churned up the muddy waters. Everything was different and strange.

Sometimes she wandered through the elegance of the fine streets round the Faubourg Saint Honoré and even crossed the river to the old aristocratic enclave of Fauboug St Germain. City bred, she felt at ease in the traffic and the bustle, never tiring of seeing the great houses and the fine buildings that Paris wore with grace. And when her feet wearied, she would sit in one of the fine public gardens the Parisiens took so much for granted. And just sometimes when she closed her eyes and listened to bird song in the far corner of some great shady park, she could almost think she was back in Craigdrummond.

Chapter Thirteen

Sandy Ramsay disciplined himself not to open the letter from Annie till the shop was closed for the night and the weary family gathered round the big iron cooker.

'Come on, our Sandy,' Mrs Ramsay was on the edge of her chair with excitment.

'Here we are, then' he said importantly and began, 'Twenty-ninth March, nineteen-ninety-four, Paris ...'

'Och would ye believe it? Jist think, oor Annie in Paris!' Mrs Ramsay sighed. She said exactly the same things every time Annie's occasional letters arrived.

'Mammy, let Sandy read!' the twins chorused.

'Dear Mammy, Sandy and the twins. Thank you for the letter, Sandy. That is good news about Eddie and the lassie from the pub. You are well shot of him.'

'Ye can say that again,' Mrs Ramsay nodded.

'... "Things are fine with Miss Alexandra, or as fine as they can be with her. She is not missing Craigdrummond. Now she's full of Paris and dresses and that. She nearly never talks about home these days. I think what makes her so happy is being so beautiful. You should see her now, she turns every head in Paris. Being dressed in the mode suits her though some of the other ladies just look daft. Remember I said when I wrote at New Year, that the Laird has taken to sending messages with that Lord Ballantyne, well he is never off the doorstep and she seems to like that and is not too nasty about Lady Cameron at least when he is about, which is better.

'Paris is lovely in spring, but the backstreets are dark and dirty any time. In fact they're no different from the Gallowgate. The same is not true of the big main streets, especially the boulevards which are much finer than in Glasgow and are full of people all the time, even on the Sabbath which is nearly like any other day except for the bells that keep ringing.

'I go home sometimes with the senior maid, a nice lassie about my own age called Francine. Her parents are dead, but she has a brother, Louis, who is a very nice man. He has a cafe in a part of Paris called Montmartre which is an awful strange place, a bit like being in the country and a bit like the city. It even has wind-mills and once I saw some wee stunted cows grazing in a garden. Between the Misses Berry's and the cafe are some streets where you have to be careful. Like I said, there is not much difference between Paris tenements and the Gallowgate.

'Louis's cafe is also a pub and a sort of music hall with turns, dancers, plays and shows at night. A lot of artists come here. Most of them are nice enough and some are right clever at drawing folk exactly as they are. I will get one to draw me and you can have it so you don't forget what I look like. The other folk are a right mixed bunch. I've seen workers like Daddy was with hardly a bawbee to their name, rubbing shoulders with writers who behave worse! Even rich ladies and gentlemen, gentry some of them, come in when there is a good show. By here, you'd never see the likes of them in a music hall in Glasgow. One thing about Paris, though, is that whatever they do, everybody gets excited about politics and yells and shouts. The goings on of the day are the talk of the bars. Can you imagine our Eddie, or even Sandy, arguing like mad about what the Prime Minister said last week?

'Though his cafe is doing well, the same is not true of Louis who works too hard and gets tired. To tell you the truth, he looks as if a good wind might blow him over. I was just thinking writing this that maybe you're worried about me going to Louis's cafe. Please do not bother your head about me, they are all very kind people, and though the cafe is not the sort of place you'd find in Glasgow, it is quite a nice change to go there. Of course, I do not drink booze, but Francine told me that some horrible smelling stuff the artists and other folk drink, which they call the "wee green peril", is a terrible hooch called absinthe that rots folk's guts out. Maybe it's as well our Eddie isn't here or he would be drinking it too for it's very cheap.

'You asked if I think about Ayrshire, Sandy, and the farm. Well I have not heard any news from the farm and I try not to think about the folk back there at Clachan's too much. It brings tears to my eyes so it does. This big world is fine, but I would trade it all in a minute for a walk along the heathery cliffs above Craigdrummond strand and a supper in the big kitchen with folk laughing and chaffing.

'Now I must stop because a letter has come for Miss Alexandra, it is likely from the Laird since it has an Ayr mark on top.

'Please send me your news when you have a chance, Your dutiful sister and daughter, Annie Ramsay"'

'By here, Annie writes well,' her mother sniffed into a big hanky. 'Och and all they famous folk she kens, Lord this and Lady that. I can hardly credit she's my ain wee lassie!' Hearing from Annie was something that always made her emotional. It was like a fairytale, or a something you could see in a play on a Saturday night at the music hall. 'But she better watch it in that cafe place.' She frowned then cheered up, 'Och, if Annie says, it's better than a pub in the Gallowgate, then it's likely no that bad.'

Annie had not been as economical with the truth to her family as she had with Alexandra, but even then she had been careful not to give them cause for worry. Cafe Chat Roux was typical of the roughish, multi-faceted 'Belle Epoque' of Paris. Its gay, artistic façade covered an underbelly of anarchists, writers and would be subversives, all inextricably intertwined with the even less salubrious world of pimps and prostitutes. Perched high on Montmartre, a fair walk from the already notorious and fashionable Moulin Rouge, it was no worse than it had to be and better than many of its rivals.

Despite the savaging Montmartre had suffered during the siege of Paris and the civil war of 1871, it showed little signs by the time Louis Lamarche opened his Cafe Chat Roux in 1888. Like the resilient people who lived there, Montmartre had picked itself up and got on with the life it knew. Gaps left by bombardment and fire closed rapidly as apartments sprang up on the hill, cafes like Louis's multiplied since they were popular with artists, poets and radical thinkers, as well as some of the more questionable elements in the city.

'Francine, Annie! Comment ça va? How's it going?' When they arrived after their long walk, the girls were greeted with the rough and ready warmth that always enveloped them at the Chat Roux.

'Chocolate pot is on, Annie,' Jules the barman teased. 'Leave a drop for the rest of us, eh?'

'I'll try,' Annie replied with a grin and made her way into the kitchen at the back.

Pots and pans stood higgledy-piggledy everywhere as usual. Mistress Crawford would have a fit! Annie always thought when she compared this muddle with the order back on Clachan's Farm. 'Oh, what's on today?' she sniffed appreciatively as a rich odour wafted out from a giant iron casserole on the great blackened range. That's one thing the Missus would not have criticised, she thought. These folk can cook!

Francine lifted the lid and with the air of a connoisseur, murmured, 'Pot au feu a la Normandienne.'

'How do you know that?' Annie gasped in admiration.

'It's a stew and the cook comes from Normandy!' Francine giggled.

'Come on out, you two,' Jules bawled in the back. 'There's a lad here who walked barefoot all the way from Marseille to hear Annie sing!'

'Oh, get away, Jules!' Annie knew he was teasing, but now there was always a request for 'la Petite Ecossaise' when she came with Francine.

The first time Annie sung was when someone had requested 'something English' and Louis had turned to her jokingly demanding a song. There was a growing vogue in Paris for English songs, or risqué French songs sung with a mock English accent. Louis insisted the Chat Roux couldn't be left behind.

Annie had responded with her usual cheery willingness and, bright curls escaping from their pins, jumped up onto the platform stage set at the back of the cafe. Acts had to be short, for the low roof and the simple gas footlights made it so hot, singers could only take about ten minutes before they had to jump down and recover.

Annie had stood there for a moment looking at the sea of faces below and hearing the high chatter of their French, so different from the couthy tones of Ayrshire. A great wave of nostalgia for

Craigdrummond gave her inspiration. In her clear lovely soprano that rang round the smoky bar, she sang as if she was walking along the cliffs on a summer day with the breeze in her face and the seagulls wheeling and skimming down towards Galloway.

'For I say bonnie lassie will ye come wi' me,
To share my fate in a far country,
To share my lot when doon falls a'
And to gang out o'er the hills to Gallawa'?'

'Oh the Gallawa hills are covered wi' broom
Wi' heather bells in bonnie bloom,
Wi' heather bells and rivers a'
And we'll gang out o'er the hills to Gallawa''

'Quiet, you idiots!' Louis had snapped to Jules and Marcelle who were chatting loudly when Annie began, but he hardly had to call for silence as her first notes rang out. Not a single soul in the cafe had understood a word, but with Gallic insight and sentiment, they had all heard real feeling and the longing of a hungry soul in the sweet but powerful voice and lovely haunting tune. Not a sound was heard till she had finished then, to thunderous applause, Louis had helped her down from the platform. His eyes glistened and he had kissed her warmly on both cheeks. 'Now you will sing everytime you come here, Annie,' he had said.

'Och, with pleasure, Louis, though you'll soon be tired of me.' Annie felt it was little to give in return for the undemanding camaradie that was offered so generously.

'Never,' Louis had replied with a gentle, enigmatic smile. 'Never.'

'Never is a long time, Louis,' she had replied with a cheery grin.

'But eternity is longer,' he had said and lifted her fingers to his lips.

She'd watched as he disappeared confidently into the crowd round the bar. Louis Lamarche was an enigma. A cultivated man, he had a passionate interest in the extreme French politics of the day, which as Annie had remarked in her letter home, were most turbulent in 'fin de siècle' Paris. He and Francine had inherited a small printing business in Picardie when his parents died, and he had been expected to follow his father in the industry. But Louis

151

was already a lost soul. After one visit with an uncle to the Moulin Rouge some years before, surrounded by dancers, artists, thinkers, radicals and dreamers, rich and poor milling in chaotic democracy, he had found a metier that excited and stimulated his own complex nature. Louis bided his time, secretly longing to run somewhere in Montmartre himself to rival the Moulin, a place where the entertainment would be superb and where people could express their views without restraint over a coffee or a drink.

After his father's funeral, he sold up with almost indecent haste. Then he paid for Francine to train as a lady's maid and saw her settled with a good Mistress before he sank everything he possessed into the Cafe Chat Roux. The Chat Roux was typical of its genre, embracing the crudity of the chahut or cancan, with the same fervour as it did the finer spirit of the nineteenth century's last wild, schizophrenic decade.

Francine had since changed employer, moving to Paris and the Berry establishment. Louis was always glad to see her, and more so now she usually brought Annie.

Annie looked forward to her visits with a lift of her heart. It was a perfect antidote to the tense and finicky world of the Misses Berry and Alexandra's exciting but unpredictable temperament.

'Annie! Give us a fast one today!' Marcelle shouted as she passed, flushed and laughing. 'I need cheering up. Last time, you made me weep so much I had salt in my "petit vert" ... what a waste!'

'Right you are, Marcelle,' Annie had an easy way with these ordinary folk who were little different from those she had grown up with. 'I promise nobody will cry tonight ...'

With a toss of her head, she gave a rough translation of what the song was all about, 'This is a song about a girl who goes to marry her gentleman friend and finds he has run off with another. So here is what she does ...' Then hands on hips, she began a music hall tune her mother loved her to sing. Some of it she sang in English, then repeated in French, by the end she was wiping tears of mirth from her own eyes, as with gusto, artisan, artist, anarchist, pimp, player and prostitute gaily made mincemeat of the English chorus.

Ignoring calls for more, she jumped down and pushed her way

back through to the kitchen where Francine was huddled in a corner, looking unusually serious as she talked with her brother.

'Bonjour, Louis,' Annie joined them with a smile. 'Jules thought we might miss you tonight since we have to be back early.'

'I wouldn't miss you both for the world.' He kissed her on both cheeks. 'Oh you were wonderful again, tonight, Annie. I watched till you finished, didn't you see me? You could make a career of this, you know,' he concluded gallantly.

'I've no inclination,' Annie replied thinking of the long evenings and hard life of the women who sung in the 'cafe concs', the rough music halls of Paris, or even those few who made it to the bigger stages of the Moulin Rouge or Les Ambassadeurs.

'Probably wise, it's not easy to make a living,' Louis agreed.

'Chocolate as usual, or maybe a little coffee? Just brewed.' Francine held up the long-handled coffee can stewing gently by the open fire on a blackened trivet.

'Chocolate, please, Francine,' she replied.

'Me too,' Louis said, 'it fills me up better and I've a lot still to do tonight.'

'And you need to take a rest,' she frowned at his slight frame, so different from the sturdy lads on the farm. 'You work hard, mon ami, too hard,' Annie chided. She had become fond of Francine's delicate-looking brother who nevertheless still managed to run the Chat Roux and its curious mix of artistes and clientele with a firm hand.

'At least I'm getting results, not like some of those poor sods!' He nodded towards a group of workers building the new Paris Metro, dirty, ragged and exhausted after long shifts underground, drinking their pittance of pay. They would have cleared off to cheaper places once the night's more sophisticated entertainment began. 'The Cafe Chat Roux is becoming one of the best in Paris! Soon we will be better than the Chat Noir or Le Mirilabis!' His eyes glistened in the gas light, then he relaxed. 'Anyway, I've almost finished my plans for the next month. I was talking to a great singer, a young man ... what feeling, what quality ... hope I get him before the others! But now, there are some books I must close.'

'So you're doing well, businessman?' Francine teased.

153

'Very well ... double the bookings from last week and good quality acts. Yes, ma chère soeur, things are going well for my little enterprise. Soon I'll be opening another cafe ... or more likely expanding ... the place next door is coming up for lease soon.'

'Hard work always pays!' Annie broke in, then hesitated remembering Mistress Crawford's words as if from another life. 'Or so they say.'

Francine laughed. 'Maybe I'd be tempted to join you one day, mon frère,' she said with an odd tone in her voice. 'But now I have other plans.'

'Other plans?' Annie asked.

'That's what I was telling Louis when you came in. I've been offered a new job in Tours. A very good job, far better than the one at the Berrys,' Francine said quietly.

'You didn't say a word!' Annie looked hurt.

'I didn't know till yesterday,' Francine took her hands. 'The offer came through my old employer who recommended me. I wanted to tell you and Louis at the same time.'

'Oh, Francine, what will I do without you?' Annie felt overwhelmingly sad. 'When do you go?'

'June, if all's well.'

'At least there's a little time left,' Annie replied.

'And maybe you will be leaving with Miss Alexandra by then too.'

'Maybe.'

'But while you are in Paris, you will still come here?' Louis asked Annie anxiously.

'Of course, if you want, at least during the day,' Annie replied, but in her heart she couldn't see herself making the long trek up to Monmartre alone especially in the evenings.

'If I want?' Louis deep brown eyes burned in his pale face, but he understood her concern. 'I can come for you if you wish, the way is dangerous for a woman on her own.'

'Oh, don't worry, Louis, we can cross that bridge when we come to it, I must go and say goodbye to the others.' Annie was still sad to be losing Francine and didn't want to dwell on it now. 'We need to get back to work soon.'

'But do come, I think you bring me luck, chérie, things have gone well since you began to come,' Louis persisted, following

her through into the noisy bar which was already almost full and
waiting for the main show. 'Oh and here, these are for you.
Thank you for the song.' From the shelf behind the bar he
produced a bunch of glowing flowers and presented them to
her in front of the barstaff and customers. 'Straight from the
market before they closed ... I just happened to see them and
they would have been for the bar if you and Francine hadn't
come tonight ...'

'Oh, look at those big soft eyes! What a man ... struck
through the heart and dying of love! Cupid has hit our boss at
last!' Jules the barman and the others grinned and poked fun as
Annie took the bunch and Louis kissed her hand.

Annie blushed, it wasn't the way in Ayrshire, or the
Gallowgate, for a man to carry bunches of flowers through the
town and present them to lassies in public ... or to kiss hands in
front of the world and his wife, but she didn't want to hurt Louis'
feelings by pulling away. He and Francine had been so kind.
Annie had long suspected Louis was sweet on her, but Francine's
sudden announcement seemed to have precipitated him into
action.

'Oh, Louis, there's no need, I sing for free because I like you
all,' she protested, but he just smiled at her, eyes shining.

Craigdrummond was far from Paris and the life she led here,
but it was still in her heart and anyway, no one could replace Ian.
I'll have to be careful not to lead the lad on, he's too nice for
that, she mused, as she and Francine walked the long way back.
For once they hardly spoke, each lost in her own thoughts.

'Is my little brother much like Papa?' Alexandra asked Lord
Ballantyne.

'Er ... I suspect so,' Ballantyne couldn't for the life of him
think who the child he had seen so briefly resembled. 'At four
months, it's hard to tell. But you'll see for yourself at the christening in June.'

'It is so good of you to come personally with all these little
messages from Craigdrummond. You must go out of your way.'
Alexandra looked at him from under long, dark gold lashes.

'Oh, not a bit!' He dismissed her comment with an indulgent
wave of his hand. 'I'm in Paris regularly as you know, on er ...
business ...' He hastily pushed away a picture of the coquette who

had spent the previous afternoon amusing him in a silken salon. 'And visiting the prettiest young lady in the city is hardly a chore!'

'How kind you are,' Alexandra laughed. This was the fifth time the peer had visited her in the past year and a half, mostly, but not always, with the knowledge of her father. Alexandra knew very well that Lord Ballantyne was not driven by pure kindness, but doted more and more on her. Most men did. And though he was far too old to be a beau, she loved the power she so clearly wielded over him.

'And Stepmother, how is she?' Alexandra remembered to ask, knowing it was expected.

'Lady Cameron is very well. It was she who insisted that the christening be in June when you could come home.'

'How kind.' She sounded genuinely pleased. 'Do thank her for me.'

'I will.' Ballantyne had heard rumours that all was not well between the two Cameron women, but clearly tongues had been wagging erroneously. 'You know, Alexandra, I think Paris has done you good. You make all the women in Scotland seem ... er ...' he fumbled for the words, '... quite provincial ... you'd even turn heads in London ...' He flushed deeply. 'Oh, do excuse my familiarity, but it only seems yesterday since you were in short skirts,' he took refuge in an avuncular tone.

'Yes, quite.' The humiliation of that first meeting still rankled and was one of the reasons she loved to flirt with the older man.

'But are you happy here?' he asked gently.

'Very, I adore Paris,' she nodded. 'And Papa has promised that I can make my official debut soon. That will be wonderful!' Her blue eyes shone.

'I just hope you don't decide to marry too quickly and leave the rest of us bereft,' he cautioned. 'I believe your stepmother would enjoy your company for a time at Craigdrummond before you disappear to become lady of some castle.'

'Hmmm ...' Alexandra sounded sceptical.

'Shall we take some air?' he asked.

'Delighted.' Alexandra enjoyed Ballantyne's visits. The Misses Berry treated him with greatest deference, allowing them the use of the private front parlour, in full knowledge of Lord Cameron's approval. 'I'll just call Annie to fetch my jacket.'

Annie came at once with the finely-tailored garment, having

anticipated what Alexandra would want and helped her mistress into the jacket. 'Ah, yes, Annie, that reminds me,' Edward Ballantyne said brightly in the condescending tone he habitually used with inferiors, 'I have some news for you too, girl.'

'For me?' Annie echoed in surprise.

'Yes,' he went on cheerfully. 'I was out hunting accompanied by Lord Cameron's keeper ... fine fellow ... across Rannoch's farmland. He mentioned that the tenancy was being changed. It seems there will be celebrations at the farm where you used to work because of it. Thought of you. Almost forgot to tell you. Now I have.' He flushed at his own magnanimity. 'Pity you can't be there, eh, girl?'

'Celebrations?' Annie felt a cold hand grasp her heart.

'Yes, your farmer's son, Clachan, isn't it? Yes, young Clachan is marrying the daughter of Rannoch and taking over. Good bit of business there, eh?'

'Taking over?' Annie heard herself repeat him again like an idiot.

'Quite a to do when Farmer Rannoch dropped dead, but they seemed to have sorted things out well between them all.' He turned to Alexandra, 'Excellent people, your father's tenants.'

'Certainly,' Alexandra dismissed the comment with a wave of her hand and, ignoring Annie who stood rooted to the spot, the two of them left.

Annie remained gazing into space, sick to the stomach and white as her starched pinny. At least I don't have to see them together, was all the comfort she could derive from the news.

'When do you go back, Lord Ballantyne?' Alexandra asked as they walked among the other strolling couples through the fashionable Bois de Boulogne.

'Tomorrow,' he answered. 'But do call me Edward, dear girl, no need for formality now, eh?' He smiled. 'I will be visiting your parents next week, Alexandra, may I deliver a return message from you?'

'Of course ... Edward,' Alexandra replied demurely. 'Tell them I look forward eagerly to June.'

'And I, Alexandra.' Ballantyne was to be godfather. 'Shall we take some refreshment?' he suggested.

'Yes, please.'

157

Alexandra has grown into a stunningly elegant young woman, he thought as her skirts swished softly on the gravel. Aloud he said heartily, 'Here we are, my dear,' and led the way towards a cafe frequented by the elite of Paris society.

'You know Annie is strange sometimes,' Alexandra mused.

'Your little milkmaid?' he asked, raising his eyebrows.

'Yes,' Alexandra nodded. 'She almost seems more at home in Paris than I am ... though not in the same way, of course ...' she floundered looking for the right words.

'I should hope not!' Lord Ballantyne commented sharply. He turned and ordered a coffee for himself and hot chocolate for Alexandra.

'No, I mean it,' she went on in a thoughtful tone. 'In a way Paris has changed her ... somehow I don't feel I know much about what she does when she is not with me ... and that is rather often now we are so busy with, er ... cultural matters,' she added demurely.

'Well, good grief, Alexandra, one should not get too close to servants in any case!' Lord Ballantyne frowned, 'What does it matter what the girl does off-duty as long as she is clean, efficient and in attendance when she should be?'

Alexandra went on as if he hadn't spoken. 'You know that she speaks French ... just like the natives ... and with some expressions which make the Misses Berry turn pale, I believe!' Suddenly she laughed so the feathers on her hat bobbed. Underneath, her hair was arranged becomingly in the latest style and shone like gold.

Forgetting his momentary disapproval, Lord Ballantyne was enchanted, Alexandra wasn't just elegant, she was very beautiful. Others thought so too. With a jolt he noticed the admiring glances his lovely companion drew from almost every man in the room. 'So all's well with your milkmaid,' he murmured absently.

'Yes,' Alexandra nodded, then said unexpectedly. 'No one understands me like Annie Ramsay. I would be lost without her.'

'Don't exaggerate, my dear Alexandra!' The peer was shocked out of his absent mood by her vehemence. 'Maids are servants, they are not meant to be companions. In any case, I'm sure you will have the girl for a long time yet. She couldn't possibly get a position which pays as well. Cameron has been exceptionally generous with her, I believe.' Ballantyne shrugged, dismissing the subject.

'Annie is staying with me for ever!' Alexandra's eyes were narrowed and possessive.

Young women, thought Lord Ballantyne with a sigh, even utterly lovely ones, are always so dramatic. He replied soothingly, 'Well, when you have your own household, perhaps your husband will let her continue with you and she will no doubt be monarch over a whole bevvy of maids. It was certainly a good day's work for her when she helped you on the Moss.' In his closeness to her father, Edward Ballantyne was one of the few people who knew the full story.

'And for me!' she said. 'I owe my life to her.'

'Ah well, that is all best forgotten, Alexandra. The incident was a long time ago now.' Ballantyne, like Cameron, had never felt comfortable with the idea that a daughter of Cameron of Craigdrummond owed her life to a milkmaid. 'Whatever happened that evening, the girl has been handsomely rewarded for it.'

'Oh I suppose so,' Alexandra replied in a more subdued tone and sipped her chocolate. She had spotted one of the young men who paid secret court to her, and hoped he would not make a move, not now, not with Lord Ballantyne guarding her like a lion with his favourite lioness.

The two of them sat quietly for a moment lost in their own thoughts.

Alexandra shouldn't become too attached to that farm-girl, it's not the thing! Don't know why Cameron agreed to it in the first place. Ballantyne frowned to himself. But once she marries she'll have more to think about than a maid. And if her father agrees to me offering my suit to Alexandra when she is eighteen then that will be very soon. Cameron has not rebuffed my moves there ... he even seems quite pleased. The peer looked indulgently at Alexandra, sitting demure and lovely opposite him, a smile playing round her delightful lips.

Edward felt a surge of sheer desire. Indeed the lass is lively and she could greatly benefit from the influence of an older man in her life ... someone who could teach her a thing or two ... not to mention the wealth and position she would have as my wife. But don't rush the fences, Edward Baird, he told himself. Patience man, or you'll make the filly shy!

'Finished, my dear?' he said out loud after a few minutes. And arm in arm they continued their stroll.

'We're going back to Craigdrummond!' Alexandra announced throwing her jacket over the chair.

'For good?' All afternoon Annie had fought to keep from dwelling on the news delivered so carelessly by Lord Ballantyne earlier. And now this! Her heart started to pound so hard in her chest, she could hardly draw breath.

'No, silly!' Alexandra replied. 'For my little brother's christening ... we're going in June! Lord Ballantyne told me since he will be godfather. And he delivered a letter from Papa to the same effect.'

'Imagine that!' Annie still stood like a statue.

'Is that all you can say?' Alexandra was disappointed that her news had not brought more reaction. 'There will be celebrations on the estate, I'm told. Maybe you'll even get a chance to sneak off to your little farm!'

'Aye, maybe so,' Annie said evenly and turned away, eyes suddenly filled with tears. She rummaged in a cupboard till her body stopped shaking and her feelings were more under control.

As soon as Alexandra mentioned the celebrations, Clachan's kitchen came to mind, smelling of pastry and pies, with home-made ale frothing in tankards and maybe a whisky or two for the men to toast the head of the heir to Craigdrummond. The vision hit her with a presence so physical it ached like a stone in her heart.

'Papa will surely hold a celebration dinner for his friends. Oh, I'm so glad I can be there. I have such lovely things to wear!' Alexandra had forgotten all about Annie. 'Now where is my new boater ... the one with the double ribbon and pink roses?'

By the end of the next week Annie was glad to escape to the Chat Roux. Francine was still on duty, but she braved the long walk alone since it was afternoon and there were plenty of people about even in the meanest streets. Alexandra was so full of the christening and what she would wear, that Annie felt her nerves rubbed raw by her excited, demanding moods.

'Annie, you look quite exhausted,' Louis exclaimed when he saw her drawn face. Concerned, he put his arm round her shoulders, 'Come into the kitchen and we can take some chocolate. The bar is quiet yet … anyway, Jules can take care of things for a while.'

'It's nothing, Louis, I'm just tired, it's been a heavy week,' she began, then sighed so sadly, he came over and sat beside her on the bench by the fire.

'What has happened, ma chérie? Oh excuse me!' He raised a hand and stifled the cough that seemed to be more frequent these days.

Despite her own worries, Annie noticed his pale face flush. I hope he's not heading for the same thing that worried Doctor Murchieson when he got me out of the 'baccy factory. Poor Louis, she thought, he doesn't deserve that.

'Ma chérie?' he insisted. 'Tell me.'

'I'm not sure you'd want to know,' she knew by now he harboured hopes of the two of them getting together.

'Of course I want to know! Is it a man?' Louis asked, flushing. 'Has someone been unkind to you? If he has, I would like to kill him!'

'Yes, it's a man,' she admitted, 'but no, he's not been unkind … at least not deliberately, so you don't have to kill him, Louis.' Despite her sorrow, she was amused at Louis' Gallic vehemence. 'He's doing his duty, that's all … so he can't marry me.'

'Mon Dieu! He is putting someone before you?' Louis's genuine incredulity was balm to her sad heart.

She managed a wan smile. 'I told him long ago he must. I just didn't expect it would hurt so much to hear that it is happening at last after nearly two years.'

'Tell me,' he insisted. 'Tell me the whole story.'

'Well, if you're sure …'

'I'm very sure!' he insisted.

As simply as possible she told him of the farm, of her feelings for Ian and the fact that he was to marry Betty.

'Love is not something that can be controlled by us at will, Annie. We French understand that love is a force which writes its own rules,' Louis said quietly. 'But even so, though you may still love this man, from what you say, he does not have the courage to fight for you.'

'Oh, I'm sure it's not a question of courage,' she said, stoutly defending Ian.

161

'Well,' Louis said kindly, 'then let us just say it is too late.'

'Yes, I know it is too late,' she agreed with such pain in her voice Louis really did want to kill the man who had been stupid or weak enough to let her go, but for her sake he smothered his feelings.

'So, just go back and do what you have to do with dignity,' he advised. 'Keep away from the farm. You will only stir up painful memories. And if you are lucky, maybe you won't have to meet him or his fiancée.'

'You're right, Louis.' Annie took his hand and squeezed it. 'I feel better now. It helps just to be able to talk to someone as sympathetic as you.'

'I'm always here if you need me,' he kissed her cheeks gently.

'And I'm grateful to have such a friend,' Annie replied sincerely.

Chapter Fourteen

Journeying back to Ayrshire took two long days, though express train and steam boat made it simple and extremely comfortable. Alexandra Cameron, her maid and a chaperone provided by the Berry sisters, travelled in luxury, with first-class facilities and all the modern technology available. Annie wondered as they sat in their fine private compartment reading by gas-light, on the last long leg of the journey north from London to Glasgow, how many miles they had covered together over the previous years round Europe. Odder still was how much she, the wee lass who at nearly sixteen had never been outside Glasgow, took such things as international travel quite for granted.

At Glasgow they were met by the Laird and escorted on the final short train journey to Craigdrummond. Annie could hardly contain herself as the dirty backyards of Glasgow gave way to countryside and then finally to the bonnie hills of Ayrshire.

'Och, here it is, at last!' she murmured as they pulled up at the very same platform she had tumbled onto, bundle in hand, just a few years before. A lifetime ago, she felt. That memory made her unexpectedly sad. Despite the grandeur of a waiting liveried carriage instead of a rough carter's cart, she knew she was bereft of something important.

It took her a fair bit of thinking as the carriage wheels spun towards Craigdrummond to realise what was missing. Annie Ramsay had lost her innocent optimism that the future would somehow work itself out and all would be well.

'Isn't Miss Alexandra bonnie as the day?' Mistress Crawford whispered to Doctor Murchieson as Alexandra, godmother to her new brother, swept down the aisle with Lord Ballantyne a supportive and handsome godfather. Outside as she had passed from carriage to kirk, rich and poor folk alike gasped and whispered their admiration for her Paris chic, the likes of which had rarely been seen in Glasgow, let alone Craigdrummond.

Archie Murchieson squeezed her arm meaningfully. 'In my eyes you are twice as bonnie, Bess.'

'Och, Archie.' She blushed like a girl and dabbed her eyes as the solemn words of the christening service began.

Today none of the farmers were in their usual pews. Only major tenants and a few others had been allocated places at all on one side. Opposite were senior staff from Craigdrummond. The front benches of the flower-strewn kirk were crammed with gentry from all over the country. In the row second from the back, Betty Rannoch stood beside Ian as his fiancée, together with her mother, Geordie, the housekeeper and Doctor Murchieson.

Betty's heart sang. It was sad her father had died and she truly missed him, but at least one good thing had come of it. Ian Clachan had named the day. Betty had begun to give up hope that they would wed this side of thirty. She had hoped for some promise from Ian when she turned twenty, but though pleasant as ever with her, he seemed disinclined to make the necessary commitment. But now in the wake of all tragedy, their wedding was fixed for next month and she stood beside him by right. I know he doesn't love me, the recurring thought disturbed her a little, but I'll be a good wife. And once the bairns arrive, Mamma says that romance dies anyway, Betty reassured herself.

Ian Clachan couldn't take his eyes off Annie Ramsay from the moment he realised she was standing in the pew opposite him. He was glad the attention of everyone was on the godparents and the bairn and he could feast on the sight he had longed to see once more.

Och, she's bonnier than ever, he thought admiringly as he noticed the proud carriage and confident bearing. The years away had added character to Annie's pert, lively face with its neat features and mouth that had always seemed on the point of laughter. 'Och, Annie, Annie!' Everything about her was achingly familiar, yet so womanly and so subtly changed. Only the chestnut curls were untamable, even now threatening to spill from under the smart new hat with the little decoration of flowers she wore in honour of her Mistress's baby brother.

Annie felt the intensity of someone watching her. Compelled, she sought out the source. With a shock that jolted her whole body she suddenly located it. Her face flushed then blanched before she had herself under full control. Ian Clachan, her Ian, was there with Betty possessively by his side.

'And why not?' Annie asked herself sadly. 'Betty is to be his wife, she has every right to be in my place. My place? Och, Annie Ramsay, what are you saying?' After all that had happened, her instinctive reaction astounded her.

From under lowered lashes, she glanced up again. At first she thought he hadn't changed at all, then she saw that manly lines of face and body had replaced the callowness of youth. Ian cut a fine figure in his Sunday best. As he turned towards her, she could see the old openness was still there. Brown eyes that had shone with love up on the long-rigg that summer evening two years ago, were looking at her now with naked longing.

Betty felt his attention wander, but thankfully didn't seek to see where. 'Ian!' She nudged him and he picked up his psalter with strong, capable hands that Annie knew could deliver a lamb with the gentlest of touches.

Annie dropped her gaze completely and tried not to look again, but she felt his presence burn like a flame. She knew, as she had always done, that she loved him. But it was too late, far too late to tell him so and far too late to ask him to do anything about it if she did.

Maria was glad when Urquhart slipped into the Cameron pew, leaving his lovely daughter with their new child. I always feel safe when he's with me, she thought. Still fragile from the birth and its traumas, she smiled lovingly at the man who shared her life. Although Maria still felt tears prick behind her eyes when she remembered how hostile Alexandra had been, but she pulled herself together sharply.

Lord Ballantyne, handsome and attentive as godfather, kept a possessive hand under Alexandra's elbow as she did her duty and together they made their responses. Watching the scene, Urquhart Cameron felt a deep sense of relief. The Misses Berry sent him regular reports. Alex was doing very well, but she needed strong guidance to hold her nervous disposition in check. She did not seem to find Ballantyne disagreeable, he thought. Maybe Edward is right. Early marriage to an older man could be the best thing for his difficult, lovely daughter. And Alexandra could do much worse than one of the richest and best pedigreed peers in Scotland.

The music rose and fell. The ceremony was over. As the choir sang like angels, slowly the procession from Craigdrummond House walked the length of the waiting congregation. Familiar faces watched from every corner of the crowded kirk. Outside, the rousing cheers of gathered villagers and tenants welcomed them with a skirl of pipes into the sunshine.

'Annie! I've been looking for you!' Doctor Murchieson, a little stouter but cheerful and kind as ever, puffed across the kirkyard. 'How are you, lass? Goodness me, you're the picture of health,' he said, shaking her hand.

'I'm fine, and you're in the pink yourself, Doctor, I can see,' Annie replied with a smile. 'Being back in Ayrshire is doing you good.'

'Aye, I was happy to hand over the old practice with those endless tenement stairs to young Chisholm ... in fact he's here somewhere ... we've been doing a wee bit of fishing together while he's on holiday.' He peered about. 'Not a sign. Och, the man must have been cornered on his way out ... he did a wee surgery with me last week ... just to keep his hand in, Annie.' Archie Murchieson had the grace to blush.

'Right enough,' Annie agreed, but doubted poor Doctor Chisholm had done it entirely voluntarily.

'Aye, that'll be it, some auld maid will be discussing her corns! The minute folk know your profession they're telling you all about their aches and pains.' He shook his head and sighed, but his smile was indulgent.

'Is that the doctor I've heard about from Mammy, Doctor Murchieson?' Annie asked.

'Indeed it is, lass. And what do your folks think of the lad?'

Annie smiled broadly. 'Mammy thinks the sun and moon rise and set in him ... after yourself ...' she added quickly.

'Don't worry about my feelings, lass,' the doctor chortled, 'that kind of comparison I can readily accept if it means I don't have to do the job! Talk of the devil, here he is ...'

'Phew! There isn't a thing I don't know about the medical history of that lady in the green bonnet!' John Chisholm groaned as he joined his colleague.

'Don't count on it, John, that was Miss Storey you were talking to,' Archie Murchieson warned. 'Storey by name and by nature. What you've just had is only part one. There's plenty more episodes where that came from, believe me. And there's nothing ageing spinsters enjoy more than cornering a handsome young doctor ... unless it's a fine young Minister, fresh from the Presbytry, starched collar and all.'

'Maybe that, though you're generous in your description of me, Archie,' Doctor Chisholm laughed and his questioning gaze fell on Annie standing by the doctor's side, smiling in amusement at the exchange.

Archie Murchieson noticed his glance and said, 'Oh aye, I'm lacking in my social graces as always.' He drew Annie forward. 'Now here is someone I've been hoping you would meet, John.'

'A pleasure,' John Chisholm smiled at the attractive, neatly dressed young woman by his mentor's side.

'Annie, this is Doctor John Chisholm. John, may I introduce Miss Annie Ramsay. You treat her family in your practice.'

'Ramsay? Oh, I don't think I do,' he replied in a puzzled tone, trying to place her. 'The only Ramsays I have are in the Cowc ...' he trailed off.

That will be them right enough,' Annie said with a proud lift of chestnut curls crowned with her Sunday best felt hat. 'Mammy, Sandy, Eddie, the twins and all! I think they're still with you, though they've just moved away from the Gallowgate, Doctor Chisholm.'

'So they have ... er ... now I remember ... to a much nicer area off Charing Cross, I have a few patients there.' John Chisholm could have cursed himself for his ineptitude and Archie Murchieson's well meaning but naive introduction. It was hard to reconcile this self-assured lass with poverty stricken, terminally worried, Mistress Ramsay who had only recently begun to pay her medical bills.

Archie was unaware of the embarrassment he had caused. Beaming he went on, 'You know, John, when I first met Annie she was stuck in that terrible Cowcadden tenement, working in a tobacco factory and heading straight for the TB asylum. And just

167

look at what a fine lassie she's turned into.'

'Do you live in Ayrshire now, Miss Ramsay?' John Chisholm tried to deflect Archie's good-natured clumsiness which was causing Annie to blush to the roots of her chestnut hair.

'I live in Paris,' Annie recovered quickly and answered with her cheery smile. 'I'm lady's maid to Mistress Alexandra.'

'Oh?' he was puzzled again. 'So, Doctor Murchieson was joking ...?'

'Not a bit. Thanks to Doctor Murchieson, I left Gallowgate a while back and I've been lucky enough to better myself,' she said with natural dignity. 'But it's a long story. Maybe he'll tell you himself.'

'Now, where has Bess got to?' Archie, still oblivious to the awkwardness he had created, craned his neck and tried to see over the heads of the crowd. 'Oh, here she is ... Bess, Bess, look who I've found at last.' He called Mistress Crawford over.

John Chisholm took his leave. 'Nice to meet you, Miss Ramsay.' He tipped his hat and moved quickly away.

Annie murmured a goodbye, but hardly noticed him leave, her attention was fixed on the approaching formidable figure of Mistress Crawford, splendid in her Sunday best black bombazine.

'Annie, what a pleasant surprise!' Despite the friendly words, the housekeeper was ill at ease. 'Are you well?' she asked, but her eyes darted uneasily around.

'Just grand,' Annie replied stiffly, hoping the doctor would not notice the tension between them.

'We must find Ian and tell him Annie's here. Och, it's impossible to find anybody in this mêlée!' Doctor Murchieson peered across the crowded kirkyard. 'Do you know where he and Betty have got to?' Bess had clearly not confided in him and Annie was frozen to the spot, unsure of what to do. 'You remember Betty, don't you, Annie?' he asked with a cheerful beam. Then his face became solemn. 'Pity about Rabbie Rannoch, though. Attended the poor man myself. Not a thing I could do. Dead before he hit the ground, I suspect. Hearts are funny things, baffle even doctors at times. The man looked the picture of health!'

'I heard about that,' Annie said. 'What a shame.'

'Aye, well, it's nearly six months back now. Life goes on,' Bess Crawford snapped, bringing a look of surprise to Doctor

168

Murchieson's face. 'But since you've asked, Archie, I think Ian and Betty have gone off with Elsie Rannoch. I saw her corner them as they came out. Och, there's always a lot to do when weddings are afoot,' she added with a strained smile. 'Betty is off to Glasgow in the morning to buy stuff for her bridal gown.' Bess was taking no chances that Annie might not have heard that piece of news too.

'Aye, well, I wouldn't want to bother Ian now anyway,' Annie said. 'I have to go to Craigdrummond in a minute and take my place for the staff photograph with the Laird's family and the bairn. Just tell him I wish them all the best.' She made an effort to sound polite.

'Of course, lass, and may your life go on being as happy and fulfilled as it clearly is now. Goodbye.' Doctor Murchieson shook her hand warmly again, then turned to talk to a passing patient.

Annie pushed desperately forward towards where the other staff were gathering by the long line of Cameron carriages.

'Annie!' Geordie Clachan grasped her arm as she became tangled in the crowds.

'How are you, Fairmer?' she smiled, trying to hide her dismay. Everybody from Clachan's Farm seemed to be there. As long as I don't meet Ian and Betty, she thought pushing down a wave of panic, that would be more than she could bear.

'Getting older by the day!' Geordie Clachan smiled. 'Och, but it's great to see you, lass.' He had always had a soft spot for cheery Annie Ramsay with her happy laugh, sweet voice and her courage. 'The farmhands are forever asking how you are ... but we never have any news to give them, Annie, not a thing!' he chided.

'Aye, well, I better pull my socks up on that one,' Annie lied gamely. Bess had made it clear the break should be a complete one and had never replied to a tentative letter Annie had sent early on.

'Och, but now we can hear what you've been up to from the horse's mouth instead, so to speak,' said Geordie. 'Nobody turns a hair any more that you're working for the Camerons ... great folk have their ways and humble folk follow without questioning much. All the hands had heard by the time you'd been gone a few weeks or so! So, when will you be coming over to Clachan's Farm?'

'Well, I hadn't thought ...' Annie hesitated in confusion, feelings in a turmoil and not knowing how to reply.

'What's this, are ye too grand for us?' Geordie grinned. 'Of course you will. Now promise!' he insisted.

Annie's longing to see the farm and its folk just once more, overcame all other reservations and fears. 'I've a while off tomorrow afternoon, maybe I'll come then,' she replied.

'No maybes! I'll tell Bess to expect you tomorrow afternoon,' he threw cheerily over his shoulder as he disappeared into the throng.

'Och, what in the name have I done?' Mention of the housekeeper had brought her back to reality with a bump. Since they had arrived, the upheaval and celebrations of the christening had taken every minute. Annie had been glad there was so much to do. Until the meeting at the kirk, she had told herself that Louis was right, she must keep away from Clachan's Farm, but Geordie had unwittingly changed all that. 'And it's too late to back out now!' she whispered.

'Come on, Annie Ramsay, what are ye doing standing there as if ye've seen a dozen ghosts?' Davie Murray, Craigdrummond's butler called sharply. 'Hop up on the trap, the photographers are already placing folk for a photo of the family and staff.'

Annie's heart was beating like a drum as she walked the couple of miles to Clachan's Farm from Craigdrummond House. She could have gone to her old work-place in a trap with a stablehand driving, but the thought hadn't even occurred to her. Every step was precious.

In her mind's eye Annie saw herself again, a wee lass on her way to a future unknown, in a well-darned coat and clumsily patched boots, a bundle of second-hand clothes wrapped in an old shawl. So much had happened since it was sometimes hard to credit. 'And it's funny,' she mused aloud, 'I'm nearly as nervous going to Clachan's Farm this time as I was then.'

Her footsteps slowed, as she began to wonder whether Mistress Crawford would be as pleased to welcome her again as the farmer. She knew the answer to that question but she was prepared to brave it out for half an hour or so. And Ian? ... Och, maybe he'll be working and I won't see him at all, she pushed away that painful idea. Despite Louis' warning there was no use denying anymore that it was Ian, above all, she wanted to see just once more without Betty Rannoch in tow. We're leaving again in two days time for France, maybe for ever, she thought. What harm can it do? The longing to see Ian and the farm where she had been so happy, pulled her like a lode-stone and she quickened her pace again.

The sun shone high in the late June sky and little fair-weather clouds scudded here and there like lambs at play. Her steps were light and confident. Swiftly she covered the distance. Now and then a little sob of anticipation broke from her throat as her young legs carried her nearer the place she had dreamed of for so long.

Two long years, she thought. How many times in Paris or Rome, or Vienna, had she longed to walk on the moor, to breathe the pure air and smell the glorious mixture of wild flowers, heather and the sea that was her beloved Craigdrummond? Countless! Och, at last, at last!

At the brow of the hill she stopped. 'There it is, Och, I could never forget it, even for a minute!' Annie whispered aloud and stopped to drink in the sight. The farmhouse nestled below in the cosy hollow that kept the salty winter winds from biting too fiercely. In the surrounding home-fields, the big herds of cows were peacefully grazing, waiting patiently for Dougie to drive them into the byre for milking. 'I'm glad the cook told me that Maisie's left,' Annie smiled to herself. 'She's one person I don't want to meet!'

As she covered the last few hundred yards downhill, her steps quickened of their own accord till she almost ran.

Without allowing herself any hesitation, she crossed the yard and slipped in the back door as she had always done. The line of working coats hung ignored on the porch pegs on this fine summer afternoon. Annie tapped on the kitchen door, suddenly shy.

'Come in!' Mistress Crawford's familiar voice called out.

'It's me, Missus.' Annie stuck her head round the door.

Geordie Clachan sat at the table going through the accounts as he did so often. This was all as it should be. As she looked across the kitchen, for a moment Annie felt as if she had just come in from milking. Paris vanished from her mind and with it the years in between.

'Och, it's lovely to be back, so it is!' Annie felt a great wave of emotion catch her breath. She looked around, greedy for the sight she had dreamed of so long. The kitchen at least was unchanged. Despite the warm June afternoon, as always the range was piping hot and covered in pots. The windows stood wide open and the rich smells of the farmyard mingled with the tantalising odours from bubbling broth and baking bread in one great harmony. Geordie saw her and his wide smile, so like Ian's, broke across his face. 'See I told ye she would come, Bess ... it's Annie! Come in, come in, lass!'

'Aye, come in, Annie.' Mistress Crawford drew her inside. The housekeeper spoke warmly enough in front of the farmer, but her heart sank. She had counted on Annie staying away. Och well, she thought, I'll try to get her in and out before the men finish in the fields.

Geordie Clachan dashed that hope straight away. 'You'll be staying for supper, Annie?' he asked as she came hesitantly into the room. 'Ian will be pleased to see you and the other lads and lassies too. Won't they, Bess?'

'I suppose they will,' Mistress Crawford replied with a frown.

'And would you credit it?' Geordie went on, missing any tension between the two women. 'The Doctor is coming over tonight as well. He'll be staying for supper too. Och, isn't that just the thing? Mind you, he practically lives here when he's not working, doesn't he, Bess? And we all know what brings him!'

Mistress Crawford's colour deepened. 'So you say, Geordie. But maybe Annie has other things planned for this evening.' She gave Annie a meaningful look then turned back to the range.

'Er ...' Annie floundered, shooting a quizzical glance again at the housekeeper who was busy lifting a pot and didn't seem inclined to make any further comment. 'Och, maybe some other time, Fairmer ...'

'Now I'm not standing for that!' Geordie said firmly. 'Guid knows when you'll be back, if at all, with all the gallivanting fine folk do these days. And even Miss Alexandra must understand that you need a bit of time off, Annie, while you're here.'

'Och, it's not Miss Alexandra ...' Annie mumbled.

'There you are then, we're all agog to hear about what goes on in Paris. You're not expected to eat at Craigdrummond, are you?

You can surely take a bite of supper with your ain folk?' he demanded.

'My ain folk!' Clachan's Annie was back. She stood wordlessly blinking back sudden tears that threatened to spill. The farmer was right, this would be the last time she would ever be able to sit in the big kitchen and eat supper with those she had worked alongside and learned to love. Soon Betty Rannoch would be Mistress Clachan and likely to be here by right. Making up her mind and damning the consequences, she managed to say in a clear, firm voice, ignoring the shock on Mistress Crawford's face, 'No, Fairmer, I've the whole evening off. In fact I'm not on duty till tomorrow late morning. Miss Alexandra has gone visiting to Ayr with Lady Cameron and the bairn.'

'Och, that's even better, you won't have to hurry away,' Geordie beamed. 'In fact, why not stay the night?' He looked over at the housekeeper who was busying herself at the stove, her back turned to them. 'Annie's old room is still empty since she went, isn't it, Bess?'

Bess paused with the pot poised over the glowing hob, angry at the way things were turning out and wondering how she could refuse to let Annie stay without having to offer awkward explanations. Two faces watched hers expectantly, Annie with a small defiant frown, tensing herself against a refusal, and the farmer calm and sure of acceptance. After a pause while she carefully placed the pot on the hob, she said the only thing possible. 'Aye, it's empty.'

'Well, in that case we'll send word over to Craigdrummond with one of the lads that you'll be staying, Annie.' Geordie beamed happily. Unless you've become too fine for us and your old room up in the attics.'

'The day I become too fine for Clachan's Farm, attics and all, will be the day they lay me to rest in Craigdrummond kirkyard,' Annie smiled back at him.

'Come on then, what are you waiting for, Annie Ramsay?' Mistress Crawford realised she had no choice but to welcome Annie in the ways expected of her. There was no place for anger in the face of Geordie's innocent invitation. What's done is done, she thought with a resigned sigh. Surreptitiously she crossed her fingers that it would all work out. She gave in with as good grace as she could muster in the face of teasing fates that seemed to be bent on causing trouble. Handing Annie the paring knife with a smile that was almost normal, she said, 'Now get stuck into peeling those neeps and washing the new potatoes, Annie Ramsay, or supper won't be ready in time!'

'That's the ticket!' Geordie laughed. 'Set the lass to work! You know we'll not tolerate idle hands around here ... even those of a fine lady's maid!'

'Right you are!' Annie joined in his mirth. Her heart lifted and she pushed any lingering doubts aside. Gladly she took the parer, rolled up the sleeves of her blouse and tied on an apron. 'Och, it is good to be back among my "ain folk", even for a wee while.' Refusing to look beyond the moment, she smiled as her fingers flew through the old familiar tasks skilfully. With a pleasure that came from the soul, she rinsed the rich earth from glowing yellow new potatoes and cut the thick rind from golden turnips.

'I'll away to the byre for a minute to check the churn count.' Closing the books, Geordie went off and the two women were left alone.

'You'll be looking forward to going back to Paris, then?' Bess said as soon as he had gone.

'No,' Annie decided to be honest since there was so little left to lose. 'What if I asked to come back?'

'To Clachan's Farm?' Bess's face was aghast.

'No, but at least to Craigdrummond.'

'With Miss Alexandra?'

'Och, I'll be surprised if Miss Alexandra comes home once she is finished at the Misses Berrys, which will be in a couple of months time,' Annie said slowly.

'Oh? Why is that?'

'If the Laird approves, she'll likely stay with her aunt in London till she marries. She's bonnie, they'll be no shortage of suitors.'

'But then neither of you will be back in that case ... unless the Laird insists she comes home for a while anyway.'

Annie put down the parer and turned to face the older woman. 'Och, no, poor Lady Cameron has a terrible time with her and I think the Laird will choose to give his wife the peace she deserves, especially with the wee ones arriving.'

'Oh, there you are then.' Bess felt a load had been lifted from her shoulders.

'In fact, I've been thinking of leaving Miss Alexandra's service, once her time in Paris is over,' Annie said. 'She's not the easiest person to work for and I've nearly done the two years with her like I agreed to.'

'Well, I'm sure you could find another employer,' Bess Crawford replied, mouth tightening.

'I don't think I'd have to. Och, what I'm saying is that whatever is decided for Miss Alexandra, I had thought to come back anyway. Whatever I've seen and done, I miss Craigdrummond. And I like Lady Cameron, better than I like Miss Alexandra in a way, she's easier to get on with,' Annie explained. 'I know I could work for her at the big house if I asked, she's hinted as much.'

Bess stood watching Annie with an unreadable expression on her face, then said firmly, 'I don't think it would be wise for you to come back to Craigdrummond, Annie. It would cause more trouble than you think.'

'What do you mean?'

'Betty Rannoch will be living here when she becomes Mistress Clachan.'

'Like I said, it was never my idea to come back to the farm, Mistress.' Annie paused, puzzled. 'But in any case, won't they be living at Rannoch's?'

'Not right away, maybe not for many years. Elsie, Mistress Rannoch, doesn't want to leave her home for a while. Geordie and Ian are going to work the two farms together from now on. Ian will take over the lot when Geordie retires.'

'So Betty will be mistress here ...' Annie trailed off, then she asked with a frown. 'Are you staying on with her in charge?'

'I'll only stay long enough to see she can manage, then ... aye, well ...' She flushed. 'I hadn't thought to tell you this, Geordie wasn't far off the mark, I'm being wed myself.' The colour in her face deepened again.

'The Doctor?'

'Aye,' Bess's expression softened. 'Poor Archie's waited long enough for me, and with Ian being wed, the time is right.'

'Well, that's good news at any rate.' Annie began cutting the potatoes. 'But I don't see what's wrong with me working at Craigdrummond House whether Betty Rannoch lives here or at her own farm.'

'Well, there is and surely you're not that blind, Annie!' Bess said sharply. 'Just think, seeing Betty and Ian at kirk every Sunday, passing them in Craigdrummond village ... watching their bairns grow ... are you sure that's what you would want?'

'Maybe not,' Annie muttered.

'Now listen to me, Annie, there's something else you should know if you're thinking about coming back to Craigdrummond.' She left the stove and came over, leaning on the table.

'What?' Annie gave an involuntary shiver.

'Maisie told one of the Rannoch byre-lassies that you left because Ian was getting over fond and we had to get rid of you. And Maisie made sure there was more in the telling than the simple honest truth. Even when it became clear you were working for Miss Alexandra and that's why you went, it didn't help. Anything to do with that young lady, at least back then, was suspect ... it was as if the two of you were being banished together for your bad behaviour.'

'But you didn't have to get rid of me, that was just Maisie's rotten lies!'

Bess Crawford always put great store by the truth, but she felt that the situation was desperate enough to call for desperate measures. Her hopes and dreams for Ian were at stake ... 'Aye maybe,' she said slowly, 'but word got to Betty, as these things do, Annie ... and though she's a realistic lass and understands that lads must have had their wee fling before they settle down, enough is enough! Somehow I don't think Betty would want you anywhere around the Estate.'

Annie didn't pretend to misunderstand. 'Aye, I suppose there would be gossip and I don't want to live with that either.'

Annie sighed and turned back to the last of the vegetables, thinking of Alexandra's increasingly imperious moods. There was a distance between her and her mistress these days, that Annie marked from the time Lord Ballantyne became a regular visitor. It was fair enough, she thought, for she had never sought to be more than a maid, and at least it spared her Alexandra's more eccentric confidences. 'Och, well,' she told herself silently, 'Miss Alexandra always says she wants me to stay with her whatever happens, and the Laird's factor has given me a rise as well ... the family thinks I keep an eye on her. That'll be the day!' Annie gave an ironic little smile.

Bess broke the silence that had fallen, 'When is Miss Alexandra leaving?'

'The day after tomorrow.' Annie blinked hard and rinsed her hands.

'That soon?'

'Aye. She has taken to Paris and wants to go back as soon as she can. She's asked to stay there a few more months before she decides what she wants to do. I'll be packing for us both tomorrow.'

Bess stirred the bubbling pots and turned to a safer topic. 'And how are things going in Glasgow?'

'Not bad.' Annie was glad to stop all the talk about Ian and Betty and her own future. 'The bakery's doing fine and they're working all the hours God sends. In fact they want a bigger shop now ... but I'm not sure it's the right thing to do just yet. I'll know better when I see them. Sandy sent me a wee note asking me to drop in. Miss Alexandra has promised me a couple of hours free in Glasgow on the way back ... if she remembers and it still suits her.' Annie knew her capricious mistress.

'Bigger shop, eh? So it sounds as if your sacrifice has been worth it?' Mistress Crawford said quietly, looking intently at the dough in the bowl.

'Aye, I suppose so,' Annie replied in a tone that invited no further discussion. 'Right.' She dried her hands on the dish-cloth. 'If there aren't any more, then that's all the neeps and the potatoes done ... och, I can't wait to taste Ayrshire potatoes again, with some of our own butter!'

'No, that's the lot.'

Geordie came back and picked up a pitcher of water, pouring some into the big washing basin by the door. 'Still hard at it, Annie?'

'Well, at least she's not become too fine for the kitchen, Geordie,' Mistress Crawford replied in a voice she forced to sound hearty.

'Imagine coming on a visit after years away in foreign parts and having to make your own supper!' Geordie Clachan teased.

'Och, that's no bother.' Annie nodded in satisfaction at the piles of vegetables.

'Now if we just put those on the stove, you can watch they

don't boil over, Annie. I'll just away and get Ian,' Bess Crawford untied her pinny.

'Get Ian?' Geordie asked in surprise.

'I promised I'd send up the high-riggs and tell him when supper was nearly ready. The other men are in the low-riggs.'

'Send Leezie or Nellie,' Geordie threw over his shoulder as he splashed down his face and hands.

'Leezie isn't back from Craigdrummond yet with the wool I sent for and Nellie's working with the honey.'

'Then send Annie, the lad will like that,' the farmer said. 'He always talks kindly if your name comes up. I suppose he's missed you, Annie, like we all have.'

'Aye,' Bess cut in, 'though he's too busy these days to miss anybody, especially with the wedding coming up.'

Annie winced at the blatancy of the housekeeper's reminder.

'Aye, and Betty is a fine lass, with a good cantie nature,' the farmer agreed, 'though maybe not the bonniest in the country. Still like Bess says, she brings a fine tenancy with her! Ian can't wait to get his hands on it with all the new-fangled ideas he has. God help us all!' His proud smile belied the words. 'Though it's a shame everything has to be done in such a rush and in such circumstances, I wish the lad could have had a few more years before he took on a man's responsibilities. Still, that's the way of life.'

'Shall I go for Ian then, Mistress Crawford?' Annie hesitated.

Bess could have bitten her tongue out for saying a word. She regretted not just slipping quietly out and fetching Ian herself.

'Give the other lads a shout on the way back, Annie,' Geordie added.

Bess said lamely, 'Och, maybe you're too tired after all the work I've made you do ... you can't be used to it any more.'

'Tired? Not a bit of it! Looking after Miss Alexandra is harder than milking kye or peeling neeps any day!' Annie replied with a surge of rebellion. Not to mention helping out in the Chat Roux, she thought.

'Och, I still don't think ...' Bess went on objecting.

Even Annie's loyal nature was stretched to the limits. She resented the single-mindedness of the housekeeper's determined attempts to keep them apart. You'd think I was chasing Ian ... or ever did! So she tossed her curls, looked Bess straight in the eye

178

and said, 'Och, of course I'll go and fetch Ian, Mistress Crawford, and call the other lads.'

'Och, well all right ...' Secure in the fact that Annie would soon be gone and that she had done her duty by Betty, Bess felt she couldn't do more.

'You haven't forgotten the way?' the farmer teased.

'Not a step!' Annie smiled, hanging up the big apron and tucking her unruly hair under her smart Sunday boater. Though she had known as soon as she heard of Rabbie Rannoch's death, that any regrets she might have at turning Ian down were too late, it was more than she could bear not to seize the chance to see him alone just this once. Quickly she crossed the yard and sped away up the path to the upper fields.

With a worried frown, Mistress Crawford stood at the window and watched her go, sunlight glinting in her chestnut hair that still refused to be entirely tamed. Och, maybe I should have stopped her ... she worried, her thoughts racing. Aye, maybe it wasn't so wise. Annie Ramsay is even prettier now than she was a couple of years ago when she left. I ken Ian is marrying Betty from duty, little more. What if he lets that slip? Maybe I did lay a bit more butter on the bread than there really is, she concluded silently.

Annie had grown in the years she had been away, though at newly eighteen it was obvious she would never be tall. But, her neat figure and fine bearing left no doubt that she was a young woman, not a girl. The high-necked, white linen blouse and fine wool skirt in sober brown, belted in fine leather round her slim waist, paid tribute to the status of her job. And as Mistress Crawford had noticed, she had developed a presence and dignity that impressed. The years in Paris, mixing with high and lowly alike, had taught Annie much about human nature, both good and ill and it had added depth to her character.

No, thought Bess, it wasn't just Alexandra Cameron who had blossomed in Paris. 'Maybe I should follow her up ... och, don't be daft, Bess!' the housekeeper said aloud and forced herself to leave the window and get on with the supper. 'You can't keep them apart while she's here and she'll be gone tomorrow, straight back to Paris with Miss Alexandra ... then Ian will be safely wed!'

Absently she beat eggs into a batter with practised strokes.

179

Betty Rannoch is right for Ian, I believe she'll make him happy in the end, especially if they have a quiverful of bairns right away. He certainly seems more inclined to pass the time with her since he agreed to wed the lass ... you could call it becoming fond of her ... och, of course you could! With that comforting thought, she began dropping scones expertly onto the griddle and flipping them onto the wire-tray to cool.

Annie's well-shod feet flew across the familiar fields, higher and higher to where the upper riggs sheltered from the salty sea breezes behind a great ridge of rock. Suddenly she could see Ian Clachan, crouched down, carefully measuring the lengths and planning for new crops.

'Ian! Ian!' she called and waved.

The young man stood up, then froze as if he was seeing a ghost. 'Annie!' With a whoop, he broke into a run towards her. When he reached her side, he lifted her up in his arms and swung her round and round, laughing with pleasure. 'I wondered when you would come! Och, lassie, it's great to see you! And you're as bonnie as a summer's day, so you are!'

'So have ye started reading poetry yourself, Ian?' she teased. Ian Clachan wasn't going to give up easily, whatever he was doing with Betty Rannoch! His next words and actions convinced her.

'Annie, och, Annie, how I've missed you. When you never sent me a word, I nearly came to Paris to look for you myself, but I didn't know where to start.' Ian Clachan was as direct and open as ever. 'Och, and here you are, Annie, here you are.' He lifted her face to his and kissed her with all the passion and longing of his young body and soul.

Annie felt herself respond. Despite the turmoil in her heart, she wanted this moment to last for ever. Thoughts of Mistress Crawford and Betty Rannoch faded as Ian held her close. Shaking and flushed, she finally broke away, but he picked her up as if she was thistledown and carried her over to a mossy bank. There was no sign of the boy any more, Ian Clachan was a young man in the height of his strength and longing for the woman he loved.

Caught up in her own desire, for a moment she almost gave way to his insistent hands and eager body, then she remembered Mistress Crawford and the farmer's words. She stiffened and drew away. 'Stop, Ian,' she said quietly. 'Stop right now. You have no right to be doing this at all.'

'No, Annie,' he cupped her face in his hands. 'Please, Annie. Oh, Annie, how I've missed you.'

Annie shook her head. 'They're waiting for us back at the farm.' She got up, smoothing down her skirt and trying with shaking hands to tidy her hair. 'I was sent to bring you down to supper, not to lie with you in the heather!'

Ian stood up and looked at her with longing. 'Well, at least now you know how it is with me, Annie. I may wed Betty, but I'll never love anyone but you.'

'Aye, Ian, now I know.'

Before they could say any more, Dougie appeared at the foot of the hill, driving the cows from the high fields back for milking.

'I'll see you back at the farmhouse,' she called over her shoulder as she ran down to join the cowherd.

Ian stood watching, then he picked up his hoe and made his way thoughtfully back through the gloaming to the warm kitchen where the others were gathering.

Chapter Fifteen

Supper in Clachan's kitchen was full of laughter, chatter, teasing and the occasional sentimental tear. Geordie Clachan made a speech of welcome to 'Our wee milkmaid, who has turned into a fine lady's maid faster than you could say, "Jock Robinson"! And who can, she tells me, speak French like a native! It just shows you,' he concluded, 'what talent there is in all of us if only we get a chance to let it out!'

'Aye, well, I don't think you'd make a lady's maid, fairmer,' Dougie called from the bottom of the table, 'even if ye got the chance to try it!'

'And I don't give much for your chances with French either, Geordie,' said Doctor Murchieson, 'some of your English is a bit questionable at times!'

The men cheered and banged their tankards and Annie laughed emotionally till the tears came. Sitting there, feted and fussed, in her old place between Ian and Leezie, hearing the familiar voices chaffing about the kye and which fields were doing best and which kye needed watching, it was easy to forget reality. Her heart was filled to overflowing. Nothing, not the great boulevards of Paris, could make up for one moment of this farmhouse supper. Resolutely she tried to live for the evening with its tangible joys and let the morrow take care of itself.

Old Charlie had passed away the previous spring and Doctor Murchieson sat in his place next to the farmer. At the end of the meal he got heavily to his feet and held up a hand for silence. 'Farmer Clachan, Mistress Crawford, Ian, good folk ... Annie!' He looked round the table. 'I take a special interest in this young lady, since I was responsible for bringing her here,' he went on in his kindly, pompous way. 'And I have watched with pride as she has blossomed into a lovely lass.'

'Here, here ... aye, that's a fact!' More cheering almost raised the kitchen roof as Annie sat blushing.

'None of us could have predicted the hand of fate which made her what she is, the day I sent her to Clachan's Farm and Mistress Crawford nearly sent her right back again.'

'Shame on you, Archibald Murchieson!' Bess Crawford flushed pink with embarrassment as everyone laughed.

'Aye,' the Doctor continued when the noise died down, 'we have to admire Annie for what she has made of fortune's wheel as it has spun around her. Even while fickle fortune frowned in foreign fields she fought through to be with us tonight.' He paused while they cheered his eloquence and hammered on the table. 'Now, Mistress Crawford, Geordie, Ian, lassies and lads, raise your tankards in a toast to "Clachan's Annie"!'

After supper, they had called for her to sing as she had done for them so many times before. She meant to sing something gay and light, but instead she heard herself begin the saddest love song of all.

'Ae fond kiss and then we severe
Ae fareweel and then for ever
Deep in heart-wrung tears I'll pledge thee
Warring sighs and groans I'll wage thee.

'Had we never loved so kindly
Had we never loved so blindly
Never met and never parted
We had we ne'er been brokenhearted.'

As the last notes died away, every soul in the room sat still, deep in their own emotions. Doctor Murchieson broke the silence, 'Och, lassie dear, I don't know what you've been up to in Paris, but you have the gift of a performer! I could hardly keep the tears from my eyes!'

'Aye, well done, Annie,' they chorused.

'Now how about a reel?' Geordie got up and took Mistress Crawford's hand. 'Let's have ye, Dougie!'

'Places for the eight-hand reel!' Dougie picked up his fiddle and began a gay tune that set feet tapping.

Ian Clachan's eyes had rested on Annie as the timeless words of lost love rang round the back room. Now he sat, still watching. All evening she had known he wanted to talk to her alone again. Determinedly she avoided giving him the chance.

Annie looked down, unable to hold his gaze, then she got up. 'Come on then, Jamie, they need two more wi' Leezie and Wullie!' She drew one of the blushing young lads up to join in the dancing.

Annie lay awake in her old narrow bed, Leezie's familiar snores drifting through the wall in a comforting growl. The June night was short, dusk rather than darkness had fallen. Her head spun, full of the evening's music, laughter and the sharp pain of loss.

An hour later, with sleep as far away as ever, she got out of bed, pulled on a shawl over the simple nightshirt borrowed from Leezie and crept out into the moonlit farmyard. The dogs raised their heads, but recognising the sight and scent of her, tucked them again sleepily in their tails.

Annie walked, quiet as a ghost, up to where the old rowan tree guarded her favourite hollow. The night was warm and not even a chill breeze from the sea could touch her in this sheltered spot. For a long time, she sat, head on knees thinking, but finding no answers.

'Annie, it's me,' the whisper was so soft, she thought for a moment it was in her imagination.

The heather crackled and Ian appeared. 'I couldn't sleep either and was watching at the window, just thinking. Then I saw you cross the yard. I knew where you would be.' He sat beside her, a little at her feet as they had done so many Sundays in the innocent past. 'Annie, I did wrong up there on the hill, kissing you. It wasn't fair. You were right,' he sounded infinitely sad. 'Och, Annie, can you forgive me for not waiting for you like I promised?'

'It was my fault as much as yours, I told you not to,' she replied steadily enough.

'But I would have. I wanted to.'

'But you didn't,' she stated the bare truth.

Ian flushed. 'Och, Betty's a kindly lass and Rannoch's is a fine farm,' he began, then realised he was not improving his case.

'But I tried not to let things go ahead,' he added defensively. 'I was hoping she would maybe get tired and find another lad.'

Despite the poignancy of the situation, Annie smiled to herself in irony at Ian's naive optimism. 'Well, I don't think Betty is the sort to give up that easy, especially since she's been after you all this while, Ian,' she said.

'No,' he paused, looking surprised as if that idea had never occurred to him, 'I suppose not. But once Rabbie Rannoch died it was worse.' He grasped her shoulders, desperate to explain. 'Everybody had the wish and expectation that I should marry Betty and take over. Och, Annie.' He let her go with a helpless gesture. 'I couldn't let them down ... between Elsie Rannoch weeping and Aunty Bess pleading for me to name the day ... even Faither seemed to think it was the right thing to do.'

'I understand that, Ian,' she replied, 'and I'm not blaming you.'

'I don't love Betty.'

'Well, you better start,' she said tartly.

'Will you ever come back?'

'I don't think so, Ian.' Annie turned and looked directly at him. 'What would be the point?'

'I can't bear the thought of never seeing you again,' he whispered.

'And I can't bear the thought of seeing you as Betty Rannoch's husband, with your bairns around you, Ian,' Annie spoke from her heart, 'For God's sake, you great loon, what do you think I am?'

'I hope you marry a good man, Annie,' he said, head hanging. 'Don't make this turn you bitter.'

Her face was grave in the flickering leafy moonlight. 'I told you once that I won't be considering marriage for a long while yet, maybe never. And that's probably how it will be, Ian. But what happens to me from now on is nothing to do with you.' She couldn't help but cause him pain from the depth of her own. 'Look after your wife and bairns, Ian, don't grieve over a waif from the gutters of Glasgow.'

'I've never thought of you like that, Annie.' He sounded hurt.

'Och, don't pay any heed,' she said. 'It's just being back, seeing everybody, passing a fine evening in the farmhouse, being with you ... och, it's too much!' her voice trembled.

'Annie,' he touched her arm with a tentative hand. 'Just let me know what happens to you.'

'And who will you tell your wife that the letter is from, Ian?' she said bitterly. 'Don't be daft, man!'

'If this is the last time we meet, can I at least kiss you goodbye?' Ian said.

Annie turned to him in the pale light. She knew she should say no, and she knew she couldn't.

'On one condition.'

'What?'

'That you leave in the morning before I come down to the kitchen and you stay in the high-riggs till I am long gone.'

'Why?'

'I could not bear to say goodbye again.'

'I promise.'

'Then you can kiss me, Ian Clachan,' she whispered.

The kiss began as soft as the down that lined the seabirds nests on Craigdrummond's great cliffs, but it grew in intensity till she felt it would go on for ever. There was no reality, but their nearness and need for each other.

Annie and Ian made love in the mossy hollow by the rowan tree with all the power of their youth and their need for one another. When all was done, they lay close together, fulfilled at last. Annie kissed his forehead as he dozed in her arms and wished she could die so another dawn could not dim the memory.

When the first rosy light touched the hill above and sent its warming fingers into the hollow, Ian woke. Annie was gone. Only the broken heather showed where their love had been. Ian went back to the farmhouse unnoticed. Trying not to think of Annie lying above in her old room, he washed and headed up to the long-riggs. This was one promise he knew he had to keep.

Annie joined Mistress Crawford in the big kitchen when everyone had gone to work.

'So you've got up at last, I didn't think you'd take me at my word and have a lie in to half-past seven. Well, you've just missed the Doctor, he's left to catch the early train to Girvan.' The housekeeper began in her usual dry way, then stopped, noticing Annie's shadowed eyes and drawn expression.

'Has Ian gone?' Annie asked hesitantly.

'Nearly two hours ago, like a bear with a sore head, I came in to the kitchen as he left. I guess he must have had a whisky too many. Though I don't remembering him over indulging.' Annie stood looking at her and she rushed on suddenly nervous. 'Ian's usually such a moderate lad. Anyway he's over the high-riggs again planning for new crops. Geordie isn't so keen on these modern ideas, but the lad has to be given his head and so far he's more than proved himself. He can't wait to get his hands on Rannoch's fields too ...'

'Mistress Crawford,' Annie stopped the older woman in mid-flow, 'there's no need to shove Rannoch's down my throat any more, I know what's what and I won't be back. You've got your way. But I want to tell you something before I go ...'

'Indeed? Well, it can wait a minute.' Uneasy and playing for time, Bess got up and fetched a plate of bannocks from the dresser. 'Have something to eat before you start. I'd not like Craigdrummond House to think that I starved you!'

Automatically Annie helped herself to a glass of buttermilk and thoughtfully spread thick blaeberry jam onto a slice of bannock. 'Ian made it plain yesterday that he has far stronger feelings for me than for Betty.'

'Oh, I see,' Bess Crawford replied slowly trying not to show her shock. 'And what did you say to that?'

'I repeated what we all ken, that he can't let everybody down now, and that includes Betty. Anyway she's what you all want for him.'

'So you said no and he agrees with you?' She almost sighed aloud in relief.

'Not just that,' Annie said. 'I told him like I've just told you, I won't be back.'

'Well, that's maybe for the best.'

'You've always tried to make that match, whatever the consequences, haven't you, Mistress Crawford?'

The straight question took the housekeeper off guard. 'Er ... yes, I think Ian should think of the farm and the future, and of course I've encouraged him. Betty is the right wife for Ian and the lad knows that otherwise he'd have ...' she trailed off, but stood defensively, arms folded.

'Even if he doesn't love her?'

'I'd be a fool to say a man should marry without affection, even if there is no great love. Friendship and respect can be a

187

fine basis for a marriage. And Betty certainly loves Ian. It will make up for any old, er, attachments on his part.' She refused to think of her own match that had been anything but happy and of the Doctor's abiding love for her.

'I'm not sure one person's love is enough to carry a marriage,' Annie said quietly.

'Well I am!' Bess said more firmly. 'Before you came, Ian was content enough with Betty and he will be again when you go for good. What he feels for you is only puppy love, Annie.'

'Oh aye?' Annie thought of their passion of last night in the mossy hollow and doubted the housekeeper was right. But she knew her man for good and ill. Without her pushing him to do it, Ian would never stand up for her in the face of the family's opposition, however much love he felt. Alone, he would marry Betty, of that she was certain.

'Anyway it's not just Ian any more,' Bess's mouth was set and her face stubborn. 'Elsie is left bereft and needs a man to take over right away or they'll lose the lease. Geordie Clachan is pleased with the match, you heard him yourself and ...'

Annie couldn't help but add '... and now you can wed the Doctor with a clear conscience.'

Bess Crawford looked her in the eye for the first time that morning. 'Yes, now I can wed Archie Murchieson, Annie. And would you deny us that after all these years? I've sacrificed more for Ian and Geordie than you'll ever know.'

'And now I'm sacrificing too!' Annie cried from the depths of her own short-lived joy and the sorrow it had left behind.

'Annie, if you are thinking of upsetting things now, think again,' Bess Crawford said. 'I understand that you may feel nothing but bitterness towards me, and that I accept. But if you stop Ian's wedding, you stop mine too.'

'What do ye mean?'

'First there's a question of honour now everything is arranged. Betty would be crushed, though you can hardly be expected to worry about that,' she added with tart realism. 'But just think beyond romance, Annie Ramsay! Geordie would hardly be pleased to have you here in the circumstances. I would have to stay at least a while longer. And Clachan's would be honour bound to look after Rannoch's Farm till they got a new leaseholder. Joint contracts have already been signed with the big house for produce.

It could take years to sort out the mess. Even if you got Ian in the end, is it worth trampling over the debris of so many lives?'

Annie stood biting her lip, looking at her with agonised eyes. 'It might be for me ... and for Ian.'

'So, is that how you want to repay Archie Murchieson?' Bess went on relentlessly playing every card she could find.

'I don't think that's fair,' Annie cried.

'I don't think fairness is what this is all about!' As if being active was a relief, Bess picked up a dish from the dresser and began filling it with eggs.

After a long silence broken only by the sounds of the farmyard through the open window, Annie said in a low passionate voice, 'If I got up from this table and ran up the high-riggs to tell Ian that I will never forget him ... never feel the same for anybody else ... that if he shows himself to be a man and claim me as he says he wants to do, then I'll put up with the Doctor's sadness and Betty Rannoch too, because I love him ... that I will wed him gladly for better or worse, what would you do?'

Bess Crawford blanched and rich yellow yolk ran onto the table from the egg she had crushed. 'I'd never speak to you again till my dying day.' She spat out the words. 'And I'd curse the night I took you in dripping off Thampson's cart and gave you meat and hearth.' Carefully she wiped her hand clean of the yolk and went on in a calmer voice, 'I may not want you for my sister's son, Annie Ramsay, but I've been good to you when you needed it. It's no coin in which to repay my kindness to a half-starved waif, and above all, it's no coin to repay the Doctor's goodness of heart when he couldn't bear to let you rot your lungs out in that Glasgow tenement. You owe him your life.'

When she had finished, Annie said evenly, 'I thought that was the case.' She got up, leaving the half-eaten bannock on the plate. 'Well, Mistress Crawford. I thank you for yesterday and this morning. And I thank you for all you did for me, good or ill, for I suppose that's the way it was meant to be and you're just a part of the fates that steer me ... that steer all of us.' Her steady grey eyes held the other woman's. 'And believe me, I am grateful to you for taking me in. You're right, another year in the 'baccy factor would have killed me. So, we'll part without hard words, but it will be the last time we'll meet, except by accident. I wish you and the Doctor every joy.' She held out her hand.

The older woman hesitated then took it. 'Good luck to you,' she said, 'and goodbye ... Clachan's Annie.'

With a sad heart she left the farm and walked smartly back to Craigdrummond, trying resolutely not to look back, or to think of Ian ploughing the high-riggs.

As she got closer to the big house, she saw the carriage with her young mistress approach at a trot from the Ayr road. 'Ah well,' Annie quickened her step. 'I suppose I had better get packing for the pair of us.'

Maria Cameron sat on a window seat in the corridor gazing out of the window as unexpected and unseasonal rain drove across the moor. In the two years since she had married Urquhart, she had borne him a son and heir and was carrying another child. In many ways she was the most content of women, loved by her husband, praised as a fair and kind mistress by all who worked for her and admired for her serenity by those who met her.

If only Alexandra could accept me, she thought, my life would be perfect. But it just seems to be beyond her. Whatever I do to reach out, she draws back. I suppose it's as well she's going away tomorrow. These last few months in Paris might help to finish the job of maturing her. And if as Cameron says, Edward wishes to marry her, then I won't have to worry. Oh but I doubt she'll take an older man, Maria fretted to herself. At least she has been civil this time, even quite pleasant to me when people are around, though there is no depth to our relationship.

Annie passed carrying a vase of flowers. 'Good-day, Lady Cameron,' she bobbed a curtsey and made to go on.

'Annie,' Maria stopped her.

'Yes, Milady?' She waited.

Maria noticed once more what a fine young woman Annie Ramsay had turned out to be, but sometimes she wondered how she coped with Alexandra and her many caprices.

Just as Bess had done earlier, she asked, 'Are you looking forward to going back to Paris, Annie?'

'Yes, Milady.' If Annie was taken aback by the unprecedented personal interest from Lady Cameron to a maid, she was too well-trained to show it.

'And you don't miss Craigdrummond?'

Annie looked at her in surprise. 'Oh, that's a different matter altogether, Milady,' she said.

'Do you?'

'Every day I'm away from Craigdrummond, I miss it, especially Clachan's Farm and the cliffs and moors,' Annie replied honestly.

'So you still hanker after the life of a milkmaid instead of the luxury of Paris and the great wide world,' Lady Cameron's eyes twinkled and her voice was kindly, making Annie feel at ease.

'Och, Craigdrummond House is grand.' Her face clouded and she avoided a direct answer, 'It doesn't matter where I am any more as long as it's decent.'

'So Paris won't be so bad then?' she smiled. 'And maybe London, after that?'

'Och Paris is fine and so will London be,' Annie replied firmly.

'I'm glad to hear you say so.' Maria nodded approval. 'Now, don't let me keep you from your duties any longer, Annie.'

'Thank you, Milady.' Annie bobbed a curtsey and went pensively on her way.

Arranging the flowers in Alexandra's room, Annie's thoughts went on spinning relentlessly as they had since she left the farm. Finally she took herself firmly in hand. It's not the end of the world if you stay with Miss Alexandra for a couple more years ... there's worse employers around, that's for sure. Even if you can't go back to Clachan's Farm, the future still has a lot to offer, she persuaded herself as, with an effort, she forced insidious thoughts of the void without Ian out of her mind.

With careful precision, she cut the stems to size on the great tea-roses, loving the velvet feel of their petals and placed them one by one in the rose bowl so their delicate colours formed a perfect halo. Och, our Sandy getting a bigger shop isn't so daft, she mused. Once they're on their feet properly, I could maybe join them at Charing Cross. It's not like going back to the Gallowgate. Aye, that'a a good idea, she was surprised she hadn't thought of it before.

Annie slipped off for an hour or two while the Camerons visited their Glasgow lawyer. Sandy had said they all wanted to see her so she could admire the new 'Ramsay's Bakery and Fancy

Confectionery' shop near Charing Cross Station and meet the young woman who was soon to be his wife.

'Annie, Annie! Lassie mine!' Mrs Ramsay hugged her daughter. 'Och, Sandy, come here this minute!' she called, as Annie came into the little shop. 'It's our Annie turned into a fine lady, so she has!'

Sandy came out, wiping floury hands on his bakers apron, honest face beaming with pleasure. 'So ye made it,' he cried, hugging her warmly and leaving white patches on her jacket.

'Och it'll dust off, Mammy,' she said with a shrug as her mother chided him.

Amid the chaos and warmth of their welcome, Annie noticed her mother had put on weight and the haggard look had gone from her face. And Sandy had the straight back and proud bearing of a man who had achieved something in life.

'I wasn't sure till the last minute if Miss Alexandra would let me off, Mammy,' Annie explained. 'So I couldn't let you know exactly when I would come. Still, here I am!'

'Och, ye look that grand, Annie.' Her mother fingered the fine cloth of Annie's second-best uniform coat. 'This is quality stuff right enough. I've never felt the like.'

'Miss Alexandra's school had it made for me in Paris ...'

'Paris ... aye from yer letters, ye've been havin' the time of yer life, our Annie!' her mother beamed. 'And now ye're on yer way back. I'll bet ye're that glad.'

'Er ... aye,' Annie agreed. There was no point in burdening her mother with the vicissitudes of serving Alexandra Cameron.

'Say hello to yer big sister, you two,' Mrs Ramsay instructed what was surely the twins, Isa and Bella. Annie would hardly have recognized the girls had she passed them in the street, they had changed so much. 'Ye're jist standing there like gowks!'

'Hello, Annie,' they mumbled in unison and stood looking at her with great big eyes, as if she was a complete stranger.

Och, who can blame them? thought Annie to herself. They've hardly seen me for years. Michty! They're the image of our Eddie, even though they're lassies. I just hope they'll be better workers than he is!

As if he had read her thoughts, Sandy said, 'Isa and Bella are still bairns, but they do their bit in the shop after school. There's no idle hands around here now our Eddie's cleared off, Annie.

192

So, what do ye think of the shop?' he demanded, his face alight with pride.

'It's just dandy,' Annie replied, looking around, glad not to have to say any more about her situation just yet. 'That tablet would make your mouth water, so it would.' She pointed to rows of homemade fudge lying sliced in trays and turned to where rows of jars by the window showed off bright boiled sweets in colourful blobs.

'Mammy makes those. We'll be doing even more things once Phyllis and me is wed. She's in the trade as well. Look, have ye seen my fancies?' her brother asked, flushing with excitement. Sandy's special fancy cakes were neatly laid out behind the glass barrier along with piles of fluffy scones and sturdy bannocks.

Annie went over and admired the display. 'Sandy, you're a good lad,' she said with genuine feeling. 'I'm impressed, so I am.'

'Just wait till Phyllis comes,' he beamed. 'She finishes a bit early on Thursdays so she'll be here any time. We'll close the shop and all have tea ... after all it's a special occasion, so it is!'

'Och, isn't this lovely? The lot of us together again.' Mrs Ramsay dabbed at her eyes. 'Just dandy.'

'Here's Phyllis now!' Sandy smiled proudly as a plump, cheerful young woman came in, clearly at home with her surroundings. He turned to Annie, 'Come in to the back shop now and we'll make a wee cup of tea. Mammy, Phyllis and me are keen to hear yer news.'

'Do ye hear from Eddie? Is he well now after his ... er ... wee accident?' Annie tried to sound concerned out of politeness, but since the incident of running her mother and Sandy into debt, she had no time for Eddie who was nothing but a thoughtless malingerer.

'Not a word since he went wi' that lassie in Gallowgate whose faither has a pub,' her mother said with a shrug. 'Somebody telt Jeanie Brockett from doon the road that the lassie's in the family way and they're married. But naw, I've no heard a word.'

'Good riddance!' Annie said robustly.

Sandy grinned, 'And so say all of us! Aye, Eddie's fallen on his feet ...' he chortled, 'or maybe on his back. He'll drink all their profit, so he will!'

'I never asked ye Annie,' her mother asked. 'How did ye find yer way?'

'The Cameron carriage dropped me off at the Cross, the driver offered to take me further down, but I said I'd rather walk,' she replied. 'He said he would come back for me, but I told him I'll just take a tram back to Central in time for the Laird and Miss Alexandra to catch the London train.'

'The Cameron carriage! The London train? By-here, you can hold yer head up wi' the best of them, oor Annie,' Sandy said admiringly.

'Och, whit are ye standing there for? Come through, come through,' her mother's voice was full of pride as she caught her arm and drew her in. 'So, whit do ye think of the parlour then, hen?'

'It's really nice, Mammy.' She looked round. They had moved to rooms behind the shop and, though it was no palace, the sandstone building was solid and cared for. The old signs of terrible poverty were nowhere to be seen. Even her mother's precious clock was out of pawn and back in place of honour on the mantelpiece and there was a cloth and a wee glass vase on the table and the floor was covered with decent rag rugs.

'Aye, it's a lot nicer than the old room and kitchen,' her mother beamed. 'Thanks to you, hen, we've gone up in the world as well, so we have! We can even pay the doctor,' she added with pride.

Annie smothered a smile. 'Well, that just shows you. But without your own hard work and Sandy's, even my money wouldn't have made the difference I can see around me,' she added generously. 'Did I tell you I met Doctor Chisholm in Ayrshire? He was on holiday with Doctor Murchieson.'

'Is that right? Och, he's a fine lad, that so he is ... and what we owe Doctor Murchieson is nobody's business.'

'Aye,' Annie agreed, 'without his help I'd be still in the 'baccy factory ... or six feet under.'

'So ye wid,' her mother nodded. 'But I was more thinking of the bills we never paid before he left. Still it's an ill wind ...'

'Och, I'm sure he's managing without it,' Annie suppressed a giggle. 'Now, Mammy, what have you got besides the parlour?'

'There's two bedrooms, one for me and the lassies and one for Sandy and Phyllis when they are wed, the parlour like ye ken, and a bathroom, Annie! Can ye credit it, Annie, a bathroom wi' a flush toilet?'

'And a proper big kitchen round the back so we can bake and make the sweeties,' Sandy broke in, voice full of pride. 'We've fixed everything great.'

Mrs Ramsay sat back and looked as content as Annie had ever seen her. Annie could see the long hours of toil they had put in to grasp the chance her money had given them.

Mrs Ramsay echoed her thoughts, 'Sandy and me knock oor pans in to make the shop a success. We've a good lot of regulars now that would never walk past Ramsay's to buy their loaf or tattie-scones anywhere else,' she added. Her expression changed to one of embarrassment, 'But yer money is still welcome, hen, so it is, especially since Sandy and Phyllis want to rent the shop next door and make it into tearooms.'

'You've done well, our Sandy,' Annie said when her mother left the room to join Phyllis who seemed quite at home. 'And Phyllis is a lovely lass, I'm sure you'll both be right happy.'

'Aye,' Sandy nodded.

'Would you like a wee fancy, or maybe a bit of my best short-bread, Miss ... er ... Annie?' Phyllis bustled in, pink to the ears. 'I make exactly the same at Miss Stirling's, ye ken, of Miss Stirling's Tearooms ... that's where I'm working till we're wed,' she blushed and looked at Sandy, 'I've already handed in my notice.'

'Phyllis is a lassie and a half when it comes to shortbread, Annie,' Mrs Ramsay made clear her approval of Sandy's choice. 'Tell her what Miss Stirling says about it, hen.'

'Och,' Phyllis blushed, 'Miss Stirling says I make it as light as a feather ... och, it's jist the way ye rub in the butter wi' the sugar and flour that does it. Have a wee bit, Miss ... er ... Annie.' Timidly she offered the plate.

Annie took a sliver to please her and bit into it. 'And it is delicious, Phyllis, I've never tasted the like.'

'Och, imagine that!' She went bright puce ... 'And you that's eaten wi' the gentry!'

Since they sat down in the parlour, the initial familiarity had gone and the whole family seemed to be treating her with deference due to a visiting dignitary. Phyllis was openly flustered and even her mother seemed suddenly stiff and formal. Annie feared she was to blame, for her world was long from theirs and she sensed a distance even in herself that came from experiences and

195

a life they could never even guess at.

Isa and Bella said nothing at all, but stood in clean white pinnies still staring overawed at this elegant stranger who had come from nowhere bearing presents for them all.

Annie felt sad that they regarded her so. This wasn't a big house, it was her own kith and kin. An awkward silence fell and she decided to try and bridge the gap, but before she could say a word, Sandy made it worse.

'How was the christening, Annie?' he asked politely. 'I bet all the gentry were there, were they no?'

'Och, tell us whit it was like!' her mother leaned forward. 'Was there many that came? Whit did they eat?'

Annie gave in. 'You'd never credit all the folk that were there and the food was laid out on five big tables ... each one about four times as big as that one.' She looked over at where the family ate of an evening.

'Five tables that big, oh, michty!' Her mother sighed.

'Aye, and they were straining with sides of beef, capons, soup tureens, a christening cake a yard high all glistening with sugar icing ... and as much wine and port as the gentry could drink.'

'Oh, by here!' Sandy gasped in professional astonishment. 'How in the name did they get it to stand ... the cake, ye ken?'

'Aye, ye may well ask,' Annie grinned. 'For it was covered with silvered birds and rose decorations, not to mention lacy designs in royal icing all the way round. Och, it was fine, a lovely sight, with white orchids and lilies and everything piled into crystal vases on the table beside it and musicians playing the piano and the violin. The whole caboodle cost a fine bawbee.'

'And you were there as a guest! Och, our Annie,' Mrs Ramsay sighed with pleasure. 'Is that no rerr?'

'Well, not exactly a guest, Mammy.' Annie felt obliged to explain before her mother told the whole neighbourhood a pack of fairytales. 'All the senior staff were invited. We were supposed to just stand in a row till the gentry had their fill and moved into the garden to take refreshments.'

'Aye, that's whit I meant, our Annie,' her mother said sharply. 'Ye were a guest!'

'Aye, Mammy.' Annie knew better than try to correct her further.

'Whit was the best thing, Annie?' Sandy asked.

196

'The best thing was that the sun was shining, the flowers were in full bloom and the birds were singing their wee hearts out,' Annie replied. 'Aye, Ayrshire is bonnie.'

'Och, but Paris must be even better than Ayrshire,' Phyllis broke in. 'Imagine you living there wi' they fancy streets and that, Miss ... er ... Annie ... it's like a story book.'

Annie gave a rueful smile 'It depends how you look at it, Phyllis, life is mostly just as ordinary in Paris as it is here. There's poor and rich and work to do ...'

'Aye, but ...'

Annie looked so serious Phyllis and the rest fell silent, realising something important was coming. 'But listen, Sandy, Mammy,' she said hesitantly, 'I was wondering if maybe I should come back to Scotland.'

'To Ayrshire?' her mother asked puzzled. 'Whit for? Though I ken ye've always liked the place, Annie. Will yer Miss Alexandra be coming back soon then?'

'I wasn't just talking about Miss Alexandra's service,' Annie said. 'I was thinking of changing my employ.'

'Oh aye?' There was puzzlement on all their faces now and they shifted uneasily. It was nearly as bad as talking to Mistress Crawford. Annie begin to regret saying anything at all.

'But won't Miss Alexandra expect you to go on working for her?' Sandy raised surprised eyebrows. 'You always told us she didn't want anybody else as her maid but you, Annie.'

'Aye, that's what she used to say, but she's not said it for a while!' Annie grinned ruefully. 'I think she doesn't have the same need for somebody to confide in any more. But, it's not that, Sandy. I'm just not sure I want to stay with her for ever.' She looked round her grouped family. 'Listen, what do you feel about me joining the family business?' she asked bluntly. 'Now things are going well, we could surely work together.'

They looked at her and the silence grew. 'Och that would be lovely, Annie,' her mother spoke first, but her eyes were uneasy and she kept glancing at Sandy with a worried frown.

'Er ... just to ye get another job as a maid, ye mean?' he asked.

'Well ...' Annie began.

'But where wid ye sleep, hen?' Mrs Ramsay burst out anxiously. 'You could aye share wi' me and the lassies, but

197

maybe ye wouldn't want that these days being used to yer ain bed and that.'

'Of course it's your money that has set us up, Annie,' Sandy saw Annie's expression and felt ashamed. 'We owe ye right enough. It's just that things are still a bit tight. Bakin' isn't yer trade, and we've enough folk behind the counter. Maybe if we get the place next door and start the tearooms, you could help then ...'

'I've always pulled my weight!' Annie said more sharply than she intended. But she realised they were only making excuses. Sandy, Phyllis, even Mammy and the twins had planned their lives without her ... if not without her money, she thought with a touch of bitterness.

'Och I ken that, Annie ...' Sandy trailed off awkwardly, looking as if he wished the floor would swallow him up. Phyllis stood beside him, eyes wide and homely face flushed.

Annie sighed, imagining the hours they had spent working and planning. She didn't doubt that they appreciated what she had done for them, but they couldn't cope with the sudden change of roles. Without warning, she had gone from being a distant fairy-godmother to threatening to withdraw support and muscling in on what they had created. At least she could give them back their dreams.

'Look at your faces, as if you'd dropped a shilling and found a penny! I think you've all misunderstood.' She forced a bright smile. 'It was only a wee possibility, if all else fails. The likeliest is that I'll stick with Miss Alexandra.'

'Och well, is that no for the best, hen?' Her mother sounded pleased. 'And ye're always welcome if ye need a bed for the night, ye ken that well.'

'Aye, right enough,' Sandy nodded, 'and being a lady's maid is well paid. We won't have anything spare for years, everything is goin' right back into the business, if ye ken what I mean.'

'I suppose you're right,' Annie gave up altogether. 'It was just a daft idea in case I get fed up with Miss Alexandra. And if that happens, I'll find another job. Lady Cameron would give me a reference at any rate.'

'Aye,' they chorused and visibly relaxed.

'So there ye are!' Annie tried not to show her hurt as her mother and Sandy beamed at one another. It seemed that the day

Doctor Murchieson told her about Clachan's Farm and she insisted on going, there was no way back. Whatever the future held it would be alone. Alone! The word rattled emptily round in her head.

'More tea, Miss ... er ... Annie?' Phyllis fussed, glad the tension was over.

'Thanks.' Annie took the cup and smiled, but her thoughts were far away. Firmly she pulled herself back. 'Now tell me about your plans for special teas, Phyllis.' She turned to her future sister-in-law.

'Well,' Phyllis, pink to the ears, launched into an enthusiastic discourse, hardly pausing for breath, 'Sandy says even before we even start our own tearooms, which will cost a fair wee bit to fix nice and that, we could try to get kirk socials to order purveys from us and weddin's, ye ken the kind of thing. We could do tea, scones, short-bread, cakes, pies and sandwiches as well, for afternoon or evening do's. Sandy says we should be in with a shout if we offer a good price and good service.' Phyllis stopped at last and turned adoring eyes on him. 'Och, it's great havin' somebody like Sandy to share yer ideas wi'. I like Miss Stirling's and I've served a good apprenticeship there, but this will be our ain wee business and we're in it together ... like ...' she fumbled for the word, then found it '... real friends.'

Together like friends! Annie's head began to ache. Friendship! Och, it's just another empty word, Annie thought with an edge of bitterness. That's what Miss Alexandra said she needed from me, but she soon put me in my place. And Ian Clachan ... he was my best friend once ... now I've lost him.

Even Leezie isn't close any more ... and Francine will have gone by the time we get back. There's nobody. She rubbed her forehead as anxious thoughts crowded in on her. Och, that's not true, she told herself firmly, there's one friend who'd be more than willing to share his life and his dreams. But it's not fair to use somebody just to fill a lonely place in your life, Annie Ramsay. She looked at Phyllis and Sandy, sitting hand in hand. Och, it was a pity she didn't feel anything but affection for Louis. Her face became withdrawn and sad.

Phyllis jumped up, thinking she had somehow offended and tried at once to make amends. 'Och, I shouldn't go on about the business, we aye think folk should be as happy about it as we are.

199

Would ye like another cup of tea, Miss ... er ... Annie? A wee scone?'

'Nothing to eat, thank you, Phyllis, I've done justice already. But yes, I'd love another cup of your delicious brew, then I'll be on my way.' Annie held out her cup with a smile that pleased poor Phyllis, but it didn't reach her own grey eyes.

Chapter Sixteen

Ian Clachan sat among the heather in Annie's favourite mossy spot under the great rowan tree. For nearly three weeks he had tried to compose a letter. It was hard, but time was running out. Now, resolution on his face, he dipped the pen in ink, leaned his back against the rowan and began at last.

Clachan's Farm, Craigdrummond, Ayrshire
12 July, 1894

Dear Annie
You said you wouldn't give me your address, but I have to write so you know what is in my heart at this time. I will be sending it to your brother Sandy in Glasgow, since you said he was a good reliable lad and writes sometimes, in the hope that he will forward it to you.

I walked up the hill to where you and I last met and I am sitting in that very spot where we were together. It makes me feel closer to you writing from here, and there's nobody around to ask what I'm doing either. If I shut my eyes, I can see you running down the hill with that wee cap of yours nearly falling off your head and those mad curls dancing. You are everywhere here for me, not just in this place. I will remember you as long as I have breath in my body.

Annie, Betty Rannoch and I are being married tomorrow. Oh, Annie, please forgive me for that night by this rowan tree. I have tried in my heart to regret my own part, but cannot. It was the only time we let our hearts rule our heads and it will live with me for ever. But I shouldn't have kissed you, I shouldn't have loved you as I did. Betty is blooming with happiness as the wedding draws close and I am trying to be as optimistic as I can for her sake and for Faither. Aunty Bess will wed the Doctor next month. I know you will wish them every happiness, even if you cannot bring yourself to do the same for me.

Oh, Annie, I know I have not acted as a man should towards you. I wish I could have been stronger and insisted we be wed, but I could not face letting them all down. I have a feeling I will regret marrying Betty for the rest of my life.

For ever,

Ian Clachan.

'Och, Ian, Ian!' Annie cried each time she read and re-read the letter. But at least she did not have to live through anticipating their wedding. By the time Sandy had got round to forwarding it to her in Paris with a note from himself saying how busy they were, Ian and Betty Rannoch had already been man and wife for over two months.

So distracted and sad was she all week, that she did not notice Alexandra's odd behaviour till it was almost too late.

Alexandra felt this was the moment she had waited for all her life. Jean-Marc, Comte de Ledignan wanted her to meet him secretly. Much as she adored the staid, if generous, attentions of Edward, Lord Ballantyne, this was romance, real romance.

'I must see your beautiful face alone, just once, ma belle, belle Alexandra, before you leave Paris for ever. Then I can die a happy man,' he wrote.

Alexandra didn't believe the dying part, but the excitement, the thrill of having a clandestine assignation was too much for her to resist. With careful nonchalance, she dropped her reply with a coin into the cap of a beggar at the end of the street, exactly as Jean-Marc suggested.

Mondays were dull in the Berry household. As a rule, the sisters visited their lawyers and checked their accounts. They went with clockwork regularity at six, returning around nine. After early dinner the young ladies were expected to stay in their rooms, take time for reflection and sort through their wardrobes, itemise their duties and check dancing and other appointments for the week.

Alexandra usually broke the rules by disappearing into the

rooms of one of the other girls, especially a lively, worldly, newcomer called Daisy Singleton-Brown. Daisy's sister belonged to the fast set round the Prince of Wales. The Prince, like so many of the British aristocracy, frequented Paris, visiting the theatre, art galleries and, it was hinted, other more esoteric attractions of the Pleasure Capital. Edward came and went so often, one wag claimed he should be called the 'Le Prince du Gard du Nord' and his plump figure was regularly caricatured in the iconoclastic Paris press.

Whatever the truth of Prince Bertie's relationships, Daisy's sister, whom it was also hinted was very close indeed to him, kept her up to date with all the latest gossip and scandal and Alexandra adored hearing it second-hand. But tonight she had other plans while out from under the eagle eyes of her guardians. First she had to get rid of Annie.

'Annie, take this back to the laundry-room.' With a disgusted grimace, which would have done credit to Sarah Bernhardt, she held up a blouse. 'It's soiled on the back ... and I want it tomorrow ... wait downstairs till it is done.'

'If you like, Miss Alexandra.' Annie picked up the blouse with a puzzled look on her face. She was sure it had been all right when she checked the list with Marie-Claire. Och, but I'm not myself these days, she thought, maybe I just missed it.

'I'm going to see Daisy Singleton-Brown, Annie, she promised some lovely new gossip from London! The Prince of Wales has a new favourite, it's rumoured! I might be gone a few hours ... don't bother me with anything.'

'Certainly, Miss Alexandra.' Annie took the blouse and headed down into the basements, still thoughtful and glad her mistress would be busy for a while. Usually she enjoyed the lively chatter of the French staff who took care of kitchen, cleaning and laundry. And now Francine was gone, it was natural for her to turn to them now and then for company. Annie had never given herself airs or graces, like some of the other lady's maids, and she could speak French, so she was popular and welcomed. Lately, though, she hadn't felt like sharing her free time with anyone, but walked alone, head-bowed by the river, deep in thought, Ian's letter clutched in her hand or nestling next to her heart.

As soon as Annie had gone, Alex rummaged in her wardrobe for something simple she could throw over her pretty dress. Everything spoke of luxury and money. 'I'd stand out in the street as if I carried a banner declaring "Heiress at large"! Alex giggled to herself. 'Oh, I know.' She slipped downstairs and borrowed one of the servant's plain working coats which hung in the hall. The disguise added to her feeling of excitement and daring. Stealthily, she crept out of the entrance at the back of the school.

It was the first time Alex had ever been out in Paris alone. The early autumn evening was growing chilly. She was glad of the rough cloth for warmth and the anonymity of the worsted scarf that hid her golden hair. I really hope no one does see me, she thought. I must look hideous ... I'll take the scarf off as soon as I get there.

The place Jean-Marc had chosen was farther from the school than she had ever walked before. Nervous and excited she hurried first along the Faubourg St Honore, then up towards the Opera. So far she felt confident, it was a route which she had taken many times with the Misses Berry. Then she turned along the Boulevard des Capuchines and north west into an area she knew less well. For a moment she regretted not taking Jean-Marc's little hand-drawn map with her as she began to look for the small church he had designated for their rendezvous.

'Rue de St Lazare ... ah, there it is!' Her heart began to pound in her ears and her stomach tightened with apprehension.

The porch was dim in the fading light, but empty. She pushed open the heavy wooden door and slipped inside, momentarily blinded by the darkness inside. Slowly she began to make out shapes in the gloom. A candle burned dimly at the feet of a statue of the Madonna high on a plinth. Below an old lady knelt and prayed, a shadowed hump covered by a dark shawl.

There was no sign of Jean-Marc. In the dimness she could just read the time on her fob. It was exactly seven o'clock as he had asked. Belatedly, Alex began to wonder if what she was doing was wise. Despite being in church, she slipped the scarf off her head and shivered nervously. If he doesn't come in a minute, I'll go back, she thought. She began to hope he wouldn't. Then it was too late.

'Ma belle!' He must have been watching her from the shadows for suddenly he was there, looking as dashing and dangerous as ever. 'You came, how wonderful.'

Alex felt gauche and embarrassed. It was not at all as romantic as she had anticipated. 'Yes,' she choked out in a tight voice unlike her own, 'I came, Jean-Marc.'

'And you kept our little secret?'

'I told no one, just like you said.'

'Ah, très bien.' He held out his hand, 'Come then.'

'Where?' She felt more and more uneasy.

'Don't worry, ma belle Alexandra,' he replied seeing her uncertain expression, 'I just thought we might go for a little walk. We cannot stay in church, now can we?'

'I can't be long,' she answered, panic growing. 'My maid will miss me, she might come looking,' she lied.

'Yes.' He frowned. 'The formidable little maid! Not as compliant as the others ... so we had better hurry then.'

Alex, her arm held firmly in his, let herself be led from the church and into the street where the gaslights were just being lit. Feeling unreal and strange, she followed docilely enough.

He smiled down at her. 'Isn't this fun, ma belle? Now, come, there's something I want you to see. Something very special.'

'Jean-Marc, where are we going? No!' A cry of protest burst from her when they suddenly turned off the busy thoroughfare and down a narrow lane. 'Jean-Marc, I don't like this, it's too dark. Take me back to the church ... or the school at once!' Her voice sounded frightened and small.

'No, no, ma chère Alexandra.' He looked down at her with dark, inscrutable eyes. 'That would be very silly. Our little adventure is just beginning.'

'Please, Jean-Marc.' She tried to pull away, but he held her in an iron grip which made her gasp in pain. Alexandra Cameron realised that she was in a terrible predicament and that it was entirely of her own making.

Annie finally understood that Alexandra was up to something. All the signals she had come to recognise had been there, but she had been too preoccupied to notice. Every time her mistress received a letter or flirted on an outing, she went round for days giving little bursts of secretive laughter, gazing out of the window with a faraway look on her face, playing sentimental pieces of Chopin or Schubert. Annie usually ignored the mood till it passed. It was different this time and she was bothered. Alexandra had been unusually deceitful.

The matter of the blouse had shaken Annie out of her absent mood at last. They swore in the laundry room that the blouse had been delivered in pristine condition and there was no reason to doubt them. Annie understood then that Alexandra had dirtied it to get rid of her. She had never gone to such lengths before. Against instructions, Annie knocked on the door of Daisy Singleton-Brown's rooms and asked for her mistress. The maid told her Alex had never been there. When she reached their own rooms, Annie knew her fears had been justified. Alexandra had gone.

Sick with nameless fear, she rummaged in her young mistress's bedside cabinet and found the note tucked inside a little jewellery box. Alexandra was never very imaginative.

'Oh God!' As she read it, she understood that Alexandra had let herself be drawn into something by her vanity and cupidity, that might put her future, if not her life, in danger.

Memorising the map, Annie flung on her workaday plain black serge coat. All the maids were given one to use when they were not 'on display' with their mistresses. The Berry sisters insisted they dress alike within the establishment as well as outside when they wore a distinctive smart dark wine-red uniform which they had to keep in perfect condition. Underneath she wore the simple black dress issued for doing routine jobs. Tying a kerchief loosely round her hair, she hurried out into the dusk.

'If only I find her before he takes her off somewhere,' she muttered. 'Och, why wouldn't she heed my warning about him?'

Men like Jean-Marc, she had been told by Francine, were mostly harmless gigolos, but a few preyed on young single, wealthy women. Gaining their confidence, they lured them into compromising situations. Francine's eyes had grown round as she explained that the woman was then shut away in dire conditions for at least long enough to cast doubt on what she had been subjected to. Mostly the abuse was superficial but devastating ... lack of food, water, humiliation by the perpetrator or his accomplices. Occasionally it was far more serious. Some were raped or even forced through a form of marriage. Almost always they were drugged and confused, so they had little recollection of what had really happened to them. The family was blackmailed for the girl's release and for silence. Most families paid up to avoid the inevitable scandal, none involved the police.

She arrived at the church just as Alexandra and Jean-Marc were leaving. They didn't see her, so she shadowed them in case they were heading innocently back to the school. But as they turned off the main street and it became obvious from her attempts to pull free, Annie knew that Alexandra was being taken somewhere against her will.

'Oh God!' Annie muttered, 'What will I do? If I leave her to go get help, I'll never find her again. Once he's got her into the back streets it's impossible to know where she might end up.' Taking her courage in both hands, she ran full pelt after them into the dark alley.

'Arrête! Stop!' she yelled.

'Sacré!' Jean-Marc snapped. 'Tell your stupid little maid to go away, chérie!' He twisted Alexandra's arm hard up her back.

'Annie! Help me!' Alexandra was incapable of obeying.

Annie flung herself at the Frenchman. 'Let her go, you rotten swine!' She grabbed his arm and held on like grim death, kicking his shins with all her might.

'Merde!' He shook her violently and grabbed her face with one hand, but she clung hard and tried to bite as he almost blocked her breathing.

In his struggle to get rid of Annie, he slackened his grip on Alexandra and she dragged herself free. 'Run for it, Miss Alexandra!' yelled Annie, 'Run for it!'

Alexandra hesitated.

'Run!' Annie repeated, 'I can't hold on much longer. It's you he's after not me!'

With a sob, Alexandra turned and fled back to the main road. 'I'll call the police,' she shouted over her shoulder, her golden hair in disarray and face streaked with tears.

'You little bitch!' Jean-Marc grabbed the diminutive maid and shook her like a rag doll. 'You've just ruined a whole year's work and lost me a fortune!' With that he threw her against the stone wall of a house so hard she was winded and tumbled headlong into the filthy alleyway.

Alexandra ran screaming into the street. Passers-by hurried on or looked at her as if she was mad, giving her a wide berth.

'Aidez-moi! Oh God, help! Please, somebody help!' she cried and tried to grab a man's sleeve.

He shook her off with a gesture of disgust. 'Keep your hands to yourself, whore!' he snarled.

'Non! Please! S'il vous plaît! Stop! Merci!' Her French jumbled in her head and she wished with all her heart she had tried harder to learn.

'It's all right, Miss Alexandra,' Annie emerged from the alley dizzily and touched her arm.

'Where is he?' She looked around, sobbing hysterically.

'Gone. Och, we better get back.' Annie fought down a wave of nausea as she tried to smooth down her mistress's skirt and dust off the dirt stains, but she knew she could do nothing with the mess of her hair and the bruises on her wrists.

I look a sight myself, she thought, touching her own face and seeing blood on her hand from the vicious scratches he had inflicted as she struggled to free Alexandra.

'Maybe we can avoid being seen?' Alexandra calmer now, said hopefully. 'Once we're in you can fix us both, Annie.'

'Maybe,' Annie replied with a doubtful note in her voice. 'I can try.'

As they reached the school that hope faded. The Misses Berry's carriage pulled up as they limped down the street, shaken and torn. The two shocked women got out. Miss Eugenie found her voice first. 'What on earth has happened?' she gasped, one trembling hand to her lips while she grappled in her bag for smelling salts with the other.

'Jean-Marc tried to abduct me,' Alexandra whimpered.

'Jean-Marc?' Miss Eugenie's eyes narrowed. 'You had an assignation, Alexandra?'

'Yes, but it wasn't my fault. I just thought it would be amusing!' She began to cry.

'Oh, you foolish girl! This is dreadful! Dreadful!' Miss Stephanie blanched at Alexandra's tale which was reluctantly dragged from her. 'Under no circumstances has the full story to get out!' she snapped.

'Miss Eugenie! Oh, Miss Eugenie!' A wide-eyed maid rushed into the street and whispered a message. Eugenie Berry turned grimly to her sister, 'Keeping the story to ourselves might be difficult, Stephanie. Alexandra was missed almost at once, Lord

Ballantyne came and has been waiting for over an hour to see her. Everyone has been searching the house for her and for Annie. Lord Ballantyne is greatly concerned.'

Edward Baird, Lord Ballantyne, was pacing the hall, face dark with anger. 'Good God, Alexandra! What the devil is going on?' He took in her dishevelled appearance and bruised arms with one aghast glance.

'Oh, Edward, I am so glad to see you! It was dreadful! Annie and I were attacked by anarchists, just a little way from the school as we took a breath of air! I'm amazed you didn't hear our screams from here.'

'Anarchists?' Annie and the sisters Berry listened in astonishment as Alexandra flung herself at Lord Ballantyne and poured out an amazing pack of lies.

'My poor, dear girl,' he said, patting her golden hair. Turning angrily to the Misses Berry, he snapped, 'Call the police at once!'

'Now, now, Lord Ballantyne,' Miss Stephanie gathered her scattered wits first. 'As far as we can gather, no actual harm has come to Alexandra, just a little bruising. It will do her reputation no good to bring the police in after an unfortunate incident which would never have happened if she and her maid had stayed indoors as instructed.'

'I suppose you're right,' he grunted. 'But I'm not entirely happy with the way you have fulfilled your obligations in "loco parentis". There was not a responsible soul in charge when I arrived, just a gaggle of stupid maids who can hardly speak English and silly hysterical girls! I will be recommending to my friend Sir Urquhart Cameron, that Alexandra leaves here at once.'

'Oh no, Edward,' Alexandra pleaded, dabbing her eyes. 'I couldn't bear to go back to Craigdrummond in disgrace. I promise you I will be good as gold, not even take a teeny walk without a dozen bodyguards.'

The Misses Berry held their breath, then let it out in a collective hiss, as the peer looked fondly down at her brimming blue eyes and trembling lips and said, 'Oh that won't be necessary, my dear girl, I'll be staying in Paris for the next few months. Why don't I be your bodyguard myself, eh?'

Alexandra had been far more shaken by the incident than she

would admit. Jean-Marc had truly terrified her. Maybe there was something to be said for an older and very indulgent beau after all. Her lovely eyes spilled a few delicate tears. 'Oh, Edward, how good you are to me,' she whispered. 'And wouldn't Papa be so worried if he heard about this silly business? Not that we'll tell him now, will we, Edward?'

'Very worried, my dear,' he nodded, understanding that the game end was in sight at last. 'Not a word, my dear, not a word! Now how about a little trip to Cartier tomorrow to help you forget this nasty experience?'

'Wonderful,' she gave a tremulous smile. 'Wonderful, dear Edward.'

Annie cleaned the scratches as best she could, while another maid took care of Alexandra. Her body ached and the nausea refused to go away. Once she was washed and changed, she lay down on the bed and groped in her pocket for the letter from Ian. Tears slid down her torn cheeks as the words hurt all over again. 'Och, I've got to stop reading this, or my heart will break altogether,' she said to the empty room. 'I'm on my own and that's the way it is going to be from now on.'

Some two weeks later and fully recovered, Alexandra was in excellent form. She held out her arm and admired the lovely bracelet which covered the place once so badly bruised by Jean-Marc's rough courting. 'I've decided that young men are idiots!' she announced. 'I was mistaken. Dear Edward is not too old after all ... forty is no age for a man ... and he cuts a fine figure.'

'Too old for what, Miss Alexandra?' Annie looked up from the seam she was repairing on her mistress's silk shift. Deep shadows seemed to have taken residence under her eyes and she was a subdued shadow of her cheery self.

Alexandra hadn't noticed the chance in the maid she once shared so much with. Since the christening at Craigdrummond where she caused a stir with her beauty and style, and particularly following the affair of Jean-Marc, Alexandra was too preoccupied with the twists her own life was taking to discuss any more with her.

As Alexandra spent more time with Lord Ballantyne, Annie noticed and accepted that she felt the importance of her position keenly, becoming more distant and imperious. And in her own odd state of mind it was a relief not to have to humour her mistress by listening to silly tales of romance. Now to Annie's surprise, all at once she seemed inclined to chat and confide. Just like old times.

Alexandra tossed her head and tutted. 'Annie, you are stupid! He's not too old for marriage, what else?'

'Marriage?' Annie's eyes opened wide.

'Dear Edward talked to Papa when he was here last week, and Papa has said it is up to me, but that he approves the match and indeed would be very pleased. I will expect Edward to declare himself officially soon. We have already discussed some things....'

'And do you want to wed him?' Annie was puzzled at her apparent change of heart towards the peer.

'Why not?' Alexandra said with a defiant pout. 'What else is there? Papa said he will not agree to me staying in London without some horrid chaperone to protect me, so that's no fun.'

'But your Aunt Lispeth...?' Annie trailed off as Alexandra's brow darkened.

'Dearest Stepmother fears that Aunt Lispeth will give me too free a hand in London and Papa agrees ... as he does with everything that woman says!'

'Och, I'm sure Lady Cameron means well,' Annie protested, drawing a weary hand over her aching eyes.

'I am never going back to Craigdrummond ... my Stepmother is such a bore!' Alexandra snapped.

Annie saw the warning signs of a tantrum and tried to distract her, she didn't think she could cope with one of Alexandra's tempers tonight. 'So, you think marriage to Lord Ballantyne will suit you better than coming out in London? I thought that's what you always longed for, Miss Alexandra.'

'That was before Paris ... and everything,' she hesitated. 'Actually staying here these extra months has changed my perspective.'

Not to mention nearly ending up with being carted off and seeing your life in ruins! Annie thought. She had no doubt about Jean-Marc's intentions or the pseudo nature of his title.

Alexandra continued, 'I think I would find making a London debut a trifle childish now. Daisy told me that it's better to be

211

launched into Society as a young wife, with a husband who adores one. Especially a husband who is mature and likely to indulge one rather. One has far more freedom ... one can do almost anything one wants! Daisy has a lot of connections, she knows...' The worldly wisdom of Miss Singleton-Brown had found fertile ground. Aye, and we all know what they are ... Annie thought, scandalous gossip wasn't confined to above stairs! But she said sincerely enough, 'Maybe there is something in what she says. So will it be London after all if you marry Lord Ballantyne?'

'Oh yes, Edward has promised me a new town house in London as well as his family home in Dumbarton. I said I didn't want to be buried alive in Scotland while he shot grouse all day. We'll do the Seasons as they come and travel too. He says I can have as much money as I want to modernise the London house to my own taste. Edward says my taste is impeccable.'

'I just hope Edward knows what he's taking on,' Annie murmured under her breath as Alexandra went on in a rush.

'In fact, I've made up my mind, he is quite what I've always dreamed of...' The frown came back, 'Oh I do hope his family rings are pretty or he'll have to buy me new ones ... sapphires. Isn't it lucky he decided when he was young not to rush into marriage ... I would not like to follow some dead Lady Ballantyne.'

'I can imagine, especially one with grown-up children,' Annie said with a touch of irony that was wasted on Alexandra.

'Oh, yes, horrid!'

'Och well, it's fine that he's found what he wants at last.' Annie imagined that Lord Ballantyne had set up a mistress or two to pass the time while he found someone more appropriate to his taste and social standing. It was common gossip below stairs about the rich Englishmen who frequented the brothels of Paris and kept the talented belles of the 'demi-monde' in silks, satins and fine apartments. But she kept those thoughts to herself. A more urgent matter had occurred to her and she was anxious to know the answer. 'In that case when will we be leaving Paris, Miss Alexandra?' Annie laid down the fine linen and sat with a sad, introverted look on her face wondering how she could cope with a wedding in Craigdrummond kirk and just how soon it might be.

Alexandra found her expression quite unnerving, especially in view of what she had still to say. After a moment she tossed her curls and looked at her reflection in the mirror. 'Er ... Edward is not keen that you should continue as my personal maid, Annie.'

'What?' Annie blanched with shock at the abruptness with which Alexandra delivered such an astonishing statement. Though she'd thought of leaving herself, Alexandra had never given her any reason to think she wanted a change of maid. 'You've always said you'd never let me go. Didn't you mean it?'

'Well, yes, I did when I said it, of course,' Alexandra flushed. 'But dear Edward was very concerned after the attack...'

'What has that to do with me? I helped you!'

'Oh, maybe I shouldn't have mentioned anarchists,' Alexandra shrugged, 'but it was the first thing that came to mind. And the papers are always on about them ... though half the time they seem to be mistaken. Edward says most of it is just scaremongering by the French Government to their own ends...'

'I'm sorry, I don't follow at all, what have anarchists to do with me, Miss Alexandra?' Annie asked, biting her lip with impatience as Alexandra rambled on, avoiding the point.

'Well, Edward decided to talk to a private detective about what happened ... as I had told it, you understand ... anarchists and so on...'

'I understand...'

'Well, the man immediately suggested you might have been implicated.'

'What?'

'Yes, it seemed strange to him right away that both of us were outside the school at such a time of evening. He seemed to think I was lying about taking a breath of air to save your skin because I'm indulgent with you.'

'Indulgent?' Annie could hardly believe her ears.

'In fact he told Edward that you probably enticed me out and that the attacker, whether anarchist or some simple robber, was your paramour. Edward knows you go out in Paris and that you speak French ... I told him ages ago. That, I'm afraid, settled Edward's mind.' She concluded with a wave of her slim hand, 'He wants you to leave my employ before we marry. As soon as the announcements are made, in fact as soon as possible, so we can train up someone else. You'll get a reasonable reference from the Cameron estate, of course. I expect dear Stepmother will sort that out.'

'But for God's sake, Miss Alexandra,' Annie stood up shocked. 'Whether or not I go on working for you is one thing, but you and I both know what really happened that night. This is a pack of lies! It was nothing to do with me! Surely you told him that much at least?'

'Oh, I know you didn't have anything to do with it, Annie,' Alexandra agreed and went on slowly as if explaining something to a deficient child, 'But, I dare not say so now. Now dare I, Annie? It would look very bad!'

'So if somebody is to be sacrificed to keep your honour intact it's me?' Annie could not keep the bitterness from her voice. 'Has my own honour no value in your eyes?'

'How dare you, Annie?' Alexandra replied sharply. 'Remember your place.'

'Aye, what is my place?' Annie felt as furious at this unexpected betrayal as the day she had dowsed Maisie in milk. She would never have credited Alexandra with such complete self-centredness, for all she thought she knew her.

'Your place is quite clear,' she replied. 'You are a paid servant. You do as I ask as long as you are in my employ. Edward says so.'

'Is that a fact?' Annie said through clenched teeth. 'You dragged me out of the only place I was ever happy, told me long stories about your life being in my hands and how you'd always need me.' Her cheeks flared and her grey eyes sparked. 'But the minute something better comes along in the form of Lord Ballantyne's wealth and position, and you need a scapegoat to protect it, you're willing to dump me and leave my reputation in shreds. Where's my place in all that, Miss Alexandra?'

'Annie Ramsay!' Alexandra's hand flew to her throat in affront. 'I'm calling Miss Eugenie and Miss Stephanie right now. I will not tolerate such impertinence from a maid! You will serve your notice below stairs and leave when it is up. Edward is right, as Lady Ballantyne I hardly need a milkmaid to serve me!'

'There's no need to give me my notice,' Annie replied, untying her starched white pinny. 'I'm leaving right now, Alexandra Cameron. I've served you well and put up with more than anyone should have to.'

214

'Go then,' Alexandra said coldly. 'I'll tell the Misses Berry you are not in Sir Urquhart Cameron's employ any more.'

Annie could see what she was planning. 'And before you try to blame me for anything more I didn't do to explain why I've left, I'm warning you not to try.'

'How could you stop me?' Alexandra was equally angry now and she bawled back at her like a fish-wife. 'It's my word against yours ... the Cameron lawyers would make mincemeat of you.'

'There will be a letter in the post tomorrow to my brother Sandy, with the truth of what happened that night, names, times and all. I even kept the note that Jean-Marc sent you! I left it with a friend, for safety!' she lied.

'Annie! Are you trying to blackmail me?' It was Alexandra's turn for the colour to drain from her face.

'Och, you're no worth blackmailing, neither you are! But I have my insurance, that's all. If I as much as hear my name has been taken and smeared in the mud by you or yours ... and by God, I will hear ... for you high and mighty folk treat servants as if we are machines ... but we're not, we have ears and feelings ... and friends ... but if you do, I'll get him to send it to Lady Cameron and to that fancy lawyer you're talking about in Glasgow.'

'Lawyers? You?' Alexandra tried to laugh but failed.

Annie drew herself up to her full height and faced her down. 'Aye, I've learned a lot in your service, Alexandra Cameron, that included. But I'm glad to leave. Och, it's a pity I didn't let ye sink in the Moss. May Lord Edward Baird of bloody Ballantyne have joy of ye!'

With that, she swung on her heel, and angry blood pounding in her ears, climbed the stairs to her room. She packed a bag with her personal belongings, carefully leaving everything she had been given in Paris service. 'I don't want to be accused of stealing as well as arranging a robbery that didn't happen,' she muttered bitterly as she laid the fine uniform dresses on the bed. 'But I can't walk naked down the street and they made me leave every stitch behind when I came into Cameron service. This will do fine.'

With shaking hands she dressed in the simple outfit she had first been given when she left Craigdrummond. It was two years since she'd worn it and the skirt wouldn't fasten, but she pinned

215

it, tucked in the blouse and used a belt to cover the mess. It passed well enough.

She picked up her purse. In it were still most of the few francs she allowed herself from her pay before the rest went to Sandy. 'It'll be Glasgow and sharing a bed with Mammy after all,' she muttered. Carefully she counted the money, it should be about enough to get her home to Scotland if she took the cheapest fare. Aye, Sandy and Mammy will have to manage without my bawbees for a while, she thought, but they're well set up now anyway. I have my own worries to look to.

Without a word of goodbye to anyone, she ran downstairs, lifted her coat and went into the street clutching her few possessions. Dusk was gathering as she left St Honore and wandered aimlessly up the Boulevard de la Madeleine, wondering what on earth to do. Crowds milled around and passed her by, but she didn't see or hear them.

I'll find a cheap hotel and think with a clear head tomorrow, she finally decided. But it'll have to be cheap. Thank God I can speak French! Now where am I? She looked around, confused and disorientated for a moment, then recognised the district. 'Och, am I here? Well I suppose I might as well go on, the pensions are cheaper up this way.' Resolutely she turned into the rue de Caumartin and then off in the narrow streets behind the rue de Clichy. It was almost dark, but she could see the smoky lights of a bar ahead. 'I'll ask there if they know a decent wee place,' she muttered. But before she could go a step further, she heard footsteps running behind her. Born in the backstreets, she knew danger when she heard it. Instinctively she turned and threw up her hand. Her bag caught the force of a heavy blow, but the second felled her and she crashed senseless onto the cobbled alley. The street 'apache' who had hit her, skilfully located her purse and took the money, but missed the little bundle of letters she had tucked next to her heart. Without a care, he picked up her bag and went whistling on his way. As Annie lay there with blood oozing from a gash on the back of her head, two shadowy forms came from the night and stooped over her prostrate, helpless body.

'We can't do more than we've done!' Two weeks without any trace of Annie, the police gave up. 'Your photograph was impossible to use,' the weary inspector told the Misses Berry. 'The maid was just a little speck in uniform on the end of a line of others. Useless for identification purposes. Our officers have circulated the description you gave and asked some questions in the area near your establishment and even in the less salubrious parts nearby. But Paris is a big city...' He shrugged.

'For goodness sake, there can't be too many English speaking girls adrift in Paris,' Miss Eugenie snapped. 'Surely you are not just going to give up? Her employer insists we search. Lady Cameron has sent personal instructions to find the girl.'

'Madame, if she is alive but simply lost, we have to assume she would have come forward by now and identified herself to the police. Since she has not...' His shoulders rose and fell again.

'What are you suggesting?' demanded Miss Stephanie.

The inspector was blunt, 'Paris is dangerous for a young woman alone. Maybe she is being held against her will ... perhaps she is no longer in Paris ... there is a regretful trade in young girls...'

'Good God!' The Berry sisters looked horrified.

'Or, maybe she is simply dead. That is the most likely. Suicide is quite common.' The inspector looked resigned. 'I am afraid cases like this happen often and are rarely solved. Sometimes bodies turn up in the Seine, sometimes not.' He shrugged. 'We have many other calls on our time, mesdames ... the anarchists who throw bombs to kill in the streets ... art robbers...'

'This young woman is a subject of Her Majesty, the Queen of Great Britain and Ireland, Empress of India,' Miss Stephanie thundered. 'As police you have a duty to leave no stone unturned!'

'Perhaps the Queen would like to send some help in that case!' An irritated tic began twitching under the inspector's eye. 'It is impossible to send out our entire force to scour Paris for a little maid who, after all, may not choose to come back even if she is free to do so.'

'Of course she would!' Miss Eugenie was affronted.

'Are you sure, Madame?' he raised a sceptical brow. 'You say she was under notice by her mistress who is getting married and no longer needs her services. Her colleagues say she was unusually quiet even before that. She was upset, out of work, maybe crossed in love ... eh voila, the Seine!' He leaned forward. 'Or, perhaps she is already on her way home to England.'

'Scotland,' Miss Eugenie corrected him. 'But I think we would have heard something if she had.'

'Oh, I suppose the inspector is right,' Miss Stephanie sighed. 'We have done our duty. Come, Eugenie, we will inform Lady Cameron appropriately.'

'Good, a wise decision.' The inspector got up wearily and opened the door in a gesture of dismissal, 'As far as we are concerned the case is closed. Of course if she does turn up, we will let you know, mesdames.'

'Hmmmph!' The sisters swept out skirts swishing like snakes on the tiled floor.

Chapter Seventeen

After a bit Annie realised she was being half-carried, half-supported between two sturdy women. She began to groan, but the agonising walk went on and on. Then, as the movement suddenly stopped, blinding light made her cry aloud. Mercifully, she felt herself lowered onto a bench. Her head drooped as against waves of nauseating pain, she struggled to open her eyes.

Bewildered, she peered helplessly around. She could see she was in a simple 'bistro', a cheap cafe-bar of the kind to be found in any back-street in Paris, but it was completely unfamiliar. The clientele gathered round, staring and offering opinions as to what had happened in raw Parisian French.

'Where did you find her, Geraldine?' A male voice asked.

'In the alley at the back lying sprawled in the muck. I nearly fell over her. First we thought she was drunk, and we decided to prop her up against the wall so nobody would walk on her till she sobered. Then Yvette touched her hair and got blood on her hand. We realised the poor child had been hit on the head. God knows what would have happened to her if we hadn't been passing.' Geraldine felt in Annie's coat pocket. 'She hasn't a sou on her.'

'I guess the apache bastard who hit her took her sous!' Yvette said. 'Some of them don't give a working girl a chance. And this one looks too small to put up a decent fight.'

'I'd like to see someone try to take your sous!' the male voice chortled. 'You'd break their legs!'

'Not just their bloody legs!' Yvette's generous curves wobbled as she joined in the ribald laughter. 'Here wait a minute, she's coming to.'

'Qu'est-ce que tu t'appelle, ma chèrie?' Geraldine asked Annie her name.

Annie answered in the same lauguage, 'Je m'appelle Annie.'

'And where do you live?' Geraldine asked.

'Cafe Chat Roux, Montmartre,' Annie answered after a pause. There was nowhere else she could think of.

'Annie, see to the customer, I'm still trying to fix this cask!' the barman hissed. 'What's got into you today?'

'Sorry, Jules,' she apologised. 'I was miles away. The usual, Barthe?' She served a workman in broken boots with a smile.

'Merci, Annie.' He tipped his battered felt hat back on his grubby hair and knocked the harsh spirit down with a shudder that reached his feet. For a short moment he was king of the world.

'Annie, look at this.' One of Louis's friends handed her a sheet of paper and she squinted at it, making out the crabbed writing with difficulty. 'Do you think it makes the point, eh?' he asked anxiously. 'See down there at the bottom. I have called the nationalist Déroulède "the swine who licks Drumont's pig-muck boots" and see here, "I spit on their so-called League of Patriots."'

'I'm sure you've said what you want, and I don't think messieurs Drumont or Déroulède will be a bit happy about it,' she replied enigmatically. 'Just make sure the police don't find out who wrote it ... or the bullies in the League. But, look you better show it to Louis, you know I haven't a clue about politics.' She began to swill glasses behind the bar.

'Good idea, I'll just add a bit more at the end ... something about them being vile suppressors of truth and justice, eh?' he retreated to a table and began to write frantically.

'Another political nut, just like the boss,' Jules sighed. 'Don't know what they see in it myself.'

'Me neither,' Annie agreed. 'Still half our customers seem to be the same. I didn't realise till I started coming to the cafe just how many folk, ordinary folk, in Paris get mad about politics and rush out to demonstrate somewhere or another. All they ever talked about in the Berry place was dresses! It's another world in the Chat Roux.'

'Must be strange that...'

'What?'

'Suddenly having to start a new life!' Jules stood up, rubbing his hands on a grubby rag. 'Yes, very, strange. Wouldn't like it much,' he ruminated, picking tobacco-stained, uneven teeth.

'It is,' Annie answered slowly. 'Though, I seem to have done it more than most in my eighteen years.'

'Oh, I suppose you're not alone!' Jules grinned, looking around the motley bunch of regulars, 'I guess there are quite a few here who have been through it! Old Alphonse, for instance,' he nodded over to where a shabby artist sat drawing one of the evening dancers with a look of intense concentration on his face. 'When he's had a few, he claims his family have money somewhere near Bordeaux.'

'Well, pity he doesn't have some of it on him!' the dancer Madeleine, posing in her petticoats and black stockings called over. 'I could do with a few sous, but all I get are lousy drawings.'

'Not lousy, my dear. Very good drawings!' The artist raised his head and said huffily, 'And if you don't keep your damned leg still, I'll draw Jeanette instead.'

'All right! Don't get nasty, Alphie chèri!' Despite their protests and their fidgets, the girls loved to be sketched.

'Pity you lost your bag, Annie,' Jules continued to make idle conversation while Annie wiped the zinc surface of the bar. 'I like to have my own stuff around me, know what I mean?'

Annie smothered a grin. Jules's belongings amounted to little more than his working clothes and a beer tankard from his village in Alsace. 'Well, I'm only sorry about a little wooden bird my brother carved for me years ago. The apache left the papers I had stuffed in my bodice at least. And he missed a few sous I'd tucked in my drawers as well, though he got the rest.'

'But your clothes, you know...'

She managed a brave grin. 'Jules, none of the clothes I had in the bag would fit in here. They'd get mucked up with wine and dirt from those big casks. I'd never wear them.' She couldn't imagine serving all day behind the bar in the fine black serge dress and pristine white apron that had been her uniform.

'Anyway, you look better in this gear, girl!' Jules admired the cheap striped cotton dress and apron she had bought from a Montmartre stall. 'More snazzy, you know what I mean ... shows off your figure a bit ... men like that in a bar,' Jules

221

added seriously. 'It's better for singing too, I used to think you looked too standoffish in that other stuff. Like a bloody nun!'

'I'm not standoffish, whatever I wear when I sing,' Annie protested with a laugh.

'We could test that anyway, just give the nod!' Jules's piggy eyes leered.

Annie ignored the comment. 'At least the cut has healed quite well in three weeks. It's just a little tender when I touch it.' She carefully prodded the back of her head which had taken the force of the blow.

'Yes, it was pretty nasty ... lucky the girls found you when they did and brought you here, eh?'

'And lucky Louis went along with my suggestion of trying me out as a barmaid when I got on my feet.'

'Well I guess he'd have kept you here anyway,' Jules leered again and nudged her. 'Everybody knows how the boss feels about you! But anyway Louis needed a barmaid and he's a good judge of people. Too bloody good.' He grimaced.

'How do you mean, too good?'

'After he fired the last girl for trying to turn this place into a "bar close" he swore he would pick and choose more. This is a respectable bar ... more's the pity, eh?' Jules nudged her again.

'A bar close?' Annie looked puzzled.

'Mon Dieu, you're bloody ignorant of life in Paris even after living here a couple of years ... oh I suppose it was being in that aristo school that did it. You'd never get a girl from Belleville or Menilmontant ... and certainly not Montmartre, asking a question like that! He, he, he!' he gave a ribald chuckle. 'A bar close is the kind of place where the girls serve the customers with wine or a "petit vert" downstairs, then serve them something else that takes their fancy upstairs for a few extra sous! He, he, he...'

'Oh,' Annie replied, understanding at last. 'But Louis lets lots of those girls come into the Chat. Yvette and Geraldine knew exactly where to bring me.'

Louis doesn't mind working girls like Yvette and Geraldine using the bar as their base, even picking up a customer or two. And you know Marcelle, she's a fixture! Mon Dieu, if he barred all our clients who just happen to be prostitutes or pimps, we'd have to close down. He just doesn't want the barmaids slipping off every five minutes and causing havoc with the evening schedule. It's bad enough when singers get drunk and don't turn up.'

'I was so stunned and confused,' Annie said slowly, 'I don't know what would have happened if I hadn't thought of here. God, it wasn't till Louis reminded me last week, I even thought to let the Misses Berry know I'm alive.'

'Shouldn't have bothered myself. You're better here than with that lot of bourgeois-aristo bastards!' Jules knew Annie had been given the push for standing up to her mistress.

'True,' she nodded, '... but at least I didn't send them my proper address, just a tabac where I can collect messages. "Annie Ramsay, care of the Cafe Chat Roux, next to Rolande's brothel, Montmartre". Somehow it didn't seem appropriate!' She gave a rueful smile.

'Suppose not,' Jules agreed. 'They're not the kind we get here, thank God. But your folks, Annie, how about them? You have folks, don't you?'

'Sure, I wrote to them first. I don't suppose anybody had bothered to tell them I was missing before they got my letter, Jules. But I haven't heard a word from them yet.'

'Are you really thinking of going back?' he asked with a puzzled shake of his head. 'Can't understand why anybody would want to go to England. It's full of foreigners and they eat lousy food, I've heard.'

'It's Scotland, you ape! How many times do I have to tell you?' Annie grinned. 'Yes, I'm still thinking of doing it ... though I haven't said to the family yet.' She paused with a worried frown. 'And I'll have to earn the fare first, the apache took that from my purse. Oh, God knows ...' she sighed.

'Talking of God ... give me a "petit péril vert", Annie, ma chérie,' Marcelle, the prostitute Jules had called a fixture, demanded loudly as she came in from her first shift, half in disorder and a cut under one eye that had just crusted over.

'Some rough customers tonight, Marcie?' Jules watched sympathetically as Annie passed the young woman an absinthe, which she downed without diluting it or adding sugar to soften the bitter taste of wormwood and aniseed.

'You could say that. I had to get one beaten up before he'd pay up!' Marcelle gasped through a shudder as the fierce liquor hit her throat. 'He's the bastard who did this.' She touched her damaged face. 'Still better roughnecks than none at all.'

'I don't know how you have the courage to go into those dark alleys looking for custom, even with a pimp,' Annie said shaking her head. 'I couldn't do it.'

'You don't know that,' Marcelle replied with a broad grin, running shaking fingers through her hair. 'If you're hungry or desperate enough you'll do anything.'

'Not anything,' Annie insisted.

'Anything!' Marcelle peered in a little cracked mirror and dabbed away the crusted blood with a dirty handkerchief.

'How can you be so sure? Here use this.' Annie handed her a damp cloth.

'That's better.' Marcelle cleaned the cut, combed her hair and nodded in satisfaction at her reflection before going on in a matter of fact tone, devoid of self-pity. 'My mother had eight kids, I was number four. My father drank himself to death. There wasn't enough to go round, so I came to Paris at fourteen to work in a laundry. Mon Dieu, it's the old story, half the girls in here could tell you something the same.'

'But you had a job at least,' Annie said.

'After a week I got thrown out for falling asleep, still scrubbing, towards the end of a seventeen-hour shift. First night on the streets I was raped and beaten up. That was seven years ago. It's better to make the bastards pay.'

'Oh, Marcelle,' Annie's face clouded in sympathy.

'Look at you!' Marcelle went on, experienced eyes sizing Annie up like a cabbage on a stall. 'You're a pretty girl. Jules, somebody like him ... or worse ... he's not a bad old goat,' she nipped the barman playfully, '... might have taken you in alright, but demanded "payment" once you'd recovered from the blow ... or maybe before. Then, without a job or anywhere to go, you would be well on the way to where I am.'

'Mon Dieu, what a good idea ... I am so kind to this girl, I should at least claim a little bonus! I'm an idiot not to think of it before!' Jules' podgy hands went round Annie's waist.

'Get off!' Annie prised herself out of his grasp. 'And you have thought of it, you liar ... but Louis would kill you ... what would be left to kill after I had done my bit!' Jules's lechery didn't worry her. He might like the idea of seduction but he was too lazy, too scared of his boss and too easily put down to be a pest.

'She's right about Louis, though,' Marcelle nudged Jules as the young owner came in, removing his felt hat, dark eyes seeking Annie out at once. 'This is another story. Amour ... love, mon ami, true love ... what a lost case! Be seeing you!'

Marcelle wandered over to join Geraldine at a table. 'Not out tonight, love?' she asked as the other woman sat staring into her glass.

'Just thinking about it.' Geraldine stood up. 'Listen, Marcie, I'm tired of here, there's a new show at the Moulin Rouge. It's supposed to be better now La Goulue has added a few naughty touches to the "chahut". She really gets the clowns going. There should be plenty of pickings once she and the other dancers warm up their pants nicely. Le can-can!' She gave a wry, bitter grin, 'Oh la la!'

'Well...' Marcelle hesitated. 'The girls up there don't like competition. We'll need a good pimp and Jannot has just gone out with Felice.'

'Oh, come on, we can stick together and push any whore that gives us lip for poaching their patch!'

'Not without a pimp,' Marcelle insisted. 'I'm bruised enough already.' She looked around the smoky bar. 'Tell you what, let's ask Alexi the Slav to do the bit for the two of us and we can split the cost.'

'Alexi,' Marcelle yelled to a burly man sitting alone in the corner. 'Come and pimp. We're doing round the Moulin tonight and you know what the whores are like up there.'

'Forty per cent,' he growled.

'Twenty-five and be glad.'

'Thirty.'

'Alright, but make sure you're damned worth it!'

'It's a deal.' The big man got up and followed as, arm in arm, the two women wandered out into the dark, chilly night.

Annie stood looking after them. They had shown her humanity and kindness when she most needed it. Some folk would despise them for what they were and what they did, but in her heart she knew she never could. And anyway, the memory of Ian came to mind, she was no better than she should be herself ... och, but I loved him, her heart protested. Aye, but it was a mistake, her head replied. A terrible mistake.

The weeks passed and she worked in the Chat Roux, Annie

became part of the scenery, but she knew the time was coming when she would have to make a move. Louis paid generously. Soon she would have the fare saved again to go back to Glasgow.

With a practised movement, she filled a carafe with cheap wine and loaded it onto the bar tray with glasses and a jug of water. At least nobody could say she was a freeloader, she thought. I would rather die before anybody could accuse me of that. And I won't take charity, even from Louis.

But even as she thought about it, she was reassured. She paid her way not just singing, but everywhere in the Chat. Cheerfully she served behind the bar, prepared vegetables, helped to choose artistes, listened, comforted, sometimes nearly dropped from tiredness. But, she told herself, exhaustion is better than thinking. Soon her hands lost their well-kept look, but she didn't give a bent bawbee for that. No, there were other matters far more pressing to deal with, like getting back to Scotland.

Nights were worst. Sometimes she woke in the narrow bed in her tiny room at the back of the cafe crying, knowing she had been dreaming about Ian.

'Come on, Annie, it's nearly ten o'clock!' Marie from the bar cut through fathoms of deep sleep. 'Louis is hopping from foot to foot in the kitchen!'

'Coming,' Annie groaned. Louis, Annie and last night's barmaids hadn't got to bed till the last customer had gone at four-thirty in the morning. Then the bar was tidied by Marie who was on early shift to be opened again by Jules at five.

Jules moaned when it was his turn to take the morning shift serving the first workers coming in to take a coffee, or something stronger with their chunk of bread before they staggered off into the winter darkness. Few of the crumbling apartments that made up the Montmartre backstreets had kitchens, or were expected to. The locals ate for a few centimes in dozens of cheap places, or made their local cafe home from home and place of rendezvous day or night.

Within minutes Annie was down in the bar, tucking her hair under a scarf and thankfully gulping down the mug of chocolate Marie handed her.

'Ma chèrie! You look so charming.' Louis helped her into the second-hand coat she had bought at a street market. The clothes she had been wearing when she left Berry's were cleaned and

226

stored away in a box under her bed. They were her only link to the past and for sentimental reasons she guarded them well.

'Thank you,' she muttered, too tired to talk more. But by the time Louis's cart had reached the great market at Les Halles, she was wide awake. 'Oh marvellous!' She drank in the vibrant atmosphere of shouting carters, rattling churns and country smells. He had promised to show her the great Paris market and as usual kept his word.

Churns! Country smells. Annie shook her head as if that would rid her of the memories that tormented night and day.

'Are you all right, chèrie?' Instantly attentive, Louis saw her sudden pallor.

'I'm fine.' Annie forced a smile and watched him relax, she had been about to tell him that she had decided to leave Paris, but the concern on his face held her back.

'Don't try so hard, Annie. I know it's not easy for you at the Chat Roux after working as a lady's maid in fine surroundings, ma chèrie,' he said, lifting her fingers to his lips. 'But you are doing so very well, just be happy with what you are. We are all proud of you.'

'It's not the surroundings or the work, Louis! God, I'm from streets no better than Montmartre just like the rest...'

'Then what?' he insisted gently. 'Don't you think you should be honest with me? Am I not your friend?'

'Oh you're so good to me, Louis,' Annie's voice shook. 'Ever since the girls brought me in that night, you've been patient and kind. You're a good man. If I hadn't met you through Francine, where would I be now?'

'Come.' He pulled her into a quiet spot by the big archway leading to where the flowers were brought from winter hothouses for auction. Their heady smell cut through the sharp frosty air. 'Listen to me, ma chèrie, I'm not kind, I'm in love, Annie,' he whispered, lips close to her ear. 'From the moment I saw you I wanted you beside me till the day I die. Please let me be your future. You told me there was someone in the past, the farmer's son. You still love him, don't you?'

'Yes.' Annie nodded.

'But he is married now?'

'Yes.'

'Then what you felt for him, or even feel now, is nothing to me. I love you unconditionally, Annie, and I want you to marry me,' Louis said. 'I don't expect you to forget the past, just to let it go.'

'It's not that easy, Louis,' she replied, steeling herself for his disappointment. 'I can't let you marry me hoping that one day maybe I'll love you like I did Ian. I think too much of you for that. Louis, listen, it's better if I go.' She looked him in the eye, despite the pain she knew would be there. 'I've saved enough money to go home and I'm buying my ticket for Scotland tomorrow.'

'Are you?' He held her gaze without flinching then said with quiet determination and a smile playing round his lips, 'Oh no, you're not escaping Louis Lamarche that easily, Annie Ramsay. Your old love may not have fought for you, but this one will. I'll follow if you go and pursue you to the ends of the earth if I have to, pursue till you come back willingly as my wife. Your doubts are nothing ... a woman should have had her heart broken at least once. We say in France that a touch of sorrow in the eyes adds mystery! And whatever you say, one day I know you'll love me as I love you.'

'And if I never do?'

'Then I'll always know I tried.'

Annie stood silently looking at him. She had come to know the strength of character and fine intelligence that lay behind Louis's slight build and delicate constitution. He meant what he said, every word. As the traders howled and roared and the wagons laden with rainbows of fruit and flowers trundled past, she slowly reached up and touched his face. 'I'll use the train money to buy a wedding gown,' she said.

They were married in the little country-town in Picardie where he had been born. Francine took a couple of days off and made the long journey from Tours. She wept sentimental tears as her brother slipped a fine gold ring onto the finger of her dearest friend and they were declared man and wife, first in the Mairie and then in the little stone church of Sainte Filomene, next to it.

Annie was a bonnie bride in a new velvet dress and little hat crowned with flowers. With tears in his eyes, Louis declared his love and commitment. It was easy to feel happy that lovely day and inside Annie felt a gratitude so deep it could be called love for the man who had so unselfishly filled the empty shell her life had become.

Briefly she wrote and told her family about her marriage, bequeathing them the dowery banked from the time she had rescued Alexandra. The process was simpler than crossing a Paris boulevard. She sent the Scottish bank a copy of her marriage lines which she translated herself and had stamped and signed by a drunken attorney who frequented the Chat Roux. Sandy, Phyllis and Mammy were grateful for that final piece of help and still wrote now and then.

Annie was grateful too, not to have to touch the Cameron money. It felt tainted with past hopes, dreams and disappointments. Disposing of her dowery was her only and final act of deception against Louis, for reasons she couldn't bring herself to analyse, she never told him about it at all.

Annie Lamarche tipped the rubbish into the bin and leaned for a moment against the stone wall of the cafe yard, watching the great pale yellow globe that hung over Montmartre and the crazy mixture of souls who lived there. 'You know, it's strange,' she said aloud with a sense of wonder, 'the moon sheds as pure a light here as it does over Craigdrummond Strand.'

She had settled easily into busy married life at the Chat Roux and resolutely refused to allow thoughts of Ian to intrude. Louis has my loyalty and devotion, she told herself. Even if I can't love him the way I did Ian, I owe him those at least for the rest of my life.

'Come on, Annie,' Jules bawled down the yard, 'let Marie do that, the clowns inside are waiting for you to sing.'

'Every time I come out here and grab a moment to think in peace, somebody drags me back in!' she muttered then shouted back, 'All right, Jules, I'm on my way.' As she pushed open the door, familiar cooking smells assailed her from the big range. With quickly sure steps, she walked through the kitchen and into the bar.

A cheer went up as she jumped lightly onto the stage. 'Annie! Annie! Sing "Mademoiselle Valerie"!' someone yelled.

'What, again?'

'Yes!' the crowd roared.

'If you insist.' She smiled and began a popular song of the day, about a French gentleman unsuccessfully trying to seduce his English maid. Exaggerating her accent, she had them laughing helplessly.

These days she never sang the songs which had first made her so popular in the cafe. Louis forbade it. 'Annie, I can't stand it,' he had said one evening, his pale face flushed. 'You sound so sad. The customers love it, but not me. No more, eh? You do the other songs so well now in French, it's better to stick to them.'

'Maybe you're right,' she agreed and never again sang of her native land.

Now the crowd cheered and stamped their appreciation as she jumped back down and joined Jules behind the bar. However much they yelled or pleaded, she never did an encore, and they loved her all the more for that statement of individuality.

Chat Roux had become her world. The warmth, shifting smells of casseroles, wine and absinthe, the rowdiness, ribald laugher, rough kindness, constant chatter, arguments that went on for hours ... sometimes days, and always the ready wit of the clientele, were all round from when the bar opened at five in the morning till it closed at four next morning. It was easier to fit in and feel really part of the Chat now she was Louis's wife.

'You are so clever, ma chèrie, and I adore you!' Louis told her every day. He admired her drive and courage and willingly shared responsibility. They divided the main shifts, with Jules, Louis, and Annie managing a long shift each and overlapping during the busiest time of the evenings.

Their union was instantly fruitful. Within a week of marrying Louis she was pregnant. As her stomach swelled, everyone in the cafe assumed they had been lovers for some time before the wedding and teased them roundly.

Sometimes she glanced at Louis wondering how he felt, but he accepted the good-natured chaff without distress, even with a little touch of pride. When she lay in his arms his lovemaking was gentle and undemanding as if she was almost too precious to touch. But as the months passed, after a long day Louis was so tired he simply tumbled into bed beside her and fell asleep. Then she would waken and feel a great surge of tenderness as he curled up against her, trusting and secure. She never compared him with Ian. That would have been the ultimate betrayal of his love and generosity.

Chapter Eighteen

'Il est né, le divin enfant...!' warbled Marie as she cleaned the zinc bar.

Jules joined in in his lumbering bass... 'Jouez hauthois, résonnez musettes...'

'Il est né le divin enfant...' Annie sang smiling.

'Chantons tous son avènement...' they chorused.

Christmas time arrived full of gaiety and frivolity in the city of culture, sin and light. The shops along the brilliant Paris boulevards glittered with delights of every kind. Strings of electric lamps appeared and lit up all the very best streets, glaring harshly on the awestruck passers-by. And even in Montmartre the bars and halls tricked themselves out gaily with wreaths and ribbons.

Oddly enough, Annie's resolution not to think about Ian was harder now the baby was on the way. Though Louis was the father, her swollen stomach reminded her only of what had happened between her and Ian on that warm June night. What if I'd had his child? she asked herself, picking at the still raw scar of sorrow and not allowing it to heal. Och, once it's over and the bairn is here, I'll not fret as much, she told herself. Maybe they're expecting a bairn themselves by now. The idea cut her to the quick, for all she knew she had no right to feel so.

Candles lit up the bars and brothels of Montmartre as well as the holy 'creche' in the church of Sacre Coeur towering above them. Marcelle, Geraldine and tipsy Barthe, led the sentimental songs at the Chat Roux's special open show on Christmas Eve. The cafe was reserved for its motley family that night. No outside artists were invited and only the regulars came. Everybody had chipped into a kitty, so free food and drink were served liberally all day.

Annie had stopped singing now she was pregnant, since the lights and the heat made her dizzy, but she still worked hard behind the bar and in the kitchen. By the late evening, she was exhausted. Louis, concerned and vigilant saw her wilt.

'Annie, come, rest for a little while. Let the others do the work. Just let me tell you how much I love you,' Louis murmured in her ear and laid his arm across her shoulders, drawing her to him as carols were sung.

'You're a good lad, Louis.' Annie leaned against him, feeling his strength and kindness. In the void of all she had lost, she felt blessed to have found a rock solid enough to keep her safe.

On New Year's Eve the bar was filled all day and into the night with laughter and song as they waited to welcome 1895. Annie served the seasonally cheery and the totally drunk alike with her usual calm smile, as Louis watched with loving, indulgent eyes.

As the hour of midnight neared, he disappeared and came staggering back with a great box of oysters, seaweed dripping from the corner. 'Here we are!' he shouted. 'Fresh from Brittany this morning by train. Marie, cut the bread! Supper is on me, all of you! Here, Annie,' he called to his wife. 'Take a moment and have one, ma chèrie, before this greedy lot eat them up!'

She lifted an oyster and sniffed the sea smell. A sharp stab of memory stirred and she thrust it back again.

'They're from Brittany, Annie,' Louis took her hand and opened it, putting an oyster on the palm. 'Look inside, maybe there's a pearl in it!'

'Not this time!' She laughed and raised the open shell to her lips to suck out the succulent salty flesh as the others did around her.

At that moment the cry went up across the cobbled streets of the city. 'The new year has come!' All over Paris the bells pealed out.

Just like Craigdrummond kirk on Hogmanay, Annie thought. Then tears began to stream down her face and the oyster shell shattered at her feet.

'Ma chèrie,' Louis held her close. 'What's the matter?'

'Oh I'm so sorry, Louis.' Annie forced herself to smile and dry her eyes. 'Pregnant women are always too emotional. I'm just happy for us all and for our future together.'

'As am I,' he kissed her. 'Eighteen-ninety-five is to be our year, Annie. Now come to bed while these apes drink the night away, tonight I want my wife in my arms.'

One late May evening when cherry-blossom tossed over the roofs of Montmartre and showered the cobbles with soft colour, Louis came into the bar brimming with excitement. His dark eyes as always searched out his wife at once and lit up when he found her. 'Annie Lamarche, we are going to make the Chat Roux the best venue in Paris!' he announced with a boyish grin. 'And to that end, you and I are going spying!'

'Spying? We don't need to spy, we're the best already. Oi,' she turned to the bar, 'Jules, Marie, you too, Barthe, come and listen to what daft idea has my husband come up with this time!' Louis beamed, he loved when she teased about his dreams and emotions.

'Aren't we the best already then, Boss?' Jules joined in the fun.

'Not quite.' He gave a ferocious scowl and twiddled his moustaches. 'There is just one place left which can challenge us!'

'The Moulin Rouge?' Marie suggested, slapping a steaming casserole on the bar and licking spilled sauce off her fingers.

'Rubbish! Too vulgar.' Louis pretended to be horrified. 'Who wants to see La Goulue's bloomers and big fat backside every night? No, as a great sacrifice for the sake of the Cafe Roux, Monseiur and Madame Louis Lamarche will go and see what they are up to in Le Mirabilis!' he announced with a proud flourish of tickets.

'Le Mirabilis? Oh, Louis, everyone is talking about Monsieur Bruant's new show! Come here!' He was rewarded by a kiss.

'But why not Monsieur Salis' "Chat Noir"? demanded Marcelle, refusing to be left out, 'Isn't he the master still?'

'True, so maybe we are third after all,' Louis replied with a laugh. 'Until now, nothing has compared to the singers and performers Maitre Salis gathers together. But I think Guillot has the same touch as Salis, maybe better. We must see.'

'Annie!' he turned to his wife. 'All Paris is queuing to see Guillot's show, except the most bourgeois or prudish! And so, ma chèrie, will we!'

Late on Friday night, they walked arm in arm through the back streets, then up the rue des Abbesses, crossed the rue des martyres and onto the boulevard Rochechouart towards the place d'Anvers. Le Mirabilis was near the original premises of the Chat Noir which had since moved to the rue Victor Massé. Louis hoped to rival both one day.

'Look at that!' Annie said excitedly as they turned the corner. The crowd outside was already half way down the road.

'Come,' Louis put a proprietorial arm round her shoulders and steered her into the queue.

The atmosphere was as high as the great Eiffel Tower. Excited chatter, mingled with the sounds of street buskers and singers into a cacophany Annie was sure could be heard across Paris.

'And here come the circus animals!' Louis said with republican disdain, as the rich and famous passed the queue and were personally greeted by Monsieur Guillot, the mocking, eccentric and gifted proprietor. By the time they were allowed to file in with the rest of the ordinary folk and find their seats, the show was about to begin.

'What an amazing place. Creepy though.' Annie looked around at the decor, which was in the style of the palace of Francois Villon, the medieval beggar-poet.

Drapes and grotesque lighting created an atmosphere which was both threatening and intimate. Every seat was taken and people even stood or crouched in the corners. There was a feeling of lawlessness and anarchy about the place. Annie clutched Louis's arm tighter, glad she wasn't alone.

'Look, Annie,' he nudged towards a corner of the room where a group were rowdily chatting and laughing as the waitresses poured wine into their glasses.

'What about it?' she asked.

'Have you heard of Rodin?'

'The sculptor? Yes, of course, the papers are full of him. Is he here?' She looked around helplessly. 'There are too many people, Louis, which is Rodin?'

'The pale man to the left...'

'God he looks ill,' Annie thought he had one of the greyest faces she had ever seen.

'Oh yes he's ill all right,' Louis agreed. 'It's been all the problems over his statue of Balzac ... he's only asked for more time. The Society and its Subscribers are pigs! The man is a genius, no one can deny that at least.' Louis's sensitive eyes glowed. 'Everybody in Paris knows him ... even more than the painters ... talking of painters,' he said, 'did Marcelle tell you Toulouse-Lautrec painted her at Madame Kelly's "House of all Nations" once?'

'The brothel? No, she didn't ... I thought he only did the Moulin ... I wish Alphonse was as good at doing our posters ... don't tell him that, eh,' she added with a frown. 'They're not that bad?'

'No, of course not,' Louis smiled at her anxious expression. 'But you're right, Henri de Toulouse-Lautrec is the best. Everybody know that. And the Moulin want to hang on to him ... if they can.'

'What else does he do?' Annie asked half-interested as she peered around the noisy crowd.

'Oh he's done some good stuff for Les Ambassadeurs, posters for Bruant's shows, you know the kind. But he prefers doing the dancers like Madeleine, or La Goulue at the Moulin. Or pros, you know Marcie, Yvette, Geraldine ... can't blame him really,' Louis added casually. 'It's the only way he can get them to notice him, poor ugly little runt.' He paused peering around at the crowd, then went on, 'Occasionally he does respectable women too. I'm working on him, chèrie. One day we'll have him in the Chat Roux.' Louis promised. 'Then I'll get him to sketch you.'

'Not till I'm back to a reasonable shape,' Annie laughed patting her stomach. 'Then he can draw me all he likes.'

'Once you're singing again, that's when I'll commission him to sketch you.' He kissed her fingers one by one. 'Because that's when I love you best ... almost.'

Suddenly the chattering of the waiting crowd faded to deep silence as Guillot's slight figure appeared, dapper in dark tail-coat, light waistcoat and fashionably generous moustaches.

'Mesdames, messieurs, welcome.' He bowed deeply to every corner of the room. 'Tonight we have a special programme for you which will be opened by our singers and dancers. Then later, much later you will have the rare opportunity to hear ... the incomparable ... Aristide Bruant!'

'Bruant!' A roar went up. The audience at le Mirabilis were never told the complete programme till they were in place and tonight they had drawn a trump. Bruant was a legend in his time.

235

'Talk of the devil! Bruant in person! See you always bring me luck, ma chèrie,' Louis whispered.

Impatiently the audience watched and clapped politely enough, as the supporting acts juggled, danced, sang and whetted the appetite for the great man.

Annie could feel the anticipation of the crowd as they waited through the other acts. She shot a glance at her husband, but even steady, calm Louis sat almost on the edge of his seat with impatience.

Then it was time. Guillot savoured every minute of his introduction as the audience screamed for Bruant.

Bruant came in almost casually and stood looking across the crowded room, with the sharp eyes and bitter smile everyone talked about. Built like a stocky boxer, his unruly black hair sprung back from a high forceful forehead and hung down like a mane across his thick neck. 'See,' Louis whispered in her ear, 'he nearly always wears the same stage costume, black corduroy jacket and trousers, a red flannel shirt and a black neck-tie.'

Annie didn't reply, like the rest of the audience she was totally still, mesmerised by the force of his personality. He stood silently watching, playing with them even before he started. Then he spoke in a soft, commanding tone, 'Don't think you're going to sit there like sheep.' His compelling eyes picked them off one by one. 'And when I teach you a chorus you sing it so loudly the roof comes off. If you don't, I'll leave.'

'We will, we will!' the crowd yelled adoringly.

'And by the way, you herd of camels, try to bray together in tune, will you?'

'Yes! Yes!'

'I am going to sing "À la Villette".'

In a thrusting, vibrant almost metallic voice he poured out the bitter words of the street-apache's lover as she watches him die on the guillotine. The crowd roared their way through each chorus and yelled their approval when it was over.

'Isn't he marvellous, Annie?' Louis's face shone as he clapped and stamped with the rest.

'Yes.' She was stirred by the vibrance and as a singer herself, she could appreciate his immense talent. But at the same time the violent undercurrent of the performance, so typical of the times, and above all so typical of Paris, disturbed her. Och, this is not

236

my heritage, she thought ... but what is any more?

There was much about this lovely, egocentric, raw, arrogant city she lived in, that Annie felt a deep affection for and much she found alien and disturbing. And some of that comes too close to home for peace of mind, she thought, glancing at Louis who was leaning forward, hanging onto Bruant's every word and movement, dark eyes burning.

Intellectuals like Louis and his friends had a vogue for anarchist ideals now the worst violence of that day was done. A refined philosophy of anarchistic individualism had found its admirers among artists, writers and thinkers throughout the city, but especially on the Left Bank and in other bohemian districts like Montmartre.

'And that includes Louis,' she sighed to herself with resignation. Even he, the gentlest of men, was inclined to sit over an absinthe or four now and then, and plot subversion with his cronies. It didn't worry her too much, they were idealists every one and never went beyond talk. As long as the police didn't get nervy and run them in. Annie gave an ironic grin. Alexandra Cameron would faint if she knew how many so-called anarchists she served happily with a coffee or a drink in the Chat Roux and listened to their woes.

The baby kicked and she gave a little gasp, but stilled Louis' anxious look with a smile.

Silence fell again as Bruant announced his second song. 'Un Vieux ouvrier', the song of the homeless workman without a job.

'Les chiens perdus ont des fourrières ... stray dogs have their holes, swans have their shelters by the ponds ... but I have nowhere...' he sang softly, but with such power the words reached every person in the room.

Tears came to her eyes as he sang of the loneliness and emptiness of a life without meaning, or hope. She reached out in the darkness of the room and took Louis's hand. He sensed her fragile mood, kissed her fingers once more and held her small work-worn fist tight in his. 'I'll take care of you,' he whispered.

'Please.' She laid her head on his shoulder.

It was two in the morning before the crowd let Bruant go and staggered out singing and laughing into the starry night. Above the city the moon shone pure and bright as the young pair made their way, arms linked, back to the still busy bar.

Annie dreamed that night of workmen's cracked boots clacking on stone and children running barefoot in grubby streets. But though she tried to look for some indication of where she was, the place kept its secret. In the thin early twilight her pillow was damp with tears.

On the morning she became nineteen, Annie woke, struggling to frightened consciousness. A sudden sharp pain made her gasp and another shortly after forced a cry from her lips, 'Louis! Louis! I think the baby is coming.'

Louis had already arranged a special programme as a celebration for his wife's birthday, bringing in the best he could find and afford. There was little else to do but go on with the show. Jules Jouy, the singer and composer headed the bill, backed by a group of artistes he brought with him. Madeleine and the other resident dancers did their naughty 'Chahut', among the audience as always, petticoats flying. Jules bullied and yelled at the extra help behind the bar, but even so they sweated to keep thirsty trays filled for the waiters to struggle precariously with through the crowds.

'How is she?' Jules broke off to ask Louis, who, white-faced and shaking with anxiety, spent his time between the bar and the room where Annie still lay in labour.

'Terrible!' he replied. 'It's been almost twelve hours and she's no further along. The midwife says she's hardly dilated.'

'Bloody midwives! They're no bloody good!' Marie snapped, pushing Jules out of the way and filling a pitcher with wine, slapping it down on the bar so hard it spilled like blood onto the zinc. 'Give her a tumbler of gin, Louis, and put warm cloths on her belly.'

'I don't think she's in any state to take gin even if she wanted to.' Louis shook his head. 'And as for warm cloths, I think they've tried everything up there. The midwife says it's because this is her first and she's so small ... but her pelvis is good, she says ... it should be alright, she says ... God, I can't face seeing her like this ... my poor Annie...'

'I'll go up,' Marcelle had stood listening. 'Oh, don't worry, I can take a couple of hours off for a friend,' she waved Louis's half-hearted protest aside. 'I know a thing or two from when I worked in Madame Kelly's brothel. Bet me and my mates helped deliver more little bastards than any bloody midwife.'

Louis winced at the words, but knew she was only being kind. 'If you can help her, then do it, Marcelle, but don't do anything that could hurt Annie, she is my life!'

'Oh, don't we all know that, you great softie,' Marcelle tapped his pale cheek and slipped out.

As soon as the thunderous music and chatter of the bar died behind the big kitchen doors, Marcelle could hear Annie's groans from deep in the warren of rooms at the back of the building. She listened carefully as she approached, trying to gauge how close together the contractions were.

'Mammy! Och, can ye no stop it, somebody!' Annie screamed as her small frame was shaken again.

'She's beginning to open,' the midwife said as Marcelle took her place beside the pathetic sweat-soaked sight that was Annie Ramsay Lamarche. 'But she's too tense to let go.'

'Come on, ma chèrie,' Marcelle took Annie's hand. 'It'll soon be over.'

'Marcelle,' Annie moaned when the contraction eased. 'Help me, Marcelle, I can't stand it any more. Stop it, Marcie!'

'Oh la, ma chèrie,' the prostitute wiped her brow with a damp cloth. 'You're fighting too hard. Listen to Marcie, sweetheart, and we'll work with the baby to get out ... this can't be over till the little bastard's born, whatever you think you can stand. The midwife says you're nearly there. Your poor little one must be wondering what a useless thing it has for a mother, lying groaning and not doing a bloody thing to help when it needs it. Come now, when the next pain starts, hold my hand, take a deep breath and push ... screaming is just a waste of damned time!'

'Oh, Marcie, it's starting again! Tell me what to do.' Annie's forehead broke out again in a sweat as the contractions gripped her slight body once more.

'Right, girl, breathe as deep as you can, now ... push! Push! Push!'

Annie thought her body would break in two, but with Marcelle and the midwife urging, she summoned up the last of her strength and made herself work with the great primitive force that was birth. Again and again she rode the agonising contractions, but more effectively now.

'Come on! Once more! You're nearly there!' Marcelle urged.

'Oh God!' There was one final searing pain, then the baby shot into the world followed by a stillness like a deep pool below whitewater rapids. 'It's over,' she whispered, 'thank God!' Annie sank back in exhaustion. She lay still as death while Marcelle cut the cord.

The midwife picked up the silent baby. 'Blob of mucus in the throat,' she said, turned it upside down and slapped its tiny bottom till it howled in furious outrage.

Minutes later, Louis Lamarche jumped up onto the stage, his face burning with joy and pride. He held up his hand for silence. 'Ladies and gentlemen, the bar is open at my expense for the next hour. Drink till you drop! Today is my wife's birthday and today she has given birth to our first child, a fine healthy daughter! Celebrate!'

Chapter Nineteen

'Papa, squeal!' Juliette Francine Lamarche was the little queen of the Chat Roux. At two and a half she was a precocious, delight of a child who had inherited her mother's chestnut curls and charm and her father's dark intelligent eyes. Louis adored her and he glowed with pride when she climbed onto his knee and pulled his moustaches mercilessly. 'Papa, squeal!' she cried again.

'Aie, aie,' he groaned to please her.

'Again! Again!' she demanded.

'Poor Papa,' Annie tutted. 'You'll make him sad.'

'Julie not make Papa sad.' She laid her head on his breast and stroked his cheek.

'Never,' he agreed indulgently, ruffling her curls.

Annie watched them with deep pleasure. How easy it was to love Louis, she thought then smiled as she realised what she had thought so spontaneously. Louis was right after all. The passion she had once felt for Ian was gone, and what they had found between them was deep enough to be called love by anyone's measure. 'Mes choux,' she hugged them both as she passed.

Louis caught her hand and kissed it gently. It was clear he adored his wife, but there were no more children yet to rival Julie in his affections. Louis was mostly too exhausted nowadays to do more than lie in her arms and tell her how much he loved her.

Marie called from the bar, 'Julie, bonbons! Old David has come past and I bought you some.'

'Bonbons!' Juliette climbed down from Louis's knee and ran over. Louis retrieved his papers and began to scribble quickly.

'You spoil her, Marie,' Annie reprimanded but couldn't keep

her face straight as Julie perched at the bar and dug greedy little fists into the bag.

'Oh, why not?' Marie shrugged. 'Life is hard and you're only a child once. Isn't that right, Louis?'

'What?' He looked up.

'Life is hard and...' Marie began, then broke off. 'Oh, you're not writing about that man Captain Dreyfus again, are you, boss?' she demanded with the rough democracy of the Chat Roux. 'Some of our customers think he should be sent to the guillotine!'

Everyone in the cafe knew that Louis and some close friends were helping the writer Emile Zola defend Captain Alfred Dreyfus, unjustly accused and imprisoned for treason. The whole of Paris and indeed most of France, was bitterly, noisily and actively divided over his trial. Accusations and counter-accusations over his guilt ran wild, as did unbridled anti-semitism in some highly vocal quarters, including large sections of the press.

'Then some of our customers are very wrong, Marie,' Louis said quietly, but his eyes flashed. 'The man is innocent, I...' he broke off as his habitual cough caught his breath.

Annie's face clouded. The only things that marred her contentment were Louis's failing health and his increasing involvement with the fickle, violent politics of the day. He loved the intrigue, the discussion, the social agitation that was Paris in the 'fin de siécle'. Annie, practical and tolerant as ever, didn't grudge him his beliefs, even if she found it hard to understand the twisted roots of some of them. She regarded Louis's philosophy with the same calm equanimity as she did his friends and listened patiently when he sounded off about corruption or injustice. But now she could see his interest turning into a consuming obsession which she feared would burn him out as his fragile health grew worse.

His body had never been as strong as his spirit and with each passing year his strength ebbed a little. During the hard days of winter, when the snow outside sparkled on the great sails of the Moulin Rouge and lay thick on Sacre Coeur, the still air held the smoke inside the tightly closed bar. Louis's cheeks hollowed and flared with a bright colour too unnatural for healthiness. He choked and coughed, but he was glad that his strong-willed wife could carry the burden of the cafe for a while till he got better with the spring. But that was months away, Annie worried.

'You're too idealistic, Louis Lamarche,' she teased, hiding her concern, when he finally recovered from the paroxism that shook his body and left him pouring sweat.

'Well, someone has to be an idealist or what is left of life? We can't just let an innocent man rot on Devil's Island because he is a Jew, Annie, because that's what it amounts to.'

The Dreyfus affair had been dragging on for as long as Annie had been in Paris, but in the fashionable, drawing-room world of Alexandra Cameron, she had heard little of it. In the Chat Roux she heard of little else. 'Well, as long as you take care, I don't want Dreyfus to be the death of you.'

'Oh, you worry too much...' Louis stifled a cough.

'Maybe, maybe not.' She bowed her head and continued to work. At least Dreyfus kept Louis from fretting, she took comfort in that unarguable fact as she planned the next show.

'Papa, stop!' She took his pen. 'See, you can have a bonbon!' Annie looked up again in amusement as Julie pushed aside his papers and climbed back up onto his knee. There was always his joy of a daughter to console him whatever the season.

Annie folded up the programme, got up and pulled on her coat. 'Come on, Jannot,' she called to the resident 'heavy'. 'Work to do.'

'Coming, Annie.' The big man lumbered over and waited as she kissed her husband and daughter.

'Get Marie to put Julie to bed soon. I'll come straight back once I've heard the lad from Toulouse,' she promised. 'But I need to see him in action before I'll put him on our bill.'

'Take care, ma chèrie.' Louis held her hand and kissed each fingertip before releasing it.

'Of course.' She smiled and was gone, Jannot's huge form shadowing her.

As Annie went out into the Paris night, there was no sign of motherhood in her slim figure. Hard work keeps me trim, she would shrug if anyone remarked on it. And hard work stops me brooding, she told herself many times.

After Juliette's birth she had thrown herself wholeheartedly into fulfilling Louis's vision of making the Chat Roux the place to be on Montmartre. 'All ready for the Twentieth Century,' they said as their reputation grew. 'Soon we will be the best spot in the neighbourhood,' Louis claimed in triumph after a particularly good evening. 'Or at least reckoned among the top three or four,' his wife added with sturdy common sense.

'Where is it tonight, Annie?' the big man asked, each of his long strides covering two of hers.

'Only l'Etoile on St Denis. Nowhere really tough. You can wait at the bar, just not too many petits, eh?' With Louis's health declining, it was mostly Annie whose small, determined figure scoured the theatres and bars, burly guard in tow, searching endlessly for the artistes who would pull in the crowds.

Swiftly she walked through the dark streets of the city, heading down towards St Denis. Confidently entering the cheap cafe-concert, filled with smoke, and the stink of too many bodies with too little money to think of wasting it on soap, she found a seat and took out her note-pad.

A whisper went round. 'La Petite Ecossaise is here again. She must be looking.'

Madame Lamarche was known by the artistes and bar-girls alike of Montmartre and the surrounding districts. In the back street cafes the hopefuls always tried harder when they saw her sitting at the back, listening and taking notes. The Chat Roux paid well and was becoming the place to be heard.

Annie had learned the rules and the risks of the cafe business as fast as she did with everything life had thrown at her. And she was popular. Her cheery laugh and ebullient personality brightened the bar at the Chat Roux and enchanted the customers. But if those who had known her as she danced and sang across Clachan's farmyard could have seen her, they would have missed a carefree note of pure joy in being alive that had gone for ever.

Sometimes she wondered if life on Montmartre was making her too tough, but she shrugged that doubt off. They had to survive.

The verdict of others was clearer. Madame Lamarche was kind and always ready to listen when folk had problems. But she refused to suffer fools and could be unexpectedly hard when anyone whined or tried it on. When her grey eyes flashed in anger, people backed off.

Who'd have thought it? Annie grinned to herself at the irony, the first time she heard Madeleine describe her as a 'strict but fair' employer. With a Gallic lift of her shoulders, she compared her life as Patronne of Le Chat Roux to that of 'strict but fair'

Mistress Crawford and wondered what they would all say if they could see her now.

'Where's Louis?' she asked when she got back and saw his empty place. It was close to midnight, but her husband usually liked to stay up late.

Jules's chubby face clouded. 'He went to bed, Annie, I don't think he's too well again.'

Without another word, Annie crossed the bar and made her way to their bedroom. Louis sat propped up in the big bed, cheeks flaring red and the rest of his face deathly pale.

'Don't fuss, ma chèrie!' He held up his hand before she could say a word. 'It was just an idiot who smoked old socks in his pipe right beside me. I'll be fine in the morning.'

She knew better than to argue. Louis hated it when anyone talked about his illness. 'All right,' she said, sitting on the bed beside him. 'I just want you to know that the lad I saw tonight will do quite nicely for the Chat. I've had a quick word and he'll come up in the morning for a proper audition. We can try him out next weekend. The rest of the programme is good, so it won't be a catastrophe if he's not up to the mark I think he is.'

'My darling, how clever you are. They're always good if you choose them.' Louis took her hand and ran a thin finger over her palm. 'And with Yvette Guilbert to head our Easter show in a few months time! What a coup!'

'Thank you.' She bent over and kissed his forehead. It meant so much to her that he was always encouraging, and if he felt jealous at her success he hid it well.

'We're a partnership born in heaven, even if my damned lungs come from hell!' he told her with a brave attempt to play down the cough which kept him and her awake too often all winter.

'That's true, Louis,' she agreed. Annie never allowed a trace of memory to mar what they had created on the foundation of his adoration and her affectionate gratitude.

'Mon Dieu! Look at this, Annie! Fantastic, he's done it!' A few days later, on 13th January, Louis waved a copy of the paper *l'Aurore*.

'Done what? Who?' She looked up from the poster she was designing with Alphonse.

'Zola! *L'Aurore* is carrying his letter, "J'Accuse". He's

245

ripping the whole case apart. My God, it's wonderful! Senior Ministers, top brass in the Army ... Zola says outright that they're liars every one! Oh la la! This will cause trouble.' He couldn't hide his glee.

'Just keep out of it yourself. You're still not well, Louis,' she warned, but he was already gone, huddled in the corner with some cronies and didn't hear a word.

'I'm going to the trial,' he told her a few weeks later in February. 'Emile needs his supporters round him. Did you see the cartoons in *Psst*! and *le Sifflet*? The bastards are defending the army and doing it very cleverly. Mon Dieu, most cartoonists should be guillotined.'

'Then I'm coming with you!' Annie Lamarche, the least political of women, insisted.

'I don't think you should, ma chèrie, it could be rough,' Louis objected.

'All the more reason,' she said and her grey eyes hardened.

He looked at her determined face and shrugged ruefully. 'Well, I've always said you should take more interest in politics, I guess I'm hoist with my own petard.'

'Exactly.'

'Oh, if you like.' He gave in. 'I always feel twice the man with you by my side.'

'Louis!' She held him close.

They fought their way in every day as the trial deteriorated into a mockery of justice. Admittance to the court-room was restricted, but Louis as a close friend of the accused, had managed to get permission for them both. Outside was a shambles which disgusted even the most hardened of foreign observers and shocked readers all over Europe. It was Paris at its worst and its most out of control.

Annie had often wondered since she came to live in Paris and had been met mostly with rough kindness and acceptance, how there could have been a revolution, how people could have been dragged off helplessly to die. Now she knew.

'Hold on!' Louis grasped her arm as they left the court the first day and plunged into the screaming mob.

'Death to Zola!' A man roared in her ear and plunged past waving a baton at the carriage trying to take the unfortunate writer from the court.

'Death to the League!' Louis yelled and was almost mowed down.

'Move back, you swine!' the police charged the crowd and dishevelled and thoroughly frightened, Annie, still holding onto Louis like death, struggled free and they staggered away from the court.

'If you go back, I go back!' Annie insisted that night in the Chat Roux as they discussed the terrible day.

'But it's too dangerous. You saw what the crowd is like,' he pleaded.

'Then don't go either.'

'I'm going.'

'So am I.'

Each day of the trial it got worse. Over and over the police were forced to intervene to stop people from both sides being thrown into the Seine. Annie felt it was a nightmare that would never end as the process itself became a sham. Each day Louis tried to talk her out of coming, but she knew if she let him go alone he would be even more involved than he was already and it would be the death of him.

'Guilty of defamation. One year in prison and a fine of three thousand francs!'

'Oh God,' Louis groaned, head bowed into his hands as the sentence was finally passed on his friend.

Outside the crowd bayed and roared like wild animals. At seven-thirty in the dusky winter evening Emile Zola left the court, leaning on the arm of his friend and defence lawyer, Maitre Labori. Short-sighted, grey-haired, a stooped intellectual of a man, Zola climbed slowly down the stairs towards those who screamed for his blood.

'Annie, stay here, I'll be back!' Louis dumped her at the door of the palace and ran down into the Quai des Orfèvres to join a dozen or so of Zola's friends who formed a guard around him. Slowly they jostled forward from the stairs to the carriage screening the writer's stunted body. It was reported later that if the walk had been a few metres longer, the crowd screaming 'Down with Zola! Down with the Jews!' would have torn him limb from limb.

She stood at her vantage point, heart pounding, watching the painful progress of the tight-knit group. Whatever she thought of Louis's involvement in the case, she couldn't help but feel unutterably proud of him as, weakened by consumption, he stood and fought for what he believed in.

Then it was all over. The crowd had lost its victim and sullenly dissipated as the police pushed forward.

'Louis, come on, let's go home. No, you're not walking!' Despite his protests, Annie waved down a cab and bundled Louis in.

'God, how can France have such fools to judgement?' Louis leaned his bruised and battered face against the cool side of the carriage and began to cough.

By the time they got back he was gasping for breath and there were spots of blood on his handkerchief. He was almost a dead weight as Annie struggled to help him out of the carriage. 'Wait there,' she called to the driver and left her husband slumped over the seat.

'Come on, Jules. Move it, man!' She beckoned the barman.

Between them they got Louis in through the back of the cafe and into bed. Annie undressed his unresisting body. 'Fools to judgement,' he repeated and turned his face to the wall.

Zola's fall seemed to knock the heart out of Louis and Annie anxiously watched as he lay longer in bed and became apathetic. Even the terrible aftermath of the trial, as Paris hovered on the brink of anarchy, failed to stir him out of his depression.

Spring didn't bring the usual recovery to Louis's agonised lungs or his spirit. In despair Annie persuaded him to spend the worst of the summer by the sea away from the heat and clinging dust of Paris with Julie. Old Odette from the kitchen went with them as cook and minder while Annie looked after the Chat.

He came back much restored, but with autumn the cough worsened again. One dark night he offered to move to another room for fear of passing it on and so she could have some rest.

'No, you stay with me,' she insisted. 'I'd just be lying awake thinking about you and worrying. Here I can be sure you are all right. Anyway, I don't think I can get this sickness,' she added with a thoughtful frown.

'How can you say that?' he protested, folding his 'kerchief so she wouldn't see blood that came so often now. 'I know tuberculosis is contagious, especially when people live as close as we do. I make sure Julie doesn't catch the sputum when I cough ... but you and I share a pillow.'

'Doctor Murchieson said long ago that I must have had some resistance, or I surely would have come down with it, whatever he did in the Gallowgate to save me. And working with cattle too ... I heard folk in Craigdrummond say that some milkmaids can't get it ... something to do with drinking the raw milk from cows with the infection in them...'

'Then I believe you, Annie, and I'm glad you're near.' Exhausted, he leaned against her and fell asleep at once.

'You'll be fine, Louis,' she kissed his sleeping face. 'I'll make sure you are.'

'Francine, he has to spend some time in the mountains ... help me persuade him!' On Christmas Day, Annie pleaded for her sister-in-law's support. Francine plumper than before and tangibly happy, had come to present her new husband, since Louis's health had stopped the Lamarches going to the wedding in the autumn.

'I'll do my best, but you know Louis...'

'I know, but try ... here he is now,' Annie nodded over to where he was making painful progress through the bar, handkerchief held habitually to his lips.

'Louis Lamarche, you're a fool,' Francine began the minute he drew close.

'Thank you, sister,' he gave an ironic smile. 'And why in particular have you decided to remind me?'

'You're wheezing and coughing like an old engine! Go and get some help. Listen to your wife ... nobody cares for you as she does! Do you want to leave her a widow already?' His sister was more brutal than anyone else dared. 'And even if you don't give a fig for poor Annie, just think, do you want your daughter to grow up hardly remembering her father?'

'Francine, you were always unscrupulous!' Louis shook his head and gave in.

'You'll get only the best treatment, my darling!' Annie planned to raid their savings and book him into a clinic in the Alps before he could change his mind.

249

'Now you have got your way, can I eat?' he asked smilingly, 'or do you intend us all to starve?'

'Jorice, you and Louis take yourselves off to the bar,' Francine ordered after dinner was over. 'Annie and I must have a gossip, go on, there's a good lad.'

'Anything to please the women,' Jorice replied, playfully patting his wife's behind.

Jorice Dupont was a good-natured small-time wine trader from Avignon. He was more comfortably off than he should have been since a great-aunt had left him enough not to have to work too hard, which was just as well because his heart wasn't really in the business. What he really wanted was to run a place like Louis's, but he lacked the drive to get one going.

'You know, Louis,' he said as they left the kitchen. 'My father owned a cafe years ago, but Maman made him go into the wine trade. It was more respectable, she said. Pity eh?' The doors swung and the noise rushed towards them. 'Oh, la la! Just like old times, but much, much grander! How I envy you, brother-in-law!' He rubbed his hands as they went into the smoky bar.

Christmas had become afternoon maudline in the Chat as the dancers and chorus sat around telling tales of childhood that bore little resemblance to the grim truth most had left behind.

Annie closed the kitchen door after the men, shutting out the racket and sat facing her old friend. 'Now...' she said.

'Now...' said Francine settling down to enjoy a good gossip. 'Pass the chocolate, ma chèrie, and I'll tell you all about the wedding...'

'What did you decide to wear in the end?' Annie topped up their cups.

After they had picked over the wedding, fashion, work and households Francine asked, 'How about your family, Annie? Do you hear from them still?'

'Oh now and then,' Annie smiled. 'But I'm no better myself at writing, there's no spare time... But as far as I know their shop is doing well, and the tearooms. Mammy is fine, and the twins ... oh and Phyllis has produced twins, two boys. Sandy is like a "cock on a dung heap" with pride ... as they say in the country.'

'Talking of the country, do you get news of the place you used to talk about so much? What was it called...?' Francine frowned with the effort of remembering the strange foreign name.

'Craigdrummond? No,' Annie said in a tone that encouraged no more questions.

'But do you know what happened to Mistress Alexandra Cameron at least?' Francine persisted. Annie had long ago told her what had passed between them that last day in Misses Berry's Establishment and an edited version of how she had come to the Chat Roux.

'A little,' Annie flushed.

'Just a little?' Francine raised a sceptical brow.

'Oh, all right, Francine, I'll tell you the little I've heard.' Annie flushed and picked at an imaginary spot on her skirt. 'You know that Louis gets *l'Illustration* to check what is going on in the theatre world and *Le Temps* for the news ... as well as all those radical rags ... oh, I'm not complaining. Louis is a cultured man, for all the rough work we sometimes have to do here.'

'Yes, cultured, and an idiot when it comes to politics! I know my crazy brother for God's sake! But what about Mistress Alexandra?' Francine was agog.

'I read about her once or twice.'

'In *l'Illustration* or in *Le Temps*?'

'Both.'

'Oh, come on, Annie, what has she been up to?' Francine demanded. 'Don't keep me guessing!'

'In *l'Illustration* it was just a little report about who had attended a gala performance at the Comédie Francaise. The Comtesse de Greffulhe, was there with the Prince of Wales...'

'That's no surprise!' Francine, like most people who knew Paris, recognised the names and followed the activities of women such as the Countess, who were the force behind Parisian high society and its famous 'salons'. 'Everyone knows she is a friend of the Prince,' she went on in a knowledgeable tone. 'And he's here as often as he is in London, I should think. What a scandal he causes too!' The Paris press loved to follow the doings of the great, and having disposed of their own royalty, gave great coverage to those of their neighbours.' Though I don't think the Countess is one of his mistresses... But what's that got to do with Miss Alexandra?'

'The "exquisite Lady Edward Ballantyne", was among the

other guests,' Annie replied with an ironic twist to her lips. 'From the innuendo and tone of the report it seems that Miss Alexandra has made the impact she wanted to on society here and in England.'

'Oh that's who she is now. Did it mention her husband?' Francine was bursting with curiosity. 'So she married that older Milord who haunted the Berry's establishment lusting after her, after all?'

'Oh yes, I heard about that at the time through little Jennine from the kitchens. We met once at Les Halles. Anyway, since you ask,' Annie went on, 'it said something like, "The imposing devotee of Paris, Lord Ballantyne, basked in the glory of his lovely young wife who was the centre of all attention and the focus of all eyes, including those of the Prince of Wales ..." etc etc...'.

'Ohhh...' Francine sighed. 'Just imagine...'

'I'd rather not,' Annie said sharply and picked up the chocolate pot which was never far away.

'And in *Le Temps*?' Francine was not to be put off so easily.

'Oh, in *Le Temps* she was visiting a new exhibition of Cezanne's work with her husband and some other art lovers ... I can't imagine she was there for the art alone, though. Culture for its own sake was never to her taste...' Annie added tartly.

'Was the Prince of Wales there as well?'

'Not that time, but in another mention some time afterwards in *Le Temps* it said she was in his "inner circle" of close friends at Nice.'

'Do you think...?' Francine trailed off with a meaningful life of her eyebrows.

'Maybe.' Annie shrugged. 'Though he's even older than her husband ... and fat. But, Francine, believe me, I don't know and I don't care.' She tossed the chestnut curls that still defied all the pins she skewered them into place with. 'This is my life now with Louis and Julie. It doesn't matter to me what any of them do. They can all go to hell on horseback!'

'I was a bit surprised when you and Louis married so quickly ... I knew he was besotted with you, but I thought you weren't so interested ... er ... why did you suddenly change your mind and stay in France? We all imagined you'd go back to Scotland ... maybe to that farm I mentioned earlier.' The question Annie had been dreading came out at last. She had hoped that Francine would never ask.

'Ah well there isn't much to go back to any more, and as for Louis, maybe I just hide my feelings better than he does. The important thing is we're happy.' Annie replied enigmatically and got up. 'Now, woman, Jules and Marie need to have some Christmas too and our men are too busy talking vintages to be of any use. Are you going to join me behind the bar, or do you want to take a nap upstairs?'

'Oh, I'll join you,' for all her new status as the wife of a provincial wine trader, Francine always loved the cheery atmosphere in the Chat Roux bar. '... So what new plans have you got for the bar? Louis says they're wonderful.'

'Well, they may have to wait a bit if we are going to pay for a good place for Louis to be treated. Clinics cost,' Annie said. 'But yes, they are exciting.'

'My dearest wife,' Louis wrote from his 'cure' in the Alps. 'I feel so much better here. My lungs take in air and keep it there! The cough hardly bothers me these days. I sleep well and eat all day. You will hardly know your restored husband when he comes home in May. Oh, but how he misses you and petite Julie. Kiss her from her Papa and say I think of her and her Mamma every moment of every day.'

'Listen to this, Jules, Marie ... girls,' Annie read the letter aloud and everyone sighed with relief, hoping he was as well as he sounded.

The spring passed too fast to count the days. Annie scoured all Paris for new talent. She planned an Easter show excellent enough to pay for the last month of Louis's treatment and set their reputation for the rest of the year. Paris was a fickle friend, almost as bad as Alexandra with its moods and caprices, Annie mused at times, or a fish that you think you have and then it slips away. But she had learned to play Paris audiences and land them, just like the trout she had tickled in the burn at Craigdrummond.

'Oh if only you could be here to see the show,' she wrote to Louis. He constantly begged for the minutiae of their Montmartre life. Annie paused, thinking what he might like to know. She guessed for all his brave uncomplaining attitude, he was tired of the clinic and longed to come back to the noisy cheery world he had created in the Chat Roux. For the moment at least he seemed to have given up on politics altogether. 'And maybe after the Zola affair, it's thank God for that!' she muttered to herself.

Dipping her pen in the ink once more, she continued, 'I went down to St Denis yesterday and found another singer in a cafe-conc who deserves a better audience than the rubbish that listen to her there. Of course I can't top the bill with her, it's too soon ... but one day. Our top to pull them in will be Yvette Guilbert again. Yvette promised me the last time that she would do another show and I've made her stick to it. But it wasn't hard, she's a lovely woman. She told me that she may sing these days for high society in the Divan Japonais, but her heart is still in Montmartre. When she heard you were ill, she agreed immediately to come, and for a reasonable fee, not a share.

'Now I'm looking for a good male singer and I need some novelty acts. No, my dear, whatever you say, I will not have Joseph Pujol, Le Petomane! I think someone who plays tunes and blows out candles by breaking wind, is not going to bring in the class of people we're trying to attract! Though maybe I am wrong about that. I heard last week that the King of the Belgians has just come to Paris to see him. Mon Dieu, what vulgarity!' She knew that would amuse him. 'And do you know what? The regulars have insisted I sing myself at Easter. It's been so long since I had time to do anything more than make some introductions and open the show, I almost said no, but "tant pis" I'll do it!'

'Annie, I hope the extra staff are better than the last lot of donkeys!' Jules fretted as they set up the extended bar for the big show.

'They'll be fine, don't worry,' she soothed. 'Just don't roar and swear at them all the time, Jules, they get nervous.'

'Nervous? Annie, don't mention that word. I'm dying of nerves!' Madeleine moaned, flexing a sturdy ankle encased in black stockings. 'I'll make a mess of the splits and there won't be room for the summersault if they all crowd round. It's all right for the singers, they're up on stage, but we are right in among the bastards so they can look up our skirts! What if I fall?'

'Keep your knickers on and you'll be fine,' Marie said tartly as she puffed past with glasses and carafes for the tables.

'Take them off and we'll be made!' Jules grinned.

'Mamma,' Julie pulled her apron. 'Come and play.'

'Not now, Bairnie mine,' Annie took a moment to hug her. She often spoke with the child in English. 'Mamma is busy tonight.'

'I want my Papa,' she replied in French, 'he always plays.' Her little face crumpled and she began to bawl. 'I want my Papa.'

'We all do, sweetheart,' Annie agreed wholeheartedly. 'But we've got to manage without him till he's better.'

'Want Papa!'

'Marie get Odette,' she called over. 'She can take care of Julie right away.'

Julie's face lit up and the tears were gone. The old cook who sometimes watched her was a great favourite. Odette had only one tooth and smoked a foul clay pipe, but she was kind and gentle with the little girl and told her endless stories of the farm in the Limousin where she had been born.

Julie danced off happily with Odette waddling beside her, chattering in excited French 'argot'. It sometimes worried Annie that the girl was growing up in Montmartre. Once she suggested to Louis that they sell up and buy a little bar in his native Picardie, but even with his own health problems he refused to contemplate ever leaving Montmartre. 'It's where I belong,' he insisted.

'I just hope Julie's stronger than I was,' she fretted for a moment then shook herself out of the unusually low mood that had been threatening all day. 'Och, Annie Ramsay, you're an old sweetie-wife!' she told herself with Glaswegian bluntness. 'Julie's better fed and cared for than you were so she can't catch things that easy. And there's tuberculosis in every town and most villages too wherever you go, now pull yourself together and stop mithering about what you can't change.' She tidied the bar and went into the kitchen, drawing comfort from the rich cooking smells that filled the air, but the mood of nostalgia went on picking at her. 'Who'd have guessed the day Doctor Murchieson came puffin' up the tenement stairs, where it would lead you and yours? God alone knows where Julie, Louis, or any of us will end up.' With that final thought she picked up the list of artistes for the big show and pushed all other problems from her mind.

The Easter show was a great success and Annie felt by quarter to midnight she could breathe out again. Leaving the rowdy bar, she slipped into the kitchen and through into the back yard where she often grabbed a precious moment alone. A cat scuttled over the wall, screeching protest at the intrusion. From the bars and streets around noise filled the night air, but she still felt the emptiness of the little yard gave a respite. High above her, the stars shone still and cool, distancing themselves from the mad world below.

'Annie,' a voice called from the door. 'Annie, I followed you through. I've been inside over an hour, but you didn't see me in the scrum.'

She froze as a wave of icy shock engulfed her body. Finally she found her voice, 'Ian Clachan, what in the name of God are you doing here?'

Chapter Twenty

Ian Clachan had rehearsed for weeks what he would say when he finally found her. And there she was, dressed in unfamiliar clothes, in a strange place that was as far removed from Clachan's Farm as human mind could imagine. But all the fine words disappeared. All he saw was Annie, shadowy in the dim reflected light, but still Annie. Every line of her, every feature just as he had dreamed so long, deprived him of any guile or art. 'I came over to the agricultural exhibition,' he finally said prosaically. 'There's a crowd of young farmers from Scotland ... twenty of us came together to see the new machinery ... the French are good at machinery. But I couldn't leave without trying to see you, Annie. Not when I knew you were here.'

'And your wife, Ian?' Annie could feel herself shake uncontrollably. It was difficult to believe that Ian was there in front of her, but from the shadows her voice sounded steady enough. 'Is Betty with you?' she demanded.

'No,' he replied, 'she's at home, seven months gone with our second bairn...'

'Second?'

'Aye, we have a laddie, Robert,' he couldn't keep the pride from his voice. 'Betty wants plenty of bairns. She's good with bairns.'

'Aye, so her mother and Mistress Crawford always said,' Annie flinched involuntarily as she spoke.

'... Though mind you she didn't have an easy time with Robert or this one,' Ian rushed on. 'Poor lass, she blows up like a balloon and can hardly move for the pain in her legs. Doctor Murchieson keeps an eye on her. He'll be there when the time comes again.'

Annie had stopped trembling. Standing in the shadowed yard, listening to Ian describing his wife's pregnancies, she felt almost lightheaded at the daftness of the situation. 'Ian Clachan,' she said suppressing a nervous giggle. 'Have you come all this way to tell me about Betty's bairns? Now how did you find me, and for God's sake why, man?'

He came towards her across the yard. In the dim light of Montmartre windows, she could see he had aged. The look of carefree youth had gone and in its place was a man who was almost a stranger. Almost but not quite, in his eyes and the set of his mouth, was the boy whose love she had treasured and still held in her heart.

'... Through your family, that's how I found out where you were. Och, it was easy, Annie.' Ian gained confidence from the banal details. 'The last I heard from one of the maids who has a sister at the big house ... in passing, you ken ... was that you were likely to be still living in Paris.' He rubbed his hand across his sleeve in an anxious, nervous movement. 'When I knew I would be coming, I just wrote to Sandy and he sent me a wee note back with your address. Mind you, it's not been easy to find you up here in this district, me having no French and so few folk speaking English.'

'He told you I was married and have a bairn?' Annie asked abruptly.

'No, though I guessed from your name that you must be wed. Sandy wouldn't have thought to say any more, Annie.' He hung his head. 'I just made asking for you sound as if it was for the old farm records. I didn't want him to get any ideas...'

For all the tension, Annie felt a smile twitch at her lips. He looked as guilty as a lad caught filching apples. Ian Clachan would never make a spy, she thought, or survive two minutes in the intrigue that was Paris. 'But if you ken that I'm married, why are you here, Ian?' she asked.

'Och, Annie, I had to come and see you, wed or not,' he replied vehemently.

'Well now you've found me.' She tilted her head in the quizzical gesture he remembered so well.

'Aye, but I never thought you'd be running a sort of...' he was momentarily lost for words, '... a sort of music hall! Though it seems to be right popular,' he added hastily.

258

'What did you expect?' she asked with a touch of bitterness in her voice, 'A grand salon ... a dairy farm? Miss Alexandra dispensed with my services, Ian. You married Betty. Sandy and the family had their own plans that didn't include me. Without as much as a reference or enough money to get home on, I'm lucky I had anywhere to go...'

'Aye, but here,' he said with a grimace of disgust. 'Och, Annie, it's hardly respectable. Folk drinking and carousing from morning to night it seems, women and all. And those dancers in the show are indecent. They'd arrest them in Ayr!'

Annie took umbrage at the censorious tone. 'Well, it's not Ayr, Ian, it's Paris!' she snapped. 'And I'm not ashamed of what I do. Like you say, the Chat is popular and I've helped to make it so. We make a good living and I'm respected here, even if you don't think the place is worthy of a Clachan,' she said with a toss of her curls that reminded him so much of the girl she once was.

'Annie, I'm sorry, what I said was out of turn, you'd be respected wherever you are,' Ian said quickly, realising the offence he had caused. 'There's something about you that makes folk take notice. But that's nothing to do with what I'm trying to tell you.'

'And what are you trying to say?'

'Whatever you do is alright with me. You're still my Annie. I don't care if you became the Queen of Sheba! Can you understand that? But I can never forget you,' his voice was painful, raw and pleading. 'Come back to Scotland, Annie. That's what I'm trying to say and why I'm here, I've come for you, Annie. We'll work something out,' he said. In a moment he was at her side, holding her as if the years in between were nothing.

'Och, Ian.' For a moment she hesitated, shocked that the old attraction touched her heart and the physical need for him that had haunted a thousand youthful dreams threatened to flare again. Then she pulled away, angry at her momentary weakness. 'What are you on about, Ian? You're a married man, a married man with bairns.'

He rushed on, ignoring the question, '...I have money now, Annie. Faither and I run the two places as equal partners. I could set you up somewhere. Ayr maybe. Or Kilmarnock. I'd take care of you and your bairn, I swear it. You'll want for nothing.'

'Ian Clachan, I don't think you realise what you're saying.'

Outrage grew as the implications of his suggestion dawned. 'You're not serious, man! I'm married myself and I have a bairn. Do you really expect me to leave?'

'Yes, I do!' he pleaded. 'I thought about it before I came. I don't know who the devil you've married, but you can't tell me you love him like you love me.' She made to speak but he rushed on, 'It was an awful mistake letting you go. There's always been something special between us, Annie Ramsay and there always will be. I knew it long ago when I first saw you standing there in Clachan's kitchen, dressed in Leezie's apron, so long it tripped you. And I know it now!'

'I don't deny that . . .' she began, but he cut in again.

'Then just take the bairn and come with me and we'll sort all the rest out later. Once we're safe in Scotland, he can't touch you. Betty need never know. She would never believe anything was going on, even if somebody told her. We can keep our secret. I can visit you. Annie, I can't lose you again. I've dreamed of you all these years. Day and night . . .' He sounded so desperate that she thought her heart would burst with regret with what they had lost.

'Aye,' she said softly, 'and I of you.'

'Then you'll come?' He took her hand. 'Oh, Annie.'

'No,' she stood her ground. 'Louis Lamarche is a fine man and I've pledged to stand by him. I'm not denying I loved you as much as any human being can, but I promised when we wed I would never betray Louis. No, Ian, I'll not desert the man now. He's been ill, but he's getting better. We have our life here with our wee lassie. She adores her Papa and he worships her.'

'Annie . . .'

'No more, Ian.' Tears welled up in her eyes, but she forced them back with the willpower that had become her constant companion. Her voice was firm and sure. 'It's not in my nature to live as a mistress. And I'm telling you now, that whatever happens to me or mine, I won't seek you out. It's finished between us and I'm finished with Scotland, I'm never coming back. Never. Louis has my hand and my love . . .'

'Your love?' he broke in in disbelief.

'Aye!' Her chin came up in a determined gesture. 'Folk can love more than once in life and it be just as true, even if it's different each time . . . My love is with Louis and Julie and that's my last word.'

'And you always keep your word.' It was a statement not a question.

'And I always keep my word,' she echoed.

'Annie!' Marie called from the kitchen. 'Annie, where are you? The crowd is calling for you to sing.'

'Goodbye, Ian. Go home to your wife and give her the loyalty she deserves.' She stood on tiptoe to kiss him gently and before he could make a move, she was across the yard, through the kitchen and into the bar.

'Annie Lamarche! La Petite Ecossaise!' A roar went up as she jumped on stage and the gas footlights lit up her slender figure. A chestnut curl slipped the pins and dangled across her forehead. With a quick gesture of impatience, she pulled out the rest and her untamed curls danced in the light as if she was sixteen again not twenty-two, a wife and a mother.

'Tonight I will break with my rule and sing a Scottish song once more,' she announced. 'A song I have not sung for many years. A song of love ... of hopeless love! I'll tell you a little about it so you understand when I sing.'

'Bravo!' The sentimental crowd quietened down expectantly.

'Oh God,' Marcelle grabbed her well-used hanky, 'she always used to set me off with those ones.'

'I will sing "Ae fond Kiss", the song our Scottish poet Robert Burns wrote for his mistress, Agnes McLehose, whom he called Clarinda, when she went to join her husband in the Indies. It tells of hopeless, forbidden and lost love.'

It was the very song she had sung so many years ago in Clachan's parlour the night she and Ian made love on the hillside. He stood at the back of the great bar in this strange, foreign city and listened. The words rose and fell to a climax of loss...

'... Fare thee weel, thou first and fairest!
Fare thee weel, thou best and dearest!
Thine be ilka joy and treasure,
Peace enjoyment, love and Pleasure!

But before the last notes died away, the place where he stood was empty.

'Told you I'd bubble!' Marcelle sniffed. 'Told you I would!'

* * *

'Welcome home, boss!' The staff and customers cheered as Louis's cab clattered up the hill and pulled up outside.

'And it's great to be home. How I've missed you all!' He climbed down and held out his arms for Julie and Annie.

'Louis, you're looking a new man.' Annie was pleased to see how well he was after nearly six long months of treatment.

'Mon Dieu! How I've longed for this old place!' Louis wiped his eyes with joy as they went into his beloved Chat Roux. Greedily he drank in the sight of the solid zinc bar with its great bank of bottles, the clutter of chairs and tables and the familiar smell of smoke, spirits and cooking. 'Oh, Annie, I'm never leaving here again till they take me in a box!' he said as he kissed her and Julie over and over.

'Never again, naughty Papa!' Julie cuddled his leg.

'You look tired,' he remarked, touching the shadows on her face. 'You work too hard.'

'I missed you,' she replied sincerely. 'I missed you very much.'

'And here I am again,' Louis smiled. 'Now how about some champagne?'

'Good idea, boss!' roared Jules and lumbered off to obey.

They quickly settled down to their old familiar routines as if he hadn't been away. He still had to take things easy, but the racking cough had gone and the angry flush that worried her so much had left his cheeks.

Julie spent every moment playing by Louis' easy chair down one corner behind the bar where he presided over the cafe's continued success. Paris loved pathos and Paris loved clever entertainment à la mode. The Cafe Chat Roux had both. Louis' delicate physique and tragic situation fitted the mood of the times so well that on good days they could laugh about it, calling it an act in its own right. With Annie's hard work and flair, the audience and the money rolled in and out again. They leased the place next door, expanded the stage and increased the capacity of the hall.

'One of these days, we'll have the Prince of Wales here,' Marie joked. 'Just like when the old fool went "incognito" to the Moulin and La Goulue asked if he was paying for the champagne.'

'... And his dear friend, the lovely Lady Ballantyne,' Louis added, with a sly, teasing look at his wife.

'Never!' Annie's eyes flashed, 'I'll kick them out on their backsides, the lot of them!'

But Louis's improvement was superficial. With the winter smog, his remission gave way to worse than before. Annie told Francine that the doctor didn't hold out much hope of a cure even if they sent him back to the clinic. 'The doctor says there's no point in periods of convalescence if Louis won't leave Paris for good,' she explained.

'Then try again, ma chèrie,' Francine urged. 'He refuses to listen to me this time.'

'I don't care where we go, Louis, Picardie, the mountains, the sea ... we can sell the Chat and use the money to set up somewhere you can breathe!' Annie tried that night to change his mind.

'We've been through all this before and the answer is still no. I'm staying here for good or ill!' he insisted.

'Then,' the doctor shrugged when Annie told him, 'there's nothing can be done. But with care at home ... well, it's a strange disease. You never can tell.'

'If it can be done, we'll do it!' Annie resolved to beat the odds and to carry Louis through on her own determined spirit. When she wept for all that life should have been for them together, she wept among the bins and stray cats of the little backyard where no one saw. In public her cheery smile lit up the bar and kept spirits high.

Despite it all, in her heart Annie couldn't really blame Louis for wanting to stay in Montmartre. Of all people, she understood the pull of the heart to where it felt it belonged. With all the wonders she had seen in her travels with Alexandra, the dreams that she treasured still were those of the Craigdrummond cliffs and the sky glowing with orange fire as the sun set over the Isle of Arran.

If she dreamed of Ian now and then it was against her will. After his visit her nights had been haunted for a while and she had been glad Louis wasn't there beside her. But that time was over. 'Come on, Annie Lamarche,' she had finally told herself when the cafe folk began to remark on the dark circles under her eyes, 'that's enough of feeling sorry for yourself. Count your blessings instead, woman, what you have with Louis and Julie is worth far more than the tinsel dreams of a wee farm lassie.'

By December 1899, it seemed as if her care and strong will had won against the odds for together she and Louis greeted the new century with hope and optimism. In another remission, he felt better again. After the songs in the bars, they poured out with their customers to sit with so many others on the hill of Montmartre to watch and listen to the new century being celebrated all round them.

'My dearest Annie,' he pulled her into his arms as midnight struck, bells pealed and fireworks went off all over the great city, 'before I die, promise me two things...'

'Stop this rubbish! You won't die! I won't let you!' Angry tears sprang to her eyes and she held him close.

'We will all die, ma chère,' he said soothingly. 'I just want you to humour me on this special night, all right?'

'All right.' She held his face between her hands. 'All right.'

'The first promise is that the day you can say you love me and mean it from the bottom of your heart, don't wait, just tell me. Time is so precious, Annie. Promise!'

'I promise,' she said and blinked back the tears that trembled on her lashes. 'So, I'll tell you now, Louis Lamarche. I love you from the bottom of my heart.'

He looked deep into her eyes for a long moment, then drew her to him. 'Good,' he said simply. 'That's so very good.'

As they stood holding each other, he whispered, 'I know you will look after Julie, so I don't ask that, but the other promise is that you will do what is best for my little ginger cat. Will you, Annie?'

'I'll do what's best for the Chat Roux.'

'Bon. Now let's see if these idiots manage to set fire to our city tonight!' he said stepping back, face smooth and relaxed as if he hadn't a care in the world. 'Come, ma chère, we can see better from up there on the wall.' He took her hand and they joined the crowd.

'Oh la!' they cried altogether as Paris exploded again and again into light and welcomed the twentieth century.

* * *

Louis died in November 1900, when the air in Paris was choking and damp. Drugged by a compliant doctor who frequented the cafe and was well rewarded for his kindness, he suffered as little as possible. They buried him in Montmartre in the ancient cemetery among the humble, the famous and the notorious.

Draped in a black veil, Annie led the cortege with five-year-old Julie holding her hand, walking with touching dignity beyond her years. Francine and Jorice followed with family, staff and customers in a long line behind them. Bars and brothels emptied as the coffin passed, lying on the funeral carriage drawn by black-plumed horses. All along Montmartre, people stood respectfully, men with caps in hand, women dabbing their eyes, silently watching as one of their own was laid to rest.

'He'd be glad to be for ever near his little ginger cat,' Marcelle sobbed when they came back, 'He loved this place. Oh, mon Dieu, what will we do without him? Things will never be the same.'

Annie's heart was too full to reply.

For months Julie was inconsolable and wandered the cafe like a little lost soul. Annie fought bravely out of her own misery for her daughter and turned her sadness into frenetic energy. There was no question in her mind but that she should take Louis's vision forward. The Moulin Rouge was past its best. The Chat would soon be the top place in Montmartre. She would see his dreams fulfilled, she had promised him as much. And by the following autumn, the Chat Roux was in full swing.

'As long as the shows go on, the customers are happy and the staff get their pay, none of us are missed in the end, not even Louis, for all he loved the Chat Roux.' Annie was full of uncharacteristic bitterness when Francine and Jorice came for her and Julie's birthday in June.

They threw an anxious look at each other. Jorice nudged his wife and whispered, 'Told you she would end up depressed!' They had argued many times that Annie had given herself no proper time to grieve.

'But that's life, not just cafes, Annie,' Francine ignored him and tried to console her. 'One chapter finishes,' she said with banal finality, '. . . and another begins. Life goes on, ma chèrie.'

'Aye,' Annie agreed sadly. 'So they say.'

Part 3

Catch the moments as they fly

Chapter Twenty-One

'Oh no! Just when I thought things were getting better,' Annie cried as just over a year from when she had buried Louis, she received a brief, sad letter from Sandy.

'What is it, Annie?' Marie stopped polishing the brass taps, concerned by her sudden pallor. 'You've gone white as a sheet.'

'Listen.' She read, translating into French as she went, 'Annie, Mammy is sick. She has something wrong inside and the doctor gives nothing for her chances. Can you come? She's asking for you. It won't be long. Sandy.'

'That's too bad,' Jules said sympathetically. 'What are you going to do?'

'I'd better telegram Francine and Jorice,' Annie replied after a moment of panic.

They came up from Avignon the next morning, full of sympathy and practical advice. 'Don't worry, we'll take care of the Chat, it's a pleasure,' Jorice offered even before he took off his coat and hat.

'Just go,' Francine added kindly, 'We'll look after Julie too if you like.'

'No thanks, Francine,' Annie replied. 'I want her to meet her grandmother. It's likely to be the first and last time.' She blinked back tears. 'Though I'd have liked her to go to Scotland on a happier occasion.'

'How long do you think you'll be?' Francine asked.

'I don't know how ill she really is ... a week ... a month?' Annie said worriedly. 'Can you cover that long?'

'As long as you need!' Jorice rubbed his hands in anticipation.

'But your business, Jorice? I don't want to burden you.'

'Oh, I can do a bit while I'm here.' He gave a nonchalant shrug. 'Anyway there's not a lot of profit right now in selling wine to miserable barkeepers who never want to pay up.'

'We're glad of a change,' Francine nodded agreement.

'I've always wanted to run a place like this...' Jorice's eyes glowed. 'You've organised it so well. All the programmes are in place. It's a piece of cake.'

'If you're sure?'

'We're sure,' they nodded in unison.

'It's not just Louis who dreamed of Montmartre,' Francine added. 'Even his little sister has her vision.'

'And don't forget his brother-in-law!' Jorice grinned.

Annie and Juliette travelled second class on the ferry to catch the London train, then on to Glasgow. If the journey was less luxurious than the last time she'd made it, it was efficient and comfortable enough. Julie, bright eyed and excited, kept up a barrage of questions. Absently Annie answered, but her thoughts were anxious and distracted. 'I just hope I'm not too late,' she worried.

'Ye came, my ain wee lassie. And here's yer bonnie wee Julie. Och, she's yer picture, Annie.' Her mother smiled blearily, far gone on the drugs Sandy had scoured the streets to find to kill the terrible pain that was killing her.

'Can you not get stronger stuff from the doctor, Sandy?' Annie was concerned when she heard his source had dried up.

'The doctor gives her as much as he can, Annie,' her brother explained. 'But it isn't enough to keep her from screamin' when she needs more. He only gives out two days supply at a time...'

'What?'

'It's no his fault, Annie. He says the doctors have to be careful or folk would sell it, instead of giving it to the patient. Anyway she really needs jags, but none of us can use needles.'

'I'll speak to him myself,' she said and settled down by her mother's side, holding her frail, work-worn hand. So soon after Louis, it gave her a terrible feeling of déjà vu.

'Get some proper sleep, Annie,' Sandy said after her second night of vigilance at her mother's bedside.

'There's time enough to sleep when she's gone,' Annie replied, but she got up and stretched wearily, stiff from long hours in the lumpy bedside chair.

'It won't be long right enough,' Sandy whispered. His mother whimpered in a fitful sleep and gave a thin moan of pain as she tried to turn. Instantly Annie was at her side and eased her over, but even the gentlest of touches was agony for the dying woman and she cried out.

'Have ye more stuff so I can give her something if she needs it, Sandy?' Annie asked as she wiped the sweat from her mother's brow and with difficulty settled her again.

'There's jist a wee drop left in the bottle. Look,' he replied, holding up the blue corrugated phial with a defeated look on his face. 'I'm doin' my best but there's not a drop to be had...'

'If it's more money, I've got a bit with me from France.'

'I canny get any, even with the money you gave me already, Annie. It's like I telt ye, the man who sells it has been run in and I dinnae ken anybody else.'

'When's the doctor coming back?'

'The night, I think.'

'Good,' Annie sat down again and took out her worn copy of Burns. 'I'll have a word when he comes.'

'Miss Ramsay, how are you?' A vaguely familiar voice pulled her out of a fitful doze that evening and she stood up confused as the doctor bent down and held out his hand. 'Nice to meet you again,' he went on as she blinked to clear the sleep from her eyes and to gather her scattered wits.

'Och, it's you, Doctor Chisholm, how are you?' Annie finally recognised him. His calm expression and steady manner were little changed from their brief encounter all those years ago in Craigdrummond kirkyard. 'Sandy never said your name, just that the doctor was coming tonight. I should have guessed who it was.'

'It's understandable.' He smiled. 'Slum doctors come and go.'

'I'm surprised you remember me,' Annie said.

John Chisholm thought of the embarrassingly unforgettable circumstances surrounding that first meeting, but said politely, 'I have a good memory for faces, it's useful in my job, Miss Ramsay.'

271

'Mistress Lamarche,' she corrected him.

'Mistress Lamarche, I'm sorry.' Involuntarily his eyes went to the broad gold band on her hand. 'Are you home from Paris for a while, or have you moved back for good?

'I'm still living in Paris, Doctor, though not working for Lady Ballantyne any longer. I came back when Sandy wrote to say Mammy needed me.'

'Not a good prognosis, I'm afraid,' he said sympathetically, glancing at the fading woman on the bed. 'But I'm sure she's glad you're here.'

'Annie, hen, help me!' Mrs Ramsay let out the heartrending cry of agony that Annie had come to dread.

'You'll have to give her more medicine to kill the pain,' Annie said through clenched teeth. 'She's suffering the torture of the damned and it's not fair, Doctor Chisholm. It's just not fair.'

'Well...' he hesitated.

She said sharply, 'Look, if it's a question of payment there's no problem. I know the family have not paid in the past, but I have money with me.'

'It's not the money,' he said, his pleasant, intelligent face, colouring deeply. 'I wouldn't see somebody suffer because they hadn't enough to pay, though in the tenements it's often a problem for folk are very poor ... as you well know.'

'Yes, I know, and I'm sorry, I shouldn't have sounded as hard as I did,' Annie apologised. 'I'm just upset to see her like this.'

'I understand.'

'I think you do.' In the frenzied world of Montmartre, she had learned to judge people quickly and she felt instinctively she could trust him. 'Listen, Doctor,' she went on, 'I don't want you to do anything you shouldn't...'

'I won't!' he interrupted.

'I'm not asking you to.' Her grey eyes pleaded for his understanding. 'My husband died of TB last year and we were able to get stuff to ease his suffering quite easily through folk we knew in Paris. Sandy says he could only find one man here to supply more on top of what you give her and he seems to have disappeared.'

'No doubt ... they mostly do in the end, one way or the other.' The doctor sighed.

'And?' Annie looked anxiously at him, her intuitive face drawn with tiredness and worry.

272

Archie Murchieson had told him a little of her history after that first meeting, but had never mentioned her since. Though he knew nothing of her life in Paris, it was easy to see she was a woman who would face any challenge with courage. And she's bonnie into the bargain, he thought, then pushed away that non-medical observation. Still he said nothing.

'Doctor, what are you going to do for Mammy?' she repeated her demand. 'Is she just going to scream and moan till death gives her peace?'

'I'm sorry, Mistress Lamarche,' he said with a defensive note in his voice. 'I know what she gets is not enough, but I can't normally prescribe powerful drugs like morphia in the quantities she needs to deaden the pain entirely. There's a lot of abuse if we allow morphia or other opiates to circulate without strict supervision. In any case, in her present state it is most effective if given by hypodermic injection and there's no chance of sending in someone every day to do that.'

Annie's face set in the stubborn lines that the staff at the Chat Roux knew so well. 'I'll pay for a nurse.'

John Chisholm looked embarrassed. 'I haven't got anyone suitably trained in the practice. Like I said, folk are poor, I hardly get enough from the practice to live on myself, without keeping a trained district nurse as well.'

'What then? You'll have to do something!' She refused to accept a refusal.

He shrugged, 'Hospital won't take her, even if she'd go. She's too far gone. I'd have to do it myself, but I don't have the time to come the three times a day she needs. I have other patients. Some are also as sick as your mother.'

'So she just has to suffer?' Annie looked pityingly at the skeletal figure on the bed. 'Is that what you mean?'

He ran agitated fingers through his unruly brown hair. 'There is one more possibility...'

Her face lit up hopefully. 'What's that?'

'I could show you how to give an injection.'

'Well then.' Annie's steady grey eyes were compelling. 'That's what you'll have to do.'

'If you're sure.'

'I'm sure.'

'Then watch carefully.' He rummaged in his bag. 'Somewhere

273

in here I have enough for one dose and a hypodermic which I can leave with you, it's easy to sterilise.'

Mouth tight with concentration, Annie followed the procedure of loading the big heavy needle. Then with the small capable hands that had milked cows, teased Alexandra's hair into elaborate curls and tended Louis's death bed, she did what he told her with the confidence of a professional.

'Oh, well done!' His eyes widened in astonishment as she completed the job on her mother's frail veins with less trauma than he would have caused himself.

'Where you love, you care.' She stroked the frown of pain from her mother's brow.

'I'll prescribe the maximum dose I can for a week,' he replied after a thoughtful pause. 'And I'll advise you on how often to administer it.'

'A week?' Annie glanced at the figure on the bed. 'Will she last that long?' she asked quietly.

He shook his head 'Not a chance. If after you have given her the prescribed amount each day she is still suffering, use your own judgement. There should be enough. But this is not euthanasia, or mercy killing as it's called, Mistress Lamarche. Don't be tempted to play God. Can you promise me that?'

'I promise.' She knew exactly what he was asking. 'I'll just make sure she doesn't have to scream for the next dose.'

'The one she's just had will knock her out for the night, so try to get some sleep yourself.' His shrewd gaze took in the dark shadows that ringed her fine eyes. 'Come to my consulting rooms first thing tomorrow. I have my chemist supplies next door, and I've just checked the stock, so I can let you have the whole amount. If there's anything left when she goes, get Sandy to bring it round, the stuff's too dangerous to lie about.'

'You'd trust us to do that?' Her expression was quizzical.

'I trust you or I wouldn't do it.'

'Then thank you.' Her eyes glistened with tears and he had to suppress the urge to reach out and comfort her.

'Good luck, Mistress Lamarche,' he said and walked quickly out. But she was busy with her mother and didn't reply.

'Maman, Wullie's an eejit!' Julie announced over dinner a few days later as she tucked into steaming mutton pies and tattie scones from her uncle's ovens.

'An eejit! Is that a fact?' Annie smiled. Used to talking English with her mother, Julie had picked up more Glasgow street-language than Annie could credit in a few short weeks.

For Julie at least the trip was proving to be a success. Ignoring the trauma in the back bedroom, which hardly touched the children's world, she ruled her small cousins completely. Isa and Bella, though older and her aunts, were easily overawed by her pert confidence. She took their devotion totally for granted as they pandered without question to her every whim.

At least the twins talk to Julie, Annie thought ruefully, I don't think they've said more than half a dozen words to me since I came. The girls were obviously uneasy in her presence and scurried away like a pair of frightened mice when she came into the room. Even at table, they kept their eyes firmly on the plates and got up as soon as they'd finished. But I'm going to have to talk to them once Mammy goes, she pondered. After all, Sandy and Phyllis might not want them any more.

'Maman, I'm going to make her a daisy chain,' Julie broke into her reverie again. 'Isa says there's daisies in the park down the road.'

'That's nice, sweetheart,' Annie smiled. I'm glad she's happier, she thought. Glasgow's no noisier or dirtier than Montmartre. And with new experiences and people around her, Julie still talks about Louis, but I can see she's grieving less.

'Are ye going back?' Sandy asked, while upstairs Phyllis took her turn while Mrs Ramsay slept away the short time left, her agonised fading eased by the powerful opiates Doctor Chisholm had allowed.

Annie nodded. 'There's nothing for me here, Sandy.'

'Right enough, Paris is your home now.'

'Aye, so it is. Though I think Francine and Jorice will be sad to give up the cafe,' she added with an ironic smile.

'You wouldn't want to come back here? Ye once said ye might, and I don't think we were fair to ye about that.' His eyes were anxious and his face flushed. 'It was just...'

'Listen, Sandy, I don't want you to feel bad about that old business,' she replied in a firm tone. 'It was a daft idea then and it would be a daft idea now. My home is the Chat Roux. I said to somebody once that I was finished with Scotland and that's how it is.'

'Do you miss the cafe and that?'

'In a way. The folk in the Chat are cantie. We make a good living and I've worked hard to make it what Louis dreamed of.' Her brow creased in a frown. 'But I just wish poor Louis could have lived to share our life. He was a good lad, a right good lad. It's a shame you never met him.'

'I ken ye're sad about Louis, and that's right and proper. He was your man after all and, as ye tell me, a guid one,' Sandy said carefully. 'But ye're still quite a young woman, Annie, and bonnie ... I'm your brother and even I can see how ye turn heads. Ye've mentioned that you have good friends in Paris, would ye not consider marrying again? It must be a lonely life at times.'

Annie sat with a withdrawn expression on her face.

'Och, maybe I'm talking out of turn...' he trailed off uneasily.

'Sandy, I'm not offended.' Seeing his confusion, she leaned over the wax-clothed table and squeezed his hand. 'You've a right to say what you think. But no, I don't see me wanting to wed again. There's a lot to be said for being on your own, and the Chat is family to me when I need it.'

'Aye,' he agreed doubtfully.

She got up. 'Now come on, we'll spell Phyllis off. Mammy will be needing her morphia again soon and I can't hold her up to give the jag on my own.'

Days later Mrs Ramsay faded out softly just as she had lived, asking for little and grateful for what she got. All she left was her little clock which she had bequeathed to Annie. Instead of taking it, Annie insisted Sandy and Phyllis keep it on the mantelpiece where it still held pride of place.

'You gave her and the lassies a home, the pair of you, so you've more right to it than me.'

'Och that's nice of ye, Annie,' Phyllis replied, blushing with pleasure.

'In fact,' Annie went on, 'we need to talk about the lassies. Maybe you should come back with me to Paris?' She glanced uncertainly at her sisters whose faces registered horror and panic at the words.

'Och no, Annie,' Phyllis broke in. 'The lassies are welcome, here. They're no bother, neither they are, and they help wi' the bairns and the shop.'

'Please, oor Annie.' Isa found her voice at last and spoke for both of them, 'We dinnae want to go to they foreign places, Glesca is guid enough for us.'

'Aye, Annie,' chorused her sister.

'If you're sure, Phyllis ... Sandy...' Annie trailed off.

'Och aye,' they replied unhesitatingly.

'Well, if that's what you want...' Annie sighed in relief, she couldn't imagine the shy, diffident twins in the Chat Roux.

The day after the funeral, Annie packed their bags. For all the sadness of the long journey north, she was glad she had come. It had made her mother happy and it had closed a chapter in her own life. She doubted if she would ever come back to Scotland again.

'Come on now, lassie mine,' she called to Julie when everything was ready at last. 'Put on your hat and coat, Juliette Lamarche, we've a train to catch!'

Sandy took them to the station. While Annie fussed with tickets and luggage, he went off with Julie to buy her some apples for the long journey back to England, then on to France.

Sentimental, kindly Phyllis, long ago over her uncertain chant of 'Miss ... er ... Annie', had cried buckets as they left. 'Here ye are.' She handed over a hamper full of scones, cakes and anything else she could cram in. 'Ye never ken when ye might get something decent to eat!'

'Enough for an army,' Annie had laughed through her own sudden emotional tears, as she kissed her and her sisters goodbye.

The station was as crowded as ever, and while Julie skipped happily away holding her uncle's hand, Annie stood guard, anxiously checking the bags for the third time. Suddenly an astonished voice from behind her said, 'Well, in the name of all that's holy! If it's not wee Annie Ramsay, then I'm a Dutchman!'

Annie whirled round. 'Davie Murray! What on earth are you doing here?'

'I could ask the same, young woman?' Craigdrummond's formidable butler smiled. He had a soft spot for Annie and his pleasure in seeing her was obvious. 'At least I live in Scotland,' he went on, 'so I've an excuse for being in Glasgow, but the last I'd heard you stayed on in foreign parts once you, er ... left Camerons' employ!'

'Aye,' she smiled back. 'But am I not allowed to visit, Davie Murray? Do you lose that right of citizenship if you don't work for Cameron of Craigdrummond any more?'

'Not even the Laird is that powerful.' He grinned, then bent forward conspiratorily. 'And I can't say I blame you leaving Miss Alexandra, or Lady Ballantyne as we should call her these days. There was talk, of course, that she fired you, but the servants knew you must have had enough...'

'Aye, you could say I'd had enough,' she sighed.

'We knew whatever had happened, it wasn't your fault,' he added, 'especially since poor Lady Cameron was so upset about it. She kept asking the maids if anybody had heard from you.'

'Och, she's a kind lady, so she is.' Annie was touched.

'So what brings you back, Annie?'

'I came home to see Mammy,' she said quietly. 'She died last week of cancer, Davie.'

'Och, I'm sorry to hear it.'

'Is everyone well at Craigdrummond?' She wanted to ask about Clachan's Farm, but didn't dare.

'The Laird is fine, and his Lady ... as you probably know they've a couple of fine bairns of their own this while back, two lads, so Lady Ballantyne isn't the heir any more. Not that she needs to be, having married so well. Och, but what am I on about, all that stuff happened when you were still with her.'

'More or less. And how is Lady Ballantyne?' Annie asked stiffly, feeling obliged to enquire.

'Have a look for yourself,' he said jerking his head to avoid obviously turning round. 'You're looking straight at her. She's over there with the main party.' He moved her gently round. 'By the big clock. We've all been up at Lord Ballantyne's Dumbarton House for the christening of their second bairn, wee Lady Victoria, she's nearly three and they've just got round to it.' The butler pursed his lips disapprovingly. 'Och well, better late ... as they say. And now the whole caboodle, bairns and all, are heading down to Craigdrummond for another celebration there.'

'Two bairns?' Annie's eyes shot over to where the butler had indicated. Alexandra stood half turned towards her across the station. Even from this distance Annie could see she looked as lovely and elegantly slim as ever, despite motherhood. Annie felt deeply uneasy since Davie pointed her out, and she hoped Julie and Sandy would come back soon so she could make her escape.

'Well, good luck to you, Annie,' the butler's cheerful farewell broke in. 'I can see they need me over at the other side.' He turned to go then stopped. 'Och, I nearly forgot to tell you that Ian and Betty Clachan have three wee laddies. If I see them or Geordie, do you want me to pass on your regards? I ken you were right fond of the farm folk.'

'Er ... they won't remember me, Davie,' she hedged.

'Of course they will.' He looked bewildered. 'We all remember you, Annie, and you lived there, for goodness sake.'

'Aye, well do that,' she mustered a smile. 'Just wish them well and tell them I'm doing fine in Paris ... that's all.'

'Aye.' He waved and was gone, lost in the throng of Cameron staff.

Gathering her scattered wits, Annie began to look around for Julie. But reluctantly, compelled against her will, her eyes strayed back towards the group. Suddenly the whole lot, servants and gentry, began moving towards the platform next to where she was standing. She stood paralysed, unable to desert the bags, as they stopped only twenty or so yards from her. With a jolt that was almost physical, this time she met the astonished gaze of Alexandra, Lady Ballantyne.

'Annie!' She saw the name form on her former mistress's lips. 'Annie!' Alexandra took a step forward. Annie was rooted to the spot in a panic, wondering what to do.

Suddenly Lord Ballantyne stepped forward and took his wife's arm steering her towards the entrance to the platform, temporarily coming between her and Annie. Alexandra disengaged herself, hesitated and looked back. But Annie had pulled her wits together and moved the bags behind a large newstand. By the time her heart had stopped pounding and she peeped out again, Alexandra was being helped by her husband into the reserved first-class carriage of the Stranraer train.

'By-here, that was close! I couldn't face a confrontation in the middle of a Glasgow railway station.' Just as she began to regain her aplomb, she was thrown into turmoil all over again.

'Annie Ramsay!' A voice in her ear made her jump with a yelp. She turned to see Maria Cameron at her elbow.

'I thought it was you I saw.'

In watching Alexandra, Annie had not noticed Lady Cameron, or seen her slip away from the group. 'Lady Cameron, how nice to see you.' Annie did something between a nod and a bob, as she shook the graciously proferred hand.

Maria Cameron was still a handsome woman and her manner was as gentle and caring as ever. 'Annie, are you well?' Her eyes searched and held hers.

'I'm very well, Milady, thank you,' she answered, flushing awkwardly.

'Where are you living?'

'Paris, Milady.'

'And working as a maid?' Maria asked, taking in Annie's simple but stylishly smart best coat. It was cut well from good quality cloth by a Montmartre tailor, glad to have a change from sewing 'frou-frou' for the dancers.

'No, not a maid.' She wondered how to explain. 'I'm widowed and I own and run the, er, cafe my late husband set up.'

'Oh, how sad you lost your husband.' Maria's face clouded. 'But are you content in Paris still, Annie? I remember you telling me you missed Ayrshire,' she seemed genuinely anxious to know.

'Och, that was the bletherings of a callow young lass, Milady. Paris is fine, I have a lovely daughter and I'm as happy as I can be without Louis,' she said simply.

'I was so sorry over the business with Alexandra ... please believe me.' It was clear from Maria's agitation that the matter had weighed heavily on her. 'I understood you had done nothing wrong, Annie, that it must have been Alexandra's behaviour which drove you to...' she broke off in embarrassment.

'I'm grateful for that, Lady Cameron,' Annie replied. 'And I haven't forgotten your kindness in trying to find me. Most folk wouldn't have bothered. I'd been attacked and wasn't too well, that's why it took a while to let folk know I was all right...' it was Annie's turn to leave the sentence unfinished.

'How is your family?' Maria hadn't forgotten the sacrifice Annie had made when she agreed to work for Alexandra. 'I presume you've been here visiting.'

'Yes, that's right.' Annie didn't mention her mother's death. 'Sandy, my brother, has a business now near Charing Cross. "Ramsay's Bakery, Fancy Confectionary and Tearooms". They're doing well, him and his wife.'

'I'm pleased to hear it...' She glanced back at the platform. 'Oh they're getting ready to leave. So, goodbye and good luck, Annie.' She held out her hand again and Annie took it. 'I'm pleased to know how life has worked out for you, I often wondered. And just remember,' she added as she turned to go, 'I'm happy to give you a reference any time you need one.'

'Thank you, Milady,' Annie watched as Maria joined the main party. What a good-hearted woman, she thought.

Alexandra came to the carriage door and bent down to speak to her stepmother, then they both peered over to where she stood. She turned and walked away, feeling her former mistress's eyes follow her, but she didn't look back.

Chapter Twenty-Two

The meeting with Maria Cameron and the shock of seeing Alexandra had stirred up a lot of old memories that Annie had tried hard to suppress. Throughout the long journey back to France, her mind spun back over the years.

Och, I've come a long way from the daft wee lassie dancing across Clachan's farmyard singing her heart out, she mused to the rhythmic click of the iron wheels. And from the young lady's maid trying to learn a few words of French to tell off the shoeboy. Lady Cameron asked if I was happy. Am I? she wondered. That was the hardest question of all to answer truthfully. Life brings so much in joy and sorrow and everything changes you. How can you judge any more, she thought, and what do you measure happiness against?

'Maman,' Julie pulled at her arm as they drew into a station not far from Dover on the way to the ferry. 'I know what that says.' She pointed to a big advert on the wall for Nestlés full cream milk.

'What does it say then?' Annie asked teasingly. She knew Julie read everything she could get hold of in French at the Chat Roux, but doubted her untutored English could cope with the doggerel printed boldly under the picture of a stout nursemaid and her charge.

'Baby's happy, chubby, bright, Nestlés full cream put him right!'

'You're a clever wee lass,' Annie said, looking at her with a mixture of pride and astonishment. 'Just...'

'...like my Papa,' Julie finished for her.

I had better sort out some proper schooling as soon as we get back, but what kind is best, that's the problem? Annie fretted silently. Teaching her myself isn't enough, even with help from the folk at the café, though they mean well, the lot of them. Annie thought of the motley crowd of renegade lawyers, academics and writers who cheerfully tutored the bright child, using unabridged Molière, or hair-raising newspaper stories to teach her the finer aspects of French. Julie has never even seen a school grammar-book ... though she's bright enough to catch up. And she knows more about café accounts than the examples I try to get her to do from Monsieur Leysenne's *Première Année d'Arithmétique* ... not to mention what Alphonse thinks is appropriate for her to draw! Och, what am I going to do? Annie felt a stab of loneliness. Oh if only Louis were here. Sadly she twisted her broad wedding ring. 'But he's not, Annie Lamarche, so get on with it,' her commonsense replied firmly.

Annie's guilt was compounded when they arrived back to a fine welcome from the staff, and open arms, but barely hidden regret, from Jorice and Francine. 'We've enjoyed looking after the Chat so much!' Jorice said, leading the way into the familiar low smoky rooms with their pungent mixture of odours and noise that was the essence of Paris's cafe life.

Their reluctance to leave was so palpable, Annie felt obliged to sugar the pill. 'Why don't you come and run the place now and then? Spell me off?' she suggested.

'Or we could just stay and help,' Jorice broke in hopefully. 'I've got some good ideas for acts, Annie.' He leaned against the bar.

'That's kind, Jorice, but it would be a case of "too many cooks" if we're all here. And I'm not sure we would agreed on ideas, though they all seem to work,' she added hastily, trying not to look askance at the posters Jorice had plastered everywhere. Alphonse had made them far more gaudy than she liked, with Madeleine and Nathalie showing a generous view of frilly knickers.

'Are you thinking of going away again soon?' Francine added in a tone so expectant, Annie almost laughed.

'Not right now,' she said. 'But I think Julie and I will leave Paris in the hot summer months, for instance, and maybe other times too when it gets smoggy and the air is bad. In any case, I want her to know the world outside the Chat.' She glanced over

283

to where Julie, with a look of solemn concentration on her face, was helping Madeleine fasten her frilly garters for the night's show.

'Quite right,' Francine agreed in a righteous tone, laced with more than a little self-interest. 'A Montmartre bar is not the best place to bring up a child.'

'There's worse places!' offended, Jules interjected, slapping rinsed glasses onto the zinc bar with a brittle jangle. 'If it was good enough for the boss, it's good enough for his daughter.'

'You're right, Jules, and nobody's criticising the Chat Roux. We all love it,' Annie said soothingly. 'But in a way Francine is right too.'

'There's plenty of kids who grow up in Montmartre!' Marie chipped in. 'And there's nothing wrong with them.'

'The smoke isn't good for Julie's chest,' Annie decided to be diplomatic before she had a revolution on her hands. 'I have to make sure she doesn't go the same way as Louis. So far she's been fine, but you never know...'

'Well, all right, maybe you should be careful,' Jules conceded the point.

'And we're happy to help out any time,' Jorice put a brotherly arm round her shoulder. 'Francine and me get along fine with these apes!'

'Less of the apes, Jorice Dupont!' Jules growled, but without chagrin.

'I can see that,' Annie smiled. 'Now how about some champagne to welcome us home?'

Annie waved Francine and Jorice off a few days later without allowing herself the luxury of mixed feelings. The Chat Roux was their life, her and her daughter's. Soon she settled back into the old routines and within a few weeks it was as if she had never left.

'As long as you understand what the customers want, the Chat is an easy world to run,' Annie mused as she planned the programmes for the next few months.

Though she ruled her kingdom firmly, albeit with a light, cheerful touch, she had no illusions that the Chat needed her to survive. As long as someone kept the show running, with a weather eye on the cut-throat competition from the Moulin it would be popular. The staff were loyal to the Chat and Janot and Alexi the Slav stood guard against the 'apache' thugs, always on the lookout to exact protection money. I'm a lucky woman, she thought.

'Maman,' Juliette interrupted, 'You said can I go to school? So when will I start?'

'Soon, ma chèrie.'

'How soon? I'm nearly seven!' Julie pouted. 'I want to learn more!'

Julie had her mother's charm and natural wit, but she was already showing signs of a formidable intellect inherited from Louis.

Before Annie could answer, Jules called from the bar, 'Come here and show old Leo how clever you are at reading.'

Julie skipped over and perched on a high stool beside a disreputably shabby man in a worn suit who had once been a lawyer before he fell foul of the law himself.

'Listen to this, Leo!' With a flourish like a conjurer, Jules handed her a copy of *Le Temps*.

Without hesitation, Julie read it through.

'You've won!' Leo gawped. He handed Jules a couple of coins. Only six years old and she can pronounce all the big words, just as you claimed. I didn't believe you.'

'Now tell Leo what it's all about, ma petite,' Jules instructed.

'Oh la, la,' they chorused in admiration as she rephrased the shortcomings of France's politicians.

'Mon Dieu, Annie, the child can read better than a schoolteacher,' Madeleine said. She handed Julie a bonbon. 'That's for being such a clever girl.'

'And she counts better than me,' Marie said from behind the great till.

'Better than all of us!' echoed Odette, removing her clay-pipe and spitting neatly into the fire.

'Imagine that,' Annie grinned. She didn't think much of the comparisons, but wouldn't hurt the staff's feelings by saying as much.

'Yes, she's a smart little bastard. Got her Papa's mind for trouble!' Alphonse, the artist ruffled her curls. 'Give her a few more years and she'll be the talk of the town as well as the belle of the Chat Roux. As you all know, I'm an artist,' he pronounced with an important air, 'so, I can tell you she's going to be a beauty, Annie. The child has perfect bones!'

'Maybe.' That was another worry. They adored Julie, but Annie could see trouble ahead if the child was left to grow up here with no example but her own and theirs. *What on earth will become of my wee Julie?* She lay awake that night worrying. *Brought up among pimps and prostitutes and thinking it's the only way to live.*

Finally she got up and tried to clear her thoughts. *The bar folk and the dancers are kind, but most of them have tumbled here through God knows what traumas to land in this net. They're not exactly what you hope your child will copy. And the girls are as bad as the men. Most of them let themselves be used by anyone for a couple of sous, a quick absinthe and a word of flattery or kindness.*

Annie sat looking out across the rooftops of the city. *No, I have to do something, she'll soon be seven and I'm still dithering. Oh, Louis!* She allowed herself a few tears then dried her eyes. *A convent boarder is the only answer!* she concluded. *But God knows what they'd think of that in Craigdrummond kirk!*

With characteristic speed once she had reached her decision, she went ahead. By the next afternoon her daughter's schooling was arranged.

Julie cried inconsolably when Annie told her. 'Maman, I want to go to school, but not to the nuns, they look scary with those horrible big hats!'

'The convent school is the best in the area, ma petite.' Annie explained.

'I can go to school here in Montmartre if you don't want to teach me any more,' she wailed.

Annie had already rejected the crowded, rough Ecole Public down the hill. 'I want better for you than that,' she said.

Leaving Julie in that chill convent parlour two days later, clutching her little bag, with tears running down her face, was the hardest thing Annie ever had to do in her life.

'Please, Maman,' she pleaded. 'Please, take me home.'

'Now, Juliette,' Sister Agnes chided, 'we don't want cry babies here. Any more tears and you'll be left alone till you stop.'

Annie gulped. 'She's not used to being alone, Sister, she's only a baby, really.'

'Do trust us, Madame Lamarche,' Sister Agnes said with a smile more chill than the parlour air, 'Juliette is nearly seven years old, not at all a baby. We have long experience of children and we turn out excellent young ladies.'

'But not long experience of feeling a mother's love,' Annie's heart cried, but she steeled herself to say nothing. With the sound of Julie's pitiful sobs in her ears, she walked the long way back to the Chat where the staff met her with stony silence.

Annie wept into her pillow that night, failing to shut out a picture of her daughter lying desolate and afraid in the convent school dormitory.

A week later they sent a message telling her to come. She grabbed a coat and sped, heart in mouth past Sacre Coeur, down the great hill and through seemingly endless streets to the school.

'Juliette is ill,' Sister Agnes said, her starched wimple shading her face, so Annie could not see her eyes.

'What's the matter?' Annie demanded anxiously.

'Come.' The nun led the way through long dark corridors hung with gloomy religious pictures and stark crucifixes crowning every doorway.

'God, how could I have left her here?' Annie was consumed with guilt.

'Maman, I thought you'd never come back,' in the little iron bed, Julie held out her arms.

'My poor wee bairn!' Annie's eyes filled with tears and she scooped her up. After a short week, Julie had faded to a shadow of herself. Her eyes were sunken and her hair hung limply round her pale face.

'She wouldn't eat, nothing at all, whatever we offered, whatever we tried,' Sister Agnes said simply. 'I promise we did her no harm.'

'No,' Annie said sadly. 'I did.'

Lady Alexandra Baird of Ballantyne gave birth to her third child, two years after she saw Annie in Glasgow. In the early morning the waters broke and with the help of a goodly supply of chloroform, the birth was quick and easy for mother and child.

'Is my wife well?' Edward Baird's portly, ageing figure blocked the doorway as the doctor came out of the room drying his hands.

287

'Lady Ballantyne is fine, just tired, Milord, as is to be expected...' John Chisholm began, but then hesitated with a deeply concerned expression on his face.

'And the child?'

'A lass.'

'Oh well, we have one fine son already and a daughter, I suppose we can make up the score next time round,' Edward said with heavy jocularity.

Doctor Chisholm wondered how he could break the news. Edward Baird was not an easy man and it was common knowledge that his relationship with his lovely young wife was fraught. What he had to say could only make it worse. The curse of being family physician, he thought, was knowing too much about their private lives for comfort.

Lord Ballantyne's lust for women, as legendary as that of his friend, King Edward VII, had not diminished with age, nor with having a beautiful wife. Alexandra's own indiscretions at the highest level and her nervy nature, made the doctor's confidential position delicate at times. 'Well,' he began and stopped, searching for the right words.

'What are you being so mealy-mouthed about, man?' Edward Baird demanded. 'If there's something I should know, spit it out!'

'In that case, I have to be blunt with you, Lord Ballantyne,' he decided there was no way to make it easier. 'This wee lass is not entirely what you were hoping for.'

'What do you mean?'

'The signs are clear if you know what to look for, Lord Ballantyne. Your daughter is what folk commonly call a "mongol".'

Edward Baird blanched. 'Do you mean some sort of imbecile?'

'Not an imbecile. The syndrome was first clinically identified by Dr John Langdon Down in eighteen-sixty-six...'

'Oh spare me the medical clap-trap!' Ballantyne snapped in anger and disappointment. 'Is there nothing that can be done?'

'Nothing at all.' John shook his head. 'It's a condition which cannot be changed. With care, and if the bairn has no problems internally that we don't know about yet, she could live a content and long enough life, though it will be very limited of course. She'll never be what you would describe as normal.'

'And the alternatives?' Baird turned his back and stared out of the window to the lush garden below.

'Well, she may not thrive and that will be that.'

He turned. 'If she does thrive, what does one do with a ... "mongol"?' He drew his hand over his mouth as if the words left a bad taste.

'Some families care for such children at home, and maybe you'll want to do that...'

'Good God, no!' Lord Ballantyne sounded profoundly shocked.

'If not, you can put her in an institution,' the doctor said evenly. 'There are a few in the immediate area, and there's a private one near Kilmarnock which I have heard is especially well run. Or...'

'Or what?' Edward Baird's face was grim.

'Perhaps you would prefer to leave her out to a kindly family to rear in return for some agreed monetary consideration.' John went on, 'That's not a bad option. Many people in your position do that.'

'An institution is clearly best,' Edward replied shortly, 'But my wife can sort it out. Er ... how has my wife reacted to the news?' Lord Ballantyne's pouched, heavy-lidded eyes were wary.

'Lady Ballantyne doesn't know yet that the wee lass is not right,' Chisholm said quietly. 'I thought it best to tell you first in case you would prefer to break the news yourself.'

Edward Baird stood staring into space for a moment, then he said, 'No, Doctor, you do it. I'll call on her some other time.'

As the peer left, John Chisholm sighed and sat down for a moment, deep in thought.

Handing over his Glasgow practice to another young doctor needing the general experience those grim streets brought, had not been a decision John Chisholm had taken lightly but it was one which he had only occasionally regretted since. Archie Murchieson, as interested in his protégé as ever, had contacted him immediately when he heard about the vacancy through Lady Cameron.

'You've done more than your bit in the tenements, lad, but now your talents are going to waste. All that study under Freud in Vienna and with Charcot in the Salpêtrière in Paris is not being used. Take the job of personal physician to the Bairds,' he urged. 'The work isn't onerous and you'll have both the money and the time to do the research into mental health diagnosis and treatment you've always talked about.'

Archie had been right. The job was lucrative and the hours were light. The older Baird children, Eddie, who was seven and Vicky, his five-year-old sister, were healthy and had a sensible governess in Miss Somerville. John barely saw them. The household and estate's aches and pains were easily sorted with only the odd scalding from a boiling pan, or a hay fork through the foot to break productive research days.

Not that it's always easy, he thought. Especially when Lord and Lady Ballantyne visit Scotland a few times a year and I dance attendance on them and their guests. But the results of over-indulgence in food, sex and alcohol by a crowd of spoiled folk who should know better, is nothing compared with this real crisis. This is different.

Finally he got up, braced himself, opened the door and went into the chamber.

Alexandra lay in the big bed with her eyes closed though she was not asleep. Her glorious hair was spread over the pillow. Like sheaves of corn at a Harvest Festival, he thought irrelevantly.

The maid and the midwife, tidying up the debris of birth, left at his nod. He looked down at the still figure amid silk covers and satin pillows.

Aye, he mused wryly. Nature is no respecter of rank nor wealth. Such an event is no more welcome here than it is in the tenements I used to serve. Och, at least she has money and can give the poor child some kind of a life, not like those poor wee things in slums. Early death must seem like a happy release to most of them.

Alexandra opened her eyes and looked up at him with a gaze so intense and unnerving he was forced to drop his. 'There's something wrong with it, isn't there?' It was a statement, not a question.

'I'm afraid so, your Ladyship.'

A moan so primaeval it set his teeth on edge, escaped from her lips. 'It's my fault,' she wailed, 'my fault.'

'There's nothing to blame yourself about,' he said softly.

Suddenly she sat up and demanded in an angry imperious tone, which rang out in shocking contrast to the groan of despair a moment before, 'How would you know what I am to blame for or not? Don't presume, Doctor!'

John Chisholm replied in a calm, even voice despite her rudeness and her quicksilver change of mood, 'She's what we call a "mongol", Lady Ballantyne. Research into birth defects is progressing very fast these days. From Doctor Down's research and findings since, we are quite convinced that "mongolism" is nothing to do with what the mother might or might not do during the pregnancy. You are simply unlucky, since such children are more commonly born to older mothers.'

'It's my fault,' she insisted. 'I didn't want it.'

'As a physician, I'm certain it is not your fault in the physical sense at least,' he replied patiently but firmly, well used to the irrational responses of people in shock.

'Oh what does it matter?' She sank back onto the pillows. 'I don't want it. I wouldn't want it even if it was all right. And I certainly don't want a defective.' After a silence where only the singing of the birds outside in the spring garden intruded, she asked in a hesitant voice, 'What will it be like?'

'The physical characteristics are straight-forward enough and become increasingly obvious with age.' The doctor took refuge in medical precision. 'Upward slanting eyes, flat face, transverse palmar crease, short stature, usually rather limited intelligence...' He avoided any of the more extreme manifestations. 'And unfortunately there is a tendency to childhood infection and serious heart disease. Some, I'm afraid do not survive beyond childhood. They all need great care if they are to survive beyond twenty years ... I know of one case where the person reached forty-three...'

'Great care to survive beyond twenty...' she gave a harsh laugh. 'Survive for what?' She gestured towards the silent, lace-draped crib in the corner where the baby slept peacefully. 'Just tell them to remove that cradle at once, doctor, and to keep it and the child out of my sight!'

'As you wish.' John Chisholm's intelligent face was impassive, giving nothing of his own feelings away. Some women showed such rejection following the discovery that their child was not perfectly normal, but came round later. 'It's up to you, of course,' he said in the same steady voice, 'but I advise you to take time before you decide what to do with the little girl. In a few days you'll be feeling stronger and will be able to think more clearly. I can give you some options.'

'I don't want options. You arrange something!' Alexandra replied sharply, twisting the corner of the fine sheet so hard he thought she would rip it. 'As long as I don't have to see it, I don't care what you do.'

'I spoke a little with Lord Ballantyne...'

'And what did Edward have to say?' Alexandra stopped her nervous motion and looked intensely at him.

'He would prefer if you sorted out the child's future.'

She flopped back onto the pillows. 'Of course, Doctor, of course! Did you really think Edward would concern himself?' She gave a jarring, brittle laugh. 'He'll fund anything as long as people don't know the House of Ballantyne has a defective in it. Beyond that I can promise you he won't bother if it lives or dies.' Her voice rose, 'He cares for nothing beyond himself and his "amusements". Dear Edward!'

He stood watching impassively as she ranted then finally fell silent. 'But you could care,' he said quietly.

'No!' Alexandra's answer was short and uncompromising. She lay gazing for a long time at the ceiling then asked, 'Can I get up?'

'Not till tomorrow.'

'We'll be off to Baden-Baden next week with the King.' She went on in a harsh monotone that was almost more disturbing than her previous hysterical outburst. 'It wouldn't be half the fun if the Bairds don't show! Without the gallant Lord Ballantyne, who would keep the women happy behind the drawing room curtains, when our King is snoring off another giant lunch?'

'Perhaps you should stay at Baird House this time, even if Lord Ballantyne goes to Baden-Baden,' John suggested.

'Out of the question, Doctor,' Alexandra said. 'Mrs Keppel would have to entertain fat old Bertie without my help. And that won't please him. He likes young women around even if his real tastes have gone to seed.' She gave a malicious laugh that echoed round the luxurious room. 'Did you notice when they were here last March that dear Mrs Keppel is getting quite fat?'

'No, Lady Ballantyne?' John replied, wondering if Alexandra

was beginning with child-bed fever, she sounded so odd and her eyes glittered.

'They waddle together! You must have noticed that.'

'No.'

'Nor the fumblings under the tables, nor the assignations for the night? Come, Doctor, you were there. Are you so naive?' Alexandra fixed him again with intense blue eyes. 'Don't you care about how your betters pass their time, Doctor?'

'Should I, milady?' John raised his eyebrows, but his expression was inscrutable.

'Have I shocked you?'

'No, Lady Ballantyne,' he replied with a half-smile. 'Though I can't say I like the term, "betters".'

Alexandra looked at him in surprise. 'Oh, are you some sort of socialist, Doctor Chisholm?' Then she went on without waiting for a reply, 'You should be shocked. I was at first ... but that was long ago.'

'Patients often regard their doctors as priest as well as physician. I've heard worse ... much worse. And please don't imagine that it's just the upper classes who behave that way, though I don't doubt you're right about them.' He smiled. 'Especially not the King, even if he is over sixty and should know better.'

'Do the nurse and midwife know the child is defective?' she asked suddenly.

'The midwife might, but the nurse is young and inexperienced. I wouldn't imagine she'll have guessed.'

'No one must know!' Alexandra's voice rose.

John felt weary. 'I'll make sure the midwife keeps quiet. But we had thought the nurse would look after the child.'

'No! She'll gossip.'

The doctor thought for a moment. 'I can get old Jeanie to take over care,' he said. Jeanie had spent her life in Baird service helping as skivvy in the nursery for generations of Baird children and their nurses.

'Yes, Jeanie will do till we get rid of it,' Alexandra leaned back exhausted. 'I suppose we have to name it,' she said suddenly.

'The child?' John had noted her refusal to use the baby's gender.

'Who else?'

'Of course, though you may not want a public christening,' he added gently. Despite her hard words about the baby, John Chisholm felt a surge of pity for the lovely woman lying on the bed. He knew the couple's life together was difficult, but Alexandra's bitterness and rejection of their child, revealed the depth of her unhappiness.

'Jessica was the name my stepmother suggested if we had a girl. I hadn't thought to use it ... I don't like it, but it will do. A reject for a reject.' The hysterical note was back in her voice as she laughed, '... And there certainly won't be a christening.'

'Milady,' John Chisholm approached the bed and looked down. 'Jeanie can look after the child in private rooms here for the moment. But please, as your physician, I advise you to take time to get used to the idea of what she is before you think of sending her away. Many children with this syndrome are endearing little creatures who can bring great joy to families who love and care for them ...'

Alexandra broke in, her voice full of anger and bitterness, 'Oh, do what you want, Doctor, just tell Jeanie to keep everyone away from it. But don't preach about love and care! It's too late for me to love or care for anything in this life,' her tone softened, and she added, 'except for Eddie and Vicky.' Then it hardened again, 'One thing is certain.' She stared coldly into space. 'There will be no more.'

Chapter Twenty-Three

Maria Cameron's letter came inside another envelope, with a note from Sandy.

'Dear Annie, Lady Cameron sent this up from Craigdrummond by a messenger with instructions to get it to you as soon as possible,' he scribbled. 'It gave us a fair turn when this carriage arrived at the bakery door, so it did. Here we're all just dandy. Phyllis, the twins and the bairns are thriving and the shop is doing great. Your ideas on how to get the loan we needed for the new ovens worked a treat. The bank manager was that impressed the way we put our case. You have a right touch with business, Annie.'

Annie smiled, since her visit over two years before, Sandy and Phyllis had asked her advice now and then and it seemed to work as well in Glasgow as in Paris.

But what's this? She wondered, as the once familiar Cameron seal filled her with foreboding. She pulled out the slim letter, ripped off the seal and quickly scanned the letter. She had to read it three times before it began to make sense and even then she could hardly believe the contents.

Craigdrummond, September 1904
Dear Mrs Lamarche (Annie),

Please forgive me for taking the liberty of contacting you in this rather unorthodox manner, but I have thought long and hard before going ahead. I wish you to know straight away, that I am approaching you not as a servant, but as someone who has done great service to this family and whom I know can be trusted.

Alexandra gave birth to a child with serious disabilities some months ago. I have been allowed to tell you in strict confidence, that the little girl suffers what Doctor Chisholm, the Baird family physician, has diagnosed as 'mongolism'. The Doctor is, according to our own Doctor Murchieson, quite an authority on such matters and his judgement should be accepted.

The child is being looked after for the moment by a family retainer, but Alexandra seems unable to reach a decision on how it should be cared for in the long term, assuming the child survives. Indeed she refuses to see it at all. But it is about Alexandra herself, that I am writing to you, not the unfortunate child.

During her pregnancy, Alexandra was not in good spirits, but such moods can overtake anyone in that condition as you possibly know. After initially rallying from the birth and leaving to take the waters at Baden-Baden with the King, her husband and his friends, as is their custom at this time of year, Alexandra cut short her sojourn and returned alone to Baird House. Since then she had been suffering from depression so deep, I fear for her sanity if not her life.

In her despair she has repeatedly told me that she bitterly regrets letting you go. She says you were the only person who ever understood her, or who ever told her the truth. Irrationally, she also insists that all her problems lie at your door since you saved her life. This is, of course, quite absurd, but I feel you should know.

I myself pass many hours with her, but she does not, I regret to say, find comfort for the moment in the presence of her husband. Doctor Chisholm has said all of this may well be caused by delayed depression following the birth of the child and should pass given time and patience. However, he has also warned that a few cases of post-natal malaise like this never lift.

Last week, in despair when I visited and noted further deterioration, I asked her what we could do to give her hope. She sat for a very long time without replying and I believed she had perhaps not understood. Then she said, 'I want Annie Ramsay back.'

Annie, it is more than two years since we met so briefly in

Glasgow, I know you were then a widow with a child. I also know you had responsibilities of a business nature. However, you are sympathetic and generous of spirit, therefore I dare to ask the following. Could you think of coming to Dumbarton at least for a few months to see if your presence would really help Alexandra recover her will to live? You will of course be handsomely rewarded.

If you have since remarried, or find my suggestion otherwise offensive because of the treatment you received from Alexandra, please forgive me. It is anxiety for my stepdaughter and deep sympathy for her and for her other poor children, Eddie and Victoria, that emboldens me to ask you. Whatever she has done in the past, I feel she has paid a heavy price. I also feel sure that, whatever circumstances surround you, you will at least consider my proposal. I have always admired your courage and your integrity and I appeal to both now.

Your sincerely,

Maria, Lady Cameron

Annie barely slept that night. She paced the room looking at Julie, lying in the big bed, her face, framed by dark curls, sweet and innocent. Suddenly she muttered in her sleep and a little frown creased her forehead. 'My bonnie wee lamb.' Annie blinked back a tear. Sometimes Julie reminded her so touchingly of Louis.

Trust Miss Alexandra to ask for me ... and to blame me for her troubles! Oddly she did not think Alexandra's request itself was strange. She had always been unpredictable. But, Annie couldn't shake off a feeling of guilt herself, even though she knew it was irrational.

'And there's Julie to consider,' she muttered. 'I'm not sacrificing Julie for any Cameron born.'

Mind you a change could be good for Julie, she mused. After the fiasco of the convent boarding school, Julie had begun after all at the local day school in the centre of Montmartre and only a short distance from the Moulin Rouge.

It was a simple 'ecole public' and it operated as well as it could within the limitations of its environment. Annie never meant Julie to stay there. It was supposed to be a stop-gap till she found something better. But most of the good schools were too far to

297

attend every day and Julie wept every time boarding was mentioned, so she stayed on.

She's not been sheltered in the Chat and she's tough enough to cope at the ecole as long as she can come home at night. But it isn't the place for a bright wee lassie to thrive, Annie thought, as she sunk her chin into her hands. Sixty bairns to one teacher. And half of them can't write their names. Julie covered most of the year's work in the first month. She's learning nothing now,' Annie muttered aloud, in an effort to clear her mind. 'They're using her already to teach the wee ones to read. She'll end up as a monitor, not a pupil.'

Annie got up and wandered over to the window. Up here at the top of the house she could see the lights of Paris spread below. Usually she gained pleasure from the sight, but tonight the lovely city felt like a prison.

'I could buy her books and she could work in peace and quiet on her own, even if she had to stay with Sandy and Phyllis for a while. I could maybe help her myself when I have time off.

'Och, no, Annie Lamarche!' She was shocked at finding herself using Julie to rationalise the idea of going to Scotland. 'You're daft! Alexandra Cameron is bad news. Keep away.'

'But I could do with a wee change myself.' Sometimes she felt swallowed alive by the demands of the Chat, the constant noise, the arguments, the emotion. She went on and on, pacing to and fro.

The conclusion came with the first dawn light. 'I'll lay out my conditions, strict conditions,' she decided, 'and see what Lady Cameron thinks of them. But I will not go near Craigdrummond. that I couldn't bear.'

'You should have left me in the Moss,' Alexandra said in a flat monotone by way of greeting when Annie was announced by the nervous nurse. 'You told me that yourself when we had the row,' she spoke as if their last conversation had happened minutes before and the years between didn't exist.

'Aye, maybe so, but I didn't leave you, did I?' she replied, trying not to sound as shocked as she felt at the sight before her.

Alexandra sat on a window seat, her golden hair dull as straw and unkempt was stuffed straggling into an ugly snood held by a few big pins. The blue eyes were clouded and sunken in a pale, drawn face and the disarray of her afternoon dress was in horrifying comparison to the smart, fashion-conscious woman she had been.

'And look what's happened because you didn't, Annie Ramsay,' she said bitterly.

'You can go.' Annie dismissed the nurse who had been sitting guard when she came in and was staring wide-eyed at the odd exchange.

'If you're sure, Mistress Lamarche,' the nurse hesitated. 'I don't usually leave Lady Ballantyne in case ... ye ken.'

Annie said, 'You've been told I will be spending time alone with her, so go, nurse.' She didn't blame her resistance, she'd been a servant herself once and afraid to break orders. 'Don't worry, I'll take full responsibility. You can stay outside and I'll call you when I'm finished.'

'Well, if you insist, Mistress.'

'I insist.' Annie wished the woman would go. All the way from France, she had been dreading this first meeting with Alexandra, but for all the wrong reasons, she realised. Instead of the difficult nervy, charming girl she had followed to Paris and who would surely now be upbraiding her unjustly for desertion, this was a broken, emaciated shell. Annie felt pity accompanied by deep anger at whoever had done this to her.

Alexandra turned back and gazed out of the window, saying nothing, but playing endlessly with the tasselled fringe of the heavy velvet curtain.

'Your hair's a mess, Miss Alexandra,' Annie said using the old familiar form of address. She picked up a gold-handled brush from the dressing table.

'Is it?'

'Aye!' Annie walked over and picked out the clumsy pins from the back. The limp hair tumbled down her back. 'Today I'm going to brush it and rub in some rose balm. You like that. Then tomorrow I'll wash it.'

Alexandra shrugged, but didn't draw away when Annie began the brushing motion that had always soothed her in the old days. After a while, she closed her eyes and Annie saw some of the tension drain out of her neck and shoulders.

Slow and steady, Annie took her time, and when she had finally brushed out the tangles and rubbed in the scented rose

299

petal cream to condition, she tidied the long strands into the snood and pinned it neatly.

'Nobody ever did my hair like you,' Alexandra murmured.

'I'm going to leave now, but I'll be back in the morning to see to you. I'll get them to send up a wee supper tray now,' Annie said, knowing, as well as seeing from her condition, that Alexandra had been eating very little.

'I'm not hungry.'

'Aye, you are.'

'I don't want food.'

'Then I'll go home to Paris. There's no point in me trying to fix the hair on a skeleton,' Annie said firmly, but with a smile in her voice. 'What grows on your head shows what you've put in your body!'

'Just a little then ... why don't you stay longer now?' her voice was petulant.

'I've just got off the train, and I've my own wee lass to see to, she's waiting for me at our lodgings. We've got one of the gate houses all to ourselves.'

'She means more to you than me?'

'What a daft question, Miss Alexandra,' Annie decided to lay her own cards openly on the table from the start and establish the grounds for their new relationship. 'Of course she does, she's my daughter. But you still mean enough for me to come all this way just to brush your hair.'

'You'll come back tomorrow?' Alexandra turned to face her, blue eyes as uncertain and frightened as a child's.

'I said so, didn't I?'

Alexandra let out a long, deep sigh. 'Yes, you said so.'

Annie called the nurse. 'Lady Ballantyne is tired. Order some food now. Just a light supper. When she's finished, help her to bed.'

'She's not been eating,' the nurse said anxiously.

'She will now,' Annie replied and left.

The first weeks Annie was careful to take things very slowly, spending a little longer with Alexandra each day, talking about old times, keeping away from the sensitive questions of the child and encouraging her to take an interest in her appearance again. She knew if Alexandra began to bother about how she looked, there was a chance of getting some sort of stability back in her life, if not to the root of the trouble.

Bit by bit, Alexandra improved under Annie's urging and care, eventually walking in the grounds and even visiting the nursery of an evening to kiss Eddie and Vicky goodnight. Her physical health picked up fastest and she began to look more like her elegant self.

John Chisholm watched in awe as Annie chided, coaxed, spoiled and supported her out of despair and towards normality.

'We always seem to meet in the strangest circumstances, you and I,' he remarked one evening over the evening warm cup they habitually shared while she reported on Alexandra's progress and sought his advice.

'I suppose we do,' Annie agreed. 'Who'd have imagined when we met in the kirkyard at Craigdrummond, that we'd be working together on Lady Ballantyne's wee problems one day?' She gave the charming smile that lit up bright grey eyes and made her look like the lass from Clachan's Farm all over again.

Despite steadfast professional detachment, John was finding it hard to resist being captivated by Annie. Pulling himself together, he agreed, 'Who indeed? I'm simply grateful to have you here. I have to admit that when Lady Cameron said Lady Ballantyne had asked for you, we were all clutching at straws. Please don't take this amiss,' he added apologetically, 'but I never thought for a moment it could work, even if you considered the proposal.'

'Oh?' Annie tilted her head to one side, eyes dancing. 'Why not?'

'Er ... it seemed,' he fumbled for the words, 'er ... I couldn't see how a maid Lady Ballantyne had dismissed, and whom she hadn't seen for a good ten years or more, could possibly help get her out of her misery. My question, if you'll forgive me, was what could you do that I with all my training couldn't?'

'Life isn't always about training, Doctor, though I respect your learning and your work. But it's a bit special with me and Lady Ballantyne.' Annie chose her words carefully. 'Lady Cameron knows how I came to be with her in the first place.' Annie gave a rueful smile. 'I wouldn't have come now if I hadn't the notion I could help.'

John Chisholm nodded. 'In retrospect, there's nothing I can say but, happily, I was wrong.'

'Aye, we can all say that at times,' she answered from the heart. 'And talking of right and wrong, where is Lord Ballantyne? It's been a month without a sign of the man.'

'Ah well, I can't blame him entirely.' With an uncomfortable expression on his face, John put his cup of instant Camp coffee and chicory on the table and leaned back. 'Lady Ballantyne does not wish to see him, and he in turn feels she is exaggerating her plight, so he keeps away.'

'My God, that's not an act she's putting on! How can he think so?' Annie pictured the wreck of a woman that had so shocked her the first day.

'I know, but he is neither an easy nor a patient man by nature. Lord Ballantyne has never seen this kind of reaction before in anyone and it infuriates him. I have been trying to persuade him that this type of hysteria sometimes follows childbirth or severe emotional trauma. Though thankfully it is rarely as severe as in his wife's case.' The doctor paused and picked up his cup again. 'However I did stop him putting her in an asylum...'

'An asylum?' Annie asked, deeply shocked. 'That's for lunatics!'

'Well, not always.' John Chisholm smiled. He was used to the common reaction of ignorance. 'Many inmates are temporarily ill, that's all. In fact I'm one of the people trying to improve conditions in such places and change their dreadful image of hellish "bedlam" to one where treatment is given and recovery is often quite possible.' He ran his fingers through his hair in an unconscious gesture she had come to know. 'But in this case,' he went on, 'it was not appropriate for the patient. And I managed to persuade Lord Ballantyne of this. It was harder to explain why I simply don't give her sedatives.'

'Sedatives?' Annie looked puzzled.

'Opiates,' he replied. 'We don't have much else at our disposal to calm people down.'

'But you haven't done that.' Annie couldn't recall Alexandra taking anything soporific, not even laudanum.

'No,' he confirmed. 'My instinct as a modern specialist in mentalhealth, is not to keep a patient in semi-oblivion, especially by using drugs they may not be able to live without later.' He leaned forward, brimming with enthusiasm. 'There are interesting theories being developed now about what causes disturbance in the mind. Drugs are not the answer, at least not the whole answer. Under certain conditions perhaps they can help, but modern treatment also tries to find the underlying emotional causes and deal with them.'

'Aye.' Annie nodded. 'It makes a lot of sense to get something off your chest instead of carrying it around like a bomb waiting to go off.'

'In fact,' he confided, 'I would have liked to use the technique of hypnosis on Lady Ballantyne, which my colleague Jean-Martin Charcot has developed as a treatment for nervous disorders.'

'Hypnosis? I heard about that in Paris. They call it mesmerism. We were going to have an act at the Chat, but the mesmerist got into trouble with the police and we had to cancel it.'

'Yes, Lord Ballantyne had heard about it too,' John said with a wry smile. 'And he didn't like the idea at all!'

Annie laughed. 'I can believe it.' Her memories of Edward Baird were of an arrogant egoist, not someone who would discuss theories of mental health practice, or risk hypnosis to help his wife. 'I've heard you always tell the truth under mesmerism. Maybe he didn't like that idea.'

'Hypnosis is far more complex than that,' John said. 'But whatever his reasons, he certainly gave me his opinion in the strongest terms.' His face reddened at the memory of their argument. 'In fact I've been dreading his next visit,' he confessed.

'Why?' Annie smiled at his rueful expression.

'Until you came, there was little improvement in her Ladyship's condition despite my best efforts. He would almost certainly have challenged my methods if he had found no change. Maybe I'd have been looking for another position.' He leaned towards her. 'You've worked a miracle, Annie,' he said honestly. 'I'm grateful.'

'Och, I know the woman and that helps.' Annie blushed at his praise. 'When did Lord Ballantyne last come to see her?'

'Just the day before you came, but she wouldn't let him into the room. She screamed and threw things, that's why he wanted me to sedate her. Can't blame him in a way, I suppose.'

That night Annie sat in front of the fire in their little gate house, watching Julie as she read an adventure story in English without difficulty. Annie was pleased and surprised that Lady Cameron insisted Julie join the two Baird children, Edward and Victoria, in the nursery with their governess.

'There's no point in trying to place her in a local public school for such a short time,' Maria had commented with kindly good sense. 'I'm sure it will do Eddie and Vicky good to have another face in the classroom and she seems such a bright child, I'm sure she will cope very well with the change of regime.'

'Cope?' Annie shook her head. With each day Julie had blossomed. Miss Somerville, the governess, impressed by her sharp mind and innate confidence, welcomed her warmly. Lucky she doesn't know where those talents were honed, Annie smiled, thinking of the multi-faceted world of the Chat Roux and the tough 'Ecole Public de Montmartre'. And the Baird children didn't seem to mind her joining them. They could have made her feel like an intruder or a servant's upstart, if they had wanted, but they hadn't.

Annie underestimated her daughter. No one could intimidate Juliette Lamarche with impunity.

Eddie Baird, Viscount Ballantyne, found learning a bore. At nine he knew he should already be at boarding school and would have been if Mummy hadn't been sick. His young uncle Jamie Cameron told him it was jolly good fun at school, with lots of sport and midnight binges. Eddie couldn't wait. In the meantime he barely tolerated fussy, silly Miss Somerville and the schoolroom. Making Vicky cry and Miss Somerville flustered, was all the pleasure he had. So, when she told them that there would be another girl joining them till Christmas, he was torn between being angry, and glee that he would have another victim to tease.

Julie Lamarche summed him up with Montmartre shrewdness. Eddie was no more of a problem than Janot, the bullying son of Mimi the Moulin Rouge dancer. Thick but manageable, she decided. On the first day he tripped her and sniggered as she picked herself up, dusting down her new smock.

'You stupid boy!' She turned on him with an expression so fierce he dreamed about it that night. 'I'll get you back for that. And you won't know when. Just wait for Nemesis, Eddie Baird.' Alphonse the painter had told her all about Nemesis and its role in his own downfall. It seemed appropriate.

'Yah,' he said, but felt uneasy. Eddie had never been subject to subtle feminine torture before and he hadn't a clue what nemesis was, but it sounded terrifying.

Julie waged psychological warfare till he broke. Every day when she came into the schoolroom, she whispered with a gentle smile playing round her mouth. 'How did you sleep last night? Has Nemesis called yet, Eddie?'

'Oh, what is stupid Nemesis?' he demanded in desperation by the end of the week.

'It's the great spirit of revenge,' she replied. 'It comes when you're least expecting it. Like a ghost in the night. No one escapes their Nemesis!'

'I don't believe in Nemesis! You're bluffing,' he cried defiantly.

'Test me then. Do something else and see,' she said with a mysterious smile.

'Oh you're just a stupid girl!' he sulked, but didn't dare.

'That's right, very wise,' she said and stamped on his toes so hard tears came to his eyes.

After a few weeks when nothing worse happened, he forgot his fear and tore her book. She lured him to an attic and locked him in for an hour in the dark, whispering that Nemesis was on the way.

'Pax!' he howled when she finally came back. 'Please, Julie, pax!' He battered on the door. 'Pax!'

'Pax?' It was Julie's turn to be nonplussed, for she had never heard the word before. After a moment's thought, she understood. 'Pax,' she agreed, opening the door and holding out a slim, soft hand.

'Pax.' He took it.

Lady Victoria Baird was a miniature of her mother, pretty and golden haired. But for all her lovely dresses and fine dolls, she was starved of the attention she desperately craved from self-absorbed Alexandra. Vicky adored nine year old Julie from the moment she came into the room. She had never seen someone so confident and exotic, she thought, just like a foreign princess.

Julie responded kindly enough, though with the casual carelessness of childhood. But it was enough for Vicky to sit by her heroine, whose dark eyes brimmed with enthusiasm when the books came out and whose glossy curls were tied back in the French style. Even her name was different, not a bit English,

Juliette Lamarche. Juliette who could stop Eddie teasing with only a lift of her shapely eyebrows. Vicky would gladly have died for her. Fortunately in the schoolroom at Baird House, such sacrifice was unnecessary.

'Mon Dieu, someone in this barbaric country who can speak without sounding as if they are chewing mutton stew!' Julie's native French was the delight of the young tutor who came twice a week, though he decided quietly that he had to 'do something' about Julie's 'unusual' Paris argot.

Miss Somerville, far more shrewd than any of the children gave her credit for, reported much of this back to Annie. She was glad Julie had settled so well, but was afraid even more of what the future would hold when this interlude was over.

'Come on, ma chèrie.' She pulled Julie to her feet and gave her a hug. 'Time for bed.'

'Tomorrow, I'm going to learn a poem, "Young Lochinvar". But tonight,' her daughter said firmly, 'we have to go over my tables, Maman, before I sleep.'

'Julie loves studying with the Baird children. If only I could let her grow up in such an environment,' she confided in John Chisholm next day.

'It depends what you want for her,' he replied. 'A private schoolroom doesn't prepare children for the real world, which is why they almost always go on to boarding school.'

'I suppose so,' Annie agreed with a wry smile. 'But Julie's had enough of the "real world" already to last a long time.'

'Will you stay in Scotland?' he asked quietly.

'Oh no.' She shook her head. 'Jorice and Francine are only looking after the Chat for a few months. And we really should begin to think about going back quite soon. But, John, what should I do about Julie?'

'First answer a question,' he said with an expression she couldn't quite read. 'Could you settle to life again as a lady's maid? Lady Ballantyne is becoming rather dependent on you.'

'Oh I don't think she is so dependent,' Annie heard a defensive note in her voice. 'She realises my time here is limited.'

'Have you reminded her of that?'

'Oh now and then,' Annie shrugged, though she wasn't sure she was being entirely honest with herself. 'Och, she's still too fragile to make the point too strongly, John. I don't want to agitate her. But I have to say that this short time in Dumbarton has made me realise I could never go back to being a servant, even a privileged one.'

'And the Chat Roux?'

'I promised Louis I would do what is best for the Chat. And I feel I have. Jorice and Francine love the place and, from all the reports they send me, profits are staying good.'

'Do you miss it?'

She replied with a touch of embarrassment, 'I have to admit that I don't miss the Chat so much as the organisation and planning that goes into it. I have a taste for business now, John. Would you think I was daft if I said I miss the cut and thrust of it all?'

'Daft you're not!' John Chisholm felt a wave of affection for the young woman in whom he had so unexpectedly found a mind that matched his own. Full of sharp common sense, shrewdly intelligent rather than intellectual, bright, streetwise and loving. Annie Lamarche was an enigma.

Their mutual concern for Alexandra and Jessica, whom Annie was allowed to visit, brought friendship and confidences they would otherwise never have shared. Now he teased gently. 'And if your taste for business is as strong as your taste for hot chocolate, it must be formidable.'

She blushed and put down her steaming cup. 'I suppose I am addicted to this stuff. But, come now, it's your turn to tell me something.'

'If I can.' He saw her expression become serious. 'What is it, Annie?'

'You've told me that the conditions children are brought up in shape their future. John, what is the Chat Roux going to do to my daughter?'

For a moment he was silent, wondering how to explain. 'You've said that the local school is inadequate and provides a culture little different from the bar?'

'Yes.'

'Julie's older now, so perhaps boarding won't be so traumatic,' he hedged. 'I know you hate the idea but you may have to try again when you go back. Can't you find somewhere they will let you see her at weekends?'

307

'The Chat is bad for her, that's what you're saying?'

'I'm sure there are good people there and they mean Julie no ill,' he went on carefully. 'But for all its success as a business, a bar in what is a shady, dangerous district of Paris, is no place to bring up a sensitive, intelligent and, in time, lovely girl. You know that, Annie.'

Annie gave a deep sigh. 'Yes, I know that, but I can't bear to think about leaving her somewhere like the convent again. I shouldn't have asked.' She smiled ruefully. 'You're too truthful, John!'

'Would you prefer me to lie?'

'No.' Annie looked away then changed the subject. 'When are you going to ask Lady Ballantyne about wee Jessica?'

'I'm not sure,' he replied. 'Her personal progress is excellent, but she is no closer to accepting the baby than she was to begin with.'

'What will become of the wee lass?' Annie asked sadly. 'I've been keeping my eye on her, visiting the nursery when I can, but she's not my responsibility and anyway I'm going back to Paris.'

'I'll broach the subject again with Lord Ballantyne,' John grimaced. 'Though I'll get no further than before.'

'But one of them must do something,' Annie felt a surge of defensive anger on the child's behalf. 'Jessica didn't ask to be born! She needs special care and fresh air, not just being hidden in the nursery with old Jeanie and hardly another soul allowed across the threshold. Jeanie's a kind lady, but ...'

He raised a weary hand to stop her. 'As her doctor, I agree with every word you say. But my hands are tied.'

'When is he likely to come back?'

'In a few days time, I believe.'

'Well, I'd better keep out of his way,' Annie grinned. 'And if our paths do cross, I hope he's more kindly disposed towards me that he was the last time!'

'You've met him?' John was puzzled. 'I thought you only knew Lady Ballantyne.'

'He was the one who wanted rid of me,' Annie said with a wry smile. 'Didn't you know that?'

'No. Tell me more.'

Annie shook her head. 'That story can keep. But at least if he sends me packing this time, I have somewhere to go!' She got up. 'And now I'll leave you, John. Old Jeanie likes me to sing Jessica to sleep before I collect Julie from Miss Somerville.'

John Chisholm sat pensively by the glow of the library fire. From what Annie had hinted, he had a feeling this visit by Lord Ballantyne would be definitive for them all.

'Bloody quackery, Chisholm!' Edward Baird had snorted when the doctor tried to explain the theory on emotionally induced hysteria from Professors Janet and Charcot in Paris. 'If it hadn't been for Urquhart and Maria Cameron, I wouldn't have let you even try out your daft methods with my wife. Get results or I'll get a better doctor who will take proper measures to snap Alexandra out of it!'

'At least he must admit she looks better this time,' John consoled himself, 'but maybe not in the ways he wants.'

'Might as well not have a wife at all.' Baird had been hard in his judgement. 'Doesn't look good. Had an awful time explaining why she upped and off right in the middle of Baden-Baden. Bertie ... er ... His Royal Highness ... wasn't happy!'

Maria's suggestion of bringing Annie back at his wife's request made little impact on him. Edward Baird had no personal objections to Annie. He never pondered about the lives of servants and had long forgotten the circumstances of her dismissal, or his part in it.

John got up and went through the silent house to the makeshift nursery at the far end. Before he reached it, Annie's clear sweet notes wafted towards him as she sang to Jessica. She was putting in the baby's name instead of the one Robert Burns had intended. He stopped and listened, the pure sound and the tenderness in her voice touched him almost to tears.

'Flow gently sweet Afton, among thay green braes,
Flow gently, I'll sing thee a song in thy praise;
My Jessie's asleep by thy murmuring stream,
Flow gently sweet Afton, disturb not her dream.'

When she had finished he turned away, wishing that there was some way he could improve the fate of the innocent victim of its parents' inability to think beyond their own needs.

309

'Shall I stable the horses, your Lordship?' the groom asked hesitatntly when Lord Ballantyne arrived at Baird House two days later. Last time, his master had stayed less than half an hour and then had stormed out again.

'Of course, man!' he replied irritably. Turning away, he climbed the imposing stairs of his ancestral home, thinking about the task ahead. 'The latest report from John Chisholm sounds better,' he told himself. 'Though I don't suppose that means much. Doctors are always making business by pandering to neurotic women who would be better off thinking about their husbands instead of themselves.'

Handing his coat, hat and cane to the po-faced butler, he went straight to his wife's rooms, knocked lightly and entered without waiting for a response.

This is more like it, he thought. The scene was reassuring. Annie was reading Miss Austen to Alexandra, who was sitting in the window seat, looking out over the neat lawns and great banks of rhododendrons that swept down to the Firth of Clyde. She looked largely restored, hair shining and well-arranged and her afternoon dress becoming and in the mode.

Annie stopped reading and got up, 'Lord Ballantyne,' she bobbed automatically.

Edward ignored her and approached his wife, who was gazing intently out of the window.

Annie watched with a feeling of deep apprehension growing in the pit of her stomach. If only the man had spoken to John Chisholm before barging in like this, she worried. Still he is her husband. Even though she was no longer a servant, she would not presume or dare to offer an opinion.

'Glad to see you're up and about, m'dear,' Edward began cheerfully enough, but continued across the room with a wary look on his face.

Alexandra turned towards him and Annie almost gasped at the expression of pure hate distorting her lovely features. 'Keep away from me,' she hissed.

He stopped. 'Alexandra, don't start all that nonsense again!' Edward's puffy, debauched face showed only too clearly the life he led, but now the loose flesh hardened with anger.

'Get out!' she said.

Neither of them seemed to remember Annie's presence. The

310

dark strength of their emotion was palpable. She knew instinctively that she was about to find out the cause of Alexandra's troubles, and she didn't want to hear. With an apologetic cough, she murmured an excuse and headed towards the door, hoping John Chisholm was still somewhere in the house. She had a feeling he would be needed.

'Stay where you are, Annie!' Alexandra commanded in her old imperious tone.

'I don't think I should be here, Lady Ballantyne,' Annie objected, shooting an embarrassed look at Edward Baird.

'Leave us, woman.' He waved her away with as much ceremony as he would a fly on rotten meat.

Annie sighed. God how these folk think they own other folk body and soul, she thought, but made to obey.

As she reached the door in the corner, out of line of the couple's view, Alexandra's voice froze her to the spot. 'Debaucher, rapist! Foul, fornicating bastard!' she hissed.

'Alexandra, you are insane!' her husband responded sharply. 'Calm yourself.'

'You call me insane?' she replied, raising her voice. Annie felt sick, but unable to move. 'You raped me on our wedding night!' Alexandra spat. 'Then you taught me every filthy trick you know and once we had a Baird heir you pushed me onto your so-called friends, so you could go on with your own disgusting life... "Les grandes horizontales" would have missed your money, wouldn't they, Edward, if you'd been faithful much longer? If you ever were! You and dear, fat old Bertie! Two of a kind!'

'This is idiocy,' he shouted back. 'You were a willing pupil and I never had to push you, my dear, you were only too ready to oblige them all ... even Bertie!'

'Not always!' she said, 'You know that I didn't want to go to Count Scyzinski that week ... I only did it to save your filthy skin!'

'All right,' he replied, his tone suddenly conciliatory, 'But it was only once. The Count knew I had been indiscreet with his ward. If he had exposed me as he threatened, Alexandra, it would have been the end of us both in public life. You wouldn't have wanted that any more than me.'

'So I was sold to that lecher like a slave to let you off, Edward Baird,' she said bitterly.

311

'He wanted you, and he was willing to forget...'

'But I couldn't forget!' Alexandra replied, 'Do you know what he did to me for seven days and nights?'

'Yes, yes, you've told me and I'm sorry, but it's all over. For God's sake, woman, it was more than a year ago!'

'Over?' she sounded hysterical. 'Over? He was there at Baden-Baden. Looking at me. Smiling, whispering his disgusting fantasies everytime he got the chance! Anyway,' she said, 'it'll never be over, you know that. I tried to get rid of the baby, Edward.' Her voice was lower now, but shook with unfettered anger. 'After the way it was conceived I didn't want it. The nine months I carried it were a plague. And look what happened. That's God's punishment on us both, Edward Baird.'

'Alexandra,' Edward Baird's voice was ice cold, 'You are totally mad. You need locking up.'

'Try it! Do you think Maria and my Father will let you once I tell them the true cause of my illness?' Alexandra spat back.

'I'm leaving now and unless it is something to do with our own children, Eddie and Vicky,' he replied in a voice that made Annie shudder, 'I will not be alone in your company again.'

'At last you have made me happy, Edward Baird,' she answered and began to laugh hysterically. 'Now, get out!'

Annie stood back in the cover of a great oak bookcase, but he didn't even notice her. Face like thunder, he stormed past. She heard him crash downstairs, roaring at the servants. Seconds later the front door banged shut, shuddering on its great hinges.

God, I wish I hadn't heard all that, she thought, but it's too late now. And I thought folk had troubles at the Chat Roux!

'Annie! I know you're there. Annie! Come here at once,' Alexandra's voice cut across her horror.

She went over, expecting to see her mistress deeply distressed. Instead she was sitting on the window seat again, smiling to herself. 'You heard all that,' she said calmly.

'Er...' Annie went red.

'Don't worry, I wanted you to hear! I wanted someone other than him and me to know what happened.' She got up and stretched like a cat. 'And I feel so much better now for having said it. Maybe dear, clever Doctor Chisholm is right, if you let the pain out of the mind, it can heal itself.' Calmly she smoothed down the lovely silk of her skirt. 'Now why don't we walk by the river before lunch, Annie? Then tomorrow I think I might even go and pay a few calls ... starting with the modist.'

'I can't tell you what I heard, John,' Annie said that evening still distressed and shaken. 'But all I can say is they are not likely to be with each other very much. And I don't believe either of them will make proper plans for poor wee Jessica's future.'

'I feared so.' His intelligent hazel eyes darkened. He gazed into the fire, capable fingers drumming the side of the chair. 'But we have to do something. Jessica is nearly eight months old, soon her presence will be more noticeable, however they try to suppress it.' He thought for a moment. 'Annie, how do you think Lady Ballantyne would react to her staying in one of the gate houses with a proper nurse?'

'Lady Ballantyne doesn't even want people to see her, let alone have her stay around the estate,' Annie answered sadly. 'I think she'll have to go. The poor bairn is a reminder of things she would rather forget, John.' Annie thought of the circumstances of the child's conception and Alexandra's terrible bitterness and anger.

'Then I'll have to look for an institution which will take her,' he sighed.

'Will she settle? I've told you what happened to Julie.'

'That's a good question,' he replied with a grim expression she rarely saw on his face. 'I'll have to try to find a place which is truly enlightened.'

'At least you know about such things, an ordinary doctor would be quite lost.' She smiled encouragingly.

'I'm afraid you've too high an opinion of my abilities,' he said. 'I work mostly with adults, Annie. I tend to look at the medical condition, or the underlying psychiatry, but in Jessica's case that's not the most important thing.'

'Don't underestimate yourself.' She laughed at his rueful face. 'But you're right, it's making sure wee Jessica will be happy that's the key, not that every medical detail is attended to.' She thought for a moment. 'Listen, if you feel it would be useful, I'll come with you.'

'Would you do that?'

'Don't look so surprised. Why not? I'm sorry for the bairn, it's not her fault she was born that way.'

313

'Then I'll take you at your word. Your commonsense and instinct for people will be invaluable.'

'Now who's overestimating?' she grinned.

'Not a bit! We'll begin our quest next week as soon as I've finished checking the list of possible establishments.'

Chapter Twenty-Four

'The bairn has taken a right shine to you, Annie. It's not every-body she goes to.' Jeanie handed her Jessica, who clung lovingly round her neck.

'Aie ... aie...' the little girl covered Annie's face with damp kisses. 'Listen to that, I think she's trying to say Annie ... she doesn't say anything else poor wee thing, just makes wee grunts.'

'Och, I don't think she's trying to talk, she's only eight months. An ordinary bairn wouldn't be talking yet, and it can take much longer for bairns like this to start, though Doctor Chisholm says that most of them usually do fine in the end.'

'You sing to her, Annie, while I make a wee cup o' tea.'

The nurse waddled off and Annie played with the baby's stubby little fingers.

'Oh give to me a dress of red, all sewed round wi' silver thread,' she sang, 'And I will marry, arry, arry, arry, I will marry you!'

Jessica gurgled and giggled.

'Aye, she likes that,' Jeanie came back carrying two cups.

'She likes all the attention she can get,' Annie agreed.

'Oh, by here, that's better.' The nurse sat down, shifting the weight off her bunioned feet with a deep grunt of contentment.

'You've done a good job, Jeanie.' Annie sipped her tea. 'Jessica's a right wee butter-ball and that happy. It's a pity you can't just stay and look after her.'

'Aye, well,' the nurse replied, 'I'm getting too old, Annie, and she's a right handful at times.'

'I can imagine,' Annie nodded sympathetically and placed the cup back in its saucer. 'Come on my wee dumplin'.' She wiggled the feet of the plump little girl. 'Give Annie another wee hug and she'll give you a big one back. See she understands every word!' Annie gasped as the breath was practically squeezed out of her.

'Anyway, Annie,' the nurse went on, 'they wouldn't let me stay on much longer. You ken as well as I do that they don't want her here.'

'That's a fact.' Annie sighed. She got up and put Jessica back in her cot. 'I can't speak for the Laird, but I don't think Lady Ballantyne is going to change her mind about the bairn now, Jeanie.'

'Naw, Annie. Neither Lady Ballantyne, nor the Laird have put a foot in here since the wee thing was brought straight from the birthing room. Ye wouldn't treat a dog as bad!' the old nurse shook her head. 'But I thought you'd ken more, you being that close to her Ladyship.'

'I hardly see her these days,' Annie replied. 'Since she has been feeling better, she doesn't have the same need of me. She's away at Craigdrummond half the time and the other half she's meeting friends and going out again. And that's the way it should be.'

'Aye, you're right. She's more like her old self. All the servants say that.'

And maybe it's just as well we don't see each other so much, Annie thought to herself. With each day's improvement, Alexandra was regaining her confidence and with it some of her imperious manner. I've been too long in republican Paris! had to remind herself when Alexandra, quite unconsciously, had begun to treat her as the servant she once was.

'Would ye look at that!' Jeanie pointed to Jessica, she wants ye to lift her again.'

Annie felt a lump in her throat as she looked at the vulnerable, slanted eyes of the little girl hopefully looking over the rim of the big iron cot, fat little arms outstretched. 'Well, maybe it's just as well to find some place where she can get to know folk and stay out her days.'

'I hope they'll be good to her in a home. Do ye think they will, Annie?' Jeanie commented sadly. 'She's a nice wee thing in her own way. I've got right fond of her.'

'Doctor Chisholm says she'll be fine if we can just find the

316

right place. He says things are getting a lot better these days. And he should know,' Annie answered with more hope than conviction in her voice.

'Aye,' the nurse sounded equally doubtful.

Annie made an effort to be positive. 'We're off to look at another place tomorrow. It sounds quite good.'

'Some sort of poor-house for daft bairns?'

'No this is a private clinic Doctor Chisholm has found. They say it's the best on this side of Scotland.' She couldn't help her anxiety showing through. 'I just hope it's as good as it claims, some of the others have been downright diabolical, with bairns not even kept clean or tended, let alone loved.'

November wind tugging at her scarf and hat, Annie stood beside John Chisholm, looking up at the fine red sandstone building set in its own large park just outside Kilmarnock. The place was imposing enough, even on a dreich winter afternoon, she thought, as the carriage clattered off, leaving them at the front door.

Rhododendron bushes, so favoured in West Scotland, lined the long drive. In the background, the hills rolled magnificently across the skyline. John rang the bell. Deep within she heard its echo. Strange, she wondered, for a place full of bairns, it sounds awful empty.

'Ah, yes, how nice to meet you, Doctor Chisholm, and your good lady.' The matron welcomed them in her office, assuming from Annie's sober, good quality attire and confident bearing, that she was the doctor's wife.

'Er ... may I present Mistress Lamarche, my er ... colleague,' John Chisholm was nonplussed at the unexpected faux pas.

Annie smothered a grin at his discomfort, but was touched by her spontaneous elevation to equal status.

'You've come to see what we have to offer the child you spoke of. Are you, er, able to tell me which family she is from?' Matron asked delicately.

'Not yet,' the doctor replied. 'As you know, these matters are sensitive.'

'Indeed. And of course, you're right, doctor.' Matron had many inmates whose true identity even she wasn't sure of.

While they were talking, Annie looked round, impressed by the warm comfort of Matron's office with its cheery fire burning brightly. She allowed her optimism to rise. Maybe it wouldn't be so bad for Jessica after all, it certainly looked better than the other institutions.

Matron got up and addressed them both, 'Unfortunately I am not free myself just now, but I'll just get someone to show you round, and then if you have any questions, I will be delighted to answer them. But, of course, Doctor, being in the profession, you know you can't see everything,' she warned.

'Oh?' Annie raised her eyebrows.

'Some of the imbecile and idiot children we have here are very disturbed, Mistress Lamarche,' Matron explained. 'They are kept quite separate from the others and we try to keep their routines very rigid, so as not to agitate them.'

'It's all right, Matron,' John Chisholm said. 'I work with many institutions of this kind, though with adults. I assumed we would have limited access. But of course we need to see enough facilities on which to base an objective decision.'

'Do you have a lot of patients, Matron?' Annie tried to work out how many could fit into a house as huge as this. It's at least the size of Craigdrummond, she thought.

'The numbers vary,' Matron sounded unexpectedly defensive. 'Mortality among imbeciles is higher than the normal population. They have more delicate constitutions,' she explained. 'Isn't that right, doctor?'

'Unfortunately, yes. They are especially prone to blood disorders, respiratory and gastrointestinal infections. Also to hepatitis if they come into close contact with other children who are similarly handicapped, which is an added risk in an institution like this,' John replied. 'But with good hygiene and care...'

'We provide the very best!' Matron said huffily. 'All our inmates are from good families, who have the where-with-all to pay for the exceptional service we offer,' she added proudly.

'So you must heartily approve of the moves being made by parliament to reform mental institutions generally, Matron,' John Chisholm asked with a mischievous look in his eye that made Annie smile.

'Er ... yes ... on the whole, though some go a little too far,' she conceded with an uneasy frown.

318

Turning to a stout middle-aged woman in the corner, dressed in a long white uniform, pinny and cap, primed like a stumpy candle, she said, 'Nurse, take Doctor Chisholm and Mistress Lamarche over to the children's ward. Just the open ward, nurse, not the closed ones of course,' she added with heavy emphasis.

They followed the bobbing white cap through a warren of chilly corridors which reminded Annie painfully of the convent where Julie had been so unhappy. Though it was less gloomy and the terrifying pictures of beatific suffering were missing, it held additional traumas for the visitor. From behind some of the closed doors, came heart-rending moans and all the while from somewhere in the distance, a lost and desolate soul kept up a thin, eerie wail. The nurse, hardened to the sounds, walked crisply on.

'Why are these ones kept separate?' Annie asked the doctor in a low voice as they passed solitary rooms with bars on the sliding peep windows.

'Some of them have to be or they get violent,' he whispered back, 'it's quite usual, Annie.'

'Do they see daylight, go outside, walk ... that sort of thing?'

'Some never do ... others once in a while I expect, but I'd be surprised if any of them go out regularly. The home has to be sure they don't escape.'

'Excuse me, nurse, do they stay here all their lives?' Annie struggled to keep a sense of objectivity, but the clinical nature of the place was making her depressed. She couldn't imagine what quality of life these poor creatures had.

'The imbeciles in this corridor have been here for years, Mistress Lamarche, but they can only stay till they're sixteen.'

'And what happens then?'

'Imbecile children usually go to the private asylum for adults on the other side of the town.'

'How about bairns like Jessica? She's not violent,' Annie said as they came to a big wooden door which the nurse unlocked and stood back for Annie to pass. 'She's not an imbecile either, only what they call a "mongol".'

'Then we class her as "idiot",' the nurse said crisply. 'Children with that particular condition don't usually have a long life span,' she went on. 'Most of them pick up infections easily. Not too many go on till they're over twenty, so idiots usually get staying till they reach that age.'

319

'And those that do live longer?'

'... go to the same place as the others.'

'The asylum? But Jessica's not a lunatic, she's just different!' Annie felt sadness rise up to choke her.

'Well, it's not my position to decide,' the nurse said. And not yours either, her expression added.

'Is this it?' They were at the entrance to a large ward. From the noise inside, Annie realised it was full of very young children.

'Your little girl would most likely be in here,' the nurse confirmed her suspicion. 'We keep the smallest children at the back of the house so they don't get frightened by the bigger ones ... they're in another ward along the corridor. But there's fewer of them, of course.'

Annie followed the nurse inside and John went off to talk with the day sister. Two nurses were busy cleaning and dressing around fifteen or twenty small children who ranged in age from about six months to five years, she guessed. Some were like Jessica, others had various disabilities. There was a hacking, constant bronchial cacophany from every corner of the room.

'It's the time of year for splutters,' the nurse said cheerfully, as Annie winced at a harsh rasp from one of the cots. 'And these bairns pick up everything that's going and some things that aren't.'

Annie tried to get an impression of life in the ward and what she saw depressed her. Some children stood clutching the sides of their iron cots, others sat sucking their fingers, but some lay listlessly gazing into hopeless space, little bodies racked as they sniffed and coughed.

'Are they kept in these things all the time?' she asked.

'Of course not!' The nurse was horrified. 'We take them out of the cots for a few hours each morning and evening.'

'When do they play? Do they ever play?'

'Well, we don't stop them playing any time, in or out of the cots, but we can't let them play together without strict supervision in case they harm each other.' Annie's attitude was making her overly defensive. 'But they get toys in the cots now and then and there are always nurses about.'

'To play with them?'

'No, they are too busy for that.' She looked round the bustling

320

ward with a more confident air. 'These children take a lot of looking after. You can hear that we've got a right epidemic of bronchitis the now. It's the same every November. But we do our best.'

'... Aye.'

Seeing her hesitation, the nurse added sharply. 'We've been called one of the best homes for imbecile and idiot children in Scotland, you know, Mistress Lamarche!'

'I'm not criticising you,' Annie said with a weary nod. 'It's just that bairns seem to thrive better when they're happy and active.'

'Oh, are you an expert yourself then, Mistress?' the nurse asked with heavy sarcasm.'

'No, but I know the bairn in question. She's a loving wee lass that's used to attention from her nurse and from me too at times ... cuddles, songs, you know ...'

'This is an institution,' she replied huffily. 'If you want that kind of thing, you'd better keep her at home!'

'I couldn't agree more!' Annie turned to look for John who was examining the medical facilities with a deep frown. Brusquely he took his leave, turning down a chance to speak to Matron again. 'Just tell her we'll let you know,' he said.

'Well, Annie?' he demanded as soon as she got into the carriage beside him. 'Give me your honest, objective opinion ... or just the feeling from your heart!'

'As if I'd give you anything else,' she replied with a strained smile. 'It's far better than the other places we saw. It's clean, the bairns are cared for, John. And in its way it's progressive as you would call it. But I don't think Jessica will be happy there.'

'Why not? They're not cruel. There's no evidence of physical abuse, which is one of the things that folk like Dr Arbuckle Brown, Doctor Fraser ... and myself too,' he added modestly, 'are trying to get more strictly regulated by parliament. You've been with me to some other places I'll be reporting as needing investigation.'

'No, you're right, they're not cruel, not at all. But there's no fun, no laughter either, nothing that makes life worth while,' Annie tried to explain her feelings. 'The bairns are left in their cots for a large part of the day without anybody trying to get the best out of them.'

'But actual care isn't deficient, Annie.'

'No, it's not,' Annie admitted. 'They're well fed and that.'

'That's all one can really expect. I'm sure Jessica doesn't have the same expectations as an ordinary child.' He paused, for her reaction.

'Do you want to send her there then?' Annie asked slowly.

'No,' he said. 'She'd come down at once with an infection. Children like Jessica are not strong. And because she's been locked away, she has not built up her immune defences. I wouldn't give her more than six months in a place like that among so many other mentally retarded children. They cross-infect very easily for reasons we're not quite sure of.'

'You don't?' Annie let out a sharp hiss of relief. 'I'm glad to hear it.'

'But what are we going to do with her?' John thought aloud. 'I have to act soon.'

'Och, it's a shame the wee thing can't just stay among folk she could get to know ... really know, not nurses coming and going,' she reflected.

'Well, that's the reality of institutions,' John sighed. 'I could find a family to look after her, I suppose. Yes, there's a lot to be said for guardianship.' He paused thoughtfully.

'Why not then?'

'There's always a risk they would take her for the money and maybe not treat her well. Anyway,' he shrugged, 'I shouldn't burden you with any more. It's not really your problem, Annie. As house physician it's my responsibility to do something appropriate for the child ... and I will.'

'I know you will, John.'

The carriage rattled onwards. Annie gazed idly out of the window into the gloomy night, deep in thought. Trekking round the institutions had been a dfficult and depressing job, even for someone so committed to changing the archaic mental health laws as John Chisholm.

For Annie it has been traumatic. Accompanying him, she had been shocked at much of what she saw. Now she understood his drive to try and change the system where folk were locked away, sometimes from infancy, and forgotten by families who felt only shame in their existence.

She looked at the doctor. His tall form hunched in the cramped carriage, head crowned with the mop of brown hair that never stayed in order and his chin sunk on his chest, deep in thought. Aye he's a decent lad. She admired the integrity of the man. He could've dumped wee Jessica in the nearest place, good or bad, and forgotten her too. If she'd died because somebody hurt her, or just didn't care, no one would call him to account. But he wouldn't.

John sat up. Something else was bothering him and he had to know the answer, he broke the silence, 'Have you made up your mind about going back?'

'Yes,' she replied. 'Julie and I leave for Paris soon. Beginning of next month most likely.'

'So soon?'

'Yes.' She answered the next question that hovered on his lips before he asked, 'And I've already told Lady Ballantyne.'

'She wouldn't like that.'

'No, she didn't.' Annie smiled, 'Even though we see much less of each other now, she wanted me to stay. Has she told you she might move back to Craigdrummond for a while?'

'Craigdrummond? No.' John raised his eyebrows. 'Since her latest phase of recovery began, I know she's been visiting a lot, but I'm surprised if she intends to stay longer than a week at a time.'

'Aye, well, maybe she's learned who her real friends are, and I'm glad to see they include Lady Cameron at long last. Though I can't see her going back to live in the countryside either.' Annie grinned.

'Lord Ballantyne hasn't been back since the er ... row, has he?' John had pieced together some of the rift between the couple. Annie hadn't discussed what was said, and he hadn't pressed her.

'No, he's not been back.' Annie wondered how much he knew.

'Annie, I've not asked you for detail,' he said carefully, 'but as her physician, it would help me to know if Lady Ballantyne and her husband touched on the deepest causes of her illness during their confrontation.'

'Aye, they did that,' Annie replied, the expression on her face reflecting more of the trauma than she realised.

'I thought so!' John couldn't keep the satisfaction from his voice. 'So I was right all along, it was classic emotional hysteria, quite in keeping with my French colleagues' theories. Hence the rapid recovery. Pity I wasn't able to try hypnosis on her,' he mused, 'Charcot's had some wonderful results.'

'Well I'm glad somebody found the experience useful!' she said sharply. 'I thought it was a crying shame seeing her like that when I came ... and then that hellish row between the pair of them! It's been a right rotten mess, John Chisholm, and I hope I never live through the like again!'

'Sorry, Annie.' He looked so contrite she was mollified. 'I got carried away by professional interest. I forgot that it must have been painful for you. May I ask one more thing?'

'You can ask, but I might not answer.'

'Do you believe there will be a reconciliation?'

'I'm not a prophet,' Annie said with a strained smile, 'but from what I heard, there never will.'

John shrugged. 'Well, if they decide to live apart, they won't be the only ones, though I can't see them living through the scandal of divorce.'

'No,' Annie agreed. 'The King doesn't like divorce, does he?'

'So I've heard, though it doesn't stop him enjoying the wives of some of his closest friends,' John's tone was ironic. 'After that embarrassing brush with the courts while he was still Prince of Wales, he prefers not to have divorcees around him.'

'Well where I come from, nobody thinks of divorce.' Annie gave a wry grin. 'If you marry badly you just have to get on with it, or go back to your Mammy!'

'Why does Lady Ballantyne never ask you to go with her to Craigdrummond?' John asked, taking her by surprise.

Annie looked away. 'I've said I don't want to go, even temporarily.'

'But I thought you loved the place,' he probed gently. Annie was forthcoming about France, even the Gallowgate, but she rarely mentioned Ayrshire except in the briefest, though fondest, terms.

'Och, Craigdrummond is in the past, as is being somebody's servant ... it would be too difficult ... I've changed ... och, it's hard to explain, John,' she hedged. 'Our home is in Paris, Julie's and mine.'

'Will you risk the convent again?'

Annie's face clouded. 'I don't know. I have to do something.'

'And you'll go on running the Chat?'

'For now.' Annie was getting edgy under his persistent questioning. She fidgeted with the window blind.

He wasn't inclined to stop the interrogation. 'And what of your sister-in-law and her husband?'

'Jorice and Francine know they have to leave. Though they'd give their eye-teeth to stay.'

'For the money?'

'They get the lion's share of profit while I'm away, but Jorice had enough income to keep them comfortably without working. No, it's not the money.'

'What if something happened to you? Would Francine get the Chat?'

'What are all these daft questions leading to?' Annie smiled suddenly and her grey eyes danced. 'Do I look as if I might fall in a heap, Doctor?'

'Not a bit, you're the picture of health. I'm just naturally curious,' he responded in the same light vein. 'It comes with a specialism in mental conditions. Sorry, Annie.'

'All right, you're forgiven,' she said and went on, 'The Chat is Julie's. Under Louis's will, as long as I live I have the right to run it, but the actual ownership passes to Julie when she comes of age, or on my death, whichever is first ...'

'Do you think she will want it?'

Annie leaned against the padded carriage wall with a thoughtful expression on her face. 'Somehow I can't see Julie running the Chat and being satisfied. She likes her books too much ... though that didn't stop her father.'

'She's a lass,' John said. 'Would she be taken seriously if she tried to run it alone?'

'Julie's not alone. I thought we'd agreed I won't die for a while yet,' Annie replied with a grin.

'But, if you decided to stop for other reasons ... remarry maybe? After all, Annie, you'll still be a relatively young woman by the time she reaches her majority.'

'I can't see me remarrying even then. I'm fine as I am. Anyway, they took me seriously enough in Montmartre. If she wants to run the Chat herself she could!' she said and tossed her chestnut curls with the familiar gesture of defiance he had come to love.

'... I'll miss you,' he said hesitantly.

'And I'll miss you,' Annie replied. 'We've become real... colleagues,' she added with a teasing smile.

'The matron could have been right.' The leather seat creaked as he turned towards her.

'Right about what?' Their shoulders inadvertently touched in the jolting carriage, but neither drew away.

'You could be my wife,' he said.

'John Chisholm, have you taken leave of your senses?' she demanded, pulling back into the corner. 'I'm not the stuff doctor's wives are made of.'

'And what's that stuff then?' he asked with a half-smile.

'I don't know, but I'm not it,' Annie flushed. 'I told you I have no intention of marrying again.'

'Why?' he persisted. 'Weren't you happy with Louis?'

'Oh yes, we were happy,' she said quietly. 'But Louis, he was exceptional...'

'And I'm not...' John grinned wryly.

'I didn't mean that. Och, it's just that the circumstances when I married Louis were odd, otherwise, I don't know if I would have. But I came to love him very much.'

'Did you love somebody else?'

'Yes,' she didn't avoid the question.

'In Craigdrummond? Is that why you don't want to go back?'

'Yes, in Craigdrummond. But it was a long time ago.'

'Was it, Annie?' he asked, shrewd eyes probing. 'Do you still love him?'

'Don't ask that,' she replied, looking out of the carriage window.

'Then you've answered,' he said.

In silence that was no longer companionable, they finished the long journey back to Dumbarton.

Annie was angry at herself for giving so much away and angry at John for forcing her to do so by his endless questions. She knew there were many things about her past that she had never settled, but she didn't want reminding.

For his part, John wished he had been less open about his feelings towards her. From the time he gave her the morphia to ease her mother's passing, he had often thought of her as an exceptional woman, as well as a bonnie one. And since fate had thrown

326

them together at Baird House, he had come to care for her very deeply.

He shot her a covert look, but she resolutely stared out into the dark night, back firmly towards him. 'Now you've ruined it, John Chisholm,' he groaned inwardly to himself. 'If she hadn't been leaving I would have gone on building up our relationship. I know she likes me. Annie isn't one to pretend. But I've spoken too soon. Far too soon! Damn! I just hope I haven't ruined our friendship as well.' He sighed in resignation. 'Och, but it's too late for regrets.'

An hour later, in the foggy November darkness with the smoke from thousands of Dumbarton chimneys hanging chokingly in the still air, they left the carriage and climbed the polished granite stairs of Baird House.

John rang the great bell, but when the butler opened, his greeting was for Annie. 'Mistress Lamarche,' he said ponderously as befitting his station, 'A lady is waiting to speak to you in the library.'

'A lady?' Annie's eyebrows rose.

'She says she's a Mistress Ramsay,' he replied. 'She's been waiting an hour and she seems, er ... rather distressed!'

'Phyllis!' Heart full of foreboding, Annie slipped off her coat and crossed the hall.

Chapter Twenty-Five

'Och, Annie,' Phyllis thew herself at her sister-in-law. 'It's terrible, so it is!' She burst into heart-rending sobs.

'What's terrible, Phyllis?' Annie shook her gently. 'Come on, lass, tell me!'

'It's Sandy!' She gulped and rushed on, 'Ye ken we were doing fine. The tea-rooms and bakery were just dandy and we were even thinking of opening a fancy French place ... like you're always talkin' about. Eclairs, pastries, open tarts with lacing ... that would've been smashin', wouldn't it, Annie? If it hadn't been for the shipyards, it would've been fine, Annie ...' she began sobbing again.

'The shipyards?' Annie could have murdered her with impatience, but she bit her tongue, there was no hurrying Phyllis at the best of times and this clearly wasn't the best. 'Now come on, Phyllis,' she broke in between the sobs, 'what's up with Sandy? You're making no sense, lass!'

'He hasn't told ye, because he knew ye'd be mad, but when he borrowed the money for the ovens, he didn't do it from the bank like ye said he should, Annie.'

'Why in the name of the wee man not?' Annie groaned. 'I told him exactly how to go about things. And what was all that he said about the bank manager being impressed?'

'That was a wee white lie, Annie.' Phyllis couldn't look her in the eye. 'Och, whit happened was the bank wanted us to wait a wee while to make sure the books were in the black, but Sandy was that keen to get on wi' it, he borrowed from the menodge men.'

'The menodge men?' Annie was horrified. 'I thought after what happened to Eddie he'd have had more sense!'

'This one seemed to be decent enough. He came into the shop every morning for a bannock for his piece. Sandy jist happened to mention one day that we needed a bit on top of what we had for new ovens. And this man said ye could get a menodge for as much as ye like and for anythin' ye want. He set it up for Sandy, Annie, no bother at all.'

'I'll bet he did,' Annie muttered in fury. 'Och, the daft eejit! Why didn't he trust me?' She shook her head. 'I know how to do these things right.' The Chat Roux was a harsh school in street-wise finance. Louis might have been a political idealist, but he had a firm grasp of the realities of rough banking and had taught her well.

'Sandy did trust ye, Annie,' Phyllis moaned. 'It was jist he wanted you to be proud of him...'

'Aye, all right, don't cry again, Phyllis. Poor Sandy.' Despite her exasperation, she understood the motivation that had driven him to go ahead and take a chance. He had wanted to prove himself, wanted the business to flourish and then was too embarrassed to tell her what he had done. 'But the menodge men!' Annie groaned aloud. 'Imagine setting up a menodge to buy ovens! A new coat or some bed linen, that's bad enough... but ovens! They must have thought it was Hogmanay all the year round! Och, even so, I thought Sandy had more sense.' She paced the room. 'How much are you owing?'

'Sandy didn't borrow it all from them, Annie,' Phyllis stoutly defended her husband. 'We used all our savings and the money left over from when you married Louis, so we only had to borrow twenty pounds,' she said the amount quickly as if the words burned her tongue.

'Twenty pounds! That's more than a house-maid earns in a year!'

'They're great ovens. And we wid have managed,' Phyllis began weeping again in jagged gulps. 'But the man we knew packed it in and handed over Sandy to somebody else we didn't. A man called McMurtie. He's a right hard man, Annie. A bad lot, so he is. He kept pittin' up the interest. We could hardly scrape it together...'

'You hadn't a written agreement on interest?'

'Naw, and McMurtie wouldn't give us one.'

'Och, the rotten swine.' Annie sighed, for Phyllis had well

329

described the mafia-like activities of Glasgow's most unscrupulous and feared money-lenders.

Phyllis took a deep breath and went on, 'At first we were paying back three shilling a week ... then four, then five ... In the end we owed more than we had borrowed. Then the Govan shipyards went on to short-time and folk were broke. So we fell behind ourselves. That's when he sent in the frighteners.'

'Right away?' Annie was surprised. A warning, even if it was nasty, was usually sent first.

'Aye, that's McMurtie for ye. The very first time Sandy had to miss, McMurtie set the frighteners on him, Annie, the frighteners,' she repeated with terror in her eyes '... they took him in the back and kicked him stupid ... and when I tried to stop them they pushed me so I fell. And they're comin' back, Annie!' The tears ran down onto her nose, falling onto her plain black coat like silver streams, but she didn't notice. 'We've asked folk to pay their tick, but they can't.'

'You shouldn't have let folk run up tick with you, Phyllis. It's just daft!' Annie was beyond being kind any more. 'I thought you both promised me you wouldn't?'

'It's hard to say no when there's hungry bairns comin' in beggin' for a loaf!' soft-hearted Phyllis sobbed. 'And now we're in the same boat. Sandy is black and blue and his leg is hurt bad. He can hardly stand at the ovens. Och, we'll have to sell the fitments as well as the ovens to pay off the menodge. That's what they're after, they want the lot! We're ruined, Annie.'

'Not if I can damn well help it!' Annie snapped with the look on her face that Montmartre had come to respect. 'Lady Ballantyne is away at Craigdrummond this week,' she said, 'and Julie is fine in the nursery. I'll have a word with Miss Somerville and ask if she can sleep there for a few nights, she nearly does as it is! Get on your feet, Phyllis Ramsay,' she said briskly, 'we'll get the carriage to take us over to Charing Cross right this minute.

'Annie, I heard. Can I help?' John Chisholm had blatantly listened to the exchange through the open library door, though he had ordered the curious butler downstairs before the staff knew what the trouble was and added miles of drama in the telling.

'Thanks,' she said in a voice as grim as her expression, 'but I'll handle this myself, Doctor Chisholm.'

He winced at the formality, but felt he'd earned it with his heavy-handed behaviour in the carriage. 'Well, if you're sure.'

'I'm sure.'

'It's up to you, but for God's sake take care...' No doctor who had worked the tenements, had any doubt as to what she would be up against.

'I will that.' She nodded brusquely, then seeing the hurt on his face by her curt dismissal, added in a softer tone, 'and if I need help ... a witness or whatever, I know where to come.'

'Good luck, then,' he replied.

'Aye, I'll need it.'

Annie and Phyllis disappeared into the dark night. John stood watching, admiring the strength and courage built into Annie's diminutive frame. 'But I wish she wouldn't take it all on her own shoulders,' he said to himself and shook his head. 'It's too much for anyone, however brave.'

'I'm sorry I can't get up.' Sandy, sitting at the table with one leg on a chair, greeted them with a wan smile.

'Och, what in the name have they done to you?' Annie was shocked at the livid bruising on her brother's face. 'Have you seen to that leg?'

'It's no broken, just battered. See.' He tried to move it and groaned aloud. 'They kicked me wi' tackety boots. My ribs hurt worse.'

'Aye, well let's see the other real damage,' Annie knew more sympathy was misplaced, 'Get the books, Phyllis.'

Annie sat with Sandy for hours, trying to see a way out of the mess they were in. But it was a hopeless task. He was a good baker, but the books such as they were, were a chaos of old debt from countless folk round the back streets behind Charing Cross who would never be able to pay, even if they had the will. She calculated at the last rate of interest McMurtie had levied, that he and Phyllis owed somewhere over thirty-four pounds on the original twenty pound debt.

'And if we don't pay up within three days, we'll be forced to sell the stock and fittings for next to nothin' to cover it.' Sandy sunk his chin onto his hands in a gesture of black despair.

'Could you not bargain with them, Sandy?' Annie asked,

331

rubbing tired eyes. 'If we can win some more time, I can maybe get some money over from France.' Her face clouded. 'Mind you, it's a lot to ask for and the Chat isn't that well off. What comes in goes out again.'

'They've refused more time, Annie. That's what I got before and when I didn't make the payments they gave me the kickin' and upped the interest again. But they've telt me they'll leave off if I sign over all the stuff instead,' Sandy said with the hang-dog expression he had worn since she came.

'Aye, that would suit them fine,' Annie said grimly. 'Over a hundred pounds worth of stuff to cover a twenty pound debt.'

'And we'll never be able to start up again,' Phyllis buried her head in her apron and wept.

In the background, Isa and Bella, quiet and retiring as ever, stood white-faced beside their nephews who were awed into unnatural silence. They all knew that the family faced catastrophe but were unable to comprehend the extent.

'When are they coming back?' Annie demanded.

'Tomorrow wi' McMurtie himself to check out the stock. If I don't have the money by Thursday morning, he's taking the lot. Ovens take a while to sell, or I'd have sold them myself to try and save the lot going to him.'

Annie stayed that night, lying under a thin blanket, tossing and turning in the narrow passage bed vacated by the boys who were crushed in with their parents. By morning she had made up her mind, but it was a hard decision and one she regretted she had to make.

'They're here! Wee Wullie's seen them coming down Woodlands Road.' Phyllis, white as the flour on her hands, rushed in yelling for her sister-in-law. 'He says McMurtie's wi' them right enough. Oh dear heavens, we've had it! Annie! Annie! Whis in the name of God are we goin to do?'

Never one to stay idle, Annie had been cleaning glass cake covers in the kitchen. 'Right, Phyllis, I'm with you.' She put down the cloth and followed her into the front shop.

Heart pounding with apprehension, but outwardly calm, Annie watched as two burly thugs came in followed by a small weasel-faced but well-dressed man. This was without doubt the infamous McMurtie in person. 'Where's Ramsay?' he snapped at Phyllis,

332

ignoring Annie altogether. 'We've come to check the stuff. I want tae see what we'll be takin'.'

'My brother is not coming out to speak to you, Mr McMurtie,' Annie said in a quiet, firm tone.

'Oh is he no, Missus la-de-dah?' McMurtie's lip curled. 'We'll see about that. Right, lads...' his head nudged towards the back shop where Sandy, pale as death, was doing what Annie had instructed by staying out of sight.

'You've no right to come in here. I'll have the police on you!' Annie stood blocking the doorway.

'The polis? Whit a laugh,' McMurtie sniggered. 'Ye've got to be kiddin', hen.' He looked her up and down with an eye that was lecherous and appraising. 'Yer brother said he had a sister that worked for the gentry, but he didn't tell me her heid was up the lum!' He tapped his own head in a rude, meaningful gesture of contempt. 'Now move, hen, or ye'll get hurt and that wid be a pity, you're no a bad-looking lass.'

'Hurt is it, ye wee nyaff?' Annie reverted to the terms of her youth as her temper flared. 'I bloody well mean what I say, Mister. If you or yer fat-heided frighteners put one foot in the back, or touch me or mine, ye'll rue the day ... I'll take ye all the way, so I will!'

McMurtie hesitated in astonishment. Annie was angry, but she showed no fear and that unsettled him. He was used to women screaming in panic or weeping for mercy for their men when he came to make an example of somebody, but not this confident, spitting fury.

'Ye'll take me nowhere if yer brother doesnae pay up, hen,' he snarled. 'It'll be me that'll be takin what's left of him to the midden. The law's on my side, so it is. He's a debtor, and he owes me.'

'I know that,' Annie replied. 'And I want a full statement, signed by you, of what he owes. I ken you've been screwing them for more than they borrowed. Much more.'

'Whit's wrong wi' that?' McMurtie looked aggrieved. 'That's whit it's a' aboot, hen. Compound interest!'

'Aye, and that's why I want a paper stating how much it will be on Thursday to finish the debt off.'

'Ye'll no get one!'

'Aye I will!' Annie knew that without it, there was a risk they

333

would demand more even if they found the sum that was agreed today.

'Who'll make me?' he snarled. Like Pavlovian dogs, the two heavies moved forward again in response to the familiar threat in his voice.

'If you don't declare the full debt, I'll be lodging a complaint with the debtors' court that you've failed to confirm. Ye'll be done for malpractice. Ye're no above the law, though ye use it,' Annie hoped the procedure was the same in Scotland as in France.

'If there's one thing I can't effing stand it's a lassie that's too smart for her ain guid.' McMurtie looked at her stubborn defiant face with what was almost bordering on admiration. Then he began to laugh. 'But I'll tell ye whit, I dinnae ken where ye got yer daft ideas about debt collectin', but I'll gie ye ten out of ten for cheek, pure bloody cheek. Aye, ye've got nerve, hen!'

'Give me the paper,' Annie repeated.

'Och, here ye are. But it won't change a soddin' thing.' McMurtie took out a notebook from the capacious pocket of his warm coat. He scribbled a few lines with a pencil stump and handed it to her. 'That do ye?'

Annie carefully checked the figures. It was even more than she feared, but right enough when she saw the interest rate. Hiding her horror, she examined the signature. 'Aye.'

'But don't get ony ideas that I'm soft-hearted,' he said. 'If ye don't pay up on Thursday, yer brother is for the bum's rush and I'm takin the lot. Ye'll all be out in the street.'

'I don't think for a minute you're soft-hearted, Mr McMurtie,' Annie replied with a wry smile.

'Right, youse,' McMurtie nudged towards the door. Obediently, the frighteners left. In the street they fell into line, one in front, one behind McMurtie, eyes shifting continuously looking for trouble. Heads popped back into closes and window sashes clattered down. Not even the mongrels that scavenged the closes and backyards dared to bark when the menodge frighteners were teaching some wretch a lesson.

Annie watched them go. And I only needed one at a time to look after me in Montmartre, she thought of Janot and Alexi ... and wished either, or both, were there. But then Montmartre was civilized in comparison to Glasgow when the frighteners come to duff folk. It was then she noticed she was shaking.

'We cannae pay, Annie?' Sandy sat looking the picture of dejection, rubbing endlessly at his throbbing leg, staring at the paper. 'Look, he's even put the interest up since yesterday. Thirty-five pound, seventeen shillin's and sixpence farthin'. It might as well be a hundred right enough.'

'That's another reason why I wanted the paper today, by Thursday it would have been higher. We've at least saved two days interest.'

'But whit are we goin' to do?' Phyllis wept.

'There's only a couple of things we can do. This afternoon, I'm going to Craigdrummond to talk to Lady Cameron and see if she can advance me the money she promised.'

'Craigdrummond?' Sandy's eyes widened. 'By here I'd never have thought of it.'

'Aye, well it's the last place on earth I want to go,' Annie said with a resigned sigh. 'But Lady Cameron is the only one who can let me have some money fast. Och, it's right embarrassing, so it is.'

'Annie, I'm really sorry to bring this on ye.' Sandy's expression was full of shame.

'Och, what's done's done, Sandy,' Annie said with a shrug. 'I know you didn't mean it. There's a train at one if I remember right, I'll get that.'

'But even if ye get the money, it surely cannae be enough,' Phyllis moaned.

'No,' Annied agreed, 'you're right, even the Camerons aren't that generous. Then I'll head for the bank. I've still got some money left from what I brought from France.'

'Will that cover it?' Sandy asked, sounding hopeful for the first time.

Annie hated to dash the tiny glean of optimism. 'I don't think so, there's only a few pounds left. There'll likely still be a shortfall.' She made a supreme effort to be positive, 'Och, keep your head, Sandy, we're not dead yet!'

'We might as well be.' He refused to be comforted.

'Aye, well I have to get started.' Annie got up. 'There's only two days left. But first I'll have to go to Baird House to make sure that Julie is fine.' With a shiver she remembered the pathetic scene after her stay in the convent.

335

Anxious and preoccupied, she took the tram out to Dumbarton and trekked up the long drive to Baird House.

'Maman,' Julie greeted her with a hug, 'I want to stay with Eddie and Vicky tonight as well,' she demanded. 'We have pillow fights.'

'Well, if Miss Somerville agrees,' Annie replied with a great feeling of relief. That was one problem less to cope with.

'Normally I'd say she could move in for the rest of the week, if you will be away on family business,' Miss Somerville replied to her request. 'Juliette is no trouble. In fact she has such a positive effect on Eddie, I can hardly believe it.' The governess tucked a stray lock of greying hair behind her ears with a sigh. 'He used to be so naughty, I was sometimes almost in despair, but one look from Juliette and he's as good as gold.'

'Aye, she has presence,' Annie said with a wry smile then added anxiously. 'You said "normally", is it not convenient just now, Miss Somerville?'

'I'm afraid it's not,' Miss Somerville replied. 'Oh, I'm sure Lady Ballantyne wouldn't object in principle,' she went on pedantically. 'Since she has been er ... poorly, it's been left to me to run the nursery and the school-room. No, I know she wouldn't, especially since it was her dear stepmother's suggestion that Juliette should join the Baird children in the first place. "Treat her just like the other two, Miss Somerville," Lady Cameron told me.'

'Then what's the matter?'

'In fact, Annie, I was wondering what I would do with Julie if you hadn't come today,' she answered. 'You see, Lord Ballantyne came earlier this morning on an unexpected visit. He has decided to take the children with him to London for the rest of this week and the weekend. Then he mentioned that they will go to Craigdrummond.'

'For a wee holiday?'

'No ... er ... to live. Lady Ballantyne and he have apparently come to some sort of arrangement...' She coloured deeply. 'I er ... believe the children are to stay ... now ... er ... I'm not sure ... er ... I'm not privvy to ... er,' the Governess trailed off, red to the ears.

'Does that mean that Julie won't be with them any more?'

'It would seem so.'

'Oh.' Annie's heart sank but she said reassuringly, 'All right, I'll take her with me to Ayrshire now and she can stay at my brother's tomorrow. I'll try to find out what they want to do about my own position as well when I'm there. But I'm surprised Lady Ballantyne didn't say anything about the children before she left.'

'As I understand it, they hadn't decided then. I got the impression from Lord Ballantyne's demeanour that this was a new idea and that he had spoken with Lord and Lady Cameron, not directly with Lady Ballantyne.' The governess was shrewd despite her fussy ways.

'Aye, that's likely.' Annie felt less aggrieved with Alexandra. 'Are you going with the children, Miss Somerville?'

'I don't really know.' She wrung her hands. 'I think so, but no one has said anything to me either, Annie.'

'I just wish that Grand Folk would remember the rest of us have lives and rights too,' Annie seethed quietly. 'Bringing me and Julie all the way from France and then not even bothering to say we're not needed any more. Maybe it's as well I'm going to Craigdrummond after all to have this out.'

'But I want to stay with Eddie and Vicky!' Julied moaned.

'Well you can't, now come on, Julie, I'll get you a clean pinny and knickers.' Annie hurried her protesting daughter over the gatehouse. Time was pressing and she was worried about missing the train. Finally they left, clutching a bag in case they needed to find overnight lodgings.

'But what did Miss Somerville mean, Maman?' Julie insisted, dragging her feet. 'Am I going to see Eddie and Vicky later?'

'No,' Annie replied. 'Now come on!'

'So there's no more schoolroom?' Julie's face fell.

'Och, Julie,' Annie felt a surge of exasperation at the whole mess she found herself in. 'Just let me sort our Uncle Sandy and we'll talk about lessons.'

'When?' Julie asked hopefully.

'God knows,' Annie replied in a tone so final the child gave up. 'If I'm still in one piece after Thursday,' Annie added under her breath, thinking of the frighteners and the grim reaper, McMurtie.

'Annie, can I give you and Julie a lift?' John Chisholm called from a carriage as he passed them walking towards the Glasgow road and the tram-stop.

Annie hesitated, looking up.

'Don't worry.' He gave an embarrased smile. 'I promise I won't propose.'

'Is that a fact?' She laughed and the tension which had risen so unexpectedly the day before disappeared. 'Where are you off to?' she asked, holding onto her boater as the strong late autumn wind tugged wildly at the brim.

'Craigdrummond. I have to talk to Lady Cameron about Jessica, I'm getting no sense from anyone else. I've written to her explaining the dilemma and saying I would call this week...'

'Well, isn't that just dandy! This is the first bit of luck I've had in days!' Annie almost laughed with relief. 'I was beginning to think we'd miss the one o'clock train. Move over, John Chisholm, we're joining you!'

'Give me that.' He leaned down and picked up her bag. 'Now hop in, young lady.' He held out his hand to Julie.

'Why on earth are you off to Craigdrummond?' he asked as soon as they were settled in the carriage.

'It's to do with Sandy's debt,' Annie explained bluntly and in detail what faced them. Whatever temporary difficulties there might have been between her and John, she trusted the man and his discretion totally.

When she had finished, he was visibly shocked. 'Your poor brother, what an awful situation to be in!' Then he fell silent, running his fingers through his hair as he thought. After a while he went on gravely, 'I have a small amount at home, maybe as much as six or seven pounds which I can let you have tommorrow when I get back to Glasgow again. But I would need a few days to cash in some shares to help you with more. I'm a better doctor than financier.' He gave a boyish grin. 'Actually, Annie, though my circumstances are supposed to be quite comfortable, I'm eternally short-cashed. What comes in seems to flow out again.'

'That's good of you, but I hope I won't have to take you up on it.' She was touched by his generous offer. 'First I'll collect everything I have myself and put it with whatever Sandy has scraped together. I'd rather not be dependent, John, not even on you.'

'How will you get back to France, Annie?' he asked. 'Can you get more funds from the Chat Roux?'

'Lady Cameron brought me here and she's paying to take me back. I'll buy the tickets for the train today from the petty cash left over from the journey up from France. She said to keep it for emergencies and I count this as one. We'll go second class, so that should save a bit.'

'Second class?' he laughed. 'You're thrifty, Annie, even with other folks' money.'

'There's nothing wrong with second class,' she retorted with a toss of her head. 'Anyway the train is nearly empty at this time of day. We'll have the compartment to ourselves.'

'I'll join you if you don't mind, even if it is second class,' he teased. 'I prefer your company to sitting on my own in first class.'

'You're welcome to join us, Doctor Chisholm, though the seats will be moquette, not leather,' she added with a laugh that eased the tension from her face. 'And you know what that means!'

'The odd flea is an occupational hazard for a doctor,' he joined in her laughter. 'And here we are.' The carriage turned down Hope Street and pulled up outside the station.

With little time to spare they bought their tickets and hurried to the platform. Once settled in the train, he gave rein to his curiosity again. 'Why don't you just ask your brother and sister-in-law to help? The Chat is yours, you could pay back anything you took out of it.'

'John Chisholm, you would spier the bottom out of a brass pot!' She laughed.

'It's my job, to ask questions,' he replied with mock humility and a twinkle in his eyes. 'So, why don't you?'

'Jorice and Francine would move heaven and earth to get Sandy out of hock if I asked. But there isn't time. It's quite a lot of money for ordinary folk to get together, John, and then it has to be transferred.' Annie shook her head in exasperation. 'Och, even though he's a decent man, Sandy's dropped himself, Phyllis and the bairns right in it, so he has!'

'Not to mention you,' John added.

'Aye, well that's my choice,' she said defensively. 'Sandy didn't ask me.'

But Phyllis did, John thought, though he said simply, 'Your brother is like me, he needs some instruction in business.'

'You're right there,' she mused. 'In fact if we get out of this

339

mess in one piece, I think I'll stay a while to help him.'

'Oh?' His eyebrows shot up in surprise. 'That's not what you said the other day.'

'I just thought about it last night. Anyway it looks as if my job at Baird House is already over.'

'Over? Has Lady Ballantyne said so?'

'No, but Miss Somerville told me this morning that the children are moving to Craigdrummond. And I can't see Lady Ballantyne living for long on her own at Baird House.'

'They're moving now?'

'After the weekend!'

'And you didn't know?'

'Not a word.' She shrugged. 'But you asked why I might stay a while longer. I got a shock when I went over to the shop, John.' Her mouth tightened. 'There was nothing in the house. Hardly a pot or pan, or cloth on the table. They had pawned just about everything they had, everything but the clothes off their backs. It reminded me of what we had come from ... the dire, rotten poverty! I can't leave them to sink back into the muck they worked their fingers off to crawl out of!'

'What they sold wasn't enough?'

'Nowhere near. The pawn-broker pays bawbees for old clothes, worn blankets and wee bits and pieces.'

'Then why bother?'

'Desperation to pay off McMurtie without dragging me in. The pittance they did scrape together disappeared into paying off interest not the capital.' Annie looked sad. 'Just the wee clock my Mammy left me was still there on the bare mantelpiece. Poor Phyllis couldn't bring herself to put it in hock, even to save their skins.'

John was still puzzled. 'I can understand you want to save the ovens ... and their skins, but wouldn't it be better to go back afterwards?'

'If I save the ovens and the shop, that will be all, John. While I'm at Craigdrummond, they're trying to raise what they can on the few bits and pieces they've left to pawn. There's the cake stands, some chairs. I've told Sandy the clock has to go as well. I might be able to get it out again sometime.' Despite her courage, she gulped back sudden tears.

'You could send some money now and then from Paris.'

'Money isn't enough, though I could do with some now,' she added with a touch of her old humour. 'Sandy's lost his confidence, I'll have to help if they're ever going to get the business on it's feet again.'

'But if you stay...?' he nudged towards where Julie was reading and apparently paying no attention.

'I've been thinking about that. I can send her to school in Charing Cross for a while. It'll be no worse than Montmartre.' Annie wished she felt as confident as she sounded. 'She's bright and she's more adaptable than I ever thought now she's a bit older. She'll manage ... she'll have to.'

'But what about the Chat Roux? You promised Louis you'd look after it.'

'I did and I'm not just walking out of the Chat. Jorice and Francine want to stay longer.' She looked down at her hands. Her broad gold wedding band gleamed dully in the dim November light. 'Half the night I asked myself how Louis would have handled this, but in the end I realised I had to make the decisions I feel are best ... use my own judgement, not someone else's. And that's what I've done.'

'And you've thought all this through in the bare twenty or so hours since we last met?' He looked at her with a mixture of exasperation and admiration. 'You're some lass, Annie Lamarche ... but you're your own worst enemy.'

She reddened. 'What do you mean by that?'

'I've known you such a short time, but I've never seen anyone shoulder other folks' problems like you.'

'You mean I'd be better off minding my own business and keeping my breath to cool my porridge, John Chisholm.' A smile broke through the anxiety and cheered up the dusky compartment as the great steam train clattered and roared towards Craigdrummond.

'That's a bit too harsh,' he replied with a grin. 'But maybe you should think about yourself sometimes. What do you get from all this? Nothing but trouble and worry?'

She smiled ruefully this time. 'Aye, maybe you've got a point. But I don't think I'm capable of standing by when folk get in a mess, that's all!' She fell silent and turned to look out of the window. And it's brought me back to Craigdrummond after so many years, she thought.

341

Seeing she didn't want to talk any more, he picked up the *Glasgow Herald*, covertly watching as emotions too deep to discuss, chased each other across her expressive face. He hadn't forgotten her admission of old loyalties ... more than loyalty ... that still lingered in Craigdrummond.

'Now I'll read the other book!' Julie looked up, closing one and rummaging in her bag for another.

'I thought you would never take your head out of that one,' John teased. 'Look out of the window, Julie, and see what you're missing.'

Julie glanced at the rows of washing and the children playing in the dirty yards as the train flew past. 'Tant pis! It's just like Paris!' She gave an expressive shrug and went back to her favourite occupation, not noticing when the sooty alleys gave way to open green hills and rolling countryside.

God, how this places seems to haunt me! Annie thought for the thousandth time as their destination drew closer. But at least I don't have to go to Clachan's Farm, she reassured herself.

By the time they reached Craigdrummond Junction, she had herself firmly under control and ready for all contingencies. But she had forgotten one person that linked her and her companion so closely with the past.

Doctor Murchison's stout figure was unmistakable as he stood by the signalbox peering along the length of the train. 'There he is!' John smiled happily. Then he noticed Annie's shocked face. 'Oh, didn't I say I'm staying with Archie and Bess? I usually do when I'm down, Annie,' he explained too late.

Annie dismounted and lifted her daughter after her.

'Well, would you believe it!' The good doctor's astonishment would have amused her in other circumstances. 'Bess, come and see what's come in with the Stranraer ferry-train.'

Bess Murchieson, still imposing, though grey-haired as a swan, looked as if she'd seen a ghost, but she quickly recovered. 'Well, if it isn't Annie Ramsay,' she said in a tight voice.

'Annie Lamarche,' Annie corrected her.

'Lamarche? Och yes, you married a Frenchman, is he with you?' The doctor looked around expectantly, as absent-minded as ever.

'She's a widow,' Bess snapped. 'You told me that yourself, Archie.'

342

'That's right.' Annie wasn't surprised that Bess had kept herself informed.

'Sorry, lass, I forgot!' Doctor Murchieson caught up at last. 'Lady Cameron explained your circumstances when she wanted you to come and help poor Lady Ballantyne ... of course I said it was a good idea. When did your husband pass away, Annie? Was it an accident, lass?'

'Four years past,' Annie said softly. 'He died of TB,' she smiled wryly at the old doctor. 'Ironic, isn't it, Doctor Murchieson?'

'Aye, it is that,' he replied sympathetically. 'But what brings you back to Craigdrummond and in the company of John Chisholm?'

'Doctor Chisholm and I work at Baird House together as you know. I have a matter to talk about with Lady Cameron. We just caught the same train,' Annie replied, hoping John Chisholm would spare her the humiliation of explaining what her own visit was about.

She needn't have worried, with his quick sensitivity he had already picked up tensions between Annie and Bess. He held his tongue but watched with a touch of professional interest as the situation developed.

'Will you be staying a few days and maybe visiting some old friends?' Archie asked kindly.

Before Annie could reply, Bess broke in. 'Annie is likely too busy for socialising and most of the folk she knew have their own lives to lead these days, Archie.'

'I know that, Bess,' Archie replied as Annie stiffened. John Chisholm sensing deeper and more serious undertones, shifted uneasily.

'I was just meaning Clachan's Farm, not half Ayrshire, Bess,' Archie persisted.

Bess's face was strained. 'That's what I was meaning too. Ian and Betty have enough on their hands with three bairns and two farms to run to have open house for visitors arriving without as much as by your leave.'

Archie Murchieson's open face fell in astonishment. 'What in the name are you on about, Bess? Betty Clachan loves visitors. And she's got plenty of lassies to help round the place. She can spare a minute for a cup of tea with Annie. Ian would be glad to

343

see her, that's for sure, and Geordie too, even if he's getting a bit deaf.'

'I still don't think . . .' Bess began.

Annie closed her eyes for a moment. She felt as if history was repeating itself as she listened to Bess warning her off as clearly as if she spelled it out. But Annie Ramsay Lamarche wasn't a waif to be intimidated any more. She was a woman of twenty-eight who had lived through more joy and sorrow in the twelve years or so since she came to Clachan's Farm, than most folk would face in a lifetime.

'It's all right, Mistress Murchieson, just leave that kind of talk be,' she said in the calm, firm tone that could stop an argument in the Chat Roux instantly. 'I'm here for a purpose and then I'm going back to Glasgow on the next train I can. You're right, I don't have time for socialising. Once things are sorted out in Scotland, I'll be heading back to France. I have a business to run and a life to lead. And don't worry yourself on Ian's behalf, he's safe from me. Though if you'd let nature take its course, I suspect he would have been a far happier man.'

Doctor Murchieson looked in puzzlement from one to the other, there were undercurrents so strong, even he could pick them up, but had no idea what they were about. Bess paled and pursed her lips but said no more.

'Aye, well, is this your lass?' Archie said in an overly jovial tone to hide his unease.

Julie stepped out from behind her mother.

'How do you do, young lady.' He held out his hand and she took it with dignity.

'How do you do, sir?'

'By heavens she's bonnie,' the doctor added admiringly. 'Just like her Mammy! What's your name, lass? How old are you?' He hesitated. 'Does she speak much English, Annie?'

Julie gave a brilliant smile that would have melted a heart of stone and had the kindly old doctor captivated. 'I am Juliette Lamarche from Paris, and I am nine years old,' she announced confidently in the polished tones of the Baird schoolroom. 'And as you can hear, sir, I do speak English quite well.' She looked proudly from him to his wife with dark, expressive eyes.

'Nine? Annie!' Bess caught her arm. 'Annie!' Her face was grey with shock. 'Is she Ian's bairn?' she blurted out.

344

'You tell me?' Annie looked at her with a strange expression on her face.

Bess moved stiffly across to the little girl. 'Look at me, child,' she said.

Julie had been following every word of the exchange, with sharp intelligent eyes. And she had met all types in the Chat Roux, so one more odd elderly lady couldn't intimidate her. She looked Bess straight in the eye and replied with Gallic pride and formality, 'I don't know who Ian is, Madame, but I am Juliette, the daughter of Monsieur Louis Lamarche, late of Montmartre.'

Bess paled and stepped back. 'You could have told me yourself, Annie.'

'Would you have believed me if I had?' Annie answered. 'Anyway she could have been, but she's not, like she says, she's Louis's bairn.'

Bess stared at her for a long moment, then her face crumpled and she groped for a handkerchief. 'Annie, I'm sorry, lass, I'm so sorry.'

'And I'd like to know what the hell is going on?' the poor doctor blurted out.

'Och, I'll tell you ... but not the now, Archie,' Bess sniffed.

'Never, as far as I'm concerned, there's no need to dig up the remains of old sorrows and mistakes,' Annie said as kindly as she could. Whatever Bess had done, Annie knew she had believed it was for the best at the time. Maybe I'm older and wiser myself, she thought to herself, but there's much we do, that, given our time over again, we'd tar with a different brush.

'This wind would cut you in two! I think it's time we were all on our way,' John Chisholm broke in, his matter-of-fact tone hiding the acute discomfort of this unexpected turn of events. 'And, Archie, I need advice about Jessica before I talk with Lady Cameron. Have you thought about it like I asked?'

'Aye, I've been giving it some thought, and maybe better than thought, John.' The doctor was glad to be on surer ground. 'In fact something interesting has turned up.' Then he remembered Annie and Julie still standing on the empty platform. 'Have you a carriage coming to pick you up, lass?' he called over. 'Otherwise I'll take you over myself.'

'Thank you, but I'm going with the post-wagon, Doctor Murchieson. I talked to the guard before we got on in Glasgow

345

and I think he's fixed it.' She nodded towards the guard, deep in discussion with the postman who was nodding vigorous agreement.

'If you have a minute, come and pay a wee visit before you go back to Glasgow.' Doctor Murchieson came over and shook her hand. 'We live in Craigdrummond village nowadays. It's the grey stone house with the iron gates, right next to the kirk. But if you can't find it, just ask where the Doctor's house is. Anybody will tell you.'

Annie nodded. 'I ken the house,' she said. 'Mr Ronaldson, the tea-merchant from Ayr had it when I was here.'

'That's it.'

'I'll come if I have time then, Doctor,' she said, but was certain she wouldn't.

'Annie, I'd like it as well ... bring the wee lass,' Bess understanding the source of her reluctance, came forward and touched her arm hesitantly.

'Aye, well...' Before Annie could say more, John Chisholm broke in, 'If you're still at Craigdrummond House later, Annie, maybe you'd give me some support with my suggestions for Jessica?'

'If they're not too daft,' she teased gently and with a wave of her gloved hand, moved away before any more was said or done. 'Come on, Julie,' she took her daughter's arm and walked quickly without a backward glance towards the waiting post-carriage. They had only been a few minutes in Craigdrummond and already it had proved traumatic.

'Will you be all right in the back, chèrie? It's not quite the Baird carriage, but it's snug enough.' She helped Julie in beside the parcels in the covered section.

'This is fun, Maman!' Julie sat like a queen among the bundles of papers and packages destined for Craigdrummond House.

'Aye, and no doubt there will be more fun in store, before this business is over.' Annie gave an ironic shrug and jumped up front with the driver.

'At least it's not raining,' she said as they set off at a brisk pace across the moor.

'No yet, Mistress,' he replied, 'but there's a storm brewing!'

Chapter Twenty-Six

'Annie!' Lady Cameron came forward, hand outstretched as if greeting an equal. 'How pleasant to see you. And this must be your daughter. Juliette, is it not...?' She paused questioningly.

'Yes, Milady, this is Juliette Lamarche.' Annie noticed with pride how Julie bobbed a curtsey with as much aplomb as she had shown when she climbed onto the post-wagon.

'What a pretty girl, and what pretty manners!' Maria observed.

'Folk say so.' Annie hoped all the adulation she'd had in Scotland wasn't turning Julie's head.

'But what do I owe the pleasure of your unexpected visit?' Maria asked. 'I was quite taken by surprise when the butler announced you.'

Not half as surprised as Davie Murray when I told him to tell you I was here, Annie thought. Aloud she said, 'I'm really sorry to intrude without warning, Lady Cameron, but there was no time to send down and ask.'

'No matter,' Maria replied kindly. 'I'm sure you have good reason to come and I'm curious to know what it is.'

Flushing deeply Annie went on, 'I'm here for a few reasons. One is to know what is expected of me from Lady Ballantyne. There's four or so weeks till I'm supposed to leave your service, but I hardly see her Ladyship now she's much better and I don't want to take money under false pretences. On top of that, this morning I heard that the children are coming here, so...' her eyes shot towards Julie and she hesitated, 'I'd like to know what's expected in that direction too. And...' Annie tried not to look embarrassed, but she felt her colour mount.

'And?'

'... And there's a serious financial matter I'm faced with ...'

'A serious financial matter?' Maria's fine eyebrows rose. 'Come, sit down,' she waved Annie towards a chair. 'Is your establishment in Paris having difficulties?'

'Er, no, not at all ...' Annie's eyes slid again towards Julie.

'A moment.' Maria rang for the maid. 'Rosie, take Miss Juliette to the nursery. Ask Governess to give her afternoon tea with the others,' she instructed. As they left, she turned back towards Annie. 'I've heard she's a very clever child, Annie, perhaps she can show a good example to my son William.'

'Och, I shouldn't think so,' Annie smothered a proud smile.

'Now,' Lady Cameron said when they were alone, 'go on.'

'I intended to ask for an advance on the money you promised me, Milady, but now I'm wondering if I'm still entitled, since, the job with Lady Ballantyne seems to be over sooner than we agreed.'

'We can talk about the future in a moment, but of course you are entitled to your money, Annie. The full amount. Sir Urquhart and I are very satisfied with what you and Doctor Chisholm's enlightened methods have done for Alexandra. She is quite restored, if still rather fragile. The actual number of weeks you took has little to do with it. But why do you need money so badly that you came all the way to Craigdrummond in person? I thought you were quite comfortably placed.'

'There isn't time to get the money I need from France, Milady, and anyway, it's not for me. I'm afraid my brother has too soft a heart for business,' Annie explained. 'He's got himself into debt and I have to get him out of it by Thursday. Sandy's in the hands of unscrupulous folk, Lady Cameron, money-lenders who won't think twice about taking every farthing and throwing him and his family into the street.'

'But surely the law can protect them?'

'The law can't protect folk who put themselves into the hands of people like Mr McMurtie and his "frighteners", Lady Cameron, they rule by the law of the jungle.'

'And you have taken your brother's debt upon yourself?'

'Yes,' Annie's colour deepened. 'Sandy is a good man, a hard worker. He's been silly, but he doesn't deserve to be ruined, or beaten up.' Her face tightened. 'And neither he will be as long as I am able to prevent it.'

'I see. Is it a huge amount? If not I may be able to give you the entire sum, Annie.'

'No thank you, Milady. I only want what you promised me, twenty-five pounds,' Annie said with a proud lift of her head. 'I'm not here to beg.'

'Annie, I'm sorry if I offended you,' Maria hid a smile, 'it's just that maybe we can reach an agreement...'

'An agreement, Milady?'

'An agreement.' Lady Cameron began then paused, slender fingers drumming thoughtfully on the arm of the chaise longue. 'And you're quite right, we need to make some decisions, especially since Alexandra is leaving tomorrow.'

'For Dumbarton?'

'For London.'

'London?' Annie echoed in surprise.

'She's decided to stay with her Aunt Lispeth for a while. And I think maybe that's for the best ... and this is where you come in ... in fact your visit is quite timely. But perhaps we should leave it to Alexandra to explain. She's out riding, but she'll be coming in for afternoon tea any moment.'

Annie's puzzlement deepened. 'What do you mean, where I come in, Milady?'

'Ah here she is.' Before Maria could explain, Alexandra swept in. Clad in a dark-blue riding habit, face glowing from a brisk canter across the moors, it was hard to remember the pitiful wreck of only a couple of months before.

'Annie, what on earth are you doing here?' She paused in surprise. 'I thought you were in Dumbarton. You told me you wouldn't come to Craigdrummond again!'

'Annie has come to find out if we are finished with her services,' Maria interjected. 'I think it's an excellent opportunity for you to tell her yourself what you plan, Alexandra.'

'How mean of us to keep you in the dark!' Alexandra came over full of the old charm. Annie's stomach leaped in apprehension. Charm always heralded some demand from Alexandra. 'How could you imagine we're finished with you? Your work is just beginning.'

'Beginning?' Annie stiffened. 'I've a month left that you could call on me, Lady Ballantyne, under the agreement with Lady Cameron, but after that I'm my own mistress again.'

'Excuse me, your ladyships.' A maid came in bearing a laden tea-tray. Her eyes shot to Annie and she hesitated, mouth hanging, her name half forming on her lips.

'Bring an extra cup for Mistress Lamarche, Nellie,' Maria instructed. 'She will be joining us for tea.'

Despite her dismay at Alexandra's announcement, Annie had to stifle a grin at the shock on the maid's face.

'Mistress Lamarche? Och, right away, your Ladyships.' She billowed out, apron and cap streamers flying and returned at once with an extra cup and saucer. With another astonished look at Annie sitting as to the manner born between Maria and Alexandra, she bobbed and left.

That's a bit of gossip for below stairs, Annie thought. I wonder what Davie Murray and the others will make of it? Clachan's Annie has not just become a lady's maid and moved to foreign parts, but she's turned up, bold as brass in the Cameron's drawing-room, sitting with the gentry, sipping Assam and eating Peek Frean's afternoon tea biscuits off a china plate! And why not? She lifted her chin. We're all Jock Thampson's bairns.

'Tea, Annie?'

'Thank you, Milady.

Maria poured. 'Now, Alexandra, do continue.' She sat back.

'As you know, Annie,' Alexandra began without preamble, 'my marriage is over in all but name.'

Maria winced, 'Is such detail necessary, my dear?' she protested.

'Annie knows it all ... more then anyone else other than Edward and myself,' Alexandra said with bitter bluntness. 'Don't you, Annie?'

'Yes.' Annie didn't bother to deny it.

'I see,' Maria leaned back on the cushions as if for support.

'There will be no divorce of course ... too awkward for the children! Instead we will maintain separate establishments.' She waved off her marriage with a dismissive, careless hand. 'I'll keep the town house in London, and Edward will have Dumbarton.' Her voice hardened, 'He'll also be spending more time with his dear friend the King at Sandringham and on his various trips abroad.'

Two of a kind, Annie thought. Neither lecherous Edward Saxe-Coburg nor Edward Baird, was worth a bawbee in her books and she didn't pretend respect she didn't feel. That's another thing about living in Montmartre, that I'm glad I haven't lost. Aloud she asked, 'And the children, Lady Ballantyne?'

'Eddie will be joining the Cameron boys at boarding school in England.'

Maria broke in, 'My youngest son, William, is almost the same age as Eddie. We intend that he and Eddie go to Prep together after the summer. My eldest, Jamie, is already at Eton.'

'Vicky is a little too young to board and too highly strung,' Alexandra went on. 'She may go to school in Edinburgh in a year or so, but until then she will move here to Craigdrummond and continue with Miss Somerville.'

Annie recalled the Governess's worried face when she left Dumbarton. 'I'm sure Miss Somerville will be pleased when you tell her. But won't Lady Victoria feel lonely in the schoolroom, especially here where she's not so used to things?'

'Yes, and that brings us to you, Annie...' Alexandra said with a smile.

'Me?'

Maria leaned forward. 'How does Juliette feel about losing her companions and her governess and going back to France?'

'Julie would prefer the world to stay as it is, Milady,' Annie replied. 'She's taken to the Baird bairns, and as far as learning goes she's found her feet. My daughter is a right wee book-worm, just like her father.' This time she couldn't keep the pride from her voice. 'But I've told her things change and we have to go back. She accepts that ... it's the way it is.' Annie gave a rueful smile.

'Annie also has confided a little financial problem, Alexandra, I think you should know about. Her brother has got into difficulties...'

'The same brother as before?'

'No, it's Sandy this time, Milady.' Alexandra Cameron always remembers more than you might expect, Annie thought.

'You seem to have the only business-head in your family,' Alexandra commented dryly.

'Maybe,' Annie said. 'But excuse me for asking, your lady-ships, I still can't see what this has got to do with me.'

'Oh but it has a great deal to do with you, Annie,' Maria said. 'And with your brother's debt.'

351

'Sandy's debt?' Annie shook her head. 'I'm sorry, now I really don't understand.'

'We want you to allow Juliette to come here almost at once with the Baird children,' Maria explained. 'She has already shown herself to be a good influence on Eddie. And I gather that Vicky is very fond of her...'

'Vicky went through a long period of having nightmares, Miss Somerville was always complaining about it,' Alexandra interrupted. 'Quite upsetting.'

'She told Julie that,' Annie agreed, but thought to herself, and I'm not surprised, poor wee lass, with the carryings-on of you and her father!

'And Miss Somerville assures me they have stopped altogether since Juliette came,' Alexandra added. 'The influence of an older girl seems to have been just what Vicky needed. So,' she announced as if it were signed and sealed, 'I've decided that Juliette should come to stay here. She can study with Vicky for a year or so after the boys leave for Prep.'

'What?' Annie was shocked. 'Are you saying that my daughter should move in now and stay on at Craigdrummond to keep Vicky company when her brother goes to school?'

'Yes. Vicky likes Juliette and once the boys go she'll need companionship even more,' Alexandra agreed with a satisfied smile.

'Och, it's not even New Year yet. If the boys don't leave till next August for the school, by the time they come back for their long holidays, Julie will have been here eighteen months.'

'Oh, I suppose so.' Alexandra shrugged.

'Och, I'll have to think about this, Milady,' Annie said firmly. 'I had thought of staying to help Sandy for a few months ... six at the most ... but over a year ... that's another story, and I wouldn't see much of Julie if she's down here.'

'You would be free to visit her any time you wish,' Maria added her quiet voice to the discussion.

'Aye, but Julie's always been with me ... and we had a bad experience when I left her in the convent-school in Paris...' But even as she protested, Annie new it wasn't the same. It was herself who would suffer this time, not Julie.

'And there's another thing,' Alexandra said in a voice which was so suddenly and uncharacteristically subdued, that Annie was startled out of her own dismayed, spinning thoughts. 'There's the matter of the child.'

'Jessica?'

'My husband will not have her in Baird House and I do not feel any more disposed towards looking after her than he does.'

'It's not too late to change,' Annie said robustly.

'For me it is,' Alexandra said with a note of finality in her voice. 'And though I have no intention of taking an active interest in the child, I don't wish any harm to befall her. So, I want you to oversee her for the next year once she is placed by Doctor Chisholm.'

'Was this your suggestion, Lady Cameron?' Annie asked.

'Yes,' Maria admitted. 'I trust you, Annie, as does Alexandra. If the child is unhappy or badly cared for, she can be moved. The work is not onerous, just a few regular visits. You will be paid well and the amount can be advanced.'

'Was this the arrangement you talked about?'

'It was,' Maria nodded.

'I'll have to sleep on this, if you don't mind, especially the matter of Julie.' Annie suddenly felt weary. 'But if I agree, when would it be exactly?'

'The Baird children arrive Sunday evening and since Alexandra will have gone, I would like Julie to be here to comfort Vicky.'

And who will comfort Julie? Annie thought sadly. 'I've promised to talk to Doctor Chisholm before I go,' she went on. 'He's got some new ideas about Jessica. Whatever I decide about your two propositions, Lady Cameron, I can at least help with that.'

'That is good of you, Annie,' Maria thanked her courteously. 'Doctor Chisholm is coming at five, though I fear we have little to add to his own deliberations,' she went on. 'Why not stay and meet him here?'

Annie got up. 'I'll do that, Milady, but now I'd better go and find lodgings in Craigdrummond for Julie and me for the night.'

'Fiddlestocks!' Alexandra broke in. 'You will stay here. There must be rooms vacant in the servant's quarters.'

Maria saw the flush rise on Annie's cheeks. But before she could say what was on her mind, the older woman interjected, 'I would like you to stay here, Annie, in one of our guest rooms.

353

Alexandra still hasn't realised that you are no longer a servant. Nor has she understood that you would refuse to let Julie come here as a servant's child. Isn't that so?'

'Exactly, Milady,' Annie said proudly, grateful for her insight. 'Julie is not to be bought and sold. When I served you, I served you well, Miss Alexandra.' She turned towards her former mistress and looked her in the eye. 'And make no mistake about it, Cameron money wasn't what brought me to Scotland. I came back to help you in your time of need when Lady Cameron wrote. I did it out of old loyalty to you and as a mark of gratitude to your stepmother who has always shown me kindness.'

'Annie!' Alexandra made to speak.

'No, hear me out.' Annie held up her hand.

Alexandra frowned but said nothing.

Annie went on, 'If I do anything for you now or at any time, it will be because I feel it's worthwhile. And only if you ask, never if you command. I'm a free woman, Alexandra Cameron. If you can't treat me and mine as such, I'll say no to all your fancy ideas right now.'

Alexandra stood frozen, her face expressionless. Then she began to laugh. 'Have it your own way, Annie Ramsay Lamarche, and if I forget to treat you or your daughter as free women, you can remind me all over again.'

Annie's face was still solemn. 'Then I'll think about it, like I said.'

They turned, all three, as a timid knock was followed by Rosie with a letter. 'Excuse me, your Ladyships, er ... Mistress Lamarche. This is for you, Lady Cameron.' She bobbed a curtsey and added, 'There's a reply expected, Milady, the man's waiting to take it back.'

'Wait outside, Rosie.' When the door closed, Maria scanned the contents. 'This sounds excellent,' she said. 'Doctor Chishom has found a possible guardian for Jessica.'

'Wonderful! Tell the man to go ahead,' Alexandra was patently relieved that the matter would not require her involvement.

'I think he assumed that is what you would say.' Maria gave a dry smile. 'They have sent for the child. She will arrive with the nurse before they meet tonight.'

'Good God, I'm not having the child here!' Alexandra said vehemently. 'No one must ever link her with me!'

'There's no need to over-react, Alexandra,' for once Maria barely hid her irritation. 'They are meeting at Doctor Murchieson's house this evening at seven instead of here at five as originally planned. And why should anyone here think of you in connection with Jessica, unless you say so?' She re-read the letter. 'Oh and he has requested your presence, Annie.'

Annie knew it would be an ordeal to face Bess Crawford and Doctor Murchieson again so soon. But Jessica's vulnerable round face haunted her mind's eye and she knew she had to go. 'Then please say I'll be there, Lady Cameron.'

'Good.' Maria quickly penned a reply and sent it off with Rosie. Then she turned to Annie. 'I expect you will be late tonight, so tell me what is decided tomorrow morning before you leave. There is no need to bother Alexandra with it.'

'Exactly!' Alexandra smiled and swept towards the door. Suddenly she stopped and came back to where Annie stood watching her. For a moment the two young women looked silently at each other. 'Don't judge me too harshly, Annie,' Alexandra said, taking her hands in her own slender ones.

'I never have, Alexandra Cameron,' Annie replied, 'despite what happened. And I won't start now.'

'I'm no good at saying sorry or thank you.' A half-smile played round Alexandra's lips, but her eyes were serious and vulnerable. 'If I were, I would say both to you.'

Annie smiled gently. 'Then I'll take them as said.'

Despite Lady Cameron's protests that it was too dark, too far and the winter weather too inclement, Annie insisted in walking the couple of miles to Craigdrummond village. After all the traumas of the day, she needed to clear her head.

A crisp wind blew in from the sea, carrying the sharp salty smell she loved. As she walked, turning over her problems, her breath showed white in the chilly air. She knew Julie would gain much if she came to Craigdrummond for a year or so, and not just from the fresh air. Private tuition with no expense spared instead of over-crowded Glasgow or Montmartre schools. But the idea of separation was so painful, it hurt in her heart.

Miss Somerville is kindly. And Lady Cameron is goodness itself and I know from what she said today, that Julie would not be treated as a servant, she tried to persuade herself as she climbed the brow of the hill lying between the House and the village and stood for a moment looking down. It's a chance in a million for my wee lassie, she thought.

By the light of the wintry moon, she had automatically taken a short-cut she could not have consciously remembered if she had tried. 'Och, I'll ask Julie what she feels herself, after all it's her life,' she muttered as the heather crunched under her sturdy boots.

Eerily an owl hooted and the wind began to rise across the moor, but the lights of the village were already in sight. Suddenly she shivered. 'And I ken what she'll say...'

Outside the Doctor's house, Annie paused. Then, gathering her courage in her hands, she opened the gates, walked up the path and rang the bell.

'Annie?' Bess Murchieson looked aghast. 'I didn't know you were coming...'

'Doctor Chisholm asked me,' Annie said, puzzled at her change of attitude from the scene of reconciliation at the station.

'I thought that was just if you were still at the big house.' Bess hovered in the doorway.

'He wrote it in the note to Lady Cameron. But if I'm not welcome,' Annie said, her colour rising, 'then I'll go.'

'Annie, what a surprise.' Archie Murchieson had heard their voices and came to investigate. 'Don't keep the lass on the doorstep like a tinker selling pegs, Bess. Come in, come in! I didn't hear a carriage.'

'I walked.'

'You must be frozen. It's bitter when the wind rises.' Doctor Murchieson drew her into the warmth of the drawing-room where John Chisholm stood, back to the glowing fire.

'You didn't tell Doctor Murchieson and his wife that I was coming, John?' It was as much an accusation as a question.

'I thought everybody understood I wanted you here, Annie,' he raised his eyebrows. 'I never thought to say.'

Annie almost groaned aloud. Between Doctor Murchieson's well meaning intervention and John's blithe assumptions, she was in a position more embarrassing than ever.

'Well I think it's a fine idea,' Archie said jovially. 'John has been praising your judgement all day. In fact he's talked of little else. And as far as I'm concerned, the more hands to the job the better if we're going to sort out this wee lass.'

'Where is she?' Annie looked round.

'She's in the back room with Jeanie,' Bess replied, then hissed below her breath, 'Annie, I need a quiet word.'

And I've had enough of Bess Murchieson's quiet words to last a lifetime, Annie thought. Blatantly she ignored her, 'Then I'll go and say hello to them both.'

'Och, there you are, Annie,' old Jeanie greeted her warmly. 'Am I glad to see ye! You ken the bairn next best to me. And they'll take heed of what ye say ... which is more than they do wi' me.' She rushed on, 'Do ye think they'll have picked somebody kind for wee Jessica? Ye won't let her go to some midden that only wants the money and will be bad to her?' she demanded, wrinkled face anxious.

Annie looked down at Jessica dozing innocently in her carry-cot. Stubby fingers cradling her shallow chin. 'Over my dead body,' she said.

'Och, this must be them!' Jeanie cocked her head as the front door bell rang. 'Och, michty!'

'Aye,' Annie heard voices as the woman was ushered in.

Bess Murchieson opened the door with a look of doom on her face. 'Annie, come and meet the lady who wants to take Jessica. Ye've met before ...'

'Aye, so we have,' Annie's self-control never wavered as she took the proferred hand of Betty Clachan.

Chapter Twenty-Seven

'Isn't it Annie Ramsay?' Betty asked uncertainly.

'Annie Lamarche,' Annie replied.

'Oh, you're Mistress Lamarche now, are you?' Betty repeated the foreign name carefully. 'I'd heard you'd done well for yourself in France.' Her face held no guile as she went on, 'It's nice to see you, but I didn't expect you to be here tonight.'

'It's a surprise for both of us.' Annie gave an enigmatic smile. 'And how are you, Mistress Clachan?'

'Och, I'm just fine ... but just call me Betty since we ken each other of old. I'm not one for formality.' Betty's homely plumpness had gone towards fat, but her expression was as earnest and kindly as Annie remembered from the teas in Clachan's kitchen.

'The Doctor tells me you have a family,' Annie took refuge in traditional banalities.

'Aye, I've three bonnie bairns ... just three ... I wish we'd more, but this seems to be the lot ... och, I love bairns.' Her plain face glowed from within. 'Have you any bairns yourself, Mistress Lamarche?'

'Annie ... I've one. My husband died some years back, so Juliette is an only child.'

'Och, that's a shame, you losing your man,' Betty replied. 'I asked Mistress Murchieson about what happened to you a while back, but she didn't seem to know. Doctor Murchieson told me the other day that you were working for Lady Ballantyne again.'

Bess watching the exchange, nerves raw with apprehension, coloured. 'Och, I don't remember you asking, Betty ... though I'm sure you did,' she added before Betty gave her chapter and verse.

358

'Have you brought the bairn?' Betty turned eagerly to Doctor Murchieson.

'Aye, she's here.'

'Let me see her!'

'Now wait a minute! Before you go in, Betty,' the Doctor warned, 'I want you to listen carefully to what Doctor Chisholm has to tell you. He's an expert you know. A very knowledgeable man. John Chisholm has studied abroad with the greatest in the field of mental health.' He paused to let that pronouncement sink in. 'Once you've heard him out, you can see Jessica. And if you still want the wee lass, we'll need to be sure Ian agrees as well. Children like this are a handful at times. Aye, quite a handful.'

John Chisholm smiled and opened his mouth to speak, but Doctor Murchieson was well into his stride. 'In fact I have to confess I was astonished when you offered to take the bairn this morning, Betty. I only mentioned it last week after kirk because I thought you might know some worthy poor body that would exchange a roof for the bairn for a laden table at home. I hadn't thought of approaching folk as fine as you and Ian at all.'

'Doctor Murchieson.' Betty's stout shapeless figure took on a sudden dignity. 'I'm not fine. Never have been and never will be. I'm a plain, ordinary, country lass. I'm not clever like Ian and you doctors. And I'm no beauty. But I ken what I'm good at and that's taking care of bairns.' She turned to John, 'And with all due respect, Doctor Chisholm, I'm sure you're as well-learned as Doctor Murchieson says, but I know all the ordinary things about mongol bairns you need to know ... their wee difficulties and that. I've a mongol cousin over the Maidens way. And there's a few others in Ayrshire I've met as well through helping with kirk charities, ye ken.'

Face flushed and determined, she looked round, ready to take them all on. 'I've given this more thought all day, than any of you could ever know. And Ian says it's up to me. Now just let me see the bairn.'

'Well said, Mistress Clachan.' John Chisholm shot a look of surprised admiration at her. 'Your priorities are in the right order. The detail can keep. Come, the baby is in here.'

'Och, she's that bonnie! Just like I pictured her.' Betty bent over the cot. Jessica lay on her back, button nose running from

359

the beginnings of a cold and dribbling from the side of her slack mouth.

Nobody said a word.

Betty gently rubbed the baby's square flat little feet till she wriggled and opened her slanted eyes. For a while they looked at each other and Betty smiled. Jessica gave a slobbery grin and lifted her arms.

Annie choked back a sob of pure emotion as Jessica was lifted, wiped and cuddled.

'You ken what I like best about these bairns?' Betty asked the silent room.

'What?' John Chisholm was the first to speak.

'They're that loving. They give love for love. And they never leave ye. My bairns are growing up fast. The oldest lad follows Ian to the fields and byre every chance he gets and the other two will follow when they're able. One day they'll be gone, or at least they won't need me any more. But these bairns, they're different. They're wee rays of sunshine to brighten yer life for as long as they live. I'll have her if you'll let me!'

'If we'll let you?' John replied. 'What do you think, Annie?'

'Jessica couldn't find a better home,' Annie replied from the bottom of her heart.

'And this'll be Ian,' Betty said cheerily as the doorbell went again. 'He was just seeing to the horse, it was a wee bit lame, he thought. But I couldn't wait to see the bairn, so I left him with it.'

Annie felt a wave of nausea choke in her throat. She wanted to run, but there was nowhere to go.

'I'll let him in.' Bess almost ran from the room, pushing past Archie who stopped in surprise.

Annie tried to collect her courage and her wits. If Ian over-reacted or if she did herself, it would be catastrophic. She was glad the attention for the moment was on Betty, with Jessica cradled in her arms. She heard Bess's voice murmur and Ian's sharp question. There was another faint burst from Bess, then finally they both came in, Ian first, his face drawn and pale.

'Isn't she bonnie, Ian?' Betty beamed, holding the baby up.

'Aye,' he said, but his eyes were on Annie. 'How are you Annie?' he asked. 'It's been a long time.'

'I'm fine,' she replied, wishing her heart would stop pounding and the roaring in her ears would quieten.

'Can we have her, Ian?' Betty demanded anxiously, pulling on his sleeve.

He dragged his gaze from Annie. 'If you want her, Betty, then that's all right with me.'

'Och, you're a good man and I'm a lucky woman, so I am!' Betty stood on tiptoe and kissed his cheek.

'Then come and have a whisky!' Archie Murchieson for once said the right thing.

Ian Clachan hadn't changed since she saw him in Paris. But here in the bright lights of the sitting-room, she could see one or two grey strands were beginning to show in the darkness of his hair, though he hadn't turned thirty yet. With his weather-beaten face and body honed from farming, he suddenly reminded her more of Geordie, his father, than of the boy she had once loved. After the first moments, they carefully avoided looking at each other.

'Sit here beside Betty, Annie.' Bess pulled out a chair.

'Och, I'm that happy, Annie,' Betty began. 'Doctor Chisholm is going to come over to tell me about Jessica's health next week. I ken there can be problems. But he says her wee heart is fine, so that's a blessing.' She looked at Annie. 'The doctor says you've helped Jeanie with the bairn, maybe you can tip me about what she likes best to eat and that.'

Intent on Jessica, Betty seemed unaware of any tensions in the room, and if as Bess once claimed she'd heard gossip about Annie and Ian, she didn't show it, but Annie couldn't be sure. 'Och, you ken more about these bairns than I do, Betty. Why don't you ask Jeanie about Jessica's wee ways,' she suggested. 'She's having a cup of tea in the kitchen with the scullerymaid?'

'Aye, that's a fine idea.' Betty got up and made her way heavily out of the room, still carrying the child.

Annie was glad she had gone and felt grateful not to have to go on talking. She sat, staring into her tea-cup, mind in a turmoil. At least that's Jessica settled. They'll never find anyone who could care for her better than Betty Clachan. It looks as if poor wee Jessica's story has a happy ending after all, she thought. Lady Cameron will be relieved. But that's one child I'll never oversee, so I'd better think of other ways of raising the rest of the money for Sandy.

Covertly she glanced over at the men. John Chisholm sat

between Ian and Archie, relaxed and chatting. Ian's face was grave and closed, but he was asking questions and discussing readily enough. The two younger men had little in common, that she knew, but they seemed to manage.

'Thank you, Mistress Murchieson.' Annie took a cup of tea from Bess, while the men drank Archie's ten-year-old malt. Aye, when we have to, we all manage to hide our feelings, Annie thought and she admired Bess's own composure. No one could have guessed what dark emotions were swilling round beneath the surface of the comfortable scene.

Outside the wind rose to a blast and the night grew chillier. As soon as she could and still be polite, Annie got up and excused herself. 'I better be heading back to Craigdrummond House. Julie is there waiting for me and Lady Cameron has asked us to stay.'

'You can't walk across the moors now,' Archie objected. 'I'll go down to the stables and harness up.'

'There's no need,' Ian Clachan rose to his feet. 'We'll take Annie with us,' he offered. 'I can drop Betty off on the way with the bairn. Craigdrummond is only a wee bit further on.'

Bess made to protest, but stopped in time. There was no acceptable reason on earth for Annie not to go with the Clachans.

'I can walk, it's no bother.' Annie picked up her coat, avoiding meeting Ian's pleading eyes.

'Och no, Ian's right,' Betty, back from the kitchen, insisted. 'You'd catch your death walking back in this, Annie.' She picked up a stout rug. 'I'll just wrap the bairn up against the night air. It'll be a crush, but we'll fit in. We brought the covered cart. I was that certain she'd be coming home with us.' Suddenly her expression grew worried. 'You're not going to take her off me now, Doctor Chisholm?' she asked.

'Not at all, Mistress Clachan,' John assured her. 'I'll get Jeanie to send the rest of her things down when she gets back to Dumbarton. I've been given full authority to arrange Jessica's future. The child is yours to look after for as long as you care to.'

'That's for as long as she lives, doctor.'

'The only condition is that you never ask me who she is,' he went on, 'nor speculate openly, though you may well suspect the truth. Oh and I have to arrange for you to be reimbursed for her expenses.'

362

'Och, it doesn't matter where she comes from. As far as I'm concerned the bairn is mine and if anyone asks where she came from, they'll get short-shrift,' Betty insisted. 'So, good night to you, Doctor Chisholm, Bess, Archie.' With Jessica well swaddled, she led the way out. 'Ian and me aren't short of a decent bawbee,' she called over her shoulder. 'Tell whoever is offering that we don't need payment for a labour of love.'

John Chisholm watched as the carriage clattered down the main street and was swallowed by the darkness of the night. Expression inscrutable, he followed Archie and Bess back into the house. 'If you don't mind,' he excused himself, 'it feels like it's been a long day.'

'Aye,' Archie agreed, 'go to bed if you want, John. Bess and I won't be a hair behind you.'

John climbed the stairs and sat for a long time on the edge of the bed. 'For all my studies of the human mind,' he muttered aloud to the silent room, 'I still don't know what is behind the power of love.'

Annie sat behind Betty on the narrow cross bench, protected from the gusting wind by a sturdy tarpaulin laced over a frame. It reminded her eerily of the night she had first come to Clachan's Farm, though then she was cold and wet as well as apprehensive.

Betty chattered cheerfully to her husband about homely matters all the way to Clachan's Farm. Ian answered in monosyllables and Annie said nothing at all. Only when they clattered into the familiar yard, did Annie pull herself together as Betty climbed heavily down, clutching Jessica to her ample breast.

'Goodnight, Betty,' she called.

'Oh aye, goodnight, Annie,' Betty barely replied, so intent was she on getting Jessica into the warm kitchen. Clachan's big cheery kitchen where she was long since the lady.

The wind slackened to gusts and above the sky shone with millions of chilly stars.

'There'll be frost on the hills later,' Ian broke the silence as the horse clopped steadily towards Craigdrummond across the dark moor.

'Aye,' she said.

'I thought I would drop on the spot when Aunty Bess said you were in the house,' he said.

'I did myself when you came.'

'Woah!' Ian stopped the horse and looped the reins over the bar.

'I think you should go on, Ian,' Annie said quietly. Her throat felt tight, so tight she could hardly breathe. She could feel herself begin to shake.

'I need to talk to you.'

'There's nothing for us to say.'

'Tonight I asked Archie where your husband is and he said you're a widow.'

'That makes no difference at all,' she snapped, angry with herself and for the whole mess she found herself in. John's right, she thought, if I kept my breath to cool my porridge and my nose out of everyone's business, I'd be safely in Glasgow packing to go back to the Chat Roux. The bar with its noisy familiarity seemed like paradise.

'It does make a difference, Annie,' he said, turning her face towards him with a strong weather-beaten hand.

'Ian,' she shivered.

'Och, Annie!' He made to draw her into his arms, but she stiffened and pulled away.

'Have you forgotten that you're not free, Ian Clachan, even if you think I am.'

'Aye, there's Betty,' he replied and his head sunk onto his chest.

'She's a woman to be proud of,' Annie said. 'I watched her tonight with wee Jessica. How could you expect me to fall into your arms, knowing I'd be betraying a woman like that? Skurking around deceiving her. Set up like a kept woman somewhere, is that what you want for me?' Her voice rose despite her efforts to keep it steady. 'A blind man can see she thinks the sun and moon rise in you. Betty Rannoch always adored you, Ian Clachan, and she still does.'

'Betty cares more about the bairns than about me,' Ian almost sounded petulant.

'And have you given her cause to turn to you, Ian?' Annie demanded, in control of her emotions again. 'Or have you been too busy dreaming about childhood sweethearts to be a man to her?'

'I've been man enough,' he was stung by her question. 'We have three bairns!'

364

'Being a man isn't about fathering bairns,' she replied sharply. 'Any raw lad of an age can do that. Being a man is being there when you're needed, sharing the good and the bad, giving a helping hand over life's troubles and managing a kind word, even when the going is hard.' She knew this would pain him most of all, but she said it anyway, 'I've been married to a real man, Ian, so I ken what I'm talking about.'

'I've been a good husband to Betty,' Ian insisted.

'But you won't be if you betray her with me.'

'How can you see it as betrayal, Annie? You and I were meant for each other,' Ian pleaded.

'Meant for each other? Ian, I don't deny we were first love to one another, but time has passed since then.'

'First and last,' he said stubbornly.

'Love wasn't enough for you to fight for me, Ian,' she quoted Louis.

'Is that how you see it? That I gave up?'

'Didn't you?'

He hung his head. 'But I regretted it.'

'I haven't,' she said.

'Do you really mean that?' He was shocked out of his misery. 'Do you, Annie?'

'I do,' she spoke from conviction. 'I ken we might have been happy ...'

'We would, Annie!'

'I can't be sure, Ian. Mistress Murchieson once said we'd have found happiness, you and I, over the crushed dreams of other folk.'

'Was it Aunty Bess who sent you away right enough?' He demanded angrily. 'I thought she had a hand in it!'

'You're wrong!' Annie replied without hesitation. 'It wasn't her fault. There's no point in you or I looking for scapegoats, Ian. It was my own choice when all's said and done. I could have fought for you too. But I didn't.'

'But we can begin again ...' he reached out towards her, pulling her into his arms. 'Lie with me now ... at least for old times sake ... I want you, Annie ... I've always wanted you.' She sat stiff and unyielding till he finally let go and gazed bitterly ahead.

Side by side they sat, saying nothing. Only the wind sighing across the moor broke the silence. Annie knew she had to break this old fascination or they were both lost. Finally she spoke, 'Ian, I have to say this, though I know it will hurt you.'

'Och, say it, you might as well!' he muttered, voice full of anger and disappointment. 'I can't be more hurt than I am.'

'I don't regret any more that we never wed and I haven't for a long time.' Her voice was steady and sure. 'I don't want to start again. You've got to understand that. Not ever. Even if Betty was gone, I'd not want it.'

'What?' He swung round in amazement.

'Our time when we had it was precious, Ian, and I'll never forget that...' She touched his face gently with one finger. 'I only moved on then because I thought I had to. But once I married Louis, I learned to really love the man. I loved him with the love of a woman, not a lass. And now I'm my own mistress, free to make my own choices in life, without being forced into them by anybody. And I've decided it's time I did just that.'

'That's what you feel I'm trying to do, force you?' he was angry again. 'I left off, didn't I? Even a drunk on a Saturday night rolling out of "Soutar Tams" would have got the message that you didn't want me. I don't force women, Annie.'

'Och, Ian, I'm sorry if I sounded hard, but all this talk of our old feelings for one another and beginning again...' Annie sighed. 'In a way it feels like forcing, though I know you don't mean it like that. Try to understand.' It was her turn to plead. 'It's not right for us to be more than friends. If I lay with you even once for old times sake, I could never look Betty in the eye again.'

'Aye, you've made that plain.'

'Anyway,' her tone became crisp and final, 'I have other plans for my life.'

'And they don't include me.' It was more statement than question.

'Our time is past, Ian.'

'So Clachan's Annie is dead and buried?' he sounded bitter and sad.

'No, Ian, she's not dead. She'll sing and dance across the barn floor and up the hill by the rowan tree for ever, for those who remember. But she's not me any more...' Annie stopped and blinked back sudden tears.

Ian picked up the reins. The horse feeling the motion began to walk slowly forward. 'I'll always love her,' he said softly after a while.

'And Clachan's Annie will always love the lad who teased the life out of her, and followed her up the cliffs to see the waves crash below on the rocks ... the first lad she ever lay with ...'

They fell silent. The steady clip clop of the horse's hooves on the gravel road and the moan of the rising wind accompanied their journey like a funeral dirge.

As they reached the drive to the House, Ian let out a deep sigh. 'Och, Annie,' he said. 'You're right enough in what you say. The past is over. Good luck to you. If you ever need friends, there will always be a welcome at Clachan's fireplace, from me ... and from Betty.'

'I'll remember that, Ian Clachan,' she replied, keeping her face resolutely turned towards the lights of Craigdrummond House looming ahead.

Chapter Twenty-Eight

'You must let me help with your brother's debt, Annie!' Maria Cameron insisted next morning as Annie took her leave having briefed her about Jessica.

'No, thank you, Milady, I wouldn't feel right walking off with more than I'm entitled to.' Annie was adamant. Half the restless night, made more strange by being in a Cameron guest room with Julie, Annie had well considered the risk she was taking.

'I admire your honesty in saying that Jessica is well placed with Mistress Clachan and doesn't need you to oversee. But please do not punish yourself. You can pay the money back later if you wish.'

'I'm grateful, Lady Cameron,' Annie replied, but her face was set. 'I told you yesterday that this is my business and only money I feel is mine can go towards Sandy's debt.'

'Then what will you do?'

'I have the twenty-five pounds you gave me and I've seven pounds five shillings in the bank. Sandy is pawning what else they have . . .' she broke off, knowing that it probably wouldn't be enough.

'And if you can't gather the whole sum?'

'Then I'll have to bargain with Mr McMurtie.'

'From what you tell me, isn't that dangerous?'

'Well, I hope it won't come to that,' Annie tried to sound optimistic.

'At any rate, we're grateful that you are trusting Juliette with us.' Maria took her hands. 'I know she means everything to you.'

'Julie decided for herself,' Annie replied ruefully. 'As soon as I mentioned it this morning, she jumped at the idea . . . but it still worries me what will happen later on ... och,' she gave a fatalistic shrug, 'I should have learned by now that the future has a way of taking its own road and folk have to follow.'

Maria nodded. 'That's the way I feel myself sometimes, Annie. And I promise you, Juliette will be treated exactly the same as Vicky. I will see to clothes and other necessaries for both of them. That is if you have no objection,' she added hastily as Annie's face clouded.

'I suppose not,' she replied with an embarrassed flush. 'And I should be thanking you for doing this instead of jumping down your throat, Milady. But I hope you understand about Sandy. That's another matter altogether.'

'From the very first time I saw you standing in this room, with your big work boots and your darned woollen dress, carrying off your negotiations with the dignity of a queen, I admired you, Annie,' Maria said gently. 'I respected your independence and your spirit then and I still do, so good luck with Sandy's problem. At least Juliette is safe here.'

'I know that or I'd not leave her.'

'William and she are going out on the moor today to look for rabbits with the gamekeeper, so they tell me. And the Baird children come in a few days. I'm sure she will be happy.'

'Yes.' Annie swallowed tears. How many times in Montmartre she had dreamed of Julie growing up in fresh air, with books and learning and all the things money could buy? Now she had it, at least for a while, but the price for her mother was high. 'Well,' she said, 'I'll say goodbye to Julie and be away to Glasgow.'

'Annie!' As she waited in a stiff wind blowing across the moors at Craigdrummond Junction, Bess Murchieson puffed up holding onto her little black hat for dear life though it was firmly skewered by two huge jet pins.

'Mistress Murchieson, what are you doing here?'

'I just came to collect a parcel of Irish linen I ordered from Belfast. It came on the ferry. They'll be leaving it off from the train,' Bess explained at unnecessary length. 'Are you off to Glasgow, Annie?'

'Aye.'

Her expression was drawn and anxious. 'Did you get home all right last night ...?'

Annie knew what she was really asking and, though it was painful, she didn't hesitate, 'Ian understands that the past is best left where it is.'

'Och, Annie, thank God for that!' Bess let out a long sigh of relief. 'I ken a lot of it was my fault, lass, but I did what I thought was right at the time, so did Elsie Rannoch. Betty is a good woman. It's not her fault ... she doesn't deserve...'

'Neither she does,' Annie agreed. 'I wish her and Ian luck. And Jessica couldn't have found a better home. Lady Cameron wanted to pay me for checking she was in good hands, but that would be stealing. Betty Clachan will give her all she needs and more.'

'Annie, I'm that grateful. You're a generous lass. And I wish you all the best too, you know that, don't you?' Bess's eyes pleaded for understanding.

'Aye, Mistress Murchieson. I believe you never meant to cause any harm. But just tell me one thing ... did Betty really hear gossip about me and Ian?'

'No.' Bess coloured with shame, but she held the younger woman's gaze steadily enough. 'I lied, Annie, and I'm sorry.'

'Well, I'm glad it wasn't true,' Annie replied with a wry smile. 'At least I don't have to worry about that as well.' She lifted her chin. 'Och, life's too short for regrets Mistress Murchieson, and there's still a lot on offer for those with the courage to take a chance.'

'You're right, Annie!' Bess's sudden laugh wiped all the anxiety from her face. 'Och, by heavens you're right! Life still has a lot to offer, even for old folks like me and Archie. So, what will you do now, lass, are you going back to France?'

'I'm staying with Sandy for a while. Julie will be living at Craigdrummond for a year at least, she's to be company for Lady Victoria while she's in the schoolroom.'

'Well just imagine! Isn't that a turn up for the books?' Bess was astonished. 'Just wait till I tell Archie! He'll be pleased, Annie. He was just saying that wee lass of yours is something special ... just like her Mammy, he said.'

'Here's the train now.' Annie picked up her bag as a distant howl gave warning of its arrival. Above their heads, the great signal moved to stop. Annie waved to the signalman, wondering if his wife still made jammy bannocks for his piece.

370

'Good luck, lass. Goodbye and safe journey.' Bess headed down towards where the guards van usually stopped. She called over her shoulder, 'I'll pass on your regards to John Chisholm.'

'Aye, do that,' Annie yelled back over the din of the approaching train. In all the fuss and bother, she had forgotten she wouldn't be seeing him again at Baird House. She'd already told Lady Cameron she would leave the gate house and move to Charing Cross at once.

'Annie, we only managed to raise another one pound and fourpence, even wi' pawning the clock.' Sandy still barely able to walk from the brutal beating, was a broken man. 'We cannae pay unless you've managed to get the rest.'

'I've rustled up thirty-two pounds fifteen shillings altogether. Twenty-five is from Craigdrummond, seven pounds five shillings from the bank and what I had in my purse, and I pawned my best coat and dress for ten shillings on the way from the station ... I haven't anything else left ... you've had it all except my shifts and the clothes I stand up in.'

'And it's still not enough,' Phyllis wept.

'Wait till McMurtie comes, I'll try to reason with the man,' Annie said as calmly as she could, but in her heart she knew it was hopeless.

Sandy confirmed her fears. 'There's no point, Annie. If ye're a farthin' short of what he's asked for, he'll no let ye off.'

'Mammy!' One of the children ran in, face white with fear, eyes starting almost out of his head. 'McMurtie and the frighteners are on their way doon the street. Will they kill Daddy? Will they, Mammy?'

'Och, son, I dinnae ken.' Phyllis buried her head in her apron and began to sob.

'Go into the neighbours, lassies,' Annie instructed the terrified twins. 'Take the weans and don't come back till we send for you.'

'Aye, Annie,' her sisters chorused, grabbed their nephews' hands and fled.

They had barely left when the door swung open. 'Mistress Ramsay, Mistress Lamarche, Ramsay, good day to ye,' McMurtie began civilly enough. 'As ye ken I'm here to get settlement in full for the debt ye owe me. Thirty-five pounds sterling, twelve shillings and sixpence farthing,' the sum rolled like the trumpets of doomsday off his tongue. Beside him the frighteners shifted restlessly, waiting for trouble and happy if it came.

'We have thirty-two pounds fifteen shillings,' Annie said then paused, waiting for his reaction.

'It's a helluva lot more than I thought ye'd scrape the gither,' he sounded surprised. 'But ye ken it's no enough.'

'What in the name will you do with second-hand ovens and a pile of used tables and cakestands?' Annie asked boldly. 'Start a tea-room, with this pair to serve cream teas?' She shot a glance at the burly frighteners. One of them sniggered.

'Belt up, you!' McMurtie rasped. 'Listen, hen,' his voice was chill with icy menace and his eyes merciless. 'Whit I do wi' stuff I take is my business. If ovens and tea-room junk is what ye have, that's what I take.'

Annie shivered, her momentary bravado gone. McMurtie was hard as flint. 'Wouldn't you prefer something more worthwhile?' she asked.

'Like what have ye got, hen?' His small eyes shot over her comely body. 'I don't take certain types of payment ... if ye ken what I mean ...

Sandy reddened and tried to get up, wincing with pain. 'Ye've no to talk to my sister like that, McMurtie!'

'Och naw, dinnae hit him!' Phyllis shaking from head to foot, gave a scream of terror as McMurtie nodded and Big Ed lumbered forward. 'Belt up, Missus!' Big Ed pushed her aside. 'Shift!'

'Watch yerself, Annie hen, he'll do ye an all!' Sandy let out a groan as his sister moved between him and McMurtie's man.

'Back off!' Courage back, she snapped like a terrier at the burly figure.

Ed stopped, looking for guidance from his boss. 'Do ye want me tae do Ramsay or no, Mister McMurtie?'

'There's no need to show off by beating up my brother again, McMurtie,' she went on in a voice full of contempt. 'I ken only too well what ye are, you and yer frighteners. And we'd be more bloody desperate than we are the now before I'd pay you in the way ye thought. What I meant is this ...' she took off her wedding ring and placed it gently on the table beside the money they had so painfully collected.

McMurtie nodded imperceptibly and Ed moved away. He

peered down at the ring. 'Is it real?' The money-lender was used to the poverty he fed on, where brass curtain rings served as wedding bands.

'It's gold, pure gold, twenty-two carats, stamped and all,' she said. 'We can go this minute and get it checked at the pawn shop if ye doubt my word.'

'Naw, it's real enough.' He picked it up and greedily examined the fine workmanship Louis had so proudly paid for to give his beloved bride.

Annie thought her heart would break as he pawed the one thing she had from Louis and their life together that was hers alone. But she lifted her head and said without faltering, 'So, if you're satisfied, then, Mr McMurtie, shall we sign?'

'Aye.' He showed blackened teeth. 'That's the ticket, hen.'

The shop door burst open and they heard rapid footsteps coming through the back.

'Mind out, lads.' McMurtie's heavies got ready for trouble.

'Am I in time?' John strode in, his face scarlet from running all the way from the carriage. He spotted the wedding ring lying on the table. 'What the hell are you doing, Annie?'

'A blind man running for a tram can see what I'm doing, John Chisholm,' she replied. 'I'm paying Sandy's debt.'

'Not with that you're not!' He snatched the ring. 'How much do you need, you bastard?' he demanded of McMurtie. There was no mistaking which of the three men was in charge.

'Jist wait a minute, Mac, I dinnae like yer attitude...' McMurtie nodded to his frighteners who moved forward lifting their fists.

'Put one finger on me, either of you,' Chisholm said in a tone that froze them to the spot, 'and I'll make sure you never get a doctor in Glasgow, even if you're screaming in agony on your death-bed.'

'By here!' Sandy gawped in awe at the threat, despite his fear. 'That's a guid yin!'

'Och, it's the doctor.' Big Ed stopped. 'I ken him. He came tae ma wee laddie last year before the new yin took over. I dinnae duff doctors, Mr McMurtie.'

'Neither dae I,' his colleague echoed. In the grim slum streets of Glasgow a doctor was sacrosanct, even if he wasn't carrying the trade-mark black bag.

'Aye right enough,' McMurtie backed down. He ruled by the law of the jungle, and he obeyed it. 'Are ye paying then, Doctor?' his tone was conciliatory.

'How much is owing?'

'One pound, eighteen and tuppence farthing.'

'It's one pound, seventeen and tuppence farthing, McMurtie,' Sandy protested.

'Aye but the shilling's for all the time wasting ye've put me through, Ramsay, you and yer smart-arsed sister!' McMurtie snarled.

'Here's two pounds,' John Chisholm pulled notes from his wallet and threw them down contemptuously in front of the money lender. 'Give the change to your favourite charity!'

'Och, here that's kind of ye, Doctor,' Big Ed began. 'Isn't it, Mr McMurtie ... '

'Get tae hell out of it, ye bloody eejits!' McMurtie's face darkened and the frighteners headed for the door like whipped curs.

'Don't forget to sign the paper.' Annie placed it in front of him.

'As if I wid.' He gave what passed for a smile. 'Ye're lucky in yer champion, Mistress Lamarche. It's no everyone that has a doctor as a frightener! I'd gie him a job myself.' He handed it back and with a tip of his hat, he left and the crisis with him.

'Oh God.' Sandy slumped forward on his chair, shaking uncontrollably from reaction. Beside him Phyllis started weeping all over again with relief.

'A job as a frightener?' John Chisholm began to laugh. 'I wonder what Doctor Freud of Vienna would have said to that?'

'Aye, well Vienna's no Glesca! But after what you just did, you can walk tall in either city, John Chisholm.' Annie gave him a smile of gratitude and admiration. Then she turned to her sister-in-law. 'So, if you've finished howling wi' joy instead of terror, our Phyllis, how about putting the kettle on? I think there's a batch of tattie scones left from this morning's firing.'

'Bess told me you'd already left when she got back from the Junction.' In the carriage back to Dunbarton House to collect what few belongings she had left, John explained his sudden and timely arrival.

'You said it was this afternoon you had to pay and I guessed you most likely hadn't got enough together. I was going to offer again before you went, but you surprised me by catching the earlier train.'

'The next one cuts it fine and I had to go to the bank and the pawn shop. Anyway, how were you so sure I didn't have enough?'

'I assumed you had the money from Lady Cameron, but Bess told me you wouldn't take payment for Jessica, and I remembered you said that neither you nor Sandy's family had much left to pawn.'

'So you thought you'd lend me it?'

'I did.' He gave a boyish grin. 'Then I discovered I didn't have more than one pound ten and sixpence on me, so I borrowed five pounds from Archie.' John flushed. 'I ... er ... I told him I'd forgotten my wallet and he didn't ask any questions.' He went on before Annie could say anything, 'I caught the next train, but like you said it was cutting it fine. I was on the edge of my seat when we stopped to check the boiler at Kilmarnock, I thought I'd be too late.'

She smiled teasingly. 'Doctor John Chisholm, late of the Salpêtrière and other distinguished places, heading up from Ayrshire as knight errant on the Stranraer ferry-train, with a pocketful of borrowed money to take on Glasgow's menodge men!'

'I was worried they would harm you, Annie.' His own smile faded. 'I didn't think about anything else.'

'And it was good of you, John. Right decent. Och, I should have swallowed my pride and borrowed the money from Lady Cameron. It was daft to refuse,' she admitted, 'I've had to accept it from you in the end ... though you'll get it back.'

'Yes, I know.' He saw the determined look on her face and laughed. 'I'm not too worried, you're a good risk.'

She twisted the ring on her finger. 'It really hurt to give McMurtie this. You know, John,' she said with a rueful smile. 'I learn from my mistakes all the time, but I never win because I just go on making new ones!'

'That's part of your charm,' he teased in turn. Then he suddenly changed the subject, taking her off guard, 'Are you going to tell me what happened with Clachan?'

'Why do you want to know?' Annie looked away, so he couldn't see her eyes.

375

'He's the man in Craigdrummond ... the one we talked about before. I saw it in your face and in his, the minute he walked into Bess and Archie's sitting-room.'

'You can't hide much from a psychiatrist ... or whatever fancy name they call you, John.'

'It's not the doctor that saw, or that's asking, Annie,' he said quietly, 'just the man.'

'Aye.' She continued looking out of the window as they trotted along Great Western Avenue towards the outskirts of the city. After a long silence she turned and looked steadily at him. 'It's finally over between Ian and me. The ghosts are laid to rest.'

'Are you sure?'

'I'm sure ... but I'd like to leave it, if you don't mind.'

'All right. It's none of my business.' He continued in a lighter tone, 'So what will you do now? You've no money, you've done yourself out of looking after Jessica...'

'I've decided to "catch the moments as they fly, and use them as I ought",' she paraphrased Robert Burns.

'What do you mean?'

'While Julie's at Craigdrummond, I'm going to work side by side with Sandy and Phyllis. There's some flour still in stock, so first we'll get the ovens in full operation again. Then I'll help them get going and plan their business better. They've got a good reputation already, we'll build on that.' Annie's eyes lit up with enthusiasm. 'And if I'm still here next year, we'll open a French style coffee house on Argyll Street that sells eclairs, choux pastries, real ...'

'... Hot chocolate?'

She laughed. 'How well you know me, John Chisholm.'

'But with no money ...'

'Och, man, you've no head for business, right enough! You'd be in as big a mess as Sandy if you tried anything but doctoring.' She laughed at his bemused expression. 'It's quite simple, when I started to think about helping out Sandy, I telegrammed Jorice and Francine, just to find out if they would really be interested in leasing the Chat for a while.'

'And?'

'They sent me a reply right away. I got it when I came back to Sandy's this morning. Jorice is jumping with joy. In fact I think he's been praying to all the ancient gods of Montmartre for some-

376

thing like this to happen. He suggests a year to begin with, extending it later if I want. It'll still be Julie's and mine, but they're willing to pay me a fair rent, which we'll have to discuss.'

She waved her hand in a confident gesture. 'I'll invest most of that here in Sandy's business. As a partner this time. Interests in France and Scotland mean I'll spread my risks and build up capital for Julie's future, especially for a good school.'

'But how can you look after businesses in both countries?'

'Och, no bother! After my years with Lady Ballantyne stravaiking up and down Europe, travel is nothing. With good trains and ferries, I can be in Paris in a day and a half. That way I can keep in touch with the Chat and give help if it's needed, though I trust Jorice and Francine to run it well.' She waved a gloved hand. 'Like I said, simple!'

'Simple?' he echoed in disbelief.

'Aye, simple.'

'It doesn't sound simple to me,' he said. 'I never know what's happening with the investments I inherited from my father, not to mention keeping my books for the Baird fees and the patients who do pay ... I wish you would look after me as well, Annie.'

'What are you on about, John Chisholm?' she asked sharply.

As her expression changed, his heart sank. 'Och, I didn't mean...'

'Didn't mean what?' she asked, eyes narrowed, watchful.

'I wasn't propositioning you, Annie.' He ran his fingers through his hair in agitation till it almost stood on end.

'No?'

'You made it clear the last time that my advances were unwelcome.'

'Like I told Bess Murchieson this morning, life has a lot to offer to those willing to take a chance,' Annie said evenly. 'In this past couple of days, I've faced a few old ghaisties and ghoulies and, you know, John, they were nowhere near as fearsome as I thought.' She held his eyes with her own. 'And I've found some unexpected heroes too in the midst of all the trouble.'

'So?' he ventured, afraid to give vent to his feelings again in case he ruined their renewed closeness.

'So maybe I've changed my mind.'

377

'About what?' John Chisholm couldn't keep the hope from his face any longer.

Her chestnut curls tossed and she smiled like the carefree lass she had once been. 'If I'm going to "catch the moments as they fly", John Chisholm, I might consider a closer partnership than just business with one of my heroes.' Grey eyes teasing, she added with a laugh, 'If he's man enough to persuade me.'

'By heavens, I'm man enough, Annie,' he said.